Children of Promise

by

BILL CUNNINGHAM

McClanahan Publishing House

International Standard Book Number 0-913383 47 3
Library of Congress Catalog Card Number 97 074253

Cover design and book layout by James Asher Graphics

Manufactured in the United States of America

All book order correspondence should be addressed to:

McClanahan Publishing House, Inc.
P. O. Box 100
Kuttawa, KY 42055
(502) 388-9388
1-800-544-6959

McClanahan
Publishing House

Dedicated to John Ryan, Alec, Josh, Luke and Joe.

This is a work of fiction.
Nevertheless most of the names have been changed
to protect the guilty.

Table of Contents

Now we, brethren, as Isaac was, are the children of promise.

Galations 4:28

One Hundred Years Ago
Louisville Courier Journal
March 19, 1899

About forty miles from the mouth of Cumberland river, nestled among some of the most picturesque hills which border that romantic stream, is the quaint little town of Eddyville, the oldest settlement in Western Kentucky, and it would be hard to find a spot more sequestered or more thoroughly delightful. Every rock has its history, houses built a hundred years ago are still standing, and there are few of the inhabitants who can not trace their ancestry back to some distinguished name of pioneer days. To this quiet little nook their forefathers came long ago, lived, loved, married, died and here their descendants have been content to follow out, in the same place, the same peaceful destiny, even to the sixth generation, for such the children of today number from the earliest settlers. Old landmarks untouched by the desecrating hand of progress have fallen into picturesque decay, and the sun peeping over the hilltops at this, the close of the century, beholds many of the same things upon which it shone at the dawn of 1800. And the waters of the Cumberland, rippling past, seem to touch the shores which they have so long kissed, with a kind of reverence, as if conscious of the honored dead buried there, mingling in their murmur, a sort of requiem for those departed heroes, with a salutation of respect to their children's children, now living in the dear little town, which this year celebrates its centennial, and abounds in so many rare historic associations.

Chapter One

Justice Luke Cameron

The heart comes calling for a lost promise.

Luke Cameron stood at his window and looked out upon the Washington street.

It was late spring, and already the city was teeming with tourists.

In October Luke would turn fifty, but he looked more like a man of 35—slim, his full head of hair free of gray except for just a flicker around the temples. His face was virtually untouched by wrinkles. He kept in shape with jogging and frequent racquetball and tennis.

Luke's boyish looks were especially noticeable when pictured with his much older looking colleagues in the official Supreme Court photograph.

The soft tone of his intercom sounded, drawing him away from the window.

"Justice Cameron. It's the President on line one," came the silky voice of his personal secretary.

Luke moved his athletic frame swiftly across the deep carpet and fell back into the large leather chair behind the broad and substantial mahogany desk.

He picked up the phone and punched the button.

"Good morning, Mr. President." He spoke with genuine pleasantness in his voice.

"Well," came the slow, drawling voice from the other end of the line, ". . . how is my favorite Supreme Court Justice doing today?"

"Just sitting here ruminating, Your Majesty," Luke said airily.

"Oh my God!" exclaimed the President in mock concern. "This country and especially its President is at risk when a Supreme Court Justice ruminates."

"It could be worse, Mr. President. I could be writing an opinion," Justice Cameron parried as a broad smile broke across his face.

"You got a point there, my dear Honor," deadpanned the President.

Two good ole Southern boys bantering like college kids.

There was a pause, and then from the President, ". . . say, some unexpected things came up over at State and it looks like Ginger and I are going to stay here in town over Memorial Day. We wondered if you and Carolyn would like to come over to the big house on Friday night for a little get together. It will be just us, and maybe Billy and Tonya Thompson."

Luke's face darkened.

"We'd love to, Tom . . . but we already have plans. Carolyn is going to Richmond to see our son and new daughter-in-law, and. . ." there was a short pause in his delivery, ". . . I have to be in Kentucky. I'm the keynote speaker at the dedication of the new law school."

"You damn Kentuckians," boomed the President. "Every weekend you have to go home."

"Now that's not right, Mr. President. I haven't been to Kentucky in over six months. You must have me confused with the senior Senator of the Commonwealth," Luke quipped mischievously.

"I'd never get you mixed up with that asshole!" came the

reply from the chief executive. "I wish he would go home more often...maybe even permanently. Anyway . . . no big deal. We may just stay with the Kennedy Center thing and we can do it another time."

The President had the peculiar trait of simply picking up his phone, in the middle of his monumental duties and calling old friends just to chat. Luke mentioned this to him once and the head of state said it was therapy for him, a good way to keep some normalcy in his overwhelming lifestyle.

"How're Carolyn and the kids?"

"Just great," answered Luke. "You know how Carolyn is . . . gadding about and loving all this Washington stuff. And now with a new daughter-in-law, she's already talking about grandchildren."

The President chuckled mechanically as if his attention had been diverted. Luke heard the sound of shuffling papers.

"Well . . . gotta go run the country," he said breezily. "When you get back, give Marty a call here to set up a time for us to get together. Maybe after I get back from my South Africa trip."

"Sounds good, Mr. President." Luke responded. "If I don't talk to you before you leave, have a nice trip. And don't get your ass shot."

"Thanks Justice Cameron. You're full of light and laughter. Take care."

They both hung up.

Luke swiveled his huge chair around and again stared out the window.

It was too bad. He and Carolyn enjoyed immensely the company of their friends on Pennsylvania Avenue. And Luke knew these opportunities to get together intimately were few and far between.

But commitments were commitments. They don't dedicate a new law school at your alma mater every day.

Besides, he had been obsessed for weeks by a deep inner urge to get away—to go home—to get out of D.C. and back to his place of beginning, to his roots, for rejuvenation. His stale soul was crying out for some kind of rite of renewal.

Justice Cameron turned and hit the intercom.

"Yes?" came the same silky voice.

"Karla, have you got the flight booked to Nashville for Friday night and a room at the airport Hilton?" Luke inquired.

There was note-taking on the other end.

"Yes sir. And Mrs. Cameron will not be going—correct?"

Luke paused and reflected.

"That's right."

Karla smiled. His accent still amused her, the flattened vowels—"rite" for right and "fite" for fight.

Luke hung up and clasped his hands in front of him, staring straight across the room at the huge wooden seal of Kentucky on the opposite wall.

Carolyn would go to Kentucky with him without the least complaint, he thought. But he was sure she'd much rather be going to Richmond to visit their son and his new bride. She would be very disappointed, though, that they could not spend Saturday night at the White House.

Since his appointment to the Supreme Court almost a year ago, his wife had taken to Washington like a duck to water. She enjoyed the formalities, socializing, culture, and glitz of the nation's capital.

She was a city girl from Charlotte, North Carolina. It had been through her he had come to know the President when the latter had been attorney general of that state. Carolyn and the future President of the United States had been classmates and good friends in high school.

Luke and Carolyn had met in Germany where he had been reassigned after his tour in Vietnam. They were married upon his discharge from the service.

Their oldest son, Adam, had just that spring passed the bar exam of Virginia, joined a prestigious old Richmond law firm, and married a North Carolina girl of his own, all in the space of a few weeks.

Joe, his second oldest, was a Bohemian free spirit—lots of brains and creativity, but to the frustration of his parents, a little short on ambition. He was having the time of his life with the

Peace Corps in Kenya.

Luke and Carolyn's youngest child and only girl, Caroline, was a vivacious, charismatic sophomore at Winthrop University in Rock Hill, South Carolina, where she starred on the girl's basketball team.

Luke and Carolyn were close—like the pillars of the temple, as Kahlil Gibran would say—close, yet still apart. They understood and appreciated their differences, which actually complemented the relationship.

Carolyn, the city girl, refined, polished, pretty and possessed of abundant grace—"classy," as Luke would put it. A Southern belle with the honeyed Carolina accent in her voice.

Luke, a country boy from Kentucky—rustic in his way, full of fervor and life. He spoke with the rural Southern twang of his raising which provided a constant barrier in breaking the ice of the high level Washington social life. It was a barrier, however, over which he easily bounded with his disarming charm and quick wit.

"I never knew anyone from Kentucky who was so smart," a pompous old biddy would exclaim, ". . . or for that matter, I never knew anyone from Kentucky."

"You must venture out more," Luke would deadpan, "as your age will allow."

He liked the simple life and common people.

The deep affection which he and Carolyn held for one another nurtured the mutual respect for their differences.

Yet Luke could wear his white tie with the best of them. And Carolyn could don her jeans and mingle masterfully at the chili suppers back home.

The Washington establishment, as well as most of the Northeastern media, were still not sure what to make of the Kentuckian's appointment to the highest court.

Initially, much criticism had rained down upon the President because of the close personal relationship the two men shared.

And the confirmation inquisition had tried to make much of that, as well as Cameron's mediocre academic background.

"Don't worry about all that hype," his friend in the White

House had assured him with a good-natured chuckle. "They're still getting over the shock that someone from Kentucky wears shoes."

Luke glanced over at his desk and spotted a stack of files brought in minutes before by his law clerk. He reached over and read the label on the top file. It was a utility rate case, dealing with the interstate commerce clause of the United States Constitution.

He winced. Quickly his eyes moved to a neatly bound folder atop the stack of files on his desk. He picked it up slowly, like it was some fragile treasure.

The Bikini Atoll case, and the majority opinion he had authored was being released to the media that day.

Bikini Atoll, the facts of the case unfolded, is an isolated group of islands in the northwest Marshall Island group in the Pacific Ocean. After World War II, in 1946, the United States relocated approximately 176 Bikini islanders from their homeland in order to use the tropical paradise as a nuclear testing ground. The displaced natives became nomads, with the United States moving them to three different islands in two years. They nearly starved to death on one and were eventually resettled on Kili, a tiny, solitary island with little reef and no lagoon.

There, they and their descendants remained for over fifty years. When they left their beloved Bikini Atoll, they were assured they could return when the atoll was no longer needed for testing. It ceased to be used as a nuclear punching bag in 1958. As years passed, the radiation level slowly dropped. Finally, the Atomic Energy Commission declared the islands safe for human habitation. The United States government which governed the entire Marshall Island chain as part of the United Nations Trust Territory, prepared to return the land to private ownership. Initial steps were taken for the scenic real estate to be placed upon the auction block for bidding by large private corporations. Free of contamination, the cream-like land of white beaches and swaying palms would become a luxurious new playground for the rich.

Thus, the suit by the displaced citizens of Bikini and their descendants, asking that the sale be enjoined, and they be allowed to return to their homeland.

Lower courts had thrown out the action, ruling that the

plaintiffs lacked standing because they were not U.S. citizens, and that they had been adequately compensated by the substituted lands.

The United States Supreme Court made the final decision by a narrow 5-4 vote. And Justice Cameron had written the majority opinion.

It had been difficult adjusting to the Supreme Court seat.

After all the publicity and fanfare of the swearing-in had passed, Luke found the slow moving—almost monastic—existence of a Supreme Court justice tedious.

He had spent his younger years as an elected county prosecutor. From there he was appointed Federal District Attorney, and then to a Federal judgeship. He had spent less than three months on the U.S. Court of Appeals when he was appointed to the highest court.

Justice Cameron missed the excitement and vitality of trial work. The arena of human tragedy, as he often called it. The place where people came together to grapple and struggle with their own personal Armageddons. Where they clawed for redress, life, liberty, and justice through their legal gladiators.

And juries, people with lesser problems of their own, coming together, putting aside the demands of their own daily living to wrestle with and attempt to level the terrible conflicts of others.

Luke now reflected upon it all as he peered out the window at his impressive and stately surroundings.

He missed the country courthouses with their poorly lit and age-worn hallways, the mingled scent of stale tobacco and disinfectant.

Perhaps most of all, he missed the country stores. The gathering of simple, leather-faced farmers eating their bologna sandwiches around formica-top tables. He missed their bedrock values and simple eloquence.

It was all still in his blood, a part of him. It would take a while, he reckoned, for it to be drained from him by the academic bleeding of Washington.

A deep restlessness had swept over Luke in recent days. Somehow the Bikini Atoll case had stirred a longing in his breast, an unexplained nostalgia. It had caused him to pause in his daily activities and reflect. An inner voice had inexplicably called him homeward.

He stood for a long time staring out of his window at the outward trappings of his elevated station in life. He would follow his soulful compass.

Justice Luke Cameron was going home.

⚜

The black Lexus Supreme pulled onto the ramp exiting the interstate. It was a rental car and the driver had enjoyed the leisurely drive from Nashville.

Justices of the United States Supreme Court do not travel without a retinue of aides and bodyguards. But he had managed to shake loose for the morning, and the disentanglement was exhilarating.

It was great irony, he thought, that the powerful are the most powerless when trying to shed the accessories of power.

The morning sun was beginning to warm up the windshield, and already the car's air conditioner was blasting at full speed.

He turned onto a two-lane country road and followed the highway signs.

About two miles later, he saw the sign "Kentucky State Penitentiary" with an arrow pointing to the left.

Justice Luke Cameron followed the sign, turning onto a smaller paved road. Its name, "Pea Ridge Road," was evident on a green marker. After that, the rural terrain took on a vaguely familiar look.

But . . . the way had been a gravel road, as he remembered. It wound its way through rolling farmland, tobacco barns and grazing cattle. There was an occasional mobile home, with huge television disks opened to the skies.

The passing scenery would sometimes give up tokens of the past. A familiar-looking house—amended now by additional rooms, a faded "Jesus Saves" sign, a certain barn lot—all reassured the returning pilgrim that he was on the right road.

Some newly constructed concrete block buildings began to appear. Minnow wells and fishing supplies of poles and netting were evident. Bait prices written in crayon hung from the windows. Cars parked at random in front of these places were mostly filled with restless kids and a waiting parent.

Slowly the trees began to sink beneath him as the ground dropped off to his left. The sky became wider and the horizon opened.

There, as far as the eye could see was the Cumberland River Valley, now full to the brim with Barkley Lake. It was a beautiful sight, with miles and miles of water, its shining surface glimmering and dancing to a strong breeze.

Then, almost as fast as it appeared, the scene vanished as the trees came back up and the road leaned forward to slide down a long and steep hill. The sharp grade was familiar to Luke. But he remembered it differently, on a sled and in the midst of winter.

At the bottom of the hill, the lake appeared again, as he motored across a short straightaway.

To the right of the hill was another summit. On its crest stood the massive gray walls of the Kentucky State Penitentiary.

Irregular roofs of enclosed buildings peeked above the top of the huge blocks of stone. Guard towers were perched at the corners. Black streaks of moisture meandered down the masonry.

This medieval structure, now over a hundred years old, had been a part of Justice Cameron's childhood. It stood as entrenched as ever, impervious to change.

Once again the road began to rise, still parallel with the prison. Luke slowed the car to a crawl as the lake appeared, once again, in front of him. This time the highway ended abruptly at the top of the cliff high above the water, the precipice blocked by a white and black barricade. The road to the right led to the main gate of the penitentiary.

Luke turned left, down a narrow paved street. It was a truncated street of old Currentville. Down a steep slide it went, onto a boat ramp, and into the water.

Luke eased down Penitentiary Hill.

He passed a stone wall on the left, punctuated by some steps leading up to a vacant lot where the old courthouse had once been. The picture show had stood on the right, on a grassy knoll now overlooking the water.

At the boat ramp he turned left and drove through a parking lot, which was half full of cars and empty boat trailers.

Looping halfway back up the hill, he pulled over and parked under some shade trees. He got out of the car, stretched his legs, and gazed about.

Below him past the parking lot was the small bay which covered most of what had once been Currentville, Kentucky.

At the mouth of the bay, and farther out into the open lake, ski boats and an assortment of other recreational craft churned the water.

The shoreline which rimmed the bay was a well manicured picnic area of huge oaks and maples left over from the old town.

There was a familiar mugginess in the air, even though a nice breeze rustled through the trees.

Justice Cameron spotted a picnic shelter up the hill and made for it. He was surprised to find it had not yet been captured by Memorial Day weekend picnickers.

A solidly built table was anchored onto a large concrete slab. A wooden pavilion provided cover. It was positioned near the crest of the hill, and gave him a grand vista of the valley, now mostly filled with water. Luke seated himself upon the table, his feet resting upon the bench.

Settled comfortably upon this perch, he surveyed the scene before him.

It was hard for him to imagine. There within the confines of this small embayment had once been a town, with stores, houses, churches, schools, doctors, old spinsters, and drunks.

With difficulty, he tried to reconstruct it. He stared until he could remember the details of the old village, nestled in the drooping humidity of the soggy river bottom, its white frame houses speckled from the soot of the prison boilers and passing tugs.

He looked to where Main Street now ran onto the boat

ramp and into the water. Nearby was the picture show, with its colorful and exciting preview posters of Rocky Lane westerns and John Wayne battlefields.

Next to it was Miss Annie's all-purpose clothing store. From her back window was a fabulous look at the river from one bend to the next, including the lock and dam. To her consternation, she could see over the horseweed on the riverbank, where naked boys swam next to the lock wall.

The courthouse stood across the road, leaning its solid brick shoulder into the steep hill. It was fixed in the middle of the shady lawn, leveled by the handsome stone wall. Justice Cameron smiled at the recollection of the somber place. If someone had told him as a barefoot boy scampering past the dull and dust-laden public building that he would grow up to be a lawyer and a judge, he would probably have drowned himself in the Cumberland River.

Down from the courthouse, a wide, tree-lined street branched off from the main thoroughfare. On this avenue of large stately houses lived the landed gentry, behind rambling porches and shaded lawns. Here old women, dressed and powdered to a Sunday shine, peered out from their front porches on summer afternoons. Occasionally they would even be seen working in their yards, attired in their immaculate apparel—spading flower pots or trimming roses, their hands covered with oversized garden gloves.

In this section of town, anchored only a block apart, were the large brick Baptist and Methodist churches, sluggishly vying for the souls of the community.

Back on Main Street, to the right of where the boat ramp now ran into the water, was the town's bank. It was the only air conditioned building in town. Shirtless and barefoot, Luke and his friends would slip inside on hot summer days and, with their shaggy dogs, lounge blissfully on the cool terrazzo floor.

Across from the bank was the post office. Small and musty with a dirty wooden floor, it was run by the elderly Mrs. Sable, a Republican relic from the Hoover administration. The dirty walls were plastered with "Wanted" posters, yellowed by age and mostly ignored.

At the back of the building was an old wooden slide used

for mail drops from the street level to the back door. It was also used by the local kids until either a piercing splinter or a waving postmistress would send them running down the alley.

Justice Cameron was distracted from this reverie by a boat and trailer being backed down the ramp and into the lake. Shortly the craft was afloat, the trailer pulled out, and the boaters aboard and gone.

On down the street he traveled in his mind, off the slope and into the flats to Gresham Brothers, the largest grocery and hardware store in the town. It was a century-old, family-run business. The two-story building was badly in need of paint. This fading enterprise had limped along with dusty shelves and outdated inventory, which included horse collars, wooden churns, salt blocks and zinc-plated kitchen ware.

Next to the large building was the drug store. Across an alleyway was Perkin's Feed Store, a wooden frame structure, with the cool seedy smell of grain inside. This building was seriously wounded as incessant spring floods had over the years hammered it into a Leaning Tower of Pisa.

A flying boom and the turn of a small sailboat made a sudden but graceful intrusion into his reconstruction of the old town. Quickly it slipped away, leaving only a small ripple in its wake.

Once again Luke's thoughts dropped below the water's surface.

It had been an old shanty town, colorful, but by Luke's time, run down and shabby.

Out of character from the rest of the ancient drab of downtown was a huge colonial brick home anchored between stores. It was the office of old Dr. Carey, who operated his business out of the downstairs, and lived up above. He was one ingenious human being—avid hunter, musician, writer, historian and philosopher extraordinaire.

Out back, chained to the garage, was his giant and vicious bird dog Balboa. This canine enjoyed nothing better than terrorizing people who cut through the yard on the way to the back streets of Currentville. The dog's leash ran almost to the house, but still allowed enough room for one to safely pass by, edging along the side of the house.

Late one Saturday night Stonewall Jackson, the town drunk, staggered recklessly into harm's way. It was reported later (though never confirmed because Stonewall would not admit or deny it, nor even remember) that the would-be victim got on his hands and knees and took on the animal on its own terms. Stonewall looked a mess when he woke up in jail the next day. But Balboa also showed signs of combat, and never displayed quite the same ardor again.

The thought of it caused the United States Supreme Court Justice to chuckle and shake his head.

A restaurant, two groceries, and Charlie Clark's Pool Hall led to the Standard Station on the corner. From there on out to the school a half-mile away were houses on both sides of the street.

Back up the right side of the street next to the bank was the newspaper office, *The Signal.* Luke had worked at the weekly folding papers on Thursday afternoons and taking in coal during the winter.

Next was a large charred gap in the run of buildings where a fire many years before had burned out a passage to the riverbank.

Through this parking lot, the width of two buildings, would move a mass of people for the Saturday drawings. Luke watched the drama unfold from the vantage point of his memory.

Punctually at 3 o'clock in the afternoon the town's elderly water superintendent Vester Tolin picked up the wooden keg kept at Willis Town's grocery. Carrying it on his shoulder, Vester moved down the street each Saturday toward the site. This Pied Piper, with amber trickling down his chin, was followed by old people with limps and carbuncles, barefoot kids with barking dogs, town people, farmers and their wives.

Finally, the gathering, whose size depended on the time of year and weather, reached a clearing behind the row of stores overlooking the river. There Vester gave the people time to encircle him, drawing close like metal filings to a magnet. He ceremoniously pulled the key from his pocket, the one which unlocked the latch of the keg containing the names of hundreds of the town's patrons. Vester enjoyed the attention, and made the most of this interlude of stardom in a life of tedium.

Shaking the container one last time, he dropped it down below his waist and allowed one of the small tots present to pull out a name. He raised the card to his aging eyes and bellowed out the name.

You had to be present to win. First drawing, five dollars. Second drawing, three dollars and the last dip into the cask, two dollars. All donated by local merchants.

After this event, the crowd disbursed, many heading for home. The drawing was the attraction of the day, the great divide which marked the coming and going of most of the people in this sleepy little Southern town on a Saturday afternoon.

Next to the empty lots through which Vester pulled his throng were two cavernous wooden buildings—aged and empty. They brooded over Main Street, their dust-laden windows staring blankly out over the sidewalk. Before Luke's time, they had been thriving businesses of one kind or another. Their unpainted facades were plastered with outdated political posters and circus circulars. Peering through the filmy windows with cupped hands, young boys could see the large, empty environs—scattered boxes, rusty beer cans and empty whiskey bottles. Sometimes there was evidence of an overnight stay by one of the town drunks, a discarded shirt or bologna rinds.

The sidewalk on that side of the street—the river side—was always in the afternoon shade. Dusty in summer, mud-covered in winter.

It led on down to the next place of business—Mr. Baer's clothing store. Cigar-chomping Abraham Baer and his old wife were the only Jewish family in town. They were respected, if a bit of a curiosity, and he was continually re-elected mayor of the town without opposition.

Next was a newer building, made of concrete blocks, which housed both Albert's Barber Shop and the laundry pickup service for the dry cleaners in Princeton, twelve miles away.

Toy Roberts, a squatty, tobacco-chewing, toothless little man—dirty and rough talking—served as the keeper of the pickup shop. He also operated a greasy popcorn machine, the stale yellowing heap of finished product going unsold most of the time.

In the winter Toy would sit in his cane-bottom chair next to the Warm Morning stove, peering through the plate glass window at the frosty goings on of downtown Currentville. In the summer he would move his corn maker and seat out onto the amber spattered and fly-infested sidewalk. There, leaning back against the shaded side of the building, he would religiously listen to St. Louis Cardinal baseball on his FM radio with the volume so loud one could keep up with the score all the way to the front of the prison.

Then, one hot July afternoon, Toy went to sleep and never woke up. He was buried on the rocky fringe of the town cemetery up on Pea Ridge. Only a small metal tag marked his final settling place. In a few months it had folded to the ground, and in a year it had disappeared. Nature took its course, and soon nobody knew where old Toy Roberts was—and nobody cared.

Luke Cameron's thoughts continued to drift.

There was the large, two story Currentville Hotel, which was next on that side of the street, anchoring the downtown area. It had a dreary lobby and restaurant on the first floor, seedy rooms upstairs.

The only stoplight in the village hung above the downtown intersection. Turn right and almost immediately past the DX Station, which sat on the corner, the road turned to gravel and led to the ferry. Turn left, and you were on Franklin Street, another tree-lined avenue graced by old homes.

It was there at this intersection on hot summer afternoons that itinerant preachers with loud speakers on top of their cars would park and preach the gospel to this dying town. These prophets of doom yelling and sweating profusely in the scorching sun were hard to ignore. But they were ignored.

He continued to gaze out across the water where the town had made its way out past the school, the baseball field, and abruptly came to an end as the fields and woods took over.

It was fixed in his mind, the winding little elongated town from Wrinklemeat's Grocery on the north up over Penitentiary Hill through town and out to the fork of the road on the south—one way to Nashville, the other to Louisville.

Squeezed in between the range of hills called Pea Ridge and the crooked Cumberland River, this mosaic of human inhabitation was one of the oldest settlements in the state.

Luke's mind tried to bring it all back.

Not only what it had been, but what it was. Down in its watery grave, he wondered, was there anything left, any sign of the past?

What could be left underneath the surface on the murky bottom which might give this burial place away?

Were the old streets intact, covered with silt?

Was the bottom flat, or sloping, as it was near the old lock and dam?

If the lake were drained, the plug pulled, would there be anything left to spark a memory, to remind him of the place it was?

Maybe a familiar foundation, an old fireplug, the lock gates themselves bolted together catching debris and trash?

The thought fascinated the Supreme Court Justice as he fell deeper and deeper into his nostalgic trance.

Foglike, his thoughts drifted over the years, across the imaginary landscape inside his head. The muddy flats disappeared, his footing became firm, the trees and buildings returned.

The grass, the streets, the smell, and the sounds. . . .

Chapter Two

The River

A stream not followed is a promise unfulfilled.

There is a river in every boy's life. For some it is real, and they are richer for it.

Eleven-year-old Luke Cameron stepped quickly along the riverbank on the way to town. Morning light was just beginning to shove away the darkness as the lights of the village were giving in to the gray messenger of day.

The village was Currentville, Kentucky—population 1,000—not counting the prisoners in the penitentiary on the hill. It was located on the narrow, winding, Cumberland River some 95 miles below Nashville, Tennessee. The river began as a stream in the brooks and branches of the Appalachian Mountain range far to the east. Gaining width and depth as it rolled along, it became a torrent by the time it tumbled over the Cumberland Falls and then headed south and west through the northern part of Tennessee. Finally, like a snake raising its head, it ran due north through far western Kentucky, emptying into the Ohio River at Smithland. This watery way navigated for 516 miles, and by the time it reached Currentville it was fully grown.

Twisting and turning through the tortuous times of earth's shifting crust, the course of this ribbon of rain had been fixed for thousands of years. Silently the gray stony waters slid northward, dutifully carrying its bounty to the Ohio, the Mississippi, and the sea. A good solid soldier of nature, onward through the ages it plodded its awesome and lonely way.

Sometime near the moment ancient man first worked with bronze, a resourceful spring broke loose from a cavern on the silent west bank, forty-four miles south of its mouth. From the lush meadowlands and the thick forest of hardwood and pine came varmints of varying sorts to drink of the sweet waters flowing into the river, and root out the salt deposits within the musty cave.

Moving in and out to the dreamy cadence of time, centuries of buffalo, raccoon, and deer left their mark upon the earth. Sunken paths and beaten trails cut their way through the thick forest, bringing perpetual life to the oasis.

American Indians in crude dugouts were the next to arrive at this scenic and convenient landing. Through the fertile lowlands, scenic palisades, and deep forests, they plied their way. First were the Shawnee, famed for their musical language, fine canoes, and hunting skills. Next came the Cherokees from the southeast, the Creeks from the south, and finally the Chickasaws of the west—all vying for hunting rights along the river valley.

Slowly the untainted beauty of the river valley became speckled with humanity. Crops of maize, corn, and later tobacco were hacked out of the wilderness and sporadically appeared along the ancient stream.

Indian encampments along the artery gave way to landings and log houses as the white man came upon the scene. Flatboats pulled into the settlement near the spring where several cabins had sprouted. By 1799 the grouping of hovels had become Currentville.

Soon the steamboat converted the frontier village into a bustling river town. Packet boats, laden with cotton, tobacco, molasses, and whiskey, tooted their ways in and out of the landing. Even a shipyard which hammered out sea-going vessels was established during the War of 1812. Currentville was a thriving little metropolis on the edge of the American frontier. Such American icons as Andrew Jackson, Aaron Burr, Jefferson Davis, Zachary Taylor, and Henry Clay, along with leading money moguls of the day, made visits there on their trips between New Orleans and Nashville. Union gunboats churned solemnly by on their way into the heart of the South, launching cannonballs toward the Confederate flags waving from houses along the shore. Around the turn of the century, the railroad had slackened the growth of Currentville to a crawl. With the dwindling river traffic, the town began to decline. It managed to survive, however, due in part to the construction of the main east to west highway to Louisville and Nashville. It entered Currentville to the west, climbed the large hill which overlooked the river, and dropped sharply off into the business district. From there it leveled off, running a straight course through the rest of town past the school, and eastward out of town. There the road forked. To the right led to Nashville, two hours away. Veering to the left took one on a circuitous route to Louisville, more than a half-day's journey.

By 1925, the face of the Cumberland River changed with the construction of a series of lower level navigation locks and dams. There were fifteen of them altogether from the first one at Currentville to one just twenty-nine miles below the headwaters of the Cumberland River at Burnside, Kentucky. These provided minimum pool levels even in the drought of summer to the entire stream, which at some times had become unnavigable. They also gave some new impetus to river traffic, and at least to the burgh of Currentville, the payroll for a lock and dam.

The little boy now moving smartly along the riverbank knew little of this.

Yet he knew it all. The damp, cool smell of mud and fish; a jumble of cottonwood, sycamore, hackberry, locust, and willow tilting over the concave banks; the bright evening sun, burning orange against the opposite shore; steam rising from the surface on cool October mornings; cranes, river gulls, and giant turtles; katydids and crickets chanting from the horseweed on summer nights.

By the time the stream reached Currentville, it was still scenic, but no longer spectacular. Breathtaking palisades, and mountain passes had long given way to soft and rolling farmland leveling off into vast stretches of fertile river bottoms.

This was not a lazy river. It constantly labored, day and night—moving, moving, moving.

Sometimes it worked overtime, taking its brown, surging surplus over the lock and dam, out of its banks and spreading out over the river bottoms, two miles across in some places. Even the streets, buildings, and homes of Currentville fell victim to its rage.

By late summer the low water moved almost imperceptibly. But it traveled all the time, even if sometimes at the pace of a snail. For this river had a mission, and one could not step twice into the same stream.

Luke's breeches were wet to the knees with the morning dew as he stomped his way along the edge of the cornfield. He moved out onto the neatly mowed grass of the government reservation just as the five o'clock whistle at the penitentiary moaned and groaned to a jagged end.

The hurried youth looked up to the top of the hill where the medieval-like fortress sat brooding over the river bottom.

The prison and the river: two powerful, yet subtle influences over the young lad's life. Each holding back the unknown. The massive stone walls shielding dark mysteries. The bends of the river, one upstream above the ferry, and another in the opposite direction, challenged the imagination—holding back the excitement of unknown lands.

Luke McCuistion Cameron wore the river at his side like a best friend. He came by it honestly. His father Alexander, known as Alec to all, was a lockman on the Currentville lock and dam. At the age of eighteen his father left the rigors of the farm and joined his older brother on one of the several dredge boats which plied the rivers of Kentucky and Tennessee for the U. S. Army Corps of Engineers. After several years he moved to the position of lockman, and was stationed at several locations until he returned to the one at Currentville, which he had helped to build as a young laborer on the dredge.

Alec married his childhood sweetheart Esther McCuiston, and these old friends so different in temperament and disposition forged a solid and lasting marriage—two varied limbs grafted together from a common trunk. The slender Alec with the black wavy hair was possessed of a strong and mercurial personality. His moods ranged from dark silence to flashes of tremendous warmth and humor. Esther, on the other hand, was calm, steady, and stoic. She never complained, always saw the best in people, and bore all with the deep and abiding faith of her devout father, Zachary Taylor McCuistion. Zack was widowed with ten children when Esther was only six weeks old. He farmed all week, and led singing at the Poplar Springs country church on Sunday morning. Asking no quarter, he persevered, raising a houseful of kids by himself. Taciturn, stern, yet charitable, Zack McCuistion had been one tough oak.

To Alec and Esther were born four children. Marilyn, the oldest, was married to a pipe fitter and lived in Chattanooga, Tennessee. Betty Jane was freshly betrothed to her high school sweetheart, who had been drafted. They were stationed at Fort Polk, Louisiana.

Still at home was Luke's older brother Bobby Joe. At sixteen, he was an exceptionally gifted athelete and the hope of the entire community. Tall, muscular and handsome, he could do it all. "On top of it all," people liked to say, "he's a darn good kid." Luke idolized his older brother, and Bobby Joe gave Luke about the same amount of attention most older brothers gave to their younger siblings — slightly less than the family dog.

This family of four lived in a modest white bungalow on the edge of town, just six houses up from where Wrinklemeat Hall's shabby little grocery store introduced the village. A wide hallway ran down the middle, a living room and Alec and Esther's bedroom off to the left; Luke and Bobby Joe's room, and the kitchen, to the right. It consisted of only four rooms, with a bathroom at the end of the hall.

The old house faced the busy highway, which passed only a few feet from the front door. It was split level, with a musty, dusty, but full-size basement in which Alec's workshop, the washroom, a coal bin, and other storage space found their places.

From the front porch, looking in all directions, one saw

only town—houses, sidewalks, telephone poles, front yards, and trees. Off the back porch, however, a broad panorama of river bottom opened up to the sky. Luke lived half in town, half in the country. A rutty old road led down from the street between Luke's house and his neighbor's and headed straight through cornfields and horseweed to the riverbank, less than a quarter of a mile away. It was down this roadway—used almost exclusively by fishermen and farmers—that Luke made his many treks to the river and town. A shorter route was up Penitentiary Hill and down the other side. But Luke preferred the way of the river unless time was of the essence—as it usually was when he made his long way to school on the other side of town.

Bouncing beside him on this morning was his faithful dog Soldier. A big black shaggy mutt, he possessed just enough of the Chow breed to have a purple tongue. And he had just enough of everything else to be incredibly ugly.

This loyal critter was only the canine representative of the diverse pet menagerie at the Cameron home. While the composition varied from plague to plague, stray to stray, and season to season, it was always at full strength—a bunch of cats and a litter of kittens, two parakeets, a snapping terrapin, gold fish, and a couple of tamed rabbits.

But by far the most intriguing member of this animal kingdom was Cocoa, the pet raccoon. Bobby Joe had raised this masked mascot on a bottle from a tiny baby after finding her on the side of the highway near her dead mother. It had been slow going at first, but gradually the scrawny varmint took hold and not only survived but thrived. She grew into a huge, lovable fur ball as tame as the rest of the household pets and much more engaging. While wary of strangers, she nestled in the laps of those she knew and romped in the yard with Soldier.

But a meddlesome and mischievous streak constantly kept Cocoa in hot water with Esther.

One Sunday upon returning home from church the family found the kitchen blanketed in white, with the flour canister turned upside down. The culprit had fled the scene and disappeared. After a diligent search, Cocoa was found hidden in a corner under the bed. Her beady eyes peered out through the mask at the angry faces, her coat an incriminating white.

On another occasion, Esther was washing clothes in the basement. When her back was turned, Cocoa slipped up on the open washer, cradling an egg she had taken off the kitchen table. The furry masquerader slipped and fell into the churning wash. She almost drowned before Luke's mother could pull the plug on the machine and fish the drenched intruder out of the brink. When Esther drained the machine with the rubber hose, eggshells were found in the bottom. For some time afterward, and especially to Bobby Joe's chagrin, egg spots showed up on some of the family clothing.

But the most dramatic and unexpected episode involving Cocoa had a happier ending. One morning Esther opened the large wooden quilt box in the bedroom to discover their most interesting pet lying on top of the bedding. And she had company. Snuggled up under her, barely visible, were two baby raccoons fervidly taking nourishment.

Esther's excited birth announcement both shocked and amused the family.

"Well," Alec finally drawled dryly, "it just goes to show that we don't know much about Coca's nightlife."

One coon in the house was trouble enough. So Alec advised that he was going to take the newborns to the river for a quick and painless demise. Even Esther, constantly the main victim of racoonish mischief, protested. So Alec agreed to a reprieve—but only if they could find the youngsters another home. By the time they were weaned, and before they had totally demolished the house, Bobby Joe and Luke had found two friends reckless enough to take the little urchins off their hands. Meanwhile, Cocoa was "fixed" by the vet.

On this June dawn, Luke moved from the rough ground and lashing weeds onto the easy walking of the closely cropped grass of the government reservation. Down the long slope to his right was the lock wall, which spread out to mid channel and the dam. Two lockmen, dressed in familiar khaki, leaned their bodies into the spars of the lower gate capstan, pushing and straining in a circular motion. Slowly the large steel bulwarks began to open. In the lock pit, the giant tug *The Bullfrog* rumbled impatiently as its large diesel engine labored, eager to rejoin its tow of barges tied up below.

The keepers of this lock and dam—a crew of twelve including the lockmaster—had no easy task.

Regular lockings were in and of themselves busy and strenuous ordeals. Tows had to be broken up into smaller bites to accommodate the size of the lock chamber. The crew worked feverishly, pulling the butterfly valves which controlled the flow of water into the pit, cranking open the gates, and engaging the haulage of the barges through the chamber with the assistance of a 60-cycle, electrically operated motor connected to a winch. The haulage unit was placed on a narrow gauge steel rail so it could be pulled up the riverbank during periods of high water. Sometimes a locking could take up to several hours, day and night, under the searing sun of summer, or in the biting winds of winter.

In addition to locking boats, the lock crew was responsible for raising and lowering the wickets of the dam to control the river spillway. This was especially hazardous work as the men edged out onto the narrow dam, armed with a long handle hook. There with the assistance of a winch line and hook, they would fish around in the surging water for the handle of the wicket submerged in the bottom of the stream. Once secured, another lockman would turn the hand wheel on the winch positioned on the outer wall and crank the section of the dam out of the water and into place. Upon summons from the Nashville office, this task had to be performed forthwith, without regard to time or weather.

In addition to all of this, the lock crew was responsible for the care and maintenance of the thirty-five acre reservation which included a stretch of land on the opposite bank. Mowing, weed cutting, and clearing of debris dominated all of their summer time between lockings.

Then, in the winter and early spring, when floodwaters surged over the lock and dam, there was the constant and recurring exercise of "unrigging" and "rigging" of the lock wall. This involved dismantling and removing all the locking machinery and equipment off the surface of the wall, and reinstalling them when the water had receded. Sometimes, and it might be in the darkness of midnight, the floodwaters would reverse before all the rigging could be recaptured.

Only in the midst of winter when the water would bury the lock and dam for a few continuous weeks, was there a slight reprieve from this demanding routine. Then, as the giant tugs and tows sailed over the slight ripple marking the watery grave of the dam, lockmen would retreat to the lock house to paint, retool, and overhaul their equipment.

A team of twelve men, working three shifts around the clock. It was a steady job, and it was steady work.

This configuration of river, concrete, steel, coursing water, and laboring men—this government industry, this navigational checkpoint, was a major part of Luke Cameron's life.

From the time when he was a small child, he followed his father along the precipice, staring into the darkened walls of the lowered chamber, pushing manfully against the capstan spars, harboring his secret ambition to someday wear the bright red castle symbol of the Corps of Engineers. He and Soldier would often wait patiently on the bank or lock wall near the stern of a resting tug. Invariably the cook would appear, throw the eager canine a bone and the youngster a banana from the bulging stalk which hung enticingly at the back of the ship.

Sometimes during a long summertime locking, Alec would hoist his small son over the safety line of the boat, and Luke would be treated to a sumptuous meal from the warm and spotless galley. Always there was fleeting magic as the gargantuan snake of steel and diesel reconnected and began to rumble out of the lock. Luke would stand and watch as it headed out to a world of adventure, the muscled and tanned deckhands still ratcheting the barges tight as it picked up speed. The faraway ports of "New Orleans," "Shreveport," "Cincinnati," "Davenport," "Vicksburg," and "Pittsburgh" stenciled on the sides of the barges boldly beckoned from above the turbulent wake. Luke was mystified how such large, busy creatures from such exotic points of origin could end up—even for a short time—on the remote shores of little

Currentville.

Occasionally old wooden paddle wheelers, colorful ghosts of the river's past, would come lumbering into town and through the locks. On listless summer days, the steamy air would be transformed by the distant music of the calliope, drawing all the young boys to the river. Pistons pounding, bells ringing, water spraying, passengers on the rail, these "excursion boats" painted in bright red and white gingerly felt their way into the slot. Some were show boats, staying overnight, the musical variety show pulling in a packed house from the town. And then they would disappear around the bend, the calliope bidding a joyful farewell. And so they passed away into another age, *The Cotton Blossom, The Idlewild*, the *Majestic*. But not before the boys of Currentville saw them.

The town could not escape the hovering scowl of the prison, any more than it could escape the sounds of the lock and dam. The humming of navigation, the boats blowing as they signaled their approach, metal against metal, the solid reverberating thump of fist-sized ropes slung against hollow steel decking, the clacking of the haulage motor, deckhands yelling, pilots blaring out orders from their perch. Even the oily smell of diesel would drift into town. And when the windows of the village were flung open during the torrid summer nights, the low, mesmerizing roar of the cascading dam mingled with the river breeze to provide some solace.

On the upper end of the lock wall, a concrete ramp about twelve feet wide moved up the riverbank to the lock house. Above it was more hill, and the row of houses which clung to the side of Penitentiary Hill. It was through this area that Luke now hurriedly moved.

He passed the two-story, white wooden lock house with the tin roof. On the first floor, garage size doors swung open at each end, providing a drive-through hallway. This area housed the heavy equipment, tools, and machinery such as mowers and compressors. There was also a coal bin.

The main floor, which was reached by a long flight of stairs at each end of the building, was the headquarters for the lockmen.

In the first large room was the office, with some desks, file cabinets, wooden chairs, telephones, and the two-way radio which constantly crackled with river traffic. Off to the side was a bathroom. There was a water fountain, above which hung a paper cup dispenser and canister of salt tablets—kept on hand to induce sweating and prevent overheating under the boiling summer sun.

In the back was a larger open room which doubled as a workshop and lounge for the men. A long, wooden eating table took up the center of the room, flanked by several chairs. In one corner were the stove and refrigerator. Against the back wall was a row of lockers, one for each worker with his respective name printed neatly in block letters on the door. This room had both a bathroom and a shower. A storage room housed raingear, waders, and other types of boots and clothing. On another wall hung the small hand tools, with their respective shapes painted where they hung, so a quick glance could tell what was missing—a little touch of the real army which always fascinated Luke.

The place had a manly odor about it, made cozy in the winter by coal-burning stoves and perking coffee. It was cooled in the summer by ceiling fans coaxing river breezes through the open windows and out the doors.

This was the work house for a group of men in their prime, some of them young combat veterans of World War II. Luke made it a place to be, even when Alec was not working, his place to listen, watch, and learn. These rugged but likable rivermen took a liking to Luke, teased him, bantered with him, and welcomed his company. Within this gathering of men, this nest of masculine influences, the youngster slowly constructed his own image of what manhood was all about. This picture grew from winter nights, as he sleepily nodded off to the banter of the evening shift. It took shape on summer nights lying out on the grass under the stars, as men stripped to their undershirts, drew on cigarettes, spit amber into cans, and looked out over their own river. They watched, waited for boats, and talked. These virile, vigorous creatures, grown still under the calming blanket of night spoke softly of the grist of life. From separate ships they came aboard a common shift, warriors to a common purpose, resolved to carry the simple burden of manhood with the determined visage of the river itself. They spoke of many things, from their wives, children, work, and politics to baseball and religion. And they talked of other men. Unknown to these rough-hewn laborers, they were sculptors of a sort, slowly carving, with their words and ways, the character of the yielding stone before them.

"I worked with ole Carter on the dredge. He was as strong as an ox, and wouldn't back down from anyone."

"Yeah, I saw him whup a guy twice his size down in Dover."

"But I tell you another thing. You could bank on what he told you. You could depend on him."

"His brother Tom was lockmaster up at Lock A."

"Yeah, he was a hulluva guy too. I worked under him for two years. Damn good riverman. They had that little ferry above the lock like we do here. The prop on the tug got all messed up. Tom was out of town and the assistant lockmaster Jake Lester let the owner of the ferry pull it in the lock, tie her on good and hard, and dropped the water so they could get under and fix it. Some busybody reported it to the Nashville office. In a few days old Gus Rogers from the District office went down there ready to nail sombody's scalp to the wall. Ole Tom told him, 'Listen Gus, I'm the lockmaster of this lock and I approved it. School buses use that ferry, the U.S. Mail goes across that ferry, and it's the only way the doctor and undertaker can get to those people. So you can hold me fully accountable for it. If anyone's head is going to roll, it had better be mine.' Old Gus just packed up his briefcase and went back to Nashville. After he left, Tom turned to his assistant and said, 'You did the right thing, Jake.' Boy, let me tell you, we would walk through hell for ole Tom Carter."

Lockman Hollis Hunt was a wiry little guy who been wounded at the Anzio beachhead. He was also an avid baseball fan, and a devoted follower of the St. Louis Cardinals. On summer nights when he worked the evening shift, he would plug up his old Philco radio in the open window and sit out on the lock house lawn and listen to the game. Luke would drop by when Hollis was working nights and listen to the game with him and talk baseball.

"That Musial is some kind of guy," Hollis explained to Luke one night. "He never beefs with the umpires. He's always a good sport and just goes about the business of playing his heart out without shooting off his mouth or making a scene. Williams is a better hitter, but Ted thinks more of his hitting than he does of his team. Stan's a team player, and a winner. In the '46 series between Boston and St. Louis, the Cardinals put a big shift on against Williams. Put everyone over on the right side of the field. Ted took it as a personal challenge and was too hard-headed to go the other way. So he just plowed right on, swinging away trying to drill the ball through that shift. Well he had a miserable time, and Stan and the Cardinals won the series. Ole Stan would have tore 'em up with a switch like that because he would go to the opposite field.

"Did you know Stan bought a house for one of his minor league managers? Sure did. The guy helped him become an out-fielder after he hurt his arm as a pitcher. Stan didn't forget him. A couple of years ago after Stan was making the big money, he bought the guy and his wife a house in Houston. That's loyalty for you.

"Tell you another thing about 'the Man'—and you know that's what they call him, 'Stan the Man,' A few years back some big Mexican wheeler-dealers offered him about five times what he was making to jump to the Mexican League and play baseball. Some of the major leaguers took the money and went down there and played. Not Stan. I read where he said he looked over at his little baby boy and knew that he could never explain to him some-day why he didn't honor his contract with the Cardinals."

Hollis would fall to silence, letting his words of adulation linger in the air.

Luke became enthralled with Stan Musial, that wonderful, friendly smile and the beautiful red birds perched on the front of his snow white uniform. He read everything he could find on him. Luke even tried to play like him, mimicking Stan's crooked peek-a-boo batting stance. He even tried to act like Stan.

From Hollis, Luke also acquired almost a mystic apprecia-tion for the American pastime. Hollis, on those star-studded and balmy summer nights, loved to pontificate on the sport.

"You know what the greatest single play in all sports is, Luke?" he inquired one night when he was especially reflective.

"It's the 3-6-1 double play in baseball. Think about this. A small round ball is thrown at ninety miles an hour from sixty feet and six inches to a man holding a round stick, two to three inches thick at the end. Amazingly, he hits it on the ground at about 130 miles per hour. The first baseman ranging way out of position catches it and throws it to second base at least forty-five feet away. There the shortstop is covering for the second baseman who is out of position going for the ball. He returns it to first, where the pitcher just arrives in time from his position sixty feet away to cover for the first baseman who is out of position from fielding the ball. The throw nips the runner by a step, a fraction. And all of this, all of this teamwork covering for each other—and that's the biggest part of the play, covering for each other—this baseball traveling over two hundred feet through three pairs of human hands, all of it takes place in less than six seconds. One screw up, one bobble, one man hesitating for a split second, one man not looking out for his team mate, and the whole thing gets botched."

Luke could tell Hollis had thought about this many times. The lockman lifted his eyes into the summer night and in reverent tones concluded, "It's a beautiful thing to watch."

Thus there emerged, from these casual conversations, broadening criteria for manliness which Luke absorbed into every nook and cranny of his soul.

Luke not only listened. He was also a keen and sensitive observer.

A sweat-soaked, red-faced lockman returned to the lock house with his fellow workers after a morning of cutting weeds across the river. On his left arm, a large white bandage was turning crimson, and the blood was still dripping off his hand. Casually the man went to the basement, ripped off the gauze, and doused the wound in coal oil. After rewrapping, he ascended the steps for dinner in the cool confines of the back room. Then, they headed out again, down the bank, to the skiff, and slowly pulled themselves back across the stream under the scorching sun. Not one word about the injury from anyone. No sympathy asked. No sympathy given. Grapple it to the ground on your own. To do otherwise was unthinkable, unmanly.

On rare occasions women would arrive upon the scene. A wife bringing by a forgotten lunch pail, or picking up a check. Men would stand, hats would go off, and shirts would go on; the visitor would be addressed as "ma'am" even though she might be years younger. There would descend upon these rugged and unpolished laborers a feathery and delicate manner which bordered on meekness.

Lockman Ben Cooper was about the only crew member who did not make over Luke. He did not banter and kid with him, or engage him in conversation. He was not unfriendly or hostile, just quiet and reserved.

One bright autumn afternoon Luke was leisurely making his way home from school when he stopped by the lock house. It was the evening shift change, and a half-dozen men loitered in the back room—those coming on, and those going home. The mood was light and cheerful, the replacements fresh and spirited, those departing relieved and relaxed. Ben sat at the wooden table, lunch box and thermos at his side, ready to depart for home. Their eyes met as Luke walked through the door.

"How ya doing, Pumpkin?" Ben spoke first, using the nickname Luke's father had laid upon him when he was just a baby and used exclusively by family and lockmen. It was the first time Luke could remember Ben speaking to him first and using the affectionate title. He returned the greeting, visited a few minutes with Alec who was on the evening shift, and then headed for home.

That night, Luke's father called Esther with stunning news. Ben Cooper had been killed in a car wreck on his way home from work.

Luke moved about the house as in a trance. Death, in all its awesome and overwhelming significance, came down upon him for the first time. He had lost grandparents. They had been old, expected to die. But Ben Cooper was young, energetic, strong, a father of young kids. He had been there one moment getting ready to go home from work. And within minutes he was no longer a breathing, talking, moving human being.

That night Luke did not sleep. He thrashed about in his bed until the sheets were damp with perspiration. Try as he would, he could not remove the image from his mind. In slow motion he moved time and time again through the lock house. There was Ben Cooper relaxing at the table, his eyes meeting Luke's and the friendly greeting, "How ya doing, Pumpkin?"

"How ya doing, Pumpkin?" reverberated continuously off the walls of his head as the night wore on. He heard his father come in from work around midnight and slip into his bed. Still Ben Cooper's voice haunted him.

At last he arose and went out onto the front porch. It was a cool October night with a full harvest moon giving a ghostly bright glow to the outside world. Luke settled onto the glider and stared out over the narrow yard and lonely street, into the darkened houses across the way. He felt like the only human being on the face of the planet. He and Ben Cooper. But Ben Cooper was dead. Dead and yet still not quite dead. Finally near dawn, his eyes became heavy and he began to shiver. Somehow he moved back into the house and fell into his bed.

The next day, a Saturday, Luke felt a morbid and irresistible urge to return to the lock house. When he arrived there the crew was down on the wall locking a boat, leaving the headquarters empty. Luke moved up the front steps, through the front office, and into the back room. He stared at the spot where just hours before he had seen Ben Cooper sitting, prepared to go home, not knowing he would never make it. Luke became slightly dizzy as the heavy thought rushed over him. Slowly, he turned and was drawn to the core of the emotional magnet which had pulled him into this haunted workplace. He stood in front of Ben Cooper's locker, peering breathlessly at the block letters. An avalanche of colliding and largely nonsensical questions flooded his mind. What had Ben Cooper thought when he closed the locker for the last time? Who would clean out his locker? How long would it be? Who would get the space? A new lockman? Would he know? Would he feel strange about it?

But the most riveting questions of all: Where is Ben

Cooper? What happened to him? What is death? Does it hurt? Is it good or is it bad?

Insistent was the query: Where is Ben Cooper NOW?

Instinctively, as if being moved now by some larger force than himself, Luke reached out and raised the latch on the locker and carefully pulled it open. He felt a ghoulish and exciting sensation as he looked into the coffin. A blue towel and an extra khaki shirt hung on the pegs. In the bottom was a pair of rubber boots. Luke's eyes moved to the top shelf. A pack of gum, a toothbrush, and a bottle of cough medicine. Testimony to the working day life of one who had gone on.

There was also on the top shelf a water glass, half full of pennies. Luke saw a folded piece of paper underneath. After a brief but frantic debate within himself, he reached up and pulled the paper out from under the glass. He unfolded what was a sheet of lined notebook paper. Luke viewed the large and irregular printing of a small child, written with a dim lead pencil.

"YOU are the best DaddY In the WORLLD.
I LOVE YOU.
Laura Sue."

The note went back underneath the glass, and the young boy carefully closed the locker door. Pain came to his heart, a sharp, stabbing hurt, replacing the fearful mystery which had brought him to that place. An overwhelming feeling of sadness, loss, and loneliness descended upon him as he turned and quietly walked out of the lock house, down the steps into the brilliant sun.

So all of this—the river, the lock and dam, the lockmen— were all a big part of the eleven year old's life, as he passed by the lock house on this particular morning in a big hurry.

This was one of the most important days of the summer.

The Bisbees were coming to town.

Chapter Three

The Bisbees

A mighty purpose is the soul of a great promise.

As Luke Cameron made his way along the river, a caravan of minstrels was entering town from the south.

It consisted of six large tractor trailer trucks, three panel trucks, two pickup trucks, several cars pulling house trailers, a converted school bus, and two station wagons. All the vehicles were painted bright red and white.

Each of them carried the same message emblazoned along the side: "Bisbee's Comedians."

It was a traveling entertainment group—a mix between vaudeville and the Grand Ole Opry. In 1956 it represented a vanishing segment of American entertainment.

At one time there were over 400 different "tent shows" traveling the breadth of America. Before television, they brought Broadway song and dance to the dusty back roads of the United States. Music, acting, magic, and comedy were all artfully put together in one type of extravaganza or another. Country folks poured into small towns throughout the land to catch the bright lights and painted faces which lit up their drab existence.

"Bisbee's Comedians" was one such group.

They traveled throughout Kentucky and Tennessee during the summer months and retired to Memphis for the winter. There they mainly stored their equipment, performed maintenance, disbanded most of their members for a short while and generally regrouped.

On this morning the crew of singers, musicians, comics, actors and actresses, along with the supporting cast of business manager, stagehands, and workers, were bone tired and road weary. They had just broken camp in the town of Cadiz some twenty-five miles away after a three night stand. The performers had finally made it to their bunks after midnight. The less fortunate canvasmen had labored until almost dawn, breaking down the big tent and packing up the substantial load. They were adept at folding up into a neat traveling package this brightly lit, glamorous, and colorful road show.

Asleep in the second trailer was the star of the show, Wallace Lee Paisley, known mostly by his stage name of Toby Ticklebush. His long, skinny form jostled about with the movement of the road and his feet dangled off the end of the bed.

Wallace had been born in Pittsburgh, Pennsylvania, in 1910. His mother was a teacher who was murdered by his father when he was only two. His father was convicted and hung, and Wallace went to live with various relatives until reaching the age of ten. At that time he ran away, slipping aboard a packet boat heading down the Ohio River. The captain of the riverboat *Viceroy* took him under his wing and tutored him in the ways of the river. By the time he was fourteen he could steer and navigate the huge vessel as well as a grown man.

On one fateful voyage as the *Viceroy* made its way up the Monongahela River with a load of cross ties and passengers, the boiler exploded, killing forty-five people, including his beloved mentor. Wallace escaped with hardly a scratch.

He stayed with the river, catching on with different towing lines, and finally ended up in New Orleans. There, at the age of eighteen, he met and married a beautiful young girl of French par-

ents. While Wallace worked at the port, he became interested in
the local theater and began to get bit parts. His lack of education
held him back, but through the encouragement and financial assistance of his wife, he received private tutoring as well as instruction
on manners and etiquette. Soon he became a man of learning and
style and he found that he had a real talent for acting, especially in
comedy roles. But his success led him into a new circle of friends
and temptations. Booze and womanizing finally wrecked his marriage, and he left New Orleans and headed for New York.

He went there on a whim, not knowing anyone, and
arrived with hardly a dime to his name. He was playing the bass
tuba the day it rained gold. Wallace met a professional stage director on the train, and won him over with his charm. The
roustabout went directly to work as a stagehand in one of the
Broadway theaters. Soon he met a struggling Russian born actress
and moved in with her. His was a life of bright lights, exotic people, and the throbbing excitement of the world's show town. He
became friends with Jerry Callison, a rumpled and gray old friend
of the recently late and great Harry Houdini. Sitting around
smoky and boisterous coffee houses and bars, the two would drink
and talk until dawn, mostly about the legendary magician. And
about magic. Wallace became obsessed with it. Over a period of
time, from his conversations with Callison and others, as well as
from reading all the material on the subject he could find, Wallace
Paisley decided he wanted to give magic a try.

After watching and studying the best in New York, Wallace
Paisley began to practice on his own, sometimes taking the stage in
the cavernous theater where he worked when it was empty. Finally
a few friends threw in some money, made a few phone calls, and
the deck rose beneath his feet. He was off. It was rocky going at
first, but before long he was regularly booked in night clubs and
variety shows around the Big Apple. "Wallace the Wizard" performed both on his own as well as accompanying better known
musical groups as a "warmup" to the main attraction.

So successful was his act that he signed up with an agent
and began performing up and down the Eastern seaboard. Boston,
Philadelphia, Hartford, and Baltimore were all ports of call. His

shapely girlfriend, dressed in sequin blouse and shorts, became part of his act. She was ever smiling and gesturing just right as she was sawed in half, made to disappear, and turned into a rabbit in a puff of smoke. At the age of thirty, Wallace was exactly where he wanted to be—in show business.

After confirming that his Louisiana wife had divorced him from afar, he married his Russian lover.

Over the next five years Mr. and Mrs. Paisley experienced highs and lows, but mostly highs. Then Tarinka, his wife, grew tired of the grueling pace. She wanted a child before she grew too old. So, Wallace relented and within a year a daughter, Tasa, was born to the union. Without his helpmate at his side, "Wallace the Wizard" suffered. Soon he encountered financial troubles. Then, in the pressure cooker of the large city, he began to drink excessively. He and Tarinka fought more and more, the marriage taking some staggering wounds. Finally, after weeks of secret plotting, she packed a few belongings, slung the baby on her hip, and left, leaving Wallace a short, cryptic farewell note. The spunky immigrant headed for Nashville, Tennessee, where her uncle had established himself in the hardware business after coming to this country at the time of the Russian revolution of 1917.

Wallace languished in New York. Dropping his magic show, he went back to his old job as stagehand. He was lovesick, missing his Russian blond immensely. He knew where she had gone, and wrote her long repentant letters, asking forgiveness and pledging to quit drinking if she would return. It was 1947, and finally a letter came. She would not return. But he could join her if he liked. She had an apartment, a job, and was living under the protective wing of her uncle's large family. Apparently she was also lonely.

Nashville, Tennessee.

Wallace pondered it. He had been through there a few times while working on the river many years before. Not much of a town compared with Gotham. But he was close to forty, existing in a cold-water flat, alone. So he collected his meager belongings, scraped together enough money for the train fare, and was off to the sunny South.

After a joyous reunion with his wife and kid, things worked out pretty well for a while. He got a job at a local boat yard, and made a gallant effort to curtail his drinking. But after a while he and Tarinka drifted apart and then settled into a rather strange relationship. He moved into an apartment of his own, and they became more like friends than husband and wife. It turned out to be a rather comfortable and acceptable arrangement. They visited, went out together, enjoyed their kinky-haired little daughter, and sometimes he even stayed over. But for the most part, they went their separate ways.

Wallace grew weary of the tedious job at the boatyard. Then he hooked on as a deckhand with the showboat *Cotton Blossom*. But he wasn't a deckhand for long.

One slow afternoon he began to cut up on the narrow little stage as the old paddle wheeler plodded down the muddy Cumberland. With a deck of cards and a handkerchief, interlaced with some hilarious mimicking, he had the boat crew in stitches. Sitting in the back of the empty theater was the show master, having mid-afternoon coffee.

This guy was good, really good, he thought. Better than what he had at show time. So almost overnight, Wallace Paisley graduated from scrubbing decks and oiling engines to showboat performer.

The *Cotton Blossom* plowed the rivers of the upper South. It was a brightly colored, wooden stern wheeler bringing entertainment to the landings of small river towns far away from the bright lights of the big city. Musicians, comedians, magicians, and some melodrama thrown in for good measure, made up the repertoire. The tiny keyboard of the calliope, sitting aloft on the upper deck, blasted out peppy music as the attraction approached the landing from around the bend.

It was work Wallace enjoyed, satisfying his love for the river and show business and his wanderlust. Crowds were easy to please, starving as they were for any kind of merriment and diversion from their listless lives.

But the living conditions were not the best, and most important, the pay was dismal. Each winter the boat shut down and took haven at some port, usually in Paducah. Only a skeleton maintenance crew remained as the entertainers disbanded.

Wallace always returned to Nashville. Interestingly, his life on the river seemed to have improved his marriage. He had almost quit drinking. So each winter he moved back in with Tarinka and little Tasa.

He picked up odd jobs until late March, when he would return to doing magic tricks and comedy on *The Cotton Blossom.*

Then one winter he got a call from a friend with whom he had worked on the showboat and had left to go with Bisbee's Comedians. They needed both a new magic act and a lead comic for the role of Toby, the lovable and popular star of the traveling tent show.

Wallace was familiar with the Bisbees. They were the class act of traveling vaudeville. Begun in the twenties by Jess Bisbee of Memphis, Tennessee, the show had built up a reputation of first-rate talent, clean family fun, and a loyal summer following throughout Kentucky and Tennessee. Because of their popularity, the gate was heavy, and the pay was good. Just as important, they traveled comfortably with house trailers and cars. Wallace would be able to bring Tarinka and Tasa along if he wished.

He jumped at the chance. His exuberance was so infectious that he convinced the director he could do both the magic show *and* play the part of Toby.

After a short audition, the Pittsburgh native was hired. He was a rousing success, and it didn't take long for the management and the fans to get used to the loss of the legendary Rod Brasfield who had played Toby so splendidly for many years.

As the procession made its way into sleepy Currentville, Wallace was in his fourth season with the Bisbees.

He was completely unaware of his blood ties to this small village.

The brother of Wallace's grandfather had left Pittsburgh in 1852 and traveled down the Ohio River all the way to the Mississippi River and a little town called Wickliffe on the western end of Kentucky. There he liked what he saw, got off the boat, and got a job. He eventually married the daughter of a Methodist minister and raised a family of eleven kids. One of these, a daughter, moved to Paducah, another river town about twenty-five miles away, where she became a schoolteacher.

Lorina was her name, and she married a salesman for a local drug company. Her husband traveled all over West Kentucky and Tennessee and was gone for a week at a time. They began to have children, and the constant separation became unacceptable. Then on a regular stop at Currentville, he learned that the drug-store was for sale. He arranged to buy it and he and Lorina brought their two children to settle in the quaint little river town.

One of those children was Cora Lambert, who was only a few months old when her family arrived in Currentville. There she grew up in the timeless and peaceful routine of the little town. At nineteen she married Lester Barrett, ten years her senior, an ener-getic and industrious insurance agent. Soon after the birth of their only child, and with the help of the matronly black maid Ola, she went to work as a secretary at the penitentiary.

On this morning, with the sun casting its first rays against the house tops of Currentville, as "Wallace the Wizard" crept into town, and as Luke Cameron made his hasty way along the river-bank, Douglas Lee Barrett, the young son of Lester and Cora Barrett, lay sleeping in his bed. So it was a testimony to the intri-cate quiltwork of American migration, that Wallace Paisley had no inkling he had relatives in this sleeping little town. The crawling line of vehicles was drawing him closer to a young distant cousin now slumbering, just as he was in his bed.

Douglas Lee Barrett, known as "Birdseed" by all but his immediate family, was the same age as Luke Cameron and one of his best friends. Fortunately for both of them, they were next door neighbors, separated only by the large side yards between the two wooden frame houses. A cherry tree stood on the boundary where the two boys often met and talked when they wanted to escape the ears of the adult world.

Birdseed was a precocious and effervescent child. His weak eyes required glasses, and his frail and spindly frame was com-pletely devoid of any athletic skill or dexterity. His forte was his gray matter and being the top student in his class. The term "nerd" had not yet been invented. But even so, he would not have completely fit the mold. For even if his status as long on brains, short on brawn brought him some ridicule among his peers, he was nevertheless popular because of his friendly and helpful personality. He tried unsuccessfully to cover over his superior intellect, and the effort itself endeared him to his friends. But his mind was his strength, upon which his buddies relied from time to time, especially at exam time, or on special school projects. Birdseed was—in spite of his athletic limitations and the overprotection of his parents—pretty much one of the boys.

The origin of his nickname bonded him to the community of boys early on. In the first grade he had contracted a minor scalp disease which had required shaving a part of his head, and the application of some white sticky salve. One day during a school recess, one of the boys from the upper grades came running by where Douglas Barrett and his friends were playing. Looking upon the infected scalp doctored with glistening gook, the eighth grader exclaimed in disgust, "Hey boy, what are you doing with that bird shit on your head?"

The playground erupted in giggles and laughter, to the embarrassment and chagrin of little Douglas. To the tittering of the little girls, to the horse laughs of the boys, the name stuck. Doug tried to fight back, but was soundly whipped when he protested.

One afternoon after school, while being taunted by the class bullies to the amusement of the giggling female gallery, Doug flew into a hysterical rage and began to scream and cry uncontrollably.

In stepped Luke Cameron. The future justice of the United States Supreme Court laid down an ingenious compromise. This nickname did not work, he offered, because they could not call Douglas that in front of teachers or grown-ups. At the same time, it was a pretty funny thing, even Douglas must agree. So he proposed changing the name (and he was thinking as he talked) to "uh....Birdseed. Yeah, Birdseed. And that way we can call him that all the time."

It satisfied the blood lust of the badgering roughnecks.

And it was a tremendous relief to his vanquished friend. It would-n't have been his first pick for a name, but then it was a welcome relief from what he was being called. So from then on it was "Birdseed" to everyone but his parents. They never could under-stand the label, and everyone avoided explaining it to them.

So, while Wallace the Wizard rolled into town, Birdseed continued to snooze. Luke trudged on up to the flat clearing on the riverbank just behind the row of downtown stores. It was where the Bisbees would set up shop.

Boys were already congregating near the wooden steps which led down from the sidewalk to the grassy field. Only a huge sycamore tree, spreading its branches in every direction, stood on the open plain. The strapping young lads, ranging in age from ten to eighteen were all there for one purpose. They wanted a job with Bisbee's Comedians. It was a happening. A handful of the bigger boys would be selected to assist the Bisbee canvasmen put up the large 60-by-155-foot tent which would shelter over 1,500 people. For their few hours work each would receive free passes to the show, two for each night. Younger kids would be employed to work the shows, hawking snow cones, popcorn, and candy up and down the aisles. They, too, would be compensated with passes. The jobs were highly sought, and given out on a first come basis. You had to show up early or you were out of luck.

Seated on the bottom step, peering out sleepily into the morning haze, were two more of Luke's friends.

Donnie Hawkins was a year older than Luke, his blond hair cropped into a short burr. Good natured and even tempered, his sunny face was adorned with a wealth of freckles and a crooked smile. His father ran a saw mill outside of town, and his family lived out near the school. When Donnie was born, his four year old sister had a hard time with the name, and referred to him as "Donkey." So, almost from his very beginning, that became his handle.

Sitting next to Donkey was Jack Franklin, also a grade ahead of Luke, but a close buddy. He was tall for his age, with long arms and an athletic frame. His dark eyes possessed some hint of mischief, and his angular face was crowned with dark black hair coiffured in a stylish flattop. Jack's father worked as a guard at the penitentiary, and his family lived up on a ridge behind the town.

These three young boys—Luke, Donkey, and Jack—as well as Birdseed and most every male of Currentville under eighteen, had never known life without each other. From their first recollections of church socials, school days, Bible School, or shots at the health office, these same faces and names had meshed as part and parcel of life. One could not remember when one first saw another, no more than they could remember their first step or last diaper.

They were the boys of Currentville. They had no beginning, and they had no end. Or so it seemed on this brilliant June morning in 1956.

Both Donkey and Jack were roused out of their sleepy stupor by the sight of their good friend Luke Cameron.

"Did you hear about the trade?" were Jack's first words.

"Yeah," Luke responded dejectedly.

"They're crazy," was all Donkey could muster.

They were talking about the big baseball trade of the day before when the St. Louis Cardinals had traded popular Red Schoendienst to the New York Giants for Alvin Dark.

"Frank Lane is crazy. The next thing you know, he'll be trading Musial," Luke muttered half to himself as he took his seat on the step with his buddies.

"If he trades Musial . . . " Jack's words trailed off into the unthinkable.

Luke folded his arms across his knees and looked out over the scene before him. Morning mist was rising off the river a football field away. The wide open plateau between the rear of the stores and the stream was freshly mowed, the town's green carpet rolled out for the popular Bisbees. A cloudless sky was pulling back its dark curtain, revealing a pale blue canopy. Birds were coming awake with their wide assortment of cheerful sounds.

More than a dozen boys stood around at odd angles and groups, some stifling yawns, a few older ones pulling on cigarettes. The stairway upon which Luke and his friends sat led from a narrow wooden platform which had been built in the burned-out space between two stores. Underneath and around the foundations of the existing buildings was discarded litter of empty whiskey bottles, cigarette wrappers, and other varied rubbish. A slight odor of urine permeated the air.

"Tommy Grogan got a Duke Snider and Richie Ashburn in the same pack yesterday at Graham's store" Donkey threw some baseball card talk into the conversation.

"Is that right?" Luke reacted with amazement.

"Yeah, and then he traded the Richie Ashburn to Bennie Marshall for Willie Mays."

"Are you serious! He got Willie Mays for a Richie Ashburn! Bennie must have been out of his mind!" Luke exclaimed.

Donkey shrugged and they fell silent.

"How come Birdseed didn't come?" Jack finally asked.

"Same old story." Luke responded.

"His Mom and Dad wouldn't let him." Donkey and Jack spoke in unison, and Luke nodded.

Suddenly there was a rustle of excitement in the gathering. Eyes turned toward the ferry road which led off the main street toward the river. The lead truck had arrived.

The Bisbees were in town.

Like a large reptile, the train of vehicles slithered off the gravel surface and into the waiting meadow. The huge, gleaming vehicles, with their rumbling engines and bold red lettering, brought a rush of excitement to the town.

As the huge tractor-trailer rigs began to form a large circle, the other units veered off to one side or another and pulled to a halt. The Currentville boys moved hurriedly en masse to one pickup truck, from which a squat little man with a clipboard was making his way out of the cab. A mad dash was made to him by the solicitous throng.

In a chaotic flurry repeated annually, the little cigar-chomping foreman sorted through the waving hands and beseeching pleas to pull out a crew of six of the larger boys. They joined the regular canvasmen to begin the heavy work of setting up camp for three days.

Six of the smaller boys were chosen as tent vendors. Luke

just happened to be standing in the right place at the right time. He made the cut. Donkey and Jack, to their great disappointment, did not.

"And we're a year older than you are!" Jack exclaimed disgustedly as the three made their way back toward Main Street after the selection. Luke was beaming, but knew better than to gloat. His friends were in a nasty mood. Either one of them (especially Jack) could have hammered him into the ground.

Luke showed up at the Bisbee tent at 6 p.m. sharp as directed by the show manager. Already a line was forming in front.

Show time was at eight. He and his five co-workers received about twenty minutes of instruction, the main interest being whether each of the boys could make change. And of course they were tutored in the art of barking out and hawking their product. The young boys were joined by two of the Bisbee regulars. Altogether they made up a crew of eight to canvas the opening night crowd, which would exceed one thousand people from all over Chickasaw County and beyond. Their wares would be snow cones, popcorn, cracker jacks, and candy. Drinks and cotton candy were sold in the rear.

Luke and Gordon Gray were each assigned to the candy detail. They strapped on large cardboard containers filled with small boxes, within which were individually wrapped pieces of hard taffy. Placed in every fifth box was a winning coupon which entitled the holder to one of the door prizes which would be placed on stage at one of the intermissions—dolls, lamps, bath powder, and other such merchandise.

As the sun disappeared into the red dying embers of the day, the riverbank came alive with music and color. The huge show tent was adorned with light bulbs of various hues, and a loudspeaker blasted out tunes of John Philip Sousa and other rousing composers. At seven the ticket counter opened, and people began to file into the huge tent. The smell of popcorn and cotton candy permeated the air.

The entrance, designated by a separate and smaller tent, served as the lobby where the tickets were sold. There was also a large board displaying colorful pictures of the performers. Seating was divided between the blue wooden bleachers in the back ("the blues") as general admission, and the folding wooden chairs for the reserved seats.

A stage about thirty feet long and fifteen feet deep ran across the front. It was constructed so as to accommodate the play as well as the specialty performances between acts. There was a front curtain, as well as several "street drop" screens used for the various scenes and skits. The wooden platform sat there basking in the footlights and tantalizing the gathering spectators.

Behind the stage, through the intricate arrangement of vans and trucks, were the dressing rooms and storage nooks. To the left of the stage was the orchestra pit, set apart with a string of colorful lights.

By eight o'clock, when the lights began to dim, the place was packed with a buzzing and excited sea of humanity. Cardboard fans were handed out, but there were few takers. Their keen anticipation diverted all attention from the stifling heat.

The vendors, including Luke Cameron, moved up and down the aisles, hawking their wares.

"Ladies and gentlemen," came the rich baritone voice over the impeccable sound system, "we welcome you to America's greatest and longest running traveling variety show, one that *Life* magazine has called the class of the South . . . Bisbee's Comedians!"

With that, and to deafening applause and whistles, the orchestra broke into its opening number. The curtain went up, and a line of leggy showgirls moved arm in arm to the front of the stage, singing and kicking in unison.

> *Are you from Dixie? I said from Dixie . . .*
> *Where the land of cotton beckons to me?*
> *Are you from Alabama, Tennessee, or Caroline . . .*
> *Or anywhere from 'neath the Mason Dixon line?*
> *Are you from Dixie? I said from Dixie,*
> *Cause I'm from Dixie too.*

The first number came to a thunderous conclusion as the dancing girls retreated behind the falling curtain. Immediately the orchestra moved into another popular song. After a few minutes of old standards and tunes, the music died and the stage darkened.

"Now, ladies and gentlemen, we bring to you what you have been waiting for since last summer . . . perhaps the number one act in all America . . . the one and only . . . the world-renowned . . . the legendary . . . Wallace the Wizard!"

The narrow shaft of the spotlight caught the long, slim frame of Wallace Paisley as the curtain rose. He was dressed in a black tuxedo and top hat. His face was stern, almost menacing. To his left was Tarinka, now nearing forty but still stunning and statuesque in her sequin-studded gown. His other assistant was little Tasa, as cute as a pup, dressed up in an Uncle Sam outfit. They were enthusiastically welcomed by the anticipating throng.

To the exotic background music of the orchestra, Wallace went right to work. He started with some card tricks, and then some disappearing balls. Vanishing silver dollars reappeared behind the ears of both Tarinka and Tasa. A rope was cut into four pieces, wadded up in his hand, and miraculously rejoined as one piece. There were repeated exclamations of astonishment and intermittent applause from the crowd.

After ten minutes of amazing tricks, the announcer set up the grand finale. "Now ladies and gentlemen . . . prepare for the most incredible feat you have ever seen with your eyes . . . one that has astonished thousands and one that you simply will not believe . . . only performed by Wallace the Wizard . . . Disappearing Tasa!"

Violins in the orchestra held a steady hum, and the lights dimmed even more. Wallace stepped up to a large wooden box at center stage. With exaggerated gestures the Wizard pulled open the hinged front and back sides of the carton to show that there were no hidden panels. Then Tasa dramatically bowed to the audience, and stepped up and climbed inside the box, which was then shut. Tarinka stepped forward and pulled down the hasp, and snapped a lock into place. The subject was clearly incarcerated in the box.

Tarinka then handed Wallace a large cloth which he spread over the top. Standing from behind, he then raised both hands and closed his eyes.

"Now, ladies and gentlemen . . . the great Wallace the Wizard needs your help, your mind power. To pull off this incredible piece of magic, he will need your full concentration," the announcer said in serious tones to the hushed gathering. "Please focus your eyes upon the box and think only of little Tasa. Think only of her need to be liberated from this coffin. Look . . . think . . . think . . . "

The place was so quiet that only the distant groaning of the ferry could be heard.

Then with a lightning sweep of his long arm, Wallace swept away the covering from the box, and all four sides opened and collapsed. Out of the flattened case, where Tasa had entered only moments before, hopped a small white rabbit.

There was a collective gasp and applause.

As Tarinka quickly retrieved the rabbit, there was a drum roll, and the spotlight swept all the way back to the entrance of the large tent. A rising and excited murmur followed a subject which had entered the hall, and was now sprinting down the aisle toward the stage.

It was Tasa.

The spotlight followed her as she leaped upon the stage. Like an accomplished quarterback slipping the ball to a running back, Tarinka passed the rabbit to her daughter. With bunny in hand she leaped into the air and did the splits in front of the disassembled box, smiling beautifully and holding her free hand up in the air.

The place came apart at the seams.

People were standing, screaming, clapping, whistling and going crazy. Kids stood in their chairs and stomped their feet, making the wooden seats clatter in unison.

It might have gone on for hours, if Wallace the Wizard, Tarinka, and Tasa had not moved slowly to the back of the stage, bowing and waving until they were swallowed by the falling curtain.

Calm finally returned to the show tent as the play got under way.

It was a three-act comedy, "Toby's City Cousins." The plot

entailed the story of country bumpkin Toby inheriting thousands of dollars from a long-forgotten uncle in the city. But he had to travel to the center of iniquity to collect his inheritance. His big-city relatives tried to use their slick ways to fleece what they thought to be their ignorant and hay-seed cousin out of his fortune.

Only two minutes into the play, and to the clapping and delight of the audience, Toby Ticklebush made his appearence.

Gawky, freckle faced, he wore an undersized straw hat perched precariously atop a thick mop of bright red hair. His trousers were held up by wide suspenders, and the bottom of his pant legs were high above his large brogans. His outlandish and clownish appearance was his trademark.

Even after three seasons, a large segment of the spectators did not know that Toby Ticklebush and Wallace the Wizard were one and the same. This was, to a large degree, because he contrasted the roles so well: dignified, stern, serious Wallace the Wizard, and funny, goofy, and crazy-looking Toby Ticklebush.

Wallace Paisley was born for this role. His comic expressions, forte for mimicking, and perfect timing — talents sharpened by his magic act kept the laughter rolling from beginning to end. His material, much of which he wrote himself, fit the humor of rural people like a glove.

In the big city part of the skit, he put a dime in a parking meter, stared at the numbers and turned to the audience, "How do you like that, I've lost sixty pounds."

Responding to the allegation by a city kinsman of being two-faced, Toby exclaims with surprise, "Two faced! If I had two faces, you think I'd be wearing this one?"

It always warmed the house when a little local touch was added to the show. When a city dweller told Toby he would have to take the subway, he quickly retorted, "Why? I thought Mac would take me."

Mac operated a solitary cab for Chickasaw County, mostly for the communities of Currentville and Catawba. Toby's plug brought laughter and back slapping to the blushing Mac, who was sitting on the third row.

Wallace Paisley had found himself with the Bisbees. His life, which had been one of instability and tumultuous bouts with alcohol, philandering, and unemployment, had at long last found some solid footing. Nearing fifty, he had softened the sharp edges, became more mellow and at ease with himself. Primarily through the large heart of a Russian woman, his marriage had weathered devastating storms and not only survived, but was, at long last, flourishing. He had given up booze completely.

When he reflected upon it all, late at night in some small town or riding in the car between encampments, he drew only one conclusion. He owed it all to the Bisbees.

Standing there at center stage, in some shabby out-of-the-way town, feeling the vibration of human warmth flow over him with peals of laughter, his very being rose to a higher plain. Peering out over the footlights into the sea of desperate humanity, Wallace felt a connection—an electric circuit of emotions—between himself and his fans. Perhaps it was the tortuous times of his early life, his heartaches and failures, hunger and pain—but he felt a kinship to those who had fallen upon the thorns of life, and instead of bleeding—laughing. He discovered, to his awe and amazement, that he possessed the power to transform, to liberate—if just for a while—these quiet lives of desperation.

Night after sweltering night they came. Pouring out of the hollow crevices of human existence came these people of bondage. The stooped and sunburned farmers, hereditary bondsmen of the soil. Those limping under the manacles of age, disease, injury, carbuncles, and goiters. Youngsters with angelic faces, carried to their seats by loving arms, their spines twisted by polio. Ebony faces in the distant bleachers, roped off to themselves, cheering and laughing in their exile. Those laboring in chains of ignorance and illiteracy. Merchants, vagrants, bankers, mechanics, housewives and ladies of the night, old spinsters and sparking couples, the vile and the pure—the grand menagerie of the rural South.

Wallace Paisley saw all of this. He felt their breath, smelled their sweat, and was pressed by their primal needs. In New York and Boston, Philadelphia and New Orleans, people dressed to the hilt and went to the theater. Here they were drawn to the light.

He felt a need, and in this need, a purpose for his own life. The orphan from Pittsburgh came to terms with his own secret nightmares. Through the catharsis of magic and laughter, he drove out the goblins of his life—the murdered mother, a father hung at dawn, a second father scalded to death while Wallace survived unscathed. Years of wandering, searching, unbearable loneliness and depression, all seemed to fade away into the happy faces beyond the footlights.

With the end of each act of "Toby's City Cousins," special performers would entertain the audience during the intermission. Musicians, ventriloquists, comedians, and jugglers would hold the attention of the crowd while sets were rearranged for the next act. The Bisbees even had their own rendition of Abbott and Costello's "Who's on First."

During the last intermission of the night, the prizes were brought out and the lucky holders of the candy coupons would come down front and pick out their gifts.

Finally after a great night of entertainment, the last act of the play would build to a hilarious and satisfying climax. Toby— no dummy after all—outwitted the city villains, secured his rightful inheritance, and won the pretty girl. The curtain came crashing down with the happy ending, and the orchestra blasted out the final flourish. To loud acclaim and a standing ovation, each of the stars made their curtain call, with Toby, appearing last, bringing down the house. The dancing girls returned to end it all just the way it started:

> *. . . are you from Dixie? I said from Dixie . . .*
> *where the land of cotton beckons to me . . .*

And then it was over. The lights came on, and the large crowd began to blink and stretch. It was almost 10:30. A bouncy tune from the organ serenaded the people out of the large tent. Smiling and joking, they spoke to neighbors and friends. They were lifted, felt better about themselves and about their simple and tedious lives. Each and every one was just glad to belong to the same human race as Toby Ticklebush. In the white heat of the tobacco patch, the ear-piercing bedlam of the mill, over the hot stove—the spirits would be refreshed by remembering a gesture, an expression, a line from Toby Ticklebush.

Babes in arms and old men in their dotage would never see a show again like Bisbee's Comedians.

It was almost thirty minutes after the show had ended and the large theater was empty. The regular clean-up crew was already moving in between the seats to pick up the litter. Money was being happily counted by the management. Luke and the other vendors unloaded their burdens and cleared their accounts. The floor manager thanked them for a good job and handed out their complimentary tickets for the next night's performance. Incredibly, each evening was a different show. Luke had given his first night passes to his Mom and Dad. Bobby Joe would buy the tickets for the remaining two nights for him and his girl at half price, a good deal for both Luke and his brother.

Luke moved out into the summer night and headed for home. There was a refreshing breeze coming off the river. He was finding his way through the dark, trying to maneuver past the large tent stakes and ropes.

"Hey Luke!" It was Gordon Gray coming up from behind.

Gordon was in the same class with Luke at school but much older. The youngster could hardly read and write, and was simply marking time until he turned sixteen and could drop out. He lived with his Mom and a pack of half brothers and sisters up on Oak Hill, a row of dilapidated and ruined tenements which ran down by the side of the prison wall. Gordon smoked, swore, and was constantly into some kind of trouble. While he had a terrible reputation, Luke had always found him pretty much a straight arrow. In fact, he had helped him out of a couple of tight spots that night. Gordon had worked the Bisbees before, and all the tent people knew him.

Breathlessly, the delinquent caught up with Luke.

"How would you like to meet Toby?" he inquired excitedly.

The thought hit Luke like a thunderbolt. Actually, it had been a secret reason he had wanted to work the Bisbees, to get a shot at meeting some of the performers.

"You know him?" he asked Gordon skeptically.

"Of course I know him. I know Tasa too." The last part had an amorous hint to it. "Come on. We'll go to their trailer."

They started moving through the encampment, over ropes, stakes, and in between a variety of vehicles. As they passed by an old school bus converted to living quarters for the canvasmen, they heard gruff voices inside.

"We won't be playing this place much longer. They're building a dam to flood Currentville and Catawba," one of the occupants casually mentioned.

The message stopped Luke in his tracks. He stood stunned in the darkness.

"Did you hear that?" He was finally able to speak.

"Hear what?" Gordon was trudging on.

"They said that they were going to build a dam. That Currentville was going to be flooded," Luke explained to his guide.

"Don't worry about it," retorted Gordon without slowing down, "we'll all be old men before that happens."

But Luke would worry about it. That moment, that place—on the back lot of Bisbee's Comedians—would be indelibly burned into his memory as the first time he heard about the dam.

He and Gordon reached a grouping of neat and clean little house trailers. They were cozy looking, lit up inside with the soft glow of lamp lights. The two moved to a blue trailer with the door open. Gordon knocked on the screen. Immediately, a beautiful woman in a bathrobe with her long blond hair swept down around her neck, opened the door. It was Tarinka.

"Well, hello Gordon," she said pleasantly in a heavy and husky accent.

Luke was impressed.

She invited them inside.

As soon as they stepped inside the door, Luke saw him sitting on the couch. He was long and lanky with a sad face. Wallace Paisley had changed into a pair of khaki pants and T-shirt. There was still a trace of makeup near his hairline and on his neck. In one hand he held a glass of milk, in the other a ham sandwich. Of course he looked much different than he did on stage. But one could tell it was Wallace.

Luke's heart was racing, his mind frozen, and his tongue tied to the roof of his mouth. But his raising took over, and he stuck out his hand, introducing himself first to Mrs. Paisley, and then to Mr. Paisley.

Tasa came from a back room, dressed in shorts and one of her Dad's old shirts. She was twelve years of age but was already taking on some signs of womanhood. Luke could care less, but Gordon was obviously more interested in Toby's daughter than he was in Toby.

Tarinka offered the two boys something to drink, and although they declined, she nevertheless poured them each a cold Pepsi. Luke noticed that this show business family seemed to be genuinely delighted to have company. No sooner had they been seated when Wallace Paisley's charm took over. The melancholy face notwithstanding, there was a twinkle—almost mischief—in his eyes, and he smiled easily. Instantly Luke felt at ease.

Wallace proceeded to question Luke about himself. Where did he live? What did his father do? Brothers and sisters? How did he like the show?

Luke had never met a person who asked as many questions. They were asked with such intensity, almost an interrogation, like the questioner wanted desperately to learn from this small package of life that had just walked into his trailer.

When Wallace learned that Luke's Dad had once worked on the dredge boat *Tishamingo*, he moved easily into some of his spellbinding stories of his days on the river.

"When I was on *The Cotton Blossom*, we saved the *Tish* from sinking one night. There was a terrible rainstorm. Black as pitch and the river was rising like crazy. The spuds of the *Tish* lost their bottom. Some rivets from her old bottom had come lose and it was taking on water fast. She was going down. We managed to pull the old *Blossom* up close enough, hooked on some cable, and pulled her back toward shallow water and where the spuds could hold her up. I thought the whole thing—boom, shovel and all was going to turn over on us. I was up in the pilot house trying to help out. Old Captain Miller, he was one old gritty pilot."

On and on he went. River talk. Show business. New Orleans. Pittsburgh. Houdini. Wallace Paisley was the most fascinating man Luke had ever met.

Finally Luke happened to look at an alarm clock sitting up on a shelf behind the couch. He jumped to his feet with a start. It was 1:20 in the morning.

"I've got to go," he almost yelled. "If my parents are up, they will be worried."

Only then did he realize that both Tarinka and Tasa had already slipped off to bed. Wallace seemed as awake and alert as when they first arrived.

Luke thanked him for the visit. They shook hands, and he and Gordon left.

Gordon and Luke repeated the visit the following night. This time, Tasa and Gordon took a short walk together over to one of her Bisbee friends in another trailer. Luke had Toby Ticklebush and his exotic wife all to himself. Tarinka was a good storyteller in her own right. She related how her uncle in Nashville had been a Czarist at the time of the Russian Revolution and had barely escaped to America with his life. It seemed to Luke like these two people had lived the most interesting lives one could imagine. Of course they respected his innocence and youth, and had left out the pain, the agony, the loneliness and strife.

This was Luke's last visit with the Paisleys. For after the show the next night, the place was torn apart in a frenzy. The Bisbees were breaking camp and moving on.

Amidst the flurry of activity Luke said his farewell to the tent people and started for home. Once again he heard the voice of Gordon Gray.

"Hey Luke. Wait a minute."

Just like the first night Gordon caught up with him.

"Luke," his co-worker looked around before he continued just above a whisper. "Listen, I want to tell you something. If anything ever happens to me, I want you to know you were a good friend."

With that Gordon turned abruptly and walked toward

Main Street.

Luke turned the puzzling comment over in his mind. What could happen to Gordon? And besides, yeah they had worked together, visited Toby Ticklebush together. But not really the stuff of "good friends."

Luke Cameron shrugged and headed up Penitentiary Hill toward home, wishing that he were going with Toby.

The next morning Currentville, Kentucky went into shock.

Gordon Gray had drowned himself in the Cumberland River.

After leaving Luke outside the Bisbee tent, he had gone to Charlie's Pool Hall. They said he was in terrible shape there—despondent, crying, saying strange things. He kept saying something about his Daddy not really being his Daddy. "I'm tired of living," he kept saying over and over. He had finally proclaimed he was going down on the lock wall to "sort things out."

The next morning Gordon's clothes were found scattered along the top of the upper lock wall. They were identified as those he had been wearing the night before. In one of the shoes was a note. It had been written only after a tremendous effort by the virtual illiterate. With the help of family, they were finally able to interpret the misspelled words and irregular lines. "I am sorry. But I can't go on living. Gordon."

The lock crew began dragging operations. Townspeople, friends, and relatives came down to the river and stood in silence watching. Gordon's wretched mother, eyes red from crying, stood transfixed, staring numbly out over the water.

She stood there all day, as the men changed shifts and continued the quiet and somber rowing back and forth. The wooden oars struck out a dreadful cadence over the silent river.

At supper that night, Luke picked at his food.

Alec explained the trouble with the dragging operation. "The water is fifteen to twenty feet there. On the bottom of the river there are old iron casings left over from the coffer dams when they built the lock. They are lying in there at all angles. It makes dragging a real nightmare. A body could get wedged in there and never be found . . . till it starts to swell and works lose and floats to the surface . . . ”

It was an awful thought, and cast a doleful quiet over the table.

"Was Gordon a good swimmer?" Alec asked after a long silence.

"Yes, sir," Luke answered softly.

Alec took a last sip of coffee, pushed back his chair and lit up a cigarette.

"Awful hard to drown yourself if you're a good swimmer." he stated with some conviction. "One time on the dredge, in the middle of the day, we had a guy tried to kill himself. He climbed over one hundred feet up on the boom. He then leaped into the Tennessee River. He went in feet first. He was under for a little while, and we thought sure he was a goner. Then he came to the surface. We saw him go down again. And then he came up, and swam back to the boat. We fished him out. The old man sent him to the office for his pay. Fired him on the spot."

Alec took a drag on his smoke and peered out the window, traveling back over time.

"About a year later we were working down around Dover, close to where this guy was from. He came out to the dredge to see us one night. He was all dressed up, looking great—had gotten himself back together. We were sitting around talking and he told us about that day. He said 'I meant to splatter myself on the water. But just before I landed something caused me to bring down my feet. Then when I went in the water, I went down and took a big deep breath. Then something took over, and I came up spitting and gasping for air. After I got my breath I went down and tried it again. I took another deep breath, trying to drown myself. And again, something took over and I came fighting back to the surface, gasping for air. I then decided there was somebody in that water beside me. And whatever it was, wasn't going to let me die. So I gave up.'"

Alec thumped ashes into his saucer as his wife and two sons pondered the story.

The next day they called off the dragging operations. Gordon Gray's mother retreated back to her house leaving her son to his watery grave. Currentville began to get on with life, knowing that as the weather warmed, the body would surface somewhere.

Luke was in a deep sleep two mornings later when Esther came into his room. "Luke, they found Gordon Gray!"

Luke bolted straight up in bed. They found Gordon Gray. Mangled by the surging currents against the sharp iron slabs. Caught up in the wickets, his torso twisted in two. They found Gordon Gray. Bloated and entangled in driftwood a mile downstream. Horrible images raced through his freshly awakened mind.

"I say they 'found' him," Esther went on excitedly. "Actually he came home. He had run off with the Bisbees."

Esther moved about the room straightening up and dusting. "They were over at Murray. You know what? They said that Toby himself brought him home."

A terrific rush of joy flooded over Luke Cameron. It was all too wonderful-deliriously wonderful. He let out a jubilant yell which both startled and amused his Mom.

He was happy that Gordon Gray was alive. He was especially happy for Gordon's dear old mother. And he was happy that trouble-ridden Gordon Gray, the bane of Currentville, had enjoyed three wonderful days out of bondage, with the Bisbees.

But perhaps most of all he was happy for Wallace the Wizard. For his friend had now outdone them all—even the great Houdini.

He had brought someone back from the dead.

Chapter Four

Prisoners

Tomorrow is a promise to no one.

The prison had been a part of the hamlet of Currentville for over a hundred years.

No one, however old, could remember when it wasn't there.

It was a massive structure of stone resembling a medieval fortress. High atop the hill, it sat brooding over the town and the Cumberland River Valley.

"Castle on the Cumberland" it was often called.

It was a maximum security prison, but it housed a highly diversified group of human beings. From chicken thieves and forgers, to murderous cut throats — they were all thrown in together under an antiquated classification system.

The town was as comfortable with the presence of this huge penal colony in its midst at it would have been with a large factory. It *was* a factory of sorts, employing a large number of local people and adding to the economy.

It was the largest employer in the county.

The boys of Currentville, for generations now, had grown

up with both the prison and the convicts.

Many prison "trustees" worked outside the walls—mowing grass, painting, running the prison water plant, and doing various other jobs. Most went back into the walls of the castle at night. Some however, like the warden's houseboy who had a basement bedroom in the house, were billeted at different nooks and crannies outside of the sprawling structure.

The warden's houseboy, usually black, could be seen every day, dressed in immaculately pressed whites, heading down to Gresham Brothers with his grocery list.

The boys of Currentville became friends with the "trustees."

One was Pikeen, a silver-haired old man who ran the leather shop on the sidewalk in front of the prison. His "shop" was simply a large wooden display rack with a canvas awning attached to it.

From it he sold (for the state of course) prison-made wares such as leather wallets, pocketbooks, and belts, as well as plastic rings.

Pikeen was friendly to all the kids in town and had a grand smile and charismatic personality. Except for an occasional off-color joke, he could pass as a perfect grandfather.

His crime was murder.

Luke and his friends frequently stopped to visit with Pikeen, especially in the summer time, when the shade of his awning provided a cool resting place on their arduous trek over Penitentiary Hill.

The old man was a fabulous story teller. And often, with much ado and mock secrecy, he would pull a baseball from under his prison shirt and slip it to the boys, stolen property from the prison baseball team.

The Greyhound bus stopped daily at "Harry's," a small, six-stool restaurant across the street from Pikeen's place of business.

"See that 'big dog'?" the leather man would point with a bright twinkle in his eye.

Every time the boys would turn and look, as if on cue.

"One of these days ole Pie is going to get on that 'big dog' and be gone. And you'll never see ole Pie again."

And he'd get that faraway look in his eyes, a look of total contentment on his face.

It always made them a bit sad when he said it. And at the same time they would feel a slight rush of joy.

And there was the farm truck which pulled out of the rear sally port in the back wall at 6:30 each morning full of inmates heading out to the prison farm. They came back into Currentville around 4 p.m. each day. It was a rough-looking crew riding in the large open truck. But the boys always waved.

Some would wave back.

When there was an incident at the prison during the day—an escape attempt, a hostage holding, a killing—the boys were instructed to say nothing of the incident when the truck stopped to let off guards.

And bad things did go on inside. Inmate stabbings, an occasional attack on a guard, even riots.

One Sunday afternoon, Hardin Curry, a rotund guard of considerable girth, was sitting on the yard watching a baseball game. He was nearly decapitated by a convict who slipped up behind him with a cement trowel filed down to a razor-sharp edge.

The death penalty was carried out from time to time in the electric chair which was located deep within the bowels of the prison.

The town of Currentville became somewhat subdued and somber on the day of an execution. And it was said, although Luke and his friends were never quite sure, that the lights in the old town would dim shortly after midnight when the switch was thrown and the condemned was sent into eternity with the jolt of 2,600 volts.

But the most memorable experience for Luke was the prison baseball games.

Bobby Joe played on a local summer league team composed of older boys and young men. Every now and then the team would go inside and play the convicts.

Through some artful maneuvering Luke got to go along as the bat boy.

Tall and tough Sam Mayes, the prison warden, assured Alec

that Luke would be alright. "They'll be plenty of security," he drawled. "Besides . . . inmate code. These guys hunger for women and children. If any convict laid a hand on the kid, that convict would be dead in minutes . . . and it wouldn't be a pretty death."

He was right.

The minute the ball team hit the yard, inmates would descend upon Luke—asking him questions, giving him candy and gum, telling him stories about their own families and their own kids.

One time, while Luke was tending to bat boy chores, he struck up a conversation with a sandy-haired, baby-faced young felon from the mountains of East Kentucky.

The convict disappeared for a few minutes and reappeared with a present for Luke.

It was a wallet made out of cigarette packages. Red Pall Mall wrappers were folded up in squares and tied together by string for the outer cover. Inside, white Camel packaging was used for picture frames. The bills pocket was lined with squares of silver foil.

It was an astonishing piece of handicraft.

The prison yard was actually on the very pinnacle of the towering hill upon which the prison was built. The massive administration building, the annex, as it was called, was in front, with the adjoining cellhouses and the prison walls encircling the crest—like a crown on the head of a large skull. One actually had to climb a considerable grade when coming out of the administration building or a cellhouse to reach the yard — or the flattened summit.

Thus the inmates and guards alike referred to the yard as "the hill."

When walking "the hill" one did not have the sense of being enclosed by prison walls. For the encompassing walls were down the slope, almost out of view. The pill-box guard towers on the corners were visible, but below eye level. Therefore this prison mesa, much like the deck of an aircraft carrier, had the vista of open sky, the burg of Currentville, and the scenic river valley far below.

Toward the back of the prison yard, just before it slipped drastically downward toward the back wall, was an opening about half the size and shape of a football field. Its black surface consisted of cinders, packed to a concrete hardness through years of trampling.

This was the prison baseball field.

The baseball field and the game itself were real oddities.

Just a few feet behind second base was a white, two-story concrete building, which housed the prison laundry and other inmate services. It was so substantial in size that during the game the centerfielder and right fielder were located behind it and out of view of anyone standing at home plate.

Line drives, which would have been extra bases on an ordinary field, would ricochet off the laundry to the shortstop for a double play.

An umpire was placed up on the flat roof of the laundry. His job was to trace the flight of balls hit over the building. If the ball was caught by the hidden outfielder, he would run back to the diamond side of the structure signaling the batter out. Otherwise, he would appear to the waiting players and spectators waving his arm, windmill style—a gapper, all you can get.

The umpires, all inmates, would cheat. For the visiting team, of course. They wanted to be sure their visitors felt they were treated fairly so they would return. In the same vein, the prisoners invariably rooted for the outside team. Their hospitality knew no bounds.

After each game, the outside team, along with its bat boy, would be escorted to the prison dining hall, where the soiled and exhausted visitors were feasted royally.

As the lengthening shadows began to gather, the guests would move back across "the hill" and through the annex, with the heavy metal doors clanging behind them.

Finally, the baseballers would emerge at the top of the long steps outside the front gate, back to the world of freedom, seemingly a thousand miles away from the cribbed and grim world in which they had just spent their sunny Sunday afternoon.

One of the players once commented as the team descended the steps to the street below on how nice the inmates had been.

A gruff and seasoned old guard, ending his shift at the same time remarked, "Jekyl and Hydes—-they are all Jekyl and Hydes. Put them back with their booze, their fickle women, and their problems, and they turn into monsters again. . . ."

Luke thought about that for a long time.

Behind the prison was a large open field owned by the state. For security purposes it was kept neatly clipped. This elongated meadow ran up a valley between two densely forested hills comparable in height to Penitentiary Hill.

At the end of this large clearing about a half mile from the prison and in the edge of the woods, was the prison dump.

In slow times it was a great place for the town boys to go and rummage around.

One never knew what might be discarded there—worn out tools, convict clothes, homemade barbells.

It was a real bonanza to happen upon the remains of a footlocker left behind by a departing inmate. Interesting letters, girlie magazines, a deck of cards, and an occasional painting still in a frame—all were possibilities.

Luke and Birdseed were heading to the prison dump one Saturday afternoon in late November. The best route from Luke's house was through Freewill, then up a long heavily wooded hill, along the ridge and down the other side.

They were almost in sight of the dump when they suddenly heard the rustle of leaves being kicked up on the forest floor. The hardwoods of oaks and hickories had shed their leaves, making visibility and sounds sharp and distinct. They saw someone coming up the hill from the direction of the prison.

The traveler was coming at a slow trot and quickly came into full view.

It was a convict. An old convict, donned in prison garb of pressed blue denims and work shirt.

The two boys, dumbfounded, stood gaping.

He was apparently escaping. As he drew almost even with them, they recognized the elder conman as Pokey, a trustee who worked at the outside water plant.

But his face lacked the look of the hunted and there was no sign of desperation in his movement. He looked for all the world like he was just out for a casual jog.

He saw them but showed not the least bit of concern.

Finally he stopped at their side, gasping for breath, bent over with his hands on his knees.

"Hey boys. . ." he managed to exhale, ". . .the hounds will be after me in a moment. . . ."

Pokey began to breathe easier, but Luke and Birdseed hardly breathed at all.

". . . they are training . . . training . . . some new dogs . . . and they sent me out . . . as a . . . as a guinea pig . . . you might say. . . ." Pokey straightened up and looked back down the hill.

"They told me to stay just out of sight of them." He turned to Luke and Birdseed and gave them a big toothless smile, "Great way to make a living huh?"

From a distance came the sound of the hounds.

"Oof . . . oof . . . oof . . . oof."

Pokey gave a shrug, "Welp, better get going. . . ."

With that, he turned, started ambling away through the leaves at just a bit over a fast walk. They watched until he disappeared over the ridge.

Luke and Birdseed had not said a word.

Into view from the same direction Pokey had appeared came three inmates, being pulled up the wooded hill by three bloodhounds straining at their leashes.

"Oof. . . . oof. . . . oof. . . ."

Following at a short distance were three prison guards. They were walking almost casually, and were unarmed.

The dogs arrived, and two of them went straight to Luke and Birdseed, sniffing at their shoes and legs. Then they did a curious thing—they sat down, hassling heavily with their tongues hanging to the side. The other hound circled them, his nose to the ground, and then continued on up the slope in roughly the same path Pokey had taken.

The two resting canines were then jerked from their places of rest, into the pursuit.

"Oof. . . . oof. . . . oof. . . ."

And on into the woods they went.

The three guards lingered behind for a few moments and chatted with the startled boys. They confirmed Pokey's story and moved on.

Luke and Birdseed, a little disappointed, shrugged and headed on to the dump.

They didn't even think enough of the incident to relate it to their friends or family.

Several weeks later Luke was having supper with his family and engaging in the normal evening chitchat.

Alec took a bite, laid down his fork, shook his head, and said, "The boys up at the pen had a good one pulled on them the other day."

He chuckled and went on.

"Seems they were trying out some new dogs . . . bloodhounds. Well, they thought they'd get an old trustee to use as a runner. So they told him to take off, out back of the prison. They gave him about ten minutes head start."

Luke's ears perked up as his Dad took a sip of coffee.

"Ha . . . they told him to just stay out of sight of the dogs. Well, he did that okay. In fact he didn't come back. He escaped. Apparently outran the hounds. But here's the real funny part. . . ."

Alec was now laughing as he told the story.

". . .just a few days ago the warden got a real friendly postcard from this old convict. It came from California. I mean it was just regular talk, like you would send to folks back home if you were on vacation. But here's the best part. He added a 'P.S.' on the bottom and said, 'I'm dying to know how the new dogs turned out. I hope you don't mind me saying so, but they could use a lot of work'"

They all laughed. The rest of the table then listened with great interest as Luke told them about Birdseed and him encountering Pokey on his way to California.

Everyone was savoring the story and continued eating when Luke injected, "Dad, could they charge old Pokey with escape? I mean . . . they told him to leave...."

Bobby Joe, who was wolfing his food down with both hands, froze with his mouth full and gave a moment's reflection to the question. Then he retorted, "Who gives a . . . .darn?"—almost slipping badly on the last word—and continued eating.

Luke looked toward his Dad. Alec peered at Luke with amusement, thought for a second, and then with a short laugh and a shake of his head said "I don't know," and went on with his supper.

⚜

The old Lafayette house sat across the river from Currentville. It was a ghostly looking structure standing all by itself on a slight rise in the river bottom. It sat back from the river about half a mile and was surrounded by cornfields.

From the top of Penitentiary Hill it appeared in the distant haze of summer and the mist of winter as a forlorn and foreboding sentinel of the river bottom.

It was an ancient two-story red brick building, long abandoned as a residence, and used by farmers to store hay. The window facings had fallen out, leaving dark, empty sockets in their place. A pile of slave-made bricks heaped at one end was all that was left of the old chimney, and the tin roof was rusty and dilapidated.

But it held its own, standing erect and defiant against the forces of time.

The home had once been a stately Southern mansion, the home of a plantation owner with many slaves to farm the fertile river bottom.

The landmark drew its name from the common belief that General Marquis de Lafayette of France slept there on his visit to America in the late 1700s while on his way up the Cumberland to Nashville. No one knew for sure, but there was little doubt that the house was old enough to support the claim.

The Lafayette house was haunted. Or at least that was the common belief.

Strange looking lights had been seen there at night. On one trip to the house Luke had found the picture of a little dead boy lying in a casket. He took it home and the picture vanished.

Its chilling reputation made it a favorite place to camp.

To get there from Currentville, one had to cross the river and hike up the ferry road for about half a mile. Then a spooky, narrow lane with overhanging trees turned off the main road and meandered for nearly a mile to where it flared out at the front gate of the old estate.

Only half of the old wrought iron fence which had enclosed the yard was left standing. The yard itself was a mangled mess of weeds, honeysuckle, and wild bushes. Each spring, however, evidence of labors from a more elegant past would reappear as roses bloomed bright red near the front entrance. And the apple and pear trees in the side yard still bore fruit.

On the left side of the home near the back had been a shaded gazebo. Now all that was left was the rotting and treacherous decking which covered at ground level the old well which was still deep with water. Luke and his friends stayed clear of this hazard lest they fall through into its dark and terrifying depths.

It was the first of October and school was in full swing. The days were warm, but the nights were cooling down considerably.

The boys itched for one more big camp-out before winter.

They seized upon the opportunity when it was announced there would be no school on Friday because of a teacher's conference.

All day on Thursday they plotted and schemed, and by the time school was out the plans were nailed down.

They were going to camp at the Lafayette house.

Five of them were going—Luke, Jack, Donkey, Jerry Hawkins, and Mike Terry.

Jerry was a quiet kid from a rough background. He lived on Oak Hill with his divorced mother, her boy friend, and a houseful of kids. And while he smoked and made poor grades , he was not a bad kid and was well liked by his schoolmates.

Mike, better known as "Tarzan" because of his small skinny build, was a hyperactive kid, who giggled a lot, but all in all, was fun to be around. His Dad farmed and preached part time.

Tarzan had a very coveted claim to fame within the community of Currentville boys. His special talent was skipping rocks. Standing on the sand bar, they would have contests as to who could skip a flat rock the most times on the surface of the water. No one came close to Tarzan, who with his skinny arms could fling a pebble which would skip up to eight times before dying in midstream.

They all agreed to meet in front of the pool hall at 9 o'clock on Friday morning.

The day broke clear and sunny. It was cool in the early morning with a real touch of fall in the air. By the meeting time however, the sun was already warming up things .

A perfect day for a camping trip.

They converged upon the pool hall within minutes of each other.

Packs, blanket rolls, a lantern, hatchet, knives, and other provisions were all in evidence.

The campers were excited as they compared notes and double checked their supplies.

Matches, water, and can opener were all essentials worthy of review. No tents were needed. They would be sleeping inside, hopefully on hay.

Last minute foodstuffs and cold drinks were picked up in Willis Town's Grocery.

The expedition started off down the ferry road and the crew fell into discussing the first important matter of the trip.

The matter of transportation—the amphibious part.

Normally the river crossing was done in one of two ways. One method was for one person to carry the gear and clothing across on the ferry, paying only one fare which was split by all. The others would swim across, just a short way up from the landing. Once across they regrouped.

The other way was to commandeer someone's old john boat tied to the bank, ferry everyone and the gear across, and draw straws to see who returned the boat. The loser would have to take the boat back by himself — naked of course — and then swim back across the river.

The ferry method was, understandably, the most popular.

But on this morning there was another factor to consider. The temperature of the river water was getting pretty nippy. Although it was not mentioned, no one was looking forward to swimming the river.

Their numbers complicated matters. Usually there were two travelers, three at most. Today there were five with camping gear. One person would have a hard time packing the provisions across. They would have to use two. They talked in dollars and cents, pondering the savings and the costs. The fare was 15 cents a person.

They'd save 45 cents one way, with three swimming. Almost a dime apiece.

There wasn't a one who wouldn't give a dime on that morning not to have to swim the Cumberland River.

Then they came up with the perfect solution. If there was a johnboat available, they would use it. But instead of the losing party swimming back across, they'd all pay for his fare to return on the ferry.

And that's what they did.

Above the landing, half hidden in the willows, they found a couple of old wooden john boats, used by local fishermen. Both were half full of water. The choice was made, cans went to dipping, and within a short time, the vessel was loaded and under way.

In spite of only one oar, they were across the river and unloaded in less than 15 minutes.

Jerry lost the draw, but soon was back across on the ferry to rejoin the others who were waiting patiently on the bank.

Chattering excitedly, they shouldered their provisions and headed up the ferry road away from the landing. It was late morning by the time they reached the shaded lane which turned off to the right. They stopped at the junction and rested. The sun was high and it was hot.

Donkey pulled a Mason jar full of water from a pack and they passed it around.

A cloud passed over the sun.

"I think it's gonna rain," Jack surmised as they all surveyed the sky.

"That's great! We'll be inside, and I hope she's full of hay. Hay makes a darn good bed. Hey, I can see it now, sleeping on the hay and a hard steady rain pouring down on the old tin roof." Luke exuded.

"Let's hit it," Jack commanded, and they arose and moved out.

A sense of isolation and quiet came upon them as they moved down the ghostly, tree-lined road. Streaks of sun peeped in here and there through the overhanging boughs. Grass and weeds almost knee high grew in the middle of the roadway between the ruts cut into the ground by farm vehicles.

Acres of dead cornstalks reached out from both sides of the lane. Brown and silent, these skinny ghosts of summer rattled slightly in the breeze.

Finally they arrived at their destination.

The house was full of hay—all the way to the ceiling in some of the rooms.

They dropped their packs outside and ran through its old dusty rooms, jumping up and down on the sunken floors.

Most of the furniture was gone, except for a couple of old bedposts, a table in the kitchen, and two or three old chairs. An old empty bureau with a mirror remained in an upstairs bedroom

There was plenty of room to leap across the hay and wrestle.

Only the posts remained of the railing which had once graced the winding staircase leading to the upstairs.

From the vacant window frames of the front upstairs bedroom, they enjoyed a majestic view of the river bottom, the burg of Currentville in the distant haze, and there, brooding over the entire valley, the "Castle on the Cumberland."

The river, about a quarter of a mile away, sank from view below the fields of corn.

After frolicking through the old building and over its grounds, they wolfed down a bite to eat and then headed for the river.

By now the day had grown quite hot and they stripped and went swimming. The water was chilly, but invigorating. After almost a hour of vigorous splashing, diving and wrestling, they finally laid on the bank and dried themselves in the balmy autumn sun.

The group then dressed and headed back to the house. There they gathered their packs, spread their bedding out in the side yard in the shade and amongst the fallen fruit of an apple tree. They lounged, munching the mellow apples and relishing the afternoon breeze off the river.

Tarzan raised up on one elbow and seriously studied their temporary home. "You know, this old place ain't too scary...in the daytime anyway."

"Just wait till dark. Then it's plenty scary." Jack retorted.

"Yeah," Luke chimed in, "I've heard that some people have seen some character in old-fashioned clothes walking around in the upstairs bedroom at night . . . standing at the window . . . in an old three-corner French hat — like Lafayette wore. I've heard people were murdered here, too."

The group fell silent, as the sound of the four o'clock whistle at the prison faintly made its way down the river bottom. It sounded like the moaning of a distant ghost, perhaps warning them of the impending night.

"Tell the slave story Luke," beseeched Donkey.

"Well, I don't know if it's true or not," Luke began, "but I've heard that a slave jumped into that well and drowned himself just to get away from a cruel and mean master. He supposedly cut his own throat before jumping in and there was so much blood in the well that they couldn't use it anymore. Not many years ago, they say the Health Department even found the water still had traces of blood in it. On nights when it rains and thunders, and lighting flashes across the sky, they say you can see the old slave dancing on the top of the well."

They all stared in the direction of the old well.

The taciturn Jerry broke the silence by stating dryly, "Well, he'd better be a pretty light dancer now, or he'll fall through that rotten son of a bitch, and drown again."

They all laughed and fell to discussing lighter subjects.

The shadows began to lengthen as the sun angled off to the west.

"Not too long to dark," Jack observed during a lull in their leisurely banter. "Better get our beds made and ready for supper."

With that they all jumped up, gathered their blankets and headed into the old house.

Jack, Tarzan and Jerry headed up the old steps and explored the upper rooms for their berths.

Donkey and Luke made their beds high up on the hay near the ceiling in what had once been the dining room. It was on the ground floor and on the down-river side of the house, opposite the well. There were no windows in the room, but an open doorway, its facing and door long removed, gave them a full view across large stretches of the river bottom.

The small wooden porch and steps outside the doorway had long disappeared, and now there was just a three foot drop from the threshold to the ground.

After checking out their sleeping arrangements, the quintet retreated to the yard with their packs and provisions. There, just as darkness began to fall, they built a huge fire and prepared their evening meal.

It was an assorted and varied cuisine which the five of them shared.

Canned hash, sliced potatoes, pork and beans, and Spam, all cooked in the same large black skillet.

For dessert they devoured Moon Pies and Twinkies.

All of this they washed down with Kool-Aid and Pepsi.

The night became darker, with a slight breeze kicking up the flames of the fire. Leaping shadows danced ghost-like off the pale brick structure behind them.

Full, contented and at ease, the young campers lounged around the flame as Jack fixed coffee for all. They sipped at their steaming mugs without relish, fulfilling a simple campsite ritual.

Jerry smoked one cigarette after another. Then they passed one around, Luke and Tarzan almost choking on their one and only draw.

The talk was easy and interesting.

This night they talked mostly about movies they had seen, each one relating their favorite. Appropriately, most were horror films.

Then they related funny instances from school. Goofy kids in their class, hateful teachers, paddlings in the principal's office.

A couple of hours later, the talk wore down to a murmur. Yawns punctuated the yarns. The campfire died down to a low glow, eating away at one large log.

Then from the direction of the penitentiary came a low rumble.

Again thunder broke across the sky like distant artillery.

It caught the boys totally by surprise.

Before they could get to their feet to view the sky away from the fire, large drops of rain began to fall on their faces.

The frantic campers scurried about picking up items which would not weather, throwing them in their packs and heading for the house.

They cleared quarters just as the torrent hit.

Lightning zig-zagged across the booming sky, and the deluge hammered the tin roof of the old mansion with such noise that it made it difficult for them to hear each other.

The sweet, dry smell of the hay contrasted with the soaking storm outside. Slivers of rain blowing through the open doorways and windows did not diminish the cocoon-like coziness of the old dwelling.

Charged with a new burst of energy, the boys romped and frolicked throughout the house, leaping and jumping from one stack of hay to another. Their yelling and laughter mixed with the sounds of thunder and the falling rain.

Finally they stood at the open windows in the upstairs bedroom which faced the river. There they became quiet and peered out into the rainy night. Across the wide, dark span of river bottom and through the misty screen of wind and rain they could see the faraway lights of the penitentiary.

The view, the enchanting terror of the storm, and the enveloping comfort of their den calmed them. They stood for a long time, staring into the night—each lost in his own thoughts.

After a while the thunder rumbled off to the west and the lighting followed suit. The storm had passed, but left behind a strong steady downpour which still made slumbering music against the tin covering.

Donkey and Luke left the other three at the windows and with their lantern aglow searched out their berths below.

The air was growing cooler as they crawled into their beds and wrapped their blankets around them.

Donkey put out the light. A brief flash of lightning returned to send shadows dancing across the dark room.

"Y'all keep the ghost downstairs, ya hear?" they heard Jack yell from upstairs where the others were beginning to bed down. An excited curse, laughter, some jagged conversation and then things became quiet upstairs.

Snug and comfortable on the hay, Donkey and Luke talked for a while. Donkey was on the inside next to the wall and only a couple of feet from the ceiling. Luke was on the outside ledge facing the open doorway.

The rain continued to drum upon the roof.

They talked about the past summer, baseball, the amount of money they made mowing yards. They talked about money which they would make the following summer on picking strawberries and maybe even hauling hay.

Donkey started talking about the dam.

His Dad had already spoken to some government men. Luke mentioned the signs he had found on some empty houses in town marking them condemned by the Army Corps of Engineers.

In the darkness of the stormy night, each boy acknowledged there was now little doubt that the government meant business.

All the surveying sticks placed down by the corps surveyors and which they had uprooted had come to naught.

What about a flood wall for Currentville like the one in Paducah—wouldn't it work to save the town from the dam?

They would check it out. But who would they talk to?

Then, as the dreary hopelessness of it all began to sink in, their conversation wore down and finally died. They drifted off to sleep to the sounds of nature's symphony.

It was a deep, deep sleep, as the rainy night wore on.

Then, Luke was suddenly awake.

He was awake, but his eyes remained shut. Something— some noise—had awakened him. Some sound had entered his consciousness other than the sound of the rain. He still heard a steady cadence, but the pitch had somehow changed.

It had a coarse rhythm, up and down . . . like someone breathing heavily.

The rain had stopped. But there was still a sound.

Luke was frozen with fear.

It was someone breathing—gasping almost, and it was not from the direction of Donkey who slumbered deeply beside him.

He shut his eyes even tighter—not daring to open them for fear of what he might see in the room with him.

Frantic thoughts raced through his mind as he stiffened and sweated. How long had he been asleep? What time was it?

And the awful gasping. It had to be the breathing of Lafayette's ghost.

In his delirium, Luke was able to make out that it was coming from the direction of the outside door opening.

Then in frightful panic, his eyes flew open.

He blinked and tried desperately to adjust to the darkened room. The sound was abating, becoming lower and lower. Now it was gone.

Maybe it was a dream, Luke thought hopefully.

He continued to try to focus on objects in the room.

The night was now very quiet. Luke could see through the open doorway that with the passing of the rain it had become lighter outside.

He lay still, relaxing now as he peered through the door opening.

Then he felt his hair begin to rise and his skin begin to crawl. His heart began to pound so loudly that he could hear it in the stillness.

There in the doorway a form was taking shape, silhouetted

against the lighter outside. It was the figure of a man, sitting on the floor with his legs hanging outside the door sill.

Luke blinked his eyes, hoping the apparition would disappear.

He swung his arm toward Donkey, hoping he would find his friend gone, and sitting in the doorway. The back of his hand landed on his sleeping friend's side.

Luke chose not to make a sound. Not to breathe. Maybe it would go away. Paralyzed with fear, Luke only knew that the object . . . the man . . . whatever it was had not detected that he and Donkey were in the room.

As Luke continued to stare in terror, the visitor became more apparent.

He was only about fifteen feet away, and Luke could tell it was a grown man. His hair was cropped off very short, almost shaved. Slowly the man's head turned and stared into the room, right at Luke. But his head moved on around as if he was surveying the surroundings without actually seeing anything. Then he bent forward and looked out across the yard toward the river as if he was searching for something . . . fearing something.

The intruder was tall, with a slim build. He was coatless, clad only in what appeared to be a thin T-shirt and pants.

Though no longer laboring, his breathing was still heavy, as though he had been running.

Luke wondered who he was. Where could he be going? Why was he here? Why were his actions, his movements so haunting and peculiar?

No answers would come to Luke's mind. Perhaps it was a ghost after all. Maybe a killer on the run. Strange things and strange people roamed the land between the rivers.

Luke once again trembled with fear, closed his eyes and prayed.

He prayed that he would open his eyes and the form sitting in the doorway would be gone.

Luke thought of awaking Donkey sleeping so peacefully at his side. But he was afraid of making any move or sound.

So he remained lying there like a stone—rigid and silent,

hardly breathing and his eyes shut.

Moments passed, and he began to count. One hundred...
two hundred . . .

His trancelike fixation was broken by a terrifying scream,
not from the doorway and not loud. It was from a distance, seemingly from the back of the house. It died away into a terrible low
moan and then ceased.

Cold sweat formed on his brow, and his heart pounded
against his ribs. Uncontrollably, he sprung up from his bedding,
choking on the darkness.

His eyes opened and he frantically looked to the door.

There was nothing there.

It was gone.

The cool air fell upon Luke's flushed face, and he listened
fearfully for the next sound.

There was nothing.

Quiet. All was totally quiet. The big old house was tomblike, dark and dead. Like the echo of a lone rifle shot, the remains
of the heart-stopping scream still bounced around inside of Luke's
head.

The rain had stopped and the weather had cleared. It had
grown lighter outside.

For a long while, Luke sat upright, unmoving, and con-
templating his plight.

Minutes passed, Luke strained to detect the slightest
sound.

Nothing.

Slowly, and very gingerly, he laid back down on the hay.

He looked again at the doorway. Only the light from the
outside was framed by the aperture.

After a few more moments he began to relax a bit and
breathe normally.

Maybe it was a dream, after all.

The awful gasping, the lonely figure, the scream . . . all of
it now seemed like an illusion.

Once again, Luke thought of waking Donkey and telling
him about the hideous happening.

Maybe he should get up and investigate. He was drained of all of his courage.

It would wait till morning, he reasoned, if "it" had really happened. In his fatigue, he was becoming confused, almost disoriented as he lay in the dark.

His thoughts became jumbled and slogged through his head in slow motion. He was very tired. It was time to surrender . . . just surrender.

Surrender.

⚜

"Git up! Git up!"

Luke opened his eyes to the beautifully bright sunlight streaming in across the hay.

"Git up!"

Jack was pulling at his limp and sleep-ridden body.

"Come on, there's something going on out back," he was imploring with a sense of urgency in his voice.

Donkey was sitting up wiping the slumber from his eyes.

"Come on. Right now!" Jack motioned as he stepped back and headed to the stairs. "I heard dogs, and now I hear voices."

Luke, who felt like he'd been drugged, managed to gain his feet and stumbled after Jack. Donkey followed suit.

They moved up the steps and toward the commotion.

The stairway ended in a side room with a window which overlooked the gazebo and the well. Like all the other windows in the house, it was now just an open, rectangular hole in the wall, the frame and glass having disappeared long before.

Jerry and Tarzan were already at the opening staring down on the scene below.

Jack, Luke and then Donkey moved in to fill up the window.

In order to see, Luke had to drop down on the floor and squeeze in under the others, resting his elbows where the windowsill had once been.

It was a beautiful fall morning, slightly crisp, with a deep blue sky and the bright sunshine beating down on their faces. The storm had washed the air thin and clean.

The old well was right below them and its top was flung open so that the five boys were looking straight down the dark shaft.

Gathered around the well and milling about in the overgrown side yard were several prison guards in their olive-green uniforms. Three state pickup trucks were parked in random positions from the end of the lane up into the yard. Moving slowly up the lane and parking behind one of the state vehicles came sheriff Bass Fisher's white cruiser with the red light on top.

Two inmates stood off to one side of the yard with two large hounds on leashes. The dogs pulled restlessly at their leashes and sniffed at the ground.

Luke's eyes returned to the well, where for the first time he noticed a ragged hole torn through the wooden platform which covered the pit.

The men were talking calmly with one another, if somewhat quieter than normal.

Bass Fisher moved up to the lip of the well and stared into the hole.

"Shelby on his way?" Luke heard Bass inquire of one of the correctional officers, who nodded in return.

Luke then noticed that two of the guards were pulling on lines which ran taut down into the watery hole. Others were hovering around offering instruction and watching intently.

Bass reached to help with the lines, which were now being pulled up with some effort.

An object appeared, filling the dark hole.

Upward it came. Slowly, in jerks, as the burly sheriff and two guards pulled.

Then the sunlight struck it.

Pasty white and stiff, the corpse was rising from its grave.

Other guards converged and reached out to help pull it through the canal.

Rigor mortis had set in, and the left arm was extended like

it was pointing, scraping the knuckles against the wall of the well. The grappling hooks on the end of the lines secured the body under the arms.

The rotten footing around the well was treacherous. Lifting the dead man free of the hole without them crashing through themselves was a monumental task.

Finally, with a concerted heave from several arms and shoulders, the body shot straight up above the opening of the well.

There for just a moment it was held suspended by the uplifted arms of the laboring guards.

It was at that moment that Luke and his friends stared straight into the face of death.

Young, slight, with a closely cut hair, inmate style. The drenched cadaver was dressed only in dripping denim jeans and a T-shirt, the latter pulled up under his arms, exposing his blanched and bony chest. His shoes and socks were missing.

But it was the face, now held up to them in the morning sun, which would last the boys a lifetime.

The eyes, fixed and half-closed, met Luke's. Like their last meeting, Luke could see him, but the vacant and distant stare could not see Luke.

Its mouth was open, even now in death, begging for breath. The skin wrapped around the fragile and pitiful head was white— as white in the sunlight as the belly of a fish.

And then, with a nod, it was gone.

Down it came, carefully and tenderly cradled in the arms of the guards who only hours before had been tramping through mud and rain, cursing the bastard.

Without anyone noticing, Shelby Dodd, the undertaker and coroner, had arrived and pulled his long black hearse up to the end of the lane. He and an assistant had brought a stretcher and sheets to the side of the well.

The deceased was laid upon the stretcher, face up, and his wayward arm pulled down to his side. In this position he was strapped to the litter. The sheet was neatly tucked over and around the body, as the haunting face disappeared from the boys' view forever.

There was a stillness there on the tattered grounds of this old estate as the body was borne to the hearse and placed inside. The shiny black hearse, strangely out of place there in the weeds and brush, managed to turn around and slowly head down the lane, disappearing in the undergrowth.

The prison crew, inmates, and hounds moved silently to their vehicles. Even the dogs seem subdued by the specter of death. All passengers aboard, the engines started and the trucks backed and turned into the lane.

The motorcade then headed down the road, forming a procession behind the hearse. In just a moment, they, too, were out of sight. Then, a moment or two more, out of sound.

Not a single one of them had noticed the five ashen faces peering down from the upstairs window.

An eerie hush enveloped the grounds, with only the wind chasing through the trees and the distant call of a jaybird breaking the silence around the well.

One by one the boys quietly returned to their bunks, and began to gather their belongings.

They spoke hardly at all, each one lost in his own thoughts.

At no one's suggestion, but by some tacit agreement, they all prepared to leave.

Luke kept seeing the wretched face rising from the well, and the beleaguered form cowering in the doorway.

Once packed and ready, the young campers headed down the same lane taken by the hearse and pickup trucks just a few minutes before.

The sun streamed through the green canopy as they trudged along.

Though it was a gorgeous fall morning, their collective mood was somber and quiet.

From time to time as they trudged down the old dirt roadway, someone would make a statement about what they had just witnessed. But it would go unanswered, and silence would fall heavier upon them.

On one or two occasions Luke opened his mouth to relate the terrifying story of his nighttime visitor.

But he could not bring himself to share it. An inner voice, a deep uneasiness, caused him to swallow his words and choke back the telling.

Luke kept thinking back to a past visit to the Lafayette house when he had found the picture of the little dead boy in a casket lying on the staircase. He had struggled with the same feeling, but had given in to his own morbid curiosity and carried the picture home.

It had mysteriously disappeared, convincing him that he had done the wrong thing in taking it.

His soul had quickened to the little boy in the casket and the inmate—a jarring connection with death.

He silently vowed that no one else would ever know about the last moments of the inmate's life.

That would be his feeble way of showing his last respect.

So they marched on, each lost in his own thoughts.

And that would be the last time Luke and his friends would ever visit the Lafayette house.

Chapter Five

Radio Land

A promise pursued but lost, has value greater than its cost.

It was a cold winter night.

The backwater was up a good four feet in the basement, having knocked out the old coal-burning furnace.

The grates were ablaze in each of the four large rooms as Luke's family settled in after supper.

Alec and Esther were in the living room, reading the paper and talking.

Their spirits were good. The river had crested at Nashville.

Luke and Bobby Joe were in their room. The big brother was lying on his bed with his head propped up by pillows, reading from his school literature book. Cocoa was curled up cozily on his stomach. Luke was sprawled across his bed thumbing through a copy of *The Sporting News* which he had picked up that afternoon at work at the newspaper office.

A lamp on the table between the beds and the glow from the coal fire purring brightly under the mantle gave the room ample light and warmth.

It was a school night, and Bobby Joe's unusual stay at home

for the evening could be credited to the big English test the next day.

The phone rang out in the hall.

Bobby Joe sprang from the bed and caught it on the second ring.

"It's for you, Pumpkin. It's Birdseed," he reported as he returned to his reading.

The hallway was cold, and Luke wasn't in for one of Birdseed's gab sessions.

"What's up?" he said, trying not to be rude.

"Luke. You got your radio on?" Birdseed inquired with a sense of urgency in his voice.

"Naw. Why?" Luke retorted, wondering to which program Birdseed was referring.

"Go turn it on and turn the dial to 900." There was excitement in the caller's voice.

"Why? What's on?"

"Just do it! 900! I'll hold."

Luke was moved by the tone of the command.

Placing the receiver on the table, he walked a few short steps down the hall to the large Philco radio standing in the dark against the wall.

Luke intended to make it quick as his bare feet stepped across the frigid floor.

He turned on the radio and stood waiting for it to warm up. The dial glowed in the dark, showing the names of Berlin, Paris, London, and Amsterdam on the short-wave band, which had not worked in Luke's memory.

Slowly came the hum and the static.

With the large knob he moved the line toward the middle of the set. Static and voices crackled from faraway places through the cold, dark night, lending warmth to the dismal hallway.

Fragments of "Supper Time Frolic," "Mr. and Mrs. North," "Gangbusters," and "The Arthur Godfrey Show" passed by on the way to 900.

When the needle arrived at the prescribed place, only a loud, static-free hum came out of the large speaker below.

Luke went back to the phone.

"Okay. There's nothing on."

He was ready to get back to his *Sporting News.*

"Okay," said Birdseed unperturbed, "go back and listen and see if you hear anything now."

Growing a little agitated, Luke nevertheless returned to the humming radio.

He waited.

Then he plopped down on the floor with his head close to the speaker and listened closely.

Nothing but the hum.

He was about ready to get up and hang up the phone when a screeching and scraping noise came out of the radio.

Then, "Hello there everybody, this is Harry Caray from beautiful Busch Stadium in St. Louis where it's a great day for baseball . . ."

It was Birdseed's voice!

Luke was totally aghast. He could have been knocked over with a feather.

Somehow he got to his feet and rushed back to the phone.

"How did you . . . how . . . how did you do that?" he managed to get out.

"Did you hear anything?" Birdseed inquired excitedly.

"Yeah. I heard you! How did you do it?" Luke's mind was racing.

There was a pause on the other end.

"I'll be right down."

With that Birdseed hung up the phone.

Within two minutes, Birdseed was through the front door and had breathlessly fallen into the rocking chair in front of the fire in Luke's room.

He was ecstatic. His face was flushed with excitement and he could hardly talk.

Luke could hardly think what to ask.

After a few incoherent exchanges, they calmed down a bit and Birdseed began to explain. He pulled a worn and tattered magazine out from under his coat and handed it to Luke.

It was an old copy of *Popular Mechanics,* creased back permanently to a certain page.

"I've been working on this for a long time," he explained.

"But I didn't want to tell you until I had it finished and working. The parts were simple, mostly things which we had around the house. There were a few things, like the fuses, which I had to buy. Could you hear me okay? Was it clear or fuzzy?"

"Like you were in the same room," Luke reported, unable to hide his admiration for his brainy friend.

He studied the *Popular Mechanics,* trying to make sense of the diagram and complicated language.

Bobby Joe had been distracted from his studies, finding the conversation considerably more intriguing than *The Canterbury Tales.*

"Let me see that," he interjected and almost jerked the book from Luke's hands.

The older brother studied it carefully, and then flipped it back to Birdseed.

"Well, you better have your underwear and toothbrush packed Birdseed," he remarked sarcastically, leaning back on his pillows.

"Why? Whata ya mean?" Birdseed's euphoric countenance turned serious.

"What do I mean? Didn't you read the fine print on that thing? You're not suppose to construct that thing or use it without a permit from the FCC," the older brother explained in a condescending tone. "The Feds will have you in the big house in Atlanta."

"What's the FCC?" Luke piped in.

"Federal Communications Commission," Birdseed answered the question. "Just a bunch of red tape. They'd never know about this little old transmitter. The Feds don't scare me."

"That's fine," Bobby Joe acted nonchalant as he went back to his book. "Just don't say I didn't warn you. Oh, by the way, maybe we'll come down to see ya Birdseed. In the summer, that is, when we can watch the Crackers play ball."

He smirked, and then went back to medieval literature.

Luke and Birdseed went back to their excited conversation, totally unaffected by the interruption.

"Wonder how far this thing will reach?" Luke wondered.

"I don't know. Why don't we call someone else and see?" Luke jumped up from his seat and headed for the phone.

Birdseed followed him.

They called Donkey, who lived on the other side of Penitentiary Hill and across town, about a mile away. Birdseed raced home while Luke gave directions on the phone.

In a few minutes, Donkey returned to the phone bubbling with excitement. "Harry Caray" was coming in loud and clear.

Next Luke called Jack, who lived up on a ridge going out of town. Birdseed kept transmitting.

Same result.

Now came the big test.

Billy Mason lived way out in the country near the county line.

Luke called him.

For over twenty minutes they tried. Luke giving instruction, waiting on the line. Bobby working with his radio. Birdseed transmitting.

No luck. The signal wasn't that strong.

Only slightly disappointed, Birdseed returned to Luke's house.

"Well, we at least cover the whole town. That's something," the young engineer beamed as he flopped back in the rocker.

"I think it's great, Birdseed. It's incredible!" Luke lauded his friend, still amazed by the whole thing.

"Yeah, what are you going to do, read nursery rhymes to the whole town on that thing?" Bobby Joe looked up from his reading and asked. "Or maybe give the river stages. You might even compete with Douglas Edwards."

He went back to reading as Luke shook his head at Birdseed. "Don't pay any attention to him. He's just jealous that he and his friends aren't smart enough to do something like that."

Birdseed was obviously not affected by Bobby Joe's poking.

He stared into the fire with a blissful expression on his face.

Douglas Edwards.

"Hey Luke," he jumped up from the chair, "walk me home."

On the dark, narrow sidewalk Birdseed began to talk in a very serious and deliberate tone.

"Listen Luke, I know that Bobby Joe was making fun and razzing me. He doesn't know how close he came to the truth and the whole reason that I worked so hard to set up this transmitter. You know we've talked about the dam coming and all. And we formed our club and swore an oath to do all we can to fight it—tearing down the surveying stakes and all. Well, this is our Radio Free Europe."

Luke looked at his serious young friend quizzically.

"What do you mean?"

"I mean this is our voice—our underground radio station to rally the people to fight the dam. It's our "Don't Flood Currentville" station.

"We'll broadcast every night. We'll make up leaflets and put it on everyone's doorsteps advertising our frequency . . . telling people to turn to it at night at a certain time.

"Then we will have our own programming. We'll play some patriotic music and then read some speeches and tell the people the truth. They don't know the truth. The United States of America is trying to take our land, our town, our homes . . . and we are being . . . being run out of our homes . . . just like the Indians were! And it's not right. It's not right!"

Birdseed was waxing eloquent now, his breath spurting puffs of fog into the cold night air.

"There's still time, Luke. There's still time. They're just now beginning the surveys. Politicians. They listen to voters. We'll get the people all fired up and writing their Congressmen . . . it'll work. I tell you, it will work!"

Luke let it sink in.

"What exactly is a congressman anyway? I mean . . . "

"Congressman. Congressman. The guys who go to Washington. Make our laws. Decided to build this dam. But they are elected by the people. We can change them. It's not too late."

Luke didn't fully understand. But he hated the dam. The thought of having to move. Of his Dad having to transfer to another lock. Having to leave his friends. The place where he grew up. The thought depressed him, haunted him so much that he tried not to think about it, hoping that it would just go away.

"Okay. So what do we do now?" he asked as they reached the steps leading up to Birdseed's front porch.

The porch light was on and Birdseed's mother was peering through the window of the front door, motioning to him that it was time for him to come in.

"Okay." Birdseed took a deep breath. "First we have to get my transmitter out of the house to another place. My Mom and Dad don't know about it. I mean they know that I've been working on something, but they think it's just some school project.

But we . . . I . . . have to reassemble it somewhere else. We've got to find another . . . studio. So we can broadcast anytime we want and no one will know where it is."

Luke blew out a low, soft whistle.

"Boy, that's gonna be tough. Got any ideas?" he looked hopefully at Birdseed.

"Yeah. The Benton place."

"Benton place?"

"Yeah, it's empty. The Carsons moved out two weeks ago. And I think it has electricity. I've got to have electricity."

The Benton place was an old run-down white-frame dwelling, which sat back in a group of sugar maples and was surrounded by a large yard. It was just a few houses down from Luke on the other side of the street.

At one time, years before, when it was owned by the Benton family, it had been a rather handsome home, with its gabled roof, wraparound porch and gingerbread trimming. Now it was a rundown rental house owned by some estate. There was a frequent turnover of renters, and most times it just stood there empty.

"But what if someone moves in?" Luke asked. " I mean, we can't just go down there and set up in someone else's house.....I mean......"

"You worry too much, Luke," Birdseed tried to put on grown up airs. "First of all, how often do they rent that old house? Remember the last time before the Carsons? Remember how long it sat empty? Remember the weeds growing in the yard all last summer? It'll be months before it rents. It may never rent again, with the talk of the dam and all."

There was a rapping on the window.

"We'll check it out Saturday," Birdseed bounded up the steps and toward the door. "Fifty-four forty or fight!" he smiled broadly, made a fist, and disappeared into the house.

On Saturday morning Luke and Birdseed went and checked out the Benton place.

They peered through the grimy windows, searching out the empty rooms inside.

It may have been lived in two weeks before, but already the old wooden floors were covered with dust. Coal soot from the prison and neighborhood chimneys covered the front porch.

Luke and Birdseed moved around to the rear of the house, climbed up on an old cistern, and looked through the windows of the back porch that had been closed in.

"Hey! Look here!" Birdseed exclaimed as he pushed up one of the windows. "It's open."

Luke was hesitant. The back yard was grown up in weeds even in midwinter, and an open field separated the grounds from Freewill. It was fairly secluded.

Still, he was reluctant to go inside someone's house without permission. Even if it was empty and run-down.

But Birdseed had already raised the window and crawled inside.

"Come on. Let's look around," he beckoned from inside.

Luke scanned the outside area, took a deep breath, and went through the open window.

It was bone-chillingly cold inside. Their footsteps echoed as they walked from room to room. There was trash falling out of one of the grates, and the wallpaper was peeling off the walls.

But there were a lot of windows, lighting up the rooms,

showing up their warts and cracks.

Birdseed reached and pushed one of the old-fashioned light buttons just inside one of the rooms. The light bulb hanging down from the high ceiling came on.

"Electricity!" Birdseed exclaimed in an exuberant whisper. For some reason, as if afraid they would wake up some sleeping resident, they spoke in hushed tones.

In one of the closets they found a ladder built into the wall leading up through a small crawl space and into the attic.

Up they went.

Light flowed into the attic through two dormers. Some boards were placed across the rafters to provide flooring. A few musty old jars of fruit and vegetables, a darkened funeral wreath, and a stack of *Life* magazines had been left behind.

The two adventurers went to the windows and looked down upon the front yard and out to the street.

"This is where we set up shop." Birdseed decreed enthusiastically.

"Up here?" Luke questioned incredulously.

"It's perfect. Too many windows downstairs. Nobody can see us inside, especially at night when we have lights on. We can run an extension cord up here. The equipment will be well hidden. No one will see our light . . . it's perfect!"

He was convincing. Maybe it *would* be a good place for an underground radio station.

They sat down on the rough lumber.

"Ever heard of Anne Frank?" Birdseed asked.

"The movie star?" Luke responded.

"Naw. Naw. Not a movie star. She was a Jew in Nazi Germany who some people hid up in their attic for years. Anyway, it's a great story. An attic is a great place to hide. If you can hide a person in an attic for years, we can run our radio station from here."

"But what if someone moves in?" Luke queried.

Birdseed thought long and hard.

"Listen. They finally found Anne Frank. That's the risk we take. This is war. We just have to keep an eye out. Keep an eye on the place. Looks like someone's moving in, we move in at night and move out. Each night when we sign off, we pull the extension cord up here in the attic. No one will ever know. We'll only be here at night."

Again, Birdseed was convincing.

"Here's the plan," he continued. "You leave the engineering to me. I'll get us set up here. You help me bring the stuff down and I'll need some time to put it back together. It's complicated stuff. Requires a lot of concentration. Your job will be to start planning the programming. Forget Donkey and Jack. They don't show any interest. I tried talking to them at school. All they want to talk about is having their own show, being a DJ and playing music. They'd mess up the whole thing.

"Besides," he looked around, "the less people we have coming in here the less likely we will be detected."

Luke and Birdseed spent most of that day breaking down the transmitter, packing it, and gathering accessories, including extension cords and a lamp. They even found an old record player while rummaging around in Birdseed's basement.

All the paraphernalia was moved furtively down behind the houses and through the back window. In order not to draw attention, they carried a small amount at a time.

It was all piled up in the attic on the loose boards before Birdseed was called in by his mother to do whatever Birdseed was made to do on Saturday evenings—-read, play cards with his grandmother, or attend a lecture with his parents in Paducah.

While Luke was at ball practice every day after school for the next week, Birdseed worked on the "studio."

They would meet for a few minutes at night to discuss the project. Birdseed had warned against talking about it at school.

"Too risky," he said.

Jack and Donkey, and even Billy Mason, inquired about the transmitter for a few days. Receiving cool responses from Birdseed and Luke, and with the novelty worn off, they soon forgot about it.

The mission belonged solely to Luke and Birdseed.

"One of the fuses is shot." Birdseed reported one night at

Luke's house after supper. "I think we broke it in the move. I'm in the process of getting another one. It will take a few days."

Luke had no idea where Birdseed got such things. Nor did he really want to know. He just assumed that he ordered them through some of his scientific magazines and maybe had his father buy them on his trips around the area.

"Luke, you need to work on our leaflets," he continued, "so we can start just as soon as I get us on the air. And you need to begin writing some programming. You know, stuff that will drive home the point about how unfair it is and all for the government to come in here and make us move and flood our land.

"You know the mimeograph machine that the RAs use at the church for things?"

Luke nodded.

"Think you can get in there and print out some leaflets? I'll get you the paper when we know the times when we will be on the air. But you can go ahead with writing some stuff to be read. You write pretty good, Luke. Use your imagination. But you need to get on it."

So Luke started thinking.

What could he write?

Maybe he could just write down the way he felt. He tried to imagine what the town was going to be like in the future as it began to fall apart. Luke could not conceive of things which had been a part of his life just disappearing off the face of the earth. The school, the main street, the stores. It was depressing. And it made him mad.

One night after finishing his homework at the kitchen table, he tried to visualize the undoing of his world by the dam. It was hard to imagine. He pulled out a piece of paper and began to write.

"As you look down the main street of Currentville today, you can see a real ghost town right before your eyes. The theater that used to attract many people from all over the county has now been destroyed by fire, and the remains of the old building lie on the floor in the warm sunlight.

"Gresham Brothers, the store which once brought in farmers from miles around is closed, and the old sooty doors will never be opened for business again.

"The big, colonial-type house in which the doctor's office was located is now only a rubbish pile waiting to be covered by the great waters of Barkley Lake. The street, which at one time was packed with people, especially on Saturday afternoons when farmers and townspeople would sit in the sunshine on the riverbank and talk about politics and crops and other things, is bare now except for four or five old faithfuls, occupying the old wooden bench which once was filled even in the late hours of night.

"Homes in which hospitality at one time rang, and homes where children played under big shade trees, are now condemned by the United States government. The laughter of children and the chattering of adults is gone and the wind moans through the trees by the vacant houses."

He looked through the kitchen windows, darkened by winter night, toward the river, and reflected.

"The old swimming hole sees few boys now, and the wind whistles through the willow trees. Once you could hear the loud splashing of water from a far distance.

"I was born and raised in Currentville. The place where Jenny Lind sang and Lafayette stayed are not as important to me as the other things. To the outsider it would be just the opposite.

"It is sad and it hurts to see the place where you were born and have loved crumble and die right before your eyes.

"It is so hard to see your friends that you loved so well depart, and it is hard to leave.

"This town has not been bombed by Russia nor has it been attacked by an army. This town has been destroyed by the United States government.

"It doesn't seem fair, does it? No, it doesn't seem fair for people to be run out of the homes they loved and for friends to be separated forever.

"The town is dead. It has no future. It has few dreams, and by the time they come true many of the old will be dead. They will die somewhere besides where they wanted to die because their homes will be flooded.

"The town of Currentville is one big family being broken up forever.

"When you hear *The Star Spangled Banner* and look at the missiles and jets and the mountains and meadows you think what a great country you have.

"But when you look at what is left of the little town of Currentville, it makes you think twice before you speak."

Luke showed the writing to Birdseed the next day at school.

He pushed his glasses back on his nose and read it carefully.

"Hey, that's good writing Luke, but . . ." he was groping or words, " . . . you've already thrown in the towel. I mean, this is like a white flag of surrender. It'll be okay to read, I guess. But we haven't lost yet. We need to get the people stirred up . . . to do something."

"Okay," Luke took the paper back, "I'll work on something else."

"I mean, it will be fine to read on the air," Birdseed was hoping he hadn't hurt Luke's feelings. "We can say something like, 'this is the way it's gonna be if you don't get off your can and do something' . . ."

They were walking down the basement hallway to lunch. The wonderful smell of hot rolls permeated the building.

"How are you doing on the transmitter?" Luke inquired.

"Well, I got the fuse. But I'm having a hard time getting down there to work on it. Mom's keeping a real tight watch on me. Almost dropped to a B in English these last six weeks. I try to get down every night before supper. But just about the time I get into it, I have to leave it. I'd say give me about another week."

"Can I help you? I could go down there at night and work on it," Luke offered.

"Naw. You don't know anything about it. You would mess it up big time," Birdseed said directly, not meaning to offend. "Just give me a little time."

The weather reversed itself, turned a little warmer, and it started raining again. After two days, it stopped and turned colder.

But the backwater, which was about to make its exit from Luke's basement came charging back.

The town was awash with the muddy deluge which was seeping into the side streets and alleyways. Main Street was flooded, and the stores were neck deep in water. Without much show of concern the owners had packed all of their wares and hauled them to higher ground in truckloads just before the river arrived. E. B. Hall, for instance, was running his store from the garage behind his house up on Pea Ridge.

The lowlands on each side of Penitentiary Hill were just about covered, and the main road leading into the village had disappeared. Travel to the outside world was restricted to the gravel road leading back up over Pea Ridge.

To get to school on the southern edge of town, Luke and his friends had to walk out of the way, and along the few streets still left above the flood.

The ferry was now landing up on Main Street just as it headed up Penitentiary Hill near the post office and in front of the courthouse.

The lock and dam had of course completely disappeared, leaving not even a ripple to mark their deep and murky burial. Tow boats with their barges churned right on over the submerged obstacle. Alec and the other lockmen whiled away the interlude around the Warm Morning stove in the lock house which sat high and dry above the rampaging river. They busied themselves as much as possible with repairs, painting, and maintenance.

All in all, it was a pretty dismal scene but one which the people of Currentville took in stride, stoically tolerating the mess each winter. Sometimes the store owners would move out of their businesses more than once in one season.

Each winter Perky Perkins would take a big john boat and place an old car seat on the back of it. Then he would give the girls a tour of the flooded downtown, rowing and scudding through the watery streets like a gondolier in Venice.

Coming off Penitentiary Hill it flattened out to the north and Main Street headed out of town. Houses faced the road from each side until Wrinklemeat's grocery, where the incorporated limits of Currentville came to an abrupt end.

On the river side of this thoroughfare was a row of split-level houses.   The front porch of Luke's house fronted the sidewalk and the street.   The back porch stood aloft overlooking the river valley, and the rising tide of brown water and driftwood.

Up and up it came.

For a while, Bobby Joe and Luke would feed the coal-burning furnace while wearing hip boots and shoveling the dry coal off the top in the coal bin.

Then the water would rise into the fire box and they would have to rely solely upon the grates for heat.

The water moved up the basement steps toward the kitchen door.   Soldier, Cocoa, and the cats were brought in at night to sleep on the stairway.

At night one could go to the kitchen, open the basement door, turn on the light, and stare into the Cumberland River just a few feet away on the steps.   The furry pets hovered together upon the few remaining steps.

Again everyone took it in stride.   Luke would never hear his parents talk of moving, or even consider the possibility that the three or four feet between them and the river might disappear.

Luke did overhear his mother express concern to his father once, that she was afraid someday the river might just wash the house off of its foundation.

The possibility haunted Luke.   Late at night, after his father had gone to work on the midnight shift, Luke would lie in his bed and listen to the water lapping just below the floor.

The cold wind would whistle around the windows, and the coal fire would hiss and crack.   Its bright glow filled the room with eerie shadows, and Luke would lie on his back, tracking the flickering movements on the ceiling.

Harrowing were the times when large boats plowed down the river.   Luke would hear them rumble by, way out across the dark and aqueous span.

Then he would wait.

It would take minutes for it to arrive, but even as the sound of the vessel was disappearing, the backwash came calling.   It began with small waves, simply giving off a light splash. Then they would grow larger and larger, reaching a crescendo which sent shivers through the house and made Luke's heart pound.

Each time he tensed, thinking that the house would give way and begin to float away, and sink beneath the dark, cold waters of the Cumberland.

Then the pounding would lessen and the waves tone down and finally fade away completely.

The house returned to quiet. The ticking of the Seth Thomas clock on the mantle and the hissing of the fire reclaimed the night. Bobby Joe continued to sleep undisturbed in the next bed.

Finally Luke would drift off.

The river crested, and then began to fall. It escaped from Luke's basement, and receded back across the narrow yard to the back of the garden.

One bitterly cold evening as night began to fall, Luke and his father worked at the water's edge, raking and throwing debris into the retreating stream.

Luke paused in his labor, blowing on his hands and looking out over the mile-wide, foreboding, fast-moving current. Twisted knots of driftwood and uprooted trees see-sawed along the fast lane. Dismembered planking from an old privy even bobbled past.

"Well, Dad," Luke chirped cheerfully, "looks like we got her licked."

The light of day had been swallowed by the darkening dusk, but he could still make out the form of his father, leaning on his rake and peering out at the flood.

"She'll be back," Alec replied matter-of-factly. "If not tomorrow, then the next day. If not the next day, then next year."

Then his voice dropped, as if the fifty-year-old man were staring into the dark and cold waters of his own mortality. In a low and solemn tone, and to Luke's everlasting memory, he pronounced "Nature will win . . . in the end."

It was Saturday afternoon and Luke was home alone, lying across his bed. He was writing a leaflet which would announce their first broadcast. After it was written and approved by Birdseed, he would take it to the church and put it on a stencil for mimeographing. Having access to the mimeograph machine was one of the perks of being president of the Royal Ambassadors.

When Birdseed paid a visit, he would normally knock once at the front door and then barge on in—the knock a warning rather than a request to enter.

This time Birdseed did not knock, and it startled Luke a little when he burst into the room and plopped down in the platform rocker in front of the fire.

"Birdseed!" Luke greeted his friend enthusiastically. "What ya been doing?"

His friend sat motionless, staring into the flames, and not saying a word.

Luke detected something was dreadfully wrong, and moved off the bed and into the chair beside him.

"How's the transmitter coming?" he begged for conversation.

Still nothing but silence from his guest.

Luke studied the sad and morose face of his friend. He saw his eyes begin to water, and then a large single tear rolled down his cheek.

"Birdseed. What's wrong?" Luke was becoming alarmed.

Finally, without moving his eyes away from the mesmerizing glow of the fire, he spoke.

"It's over. It's finished. They turned off the electricity and . . . " He spoke barely above a whisper, with a break in his voice.

Luke moved quickly to reassure. "So? We'll just move to another place. No problem."

Birdseed's gloomy countenance remained unchanged.

"You don't understand. They found it. It's gone. Everything. The instructions, the tubes, the equipment, everything."

The words fell like lead upon Luke's ears and a heavy

silence enveloped them.

Stunned, Luke's eyes turned and he joined Birdseed gazing into the fire.

Two shipwrecked souls watching their boat go down.

Luke searched for words, not only to bolster his own spirits, but to render aid to his pal.

No words came, and a sense of hopelessness caused him to remain mute.

After a long while and without saying another word Birdseed bolted from his chair and left the room. Luke heard him go out the front door.

It was a long time before Luke moved his eyes away from the flames and across the room to his bed. He slowly got out of his seat, walked over and picked up the half-finished leaflet. Without even looking at the paper, he crushed it into a ball and flung it into the fire.

He sat back down and watched it disappear in a flash.

Then, after wallowing around on bottom for a while, he decided it was time to come up for air. He looked up at the clock on the mantle.

He thought of Birdseed.

Luke got up from his chair and walked to the phone in the hallway.

He dialed his neighbor.

"Hey!" he yelled cheerily to the somber voice on the other end, "you don't know where a man could find a good hot monopoly game on this cold dark winter afternoon, do ya?"

There was a slight pause.

"I'll be right down."

Chapter Six

Broken Window

The only promise worth keeping is the one with an effort.

The big Gresham Brothers store sold two kinds of baseballs.

One sold for 75 cents. It was the cheapest and the one most boys bought. The more expensive ball cost two dollars, in most instances a prohibitive sum.

A new baseball was a special purchase, an annual event.

The ball would shine new and white for only a short but exciting time. Then it would begin to wear rough and brown. The stitches would start to break, then split. An extra-hard hit would send the yarn-wrapped sphere exploding from its cover.

The remnant would then take on a new lease on life, bound tightly with black electrical tape. After a while, if not lost in the corn or high weeds it would become slightly warped from constant batting and bouncing off brick walls. Lastly, in its death throes, it became water logged and heavy as a shot put, stinging the hands when caught or struck with the mended wooden bats. It would finally explode into tiny pieces off the sweet part of the bat.

The life span of a baseball.

The two dollar baseball was different. Or at least that was what was told. Only the high school boys bought the more expensive sphere. It was supposed to last longer, and be more durable.

But it was a luxury Luke and his buddies could ill afford. Until now.

He and Donkey stood at the dusty old display case at Gresham Brothers. Luke first picked up one box, and then the other. He had over two dollars of lawn-mowing money in his pocket. He had often gotten to this point before, only to chicken out at the last moment and buy the cheaper ball.

"Go for it!" Donkey urged.

So Luke took the plunge. They took the box to the counter where Luke shelled out the dough. Then they discarded the box, took the shining white baseball, and excitedly headed out onto the street.

Donkey and Luke took turns smelling the fresh rawhide and pounding it into their old darkened gloves. It was a marvelous feeling, and they were ready for a big game.

The happy pair moved down Main Street, passed the pool hall, and walked out toward the ball field across from the school on the edge of town.

They knew exactly where they could pick up a spate of boys for a big all-day game at the ball field.

Perky Perkins' house was just a block or two down the street from the pool hall toward the school. The old wooden frame house was called Noah's Ark, because each time the backwater came up, it moved around. It would change its position almost yearly.

Between Noah's Ark and Mr. Thompson's house was a large vacant lot.

This was the town sockball field, and most of the time during the summer from late morning till late afternoon, there would be a game going on.

A sockball was a couple of socks bound up into a spongy sphere with black tape. It was about the size of a baseball and was ideal for pickup games in the small confines of vacant lots and yards. It was soft, and couldn't be hit nearly as far as a baseball, and most important, it would careen off houses and windows without causing any damage.

And it was cheap. When the roundballers were bereft of baseballs, sockball would suffice.

As expected, Luke and Donkey found a sockball game in progress at Noah's Ark.

There were at least a dozen boys.

"Hey yall!" Luke yelled from the sidewalk which ran parallel with the first baseline. "Let's go to the school and have a game."

He raised the shining new baseball high over his head for everyone to see.

Play halted, and all eyes were on Luke and the two-dollar baseball.

"A two dollar ball!" Donkey announced loudly like a carnival barker.

"Hey, Luke, let me see it," pleaded Tommy Grogan, who was standing at the pitcher's rubber.

Luke proudly wheeled and fired him a belt-high fastball.

Tommy hardly had a chance to take it from his glove when Bennie Marshall, standing in from the left side at home plate waved the lumber anxiously and yelled, "Throw me one, Tommy!"

Before Luke's protest could rise from his throat, Tommy had already answered Bennie's call by sending the newly purchased baseball on its very first trip to home plate.

Bennie swung and a wooden pop echoed throughout the ball yard.

In the big sky country across from the school it would have been a beautiful sound. Here in the closed confines of the small lot between Noah's Ark and Mr. Thompson's house, it was sickening.

The ball was mashed. Really mashed.

It rose high into the air, out of the vacant lot and toward Mr. Thompson's house. Over his peach tree, over his yard, and over the hedge which ran beside the house.

Finally the ball began to descend, straight toward the multi-paned window on the side of the Thompson home.

There was a loud pop as the ball disappeared into the house, followed immediately by the sound of shattering glass. A gaping, jagged hole marked the spot.

For a long moment, there was stunned silence.

Then, like an alarm had been sounded, boys began to scatter in all directions.

Every single roughneck kid, who had only seconds before been so brazenly frolicking through a bright summer morning, was now hightailing it for cover.

Everyone, that is, except Luke.

Part of him was running away with the rest. But his feet were stuck to the same spot. His eyes were still glued on the busted window.

Within a blink, the sockball field was empty and quiet.

Luke found himself moving slowly, as if drawn by a monstrous magnet, toward the back of Mr. Thompson's house.

Trancelike, he walked across the sockball field, up through the yard, and around the corner of the house to the back door.

Slowly he opened the screen door, and raised his right fist to knock.

Suddenly and with great force the solid wooden door flew open.

There facing Luke was a tall, gray-headed old man who had turned into a monster.

Mr. Thompson's face was red and twisted, his eyes glowing white.

"Come in here!" he yelled so vehemently that his false teeth almost snapped out of his mouth.

"Come in here and see what you've done!"

Terrified, Luke slowly moved into the kitchen.

"Look at this! Look at this! You could have killed her!" Mr. Thompson swept his hand toward his wife who was standing beside the stove in front of the violated window.

What Luke saw made his blood run cold and his heart drop into his shoes.

The kitchen walls, floor and the stove were all splattered with blood. There was blood everywhere.

There was blood all over Mrs. Thompson's neatly pressed cotton dress and white apron. To his horror Luke could even see spatterings across her forehead. Her granny glasses were even sprayed with gore.

He no longer heard the invective still pouring from Mr. Thompson's popping lips.

He felt faint, the sights and sounds blurred. It was like he was passing through the misty corridors of some ghoulish nightmare.

Luke watched Mrs. Thompson turn back to the stove and begin to fish around in a large pot, steaming on the back burner.

It was directly under the broken glass.

Using a large spoon in each hand she raised a round bloody mass from the pot. She held it aloft for a few moments while the red substance drained from around it.

Luke's eyes began to concentrate on the object. It was turning from crimson to white.

It was the baseball.

Suddenly, like a fuzzy picture coming into sharp focus, Luke realized what had happened.

Bennie Marshall's gargantuan blast had sent Luke's brand-new baseball through Mr. Thompson's window and smack dab into a pot of tomato soup cooking on the stove.

Mr. Thompson's favorite midday cuisine was plastered all over the kitchen.

A heavy weight lifted off Luke's shoulder and he found himself actually breathing again.

Mr. Thompson was still rattling on, sputtering and fuming.

"I ought to call the sheriff. You could have hurt Mamma real bad." He pointed his bony finger into Luke's face.

"Now, Milton . . ." It was the first time the sweet-faced Mrs. Thompson had spoken.

"Can't you see it was an accident. The boy at least came to the house and apologized. He couldn't help it."

Her soft voice had a calming effect on her husband.

For the first time since Luke had come into the house, the

old man quit yelling. He dropped his eyes and carefully studied Luke's face. It was like he realized for the first time that the boy who had come into his kitchen was a real human being.

"What's your name, boy?" He asked in a rough but lowered voice.

Luke told him.

"What's your father's name?"

Luke told him.

"Alec Cameron. You're Alec Cameron's son."

Luke could not tell from the inflection in Mr. Thompson's voice if that was good or bad.

"He's a lockman. He works at the lock."

Luke nodded.

"Yeah, I know him."

Luke was feeling a little better.

"Well, wait till he hears about this." The old man's voice grew louder again.

Luke swallowed and decided it was time to get this whole thing moving along toward its bitter end.

"Like I said, Mr. Thompson . . . and Mrs. Thompson . . . I'm very sorry. I'll get my Dad when he gets off work this afternoon and we will come back out and fix your window. I promise."

"You bet you will!" Mr. Thompson was at last wearing down, as he now moved over and sat down in a cane-bottom kitchen chair.

Luke eyed the baseball on the table. He was now ready to make his exit out the back door as quickly as he could. But first he'd like to take his treasure with him. The gold from the mouth of the dragon.

He screwed up his courage the best he could. But at last, he didn't have the guts. Mr. Thompson's persistent and angry scowl got the best of him.

Luke muttered a few more words, backed through the doorway, and out into the wonderful fresh air of freedom.

Luke hung around the house for the rest of the day, doing odd jobs to kill the time.

He hoed the potatoes, dug up Johnson grass in the garden, and mowed the yard—even though it didn't need it.

The time passed slowly, as he waited for his father to get home from work.

Finally, a little after four, he saw him walking up the river road, his khaki shirt sleeves rolled up and his empty lunch box under his arm. The pith helmet which the lockmen wore in the summer was tilted back on his head.

It had been a long, hot day.

He could tell that Alec wasn't in the best of moods. But he had no choice. He had to grapple with the problem head on, and do it now.

Luke hoped he would notice the truck patch, the yard, the missing Johnson grass.

Luke fell in with his Dad and immediately told him about the broken window. He left out the part about the tomato soup.

Alec was obviously not too happy about the situation. But he said nothing, and went straight to the basement and his workshop.

He collected some tools, hammer, chisel, putty knife, and putty.

"Let's go," he said disgustedly as he placed the equipment on the back floorboard of the car.

They drove up over Penitentiary Hill past the prison and down into town. There they stopped at Gresham Brothers to buy a pane of glass. Luke couldn't bear to look at the counter with the baseballs.

Then they drove through town past the pool hall, and out the street to Mr. Thompson's house.

Luke noticed two things as they pulled into the driveway. The sockball field was still deserted, like a nuclear-contaminated plain. And the jagged glass had been cleared out of the pane, leaving a clean opening in that section of the window.

Alec and Luke walked up on the front porch. His father knocked on the screen door which had a treated cotton ball pinned on the outside. The main door was open.

An old man with gray hair and false teeth came to the door.

But it wasn't Mr. Thompson. This man smiled, and greeted them both with a cheerful hello, pushing back the screen and welcoming them in.

It was strange. He looked like Mr. Thompson, but it wasn't the same demented old troll that had frightened the wits out of him at this same house, earlier on this same day.

"Good to see you Alec. Would y'all like a glass of iced tea?"

Alec declined graciously just as Mrs. Thompson arrived in the living room. She was the same sweet little lady with the gray hair curled tightly on her head. But her small wire-rimmed bifocals were now clean, as was her crisply starched dress.

They moved into the kitchen which looked like the same room. But there was no evidence of the bloodshed and bedlam which had taken place there that morning.

It was neat and tidy as a pin.

Alec made small talk with the Thompsons as he moved toward the window.

The conversation finally got around to the issue at hand, as Alec looked over the damage.

"No big problem," said the old man cheerfully. "I cleaned out the broken glass, and it should be easy to take care of."

He looked at Luke and smiled benignly.

"And you should be proud of this young man, Alec. He came right up here and faced up to the music. Yes siree, you have a fine boy here."

Luke wondered where they had buried Mr. Thompson.

They moved out the back door and around to the outside of the window. Mr. Thompson fetched a small step ladder.

Alec then promptly went about his work. Like a surgeon's assistant, Luke dutifully handed his father the tools as he fixed the window.

Mr. Thompson was standing in the yard watching and talking incessantly about one thing and then another. Except for an occasional grunt or "uh huh," Alec ignored him.

In fifteen minutes it was finished.

The new pane of glass made the others look dingy.

Alec and Luke collected their tools and made their way to the car.

Fortified by the presence of his father, and the obvious transformation of Mr. Thompson, Luke found the courage he had lacked that morning.

"Uh, Mr. Thompson, do you think I could . . . uh, have my baseball back?"

"Why, of course," said the old geezer, and quickly went back in the house. Within just a few moments he was back and handed the ball to Luke.

It had lost its sheen and its innocence. But it had been thoroughly cleansed of its sins and was white as snow.

Mr. Thompson followed them, finishing up some story about when he worked at the prison.

"Sorry about this Mr. Thompson. It won't happen again," Alec finally said, throwing a quick but chilling glance at his young son as he opened the door and slid in behind the wheel.

"Oh, that's okay. Boys will be boys. Besides, I've enjoyed the visit."

Mr. Thompson was still standing in the driveway waving as they pulled out and left.

Amazing.

On the way home, Luke told his father the rest of the story. About the tomato soup.

For the first time that afternoon, Luke could see a smile break across his father's face.

After a few moments Alec turned serious. "You did the right thing, son."

Luke's father hardly ever bragged on his children. But when he did, it created magic. Luke's shoulders straightened and he felt every bit as big as the guy who was driving the car.

He picked up his old glove which had been lying on the floorboard, and pounded the baseball into its deep pocket.

Would he have gone through this ordeal if it had not been his baseball which went crashing through old man Thompson's window? Would he have even done it for less than a two dollar baseball?

Probably not. It was tough enough as it was.

As he held the clean round baseball in his hand and fingered the tight new stitches, he thought of something he had heard his Dad say many times.

Only now did he really understand what he meant. "When you hear someone say 'it's not the money, it's the principle'—it's the money."

Chapter Seven

Crime Wave

One person's promise is another person's hope.

Luke and Bobby Joe were playing catch in the side yard after supper.

The late afternoon sun had slipped below the tree line on the riverbank and struck its final rays upon the top of the house.

Cannas and four o'clocks flourished around the front porch in full summer bloom.

Alec sat in the swing reading the paper. Katydids and crickets were already conversing as the hot summer day began to cool.

Luke's Dad was sitting sideways, with both feet up in the swing like a teenager. Only the reading glasses perched low on his nose distinguished him from the boys in the yard.

Esther was inside the house cleaning up the steamy kitchen after supper.

After twenty minutes or so Bobby Joe caught Luke's last pitch and moved toward him.

"Gotta go, Pumpkin," he flipped the catcher's mitt to his little brother, who grabbed it against his chest.

"Keep that arm extended, and push off with the right foot more," Bobby Joe lectured as he bounded up on the porch and into the house.

Luke took the two gloves and ball and had a seat on the front steps, hoping that his Dad might throw a few after he finished the paper.

About that time a beat-up old Packard, loaded with dust, pulled into the driveway.

Harl Black got out and walked up to the porch.

He was a lockman who worked with Luke's Dad. He and Alec had been friends for a long time, having served time on the dredge fleet together.

Harl had a drinking problem, though he never brought it to work with him, and never missed his shift because of it.

Luke could smell liquor as he spoke and moved past him.

He was a slight little man, with a white pasty complexion and dark curly hair. He always had a cigarette dangling from his mouth and he coughed incessantly. No wonder he looked unhealthy.

But he had a nice smile, friendly manner, and an engaging twinkle in his eye.

Alec got up and greeted him, offering him a seat on the glider.

He declined, pulled his cigarette from his mouth, hacked a couple of times, and explained his visit.

"Millie is worried about Aunt Sodie. She usually calls at least once a day and she hasn't heard from her for three days now."

Harl looked troubled.

Aunt Sodie was actually the great-aunt of Harl's wife. She lived up on Pea Ridge at the end of an old lane which meandered off the main road for quite a ways. Although it wasn't that far from town as the crow flies, it was deep into the woods and isolated.

"Has she tried to call her?" inquired Alec.

"No answer. I'm afraid something may have happened to her. I'm going up to check on her and. . . ." Harl dropped his eyes, ". . well, I'd feel better if I had someone with me."

"Okay," Alec quickly responded, placing the newspaper

and reading glasses on the glider. "Let's go."

Alec stepped into the house to tell Esther where he was going and in an instant was back out the door.

The two lockmen moved toward Harl's car.

Luke sensed excitement and followed them.

He hopped in the back seat and they were off.

"She got a well? A cistern?" Alec inquired as the old car started laboring its way up Penitentiary Hill.

"A cistern." Harl advised.

"Swing by the lock house," Alec instructed. "We'll pick up some grappling hooks just in case."

After a stop at the lock house, they moved though town, down past the Baptist church and then up the steep gravel road leading to Pea Ridge. The area consisted of the summit of three large hills which came together to overlook the town and the Cumberland River Valley.

In about two miles they turned off on a seldom traveled country lane—two ruts, actually, with grass almost knee-deep in the middle.

They jostled and bounced back through dense woods and underbrush for about a mile until they came to a clearing. There stood the old wooden frame house, badly in need of paint, and with a tattered old picket fence around it.

Luke shivered as he looked at the spooky looking place. There was noticeably less light there because of all the trees and overhang.

They got out of the car and started to move toward the house.

"You'd better stay in the car," Luke's Dad admonished him somberly.

Luke was glad to oblige.

Alec and Harl moved through the broken-down gate and the weed-infested yard and up on the front porch.

The door and windows were all open, not unusual for mid-summer.

"Yo ho, Aunt Sodie!" Harl called as he peered through the screen door into the house.

"Aunt Sodie! Yo ho! Aunt Sodie!"

Alec stood on the porch and looked around the grounds, chilled by the loneliness of the place.

"She's almost ninety, you know," Harl explained, "and can't hear herself fart."

Alec didn't say it, but he knew something was wrong. There was death in that place. There wasn't even the sound of crickets and katydids, and twilight was rapidly falling upon them.

He wondered why Harl had waited this long before checking on the old lady.

"Well, let's check it out," he moved in front of Harl and opened the screen.

Two cats came running out, crying and circling their feet.

"These cats are starving," Alec noted.

They moved slowly though the house.

It was messy and full of junk.

"She was a terrible housekeeper," Harl explained almost in a whisper. "Nothing unusual here that I can see."

All the rooms were checked, and they moved through the kitchen out onto the concrete floor of the back porch.

They stood and looked around, the quiet so deafening they could almost hear each other's heartbeat.

"Check out the cistern, Harl," Alec pointed toward the end of the porch where the wooden decking and door covered the mouth of the reservoir.

"I'll check out the smokehouse."

Alec stepped down off the porch and headed the few feet to what had once been the smokehouse but had long been used just as an outbuilding.

He stopped and studied the front of the shed.

The button latch for the door was straight up and down.

He glanced at Harl who was just now opening the top of the cistern, cupping his hands and peering down inside.

Alec moved toward the door, stood in front of it for a moment, and then slowly opened it.

The stench almost staggered him.

He put his left hand over his nose and mouth as he looked

inside.

It took a few moments for his eyes to adjust to the darker environs.

Slowly things came into focus, with a long white gown in the center of the picture.

It was attached to something up above.

His eyes moved upward to an overhead beam which ran across the room.

Tied to the timber was a sash cord, pulled taut by the hanging body below.

Then the billowing white gown again, and long white hair flowing down around it.

The swollen purple face—hardly recognized as a face at all—was twisted downward, the bulging eyes blown with flies. Maggots played havoc with the wrinkled, twisted neck, where the ligature had almost severed the trunk.

Her feet dangled just a few inches off the floor, the bony toes practically scraping the wooden boards.

The floor below the suspended corpse and the lower border of the night garment itself were spattered with excrement attended to by hordes of green flies.

Holding his breath to guard against the ghastly odor, Alec moved inside. Instinctively he reached to loosen the cord from the wooden beam and free the tortured body from its suspended horror.

Then he pulled back, thinking better of it.

Stepping back to the doorway, he stood for moments and surveyed the dismal room. Light beaming through the open door gave him enough illumination to take stock of the surroundings.

Alec noticed the old wooden table in the corner covered with empty Mason jars. The musty confines also contained a closed steamer trunk, garden tools thrown haphazardly into the corner, a manual push mower propped against a wall, a horse collar hanging on a large nail, and other junk and debris.

His eyes came to rest on a three-legged milking stool turned on its side a couple of feet from Aunt Sodie's remains, apparently kicked aside with her leap into eternity.

With these mental notes taken, Alec then backed out of the doorway into the blessed air and breathed again.

"I found her, Harl," Alec summoned his friend. "Better call Shelby Dodd."

Harl came running.

"Where is she?" he asked excitedly as he approached the doorway of the smokehouse.

Then he saw her.

"Oh my God!" both the sight and the stench hit him at once.

He turned and began to retch, moved to some high weeds and threw up.

"Oh my God! Oh, Aunt Sodie. . . ." He tried to return to the scene, but once again began to heave and lament.

Harl was of no use.

Alec moved into the house to look for the phone. After a great effort, he finally found it partially hidden under a pile of newspapers.

He went through the operator for the number and called the coroner.

Luke was sitting patiently in the car with the front passenger door opened when his Dad returned.

It was almost dark, and fireflies were twinkling.

"We found her. She hung herself," Alec announced as he approached the car, as casually as if he were reporting that the Cardinals had lost in extra innings.

"Shelby Dodd and the sheriff are on their way."

He stood there by the open door next to Luke.

Alec gave a small sigh, pulled a pack of cigarettes from his shirt and calmly lit up and waited.

Harl was still wailing and retching on the back porch and Luke's Dad stood there gazing out over the summer night as cool as a cucumber.

Luke idolized his Dad.

He had a warm and charming personality, well liked by most everyone.

But Luke also feared him intensely. He had his dark moods

and a violent temper. His children watched his moods, like a haying farmer watches the gathering clouds. When the sky was dark, they knew to lie low. And always—even in the best of times—they obeyed instantly and without question.

Alec had come from a large and poor farm family, having joined his brother at eighteen on the river to escape the wretched life of the soil.

At first he had been a laborer, helping to build the very lock and dam where he was now employed. Then he went to work for the Army Corps of Engineers, first on the dredging fleet which worked the Cumberland and Tennessee rivers, and then on the locks.

His age caught him in between wars, but his life on the river, especially in his younger single days, had been one filled with close scrapes and tight spots.

Before he married Esther, he drank plenty and sowed more than his share of wild oats. His Scotch-Irish personality was full of passion—fun loving, humorous and sentimental, and he would fight over a straw if honor were at stake.

Unbeknownst to any of his children, Alec had once been the target of a criminal investigation himself.

He was twenty-one, home on leave from the dredge fleet, with money in his pockets and a shine on his shoes.

On his way out for the evening one cold winter night he stopped by the house of his old friend "Skinny" Blaine for a drink.

Skinny was a bachelor, much older than Alec and terribly obese, weighing over three hundred pounds.

He lived in an old shack, with only a couple of rooms, in the same remote part of the county as Alec's home.

The rotund friend had just fried himself a steak on the little wood burning cook stove when Alec arrived.

Delighted to see his young friend home off the river, Skinny invited Alec to sit at the table and have a drink of bonded whiskey while his host ate his supper.

Alec's glass was filled with the stout beverage, and he sat down at the end of the table opposite Skinny.

Just as he raised the drink to his lips, his host choked on a piece of steak.

Violently, he kicked the table over and fell backward in convulsions. Alec was knocked to the floor, the front of his shirt drenched by the spilled whiskey.

Skinny was kicking and choking, fighting desperately for air.

Alec, blocked by the table in the tiny room, tried vainly to get to his friend's side, not only to render aid, but also in an attempt to keep him away from the small red-hot cook stove which was aglow just an arm's reach from Skinny's flailing about.

Somehow the fat friend got to his feet and staggered into the stove.

The small fire kettle was no match for this huge hunk of humanity.

It broke loose from the flue and turned over—fire and coals spilling out into the room. The room was immediately filled with smoke as Alec struggled to free himself from the overturned table.

Still choking and thrashing madly about in the mounting chaos, Skinny reeled into the back room of the shanty.

About that time the kerosene, which had poured onto the floor when the lamp was knocked from the table, was ignited by the coals.

The room was aflame.

Alec crashed out through the front door to safety, gasping for air, and with the hair on his arms singed.

He looked around for Skinny, thinking maybe he had also escaped the inferno. But his old drinking buddy was nowhere in sight.

Alec took one step toward the shack, and was driven back by the intense heat.

The old wooden structure was quickly consumed in flames.

By the time the sheriff arrived, Skinny's charred remains lay in the smoldering rubble.

When Alec related the tragic event, he smelled like a distillery.

A nearby neighbor who was milking at the time said he had heard a shotgun blast from the direction of the house just minutes before he saw the glow of the fire.

Foul play was suspected, and Alec spent one night in jail before his brother bonded him out.

Within a week, however, an autopsy on Skinny's remains confirmed that a piece of meat had obstructed his windpipe. And there were no signs of any gunshot wounds to the body.

Alec was cleared.

Unknown to anyone, the experience had scarred the young cavalier. He would forever carry a special fear of the power of circumstances and contrivance. He had more than the usual empathy with those wrongly accused of a crime.

So, now he stood on this summer night, many years thence, calmly awaiting the arrival of the law.

Harl finally composed himself and joined Alec and Luke at the car.

In a few minutes the headlights of Shelby Dodd's long black hearse appeared in the lane. Behind him came the sheriff.

❦

Currentville settled into its summertime mode.

New lights at the ballpark across from the school created some excitement, and now Luke's Little League baseball team was playing games at night.

Arch rival Catawba as well as Sparta, Iuka, Canton, and Itta Bena, all came to town and were visited in return.

Currentville was undefeated.

Bobby Joe was playing with an eighteen-and-over men's team on Sundays. At only seventeen, he was easily their top player.

He and Luke stayed busy with their two large gardens, or truck patches. It would provide them with some good spending money toward the end of summer, not to mention the fresh vegetables for the family table.

Bobby Joe was spending most of his time in the hay fields however, leaving Luke with most of the work at home.

And of course Luke and Jack mowed yards together.

It was their second summer in partnership, and they had about five or six yards between them and a couple on their own.

In spite of the odd jobs and chores, Luke and his friends still managed to get in some baseball at the school, swimming daily in the river, and camping.

The river town drowsed in the afternoon humidity.

Old Pete Roberts, the crippled attendant for the Princeton dry cleaning pickup would pull his popcorn machine out onto the sidewalk after the sun passed mid-sky and put his side of the street in the shade.

There he would hook up his radio with the volume turned high and listen to the Cardinal games while napping in his cane bottom chair. The voice of Harry Caray describing the heroics of Stan the Man and Wally Moon blended in with the broadcast out of Charlie Clark's pool hall to provide some vicarious excitement to the sleepy streets.

On the wide, tree-lined side streets, large maples and magnolias shaded the avenues. Old women, dressed to kill and scented down, sat on their wide shady porches in the afternoon, while their black gardeners labored in the yard.

The whine of a distant chain saw mingled with the barking of a dog. Few people moved about the streets, and only in slow motion. A yellow Dr. Pepper truck parked in front of Albert's grocery, the clanking of drink bottles giving evidence of at least some industry in the town. There were the intermittent sounds of screen doors slamming shut.

Near the pool hall one could hear the crackling of billiard balls colliding.

Girls were seen only rarely. Occasionally some of the town's high school queens would doll up in tight fitting shorts and T-shirts and take a stroll through the dusty streets to the drugstore for ice cream, leaving over-sexed teenage boys lusting in their wake.

Only on Saturdays did the village come alive, as farmers came to town, stayed for the drawing and into the night.

It was the dreamlike ebb and flow of summer living.

This tranquil, almost mesmerizing routine was disrupted to some extent by a crime wave in Currentville.

The town was hit by a series of break-ins. Within a period of ten days, four different stores and the pool hall were burglarized.

Not much had been taken, mostly foodstuffs and small amounts of money.

It was no secret to Sheriff Fisher and the state police, however, who the guilty party was.

Nathan Bedford "Inky" White had gotten out of prison in the spring.

Inky, who had a rap sheet as long as his coal-black hair, was the town's convict.

He lived with his widowed old mother on Pea Ridge. Although he had held several odd jobs since his release, he was seen mostly just wandering around town, and about the woods and country lanes near his home.

The break-ins were typical of Inky's modus operandi.

Never a violent sort, the thirty-year-old hoodlum had made a career of breaking and entering, stealing, and fencing his wares.

On the break-in of Willis Town's grocery, old Dr. Carey, who had been sitting on a town bench in the wee hours of the morning, actually saw Inky make his getaway.

So Inky disappeared, and became a wanted man, only to be spotted here and there in the wilds of Pea Ridge.

The five boys laden with packs and camping gear had just passed through the cemetery. They walked along the remains of an old logging road through the dense woods. It was mid-afternoon as they trudged along the shaded path, sweating in the humidity.

Luke and his friends camped in this area often, high aloft on one of the steep hills overlooking Currentville and part of the vast Pea Ridge area.

Their destination was a small clearing and a pond which had once been an old homeplace. The house and all the outbuildings were gone, but it was an excellent place to camp—remote, shaded by large oaks, and with a water supply.

Each of the five—Luke, Donkey, Jack, Birdseed, and Bennie Marshall—was so familiar with the trail that any of them could have walked it blindfolded.

Luke's heavy pack cut into his armpits, and he stopped to drop it to the ground and take a break. His companions continued on their way.

He stood there in the weeds of the abandoned road, his pack on the ground, enjoying his short respite. The deep woods and entangling undergrowth confronted him on all sides. Luke admired the works of nature and listened to the distant cooing of a dove. As his eyes casually followed down the hill, he noticed something unusual.

After a short while it came into focus, and he was able to make out some kind of structure hidden in the trees and vines.

It was a shed, or a shack built of rough unpainted lumber. He was even able to see part of the tin roof shimmering in the spotted sunlight.

Luke had never noticed if before, even in winter with the foliage gone, and he knew it was something recently constructed.

"Hey, Luke! You coming today or tomorrow?" Donkey yelled from down the trail.

For some unknown reason, Luke remained silent, but waved frantically for Donkey and the rest to come back.

As they made their way to his side, Luke squatted down to get a better view of the lower part of the building, which was about a hundred feet away.

"Get down!" he directed in a loud whisper to the others as they arrived by his side.

"What is that? Ever seen it before?" he pointed.

All eyes turned and bore in on the partially hidden structure.

"It looks like some kind of building . . . out here in the middle of nowhere . . . an old shack or something. . . ." Jack was musing out loud while the others continued to stare.

Without saying a word, they all moved slowly into the bush and toward the object of their attention.

As they got closer, they heard a sound from inside.

They froze.

"We better get out of here!" Birdseed whispered excitedly.

Jack and Luke were so focused they didn't even notice when their confederates retreated.

Slowly, side by side, they moved closer. They dropped down and crawled through the weeds and bramble for the last few yards.

Soon they found themselves underneath the house. There was about two feet of crawl space beneath its floor, which was held up at the four corners by stacks of concrete blocks.

Suddenly Luke and Jack heard someone moving around just above them. The thin planking of a floor shook and vibrated.

A door squeaked and they saw two booted feet step down from inside.

They pressed hard against the ground, not daring to breathe.

The door was slammed shut, and the man started walking off through the clearing which had been hacked out of the forest.

As the erstwhile occupant of the shack moved away from them toward the woods, he became fully visibly.

It was "Inky" White.

He disappeared into the wilderness.

After the sound of his departure had vanished, Luke and Jack crawled forward to the front of the hideout.

Rolling out from under the floor, they stood for a moment at the door watching intently toward the direction which "Inky" had taken, and listening.

"Let's check inside," Jack nodded.

Luke was hesitant.

"What if he comes back?"

"He won't be back for a while. We'll just take a look," Jack insisted.

Luke was nervous about the whole situation, but gave in.

Jack reached high with his long arms and pulled open the door. He peered inside, and stepped high up across the threshold, and then moved inside.

Luke was right beside him.

The place was stuffy and smelled of sweat. Mildewed blankets were thrown across a dirty mattress on the floor.

There were canned goods everywhere, including some empty ones thrown in a corner.

A kerosene lantern, several cartons of cigarettes, some dirty dishes, an old alarm clock, a magazine of naked women, and that was about it.

"We need to report this." Luke finally spoke.

"Won't be any need for that!" a deep voice blasted out from behind them.

Luke and Jack jumped out of their skins and turned to see a huge bulky form filling up the open doorway.

It was Tex Jackson, the local state policeman.

The boys sagged in exuberant relief. Never had the familiar gray uniform and Smokie the Bear hat looked so good.

"We just nabbed 'Inky' at the top of the hill," Tex explained, "We've had this place under surveillance for several days. What you kids doing here anyway?"

Luke explained.

"Okay," Tex motioned with his hand. "Y'all high tail it out of here. We've got some evidence to collect."

Luke and Jack obliged gladly, jumping down from the doorway into the bright sunlight.

Sheriff Fisher and another state policeman were making their way into the clearing as Luke and Jack anxiously scrambled up the hill to rejoin their friends.

❦

School had already started when Luke first heard about "Inky" White being charged with the murder of Aunt Sodie.

He was lying on the living room floor doing his homework when he heard his Dad read the news story from the local paper.

His father was surprised with the indictment.

"They must have some other evidence," he commented to

Esther, who was crocheting in the chair next to him.

"As far as I'm concerned, it looked like a simple case of suicide."

The next time Luke heard anything about the case was on a late afternoon in early October when once again his father was sitting on the front porch in the swing.

It was a beautiful autumn day, with an invigorating nip in the air and the trees beginning to change their colors.

Luke would remember the day well. It was the same afternoon that Don Larsen pitched a perfect game for the New York Yankees in the World Series against the Brooklyn Dodgers. He heard the last inning at the pool hall on the way home from school.

Sheriff Bass Fisher pulled into the driveway in his cruiser, got out, and came up on the porch.

Luke, who was telling his Dad about the perfect game, spoke to Sheriff Fisher and then went out in the side yard and threw his baseball against the brick foundation.

He could hear bits and pieces of the conversation on the porch.

The two men exchanged small talk at first. The lawman sat on the glider. Alec remained in the swing.

After an awkward silence, Bass shifted the tobacco from one jaw to another, spit into the flower bed, and began.

"The murder trial of Inky White has been set for December, Alec . . . "

Luke stopped throwing, and eased in next to the house.

". . . and I guess you'll be one of the star witnesses."

Alec moved slowly back and forth in the swing, waiting.

"You'll have to come and tell what you saw."

A long silence.

"You know Alec . . . ole Harl says the button on that outhouse was closed when you all arrived there that night. . . ."

The sheriff let it sink in.

"Ha! How would old Harl remember?" Alec yelped, breaking his dark and brooding silence.

"He was too busy holding in his guts and coming apart at the seams."

Bass Fisher mulled over the response, leaned forward and spit again.

"Maybe so . . . maybe so. He says the house was a mess inside. Looked like there'd been a helluva struggle."

Alec's eyes narrowed.

Bass Fisher went on.

"You know Shelby Dodd doesn't remember that little milk stool in the shed Alec. Says he sure doesn't remember seeing it."

The creaking swing was the only sound.

"Sonny Jim says he remembers seeing it the next morning setting out there on the back porch."

Sonny Jim was a deputy sheriff.

"You know, Alec, people can sometimes be mistaken in what they see. Or what they think they see. I mean . . . in the excitement of the thing and all. . . ."

Luke could tell that his father was growing impatient with the conversation.

Finally Alec stopped the swing and leaned forward.

"Look, Bass, Ole Inky isn't worth the powder to blow him away. And I don't know if he killed old Aunt Sodie or not. But this much I do know. When they call me down there to the court house and swear me to tell the truth, I'm going to tell them exactly what I saw. The button on the door was straight up and down—the door unlocked. And the milk stool was inside the shed, kicked over, not two feet from the old woman's feet."

There was silence again, and after a long look into the sheriff's face, Alec went back to swinging.

Then in a softer tone he continued.

"Come on Bass. Ole Harl was drinking. He's worthless as a witness. Old Shelby is near eighty. He's blind as a bat. It was dark when he got there. She was a mess. He just wanted to get her down, and get her out of there. We didn't even use a light. There could have been an anvil sitting there and Shelby wouldn't have seen it."

Bass let it sink in. Then he slowly stood up to go.

"Well . . . we got the goods on him Alec. And it's a good thing. He's been a thorn in our side for a long time. Now we have a chance to put him away for good—in the electric chair."

Searching Alec's face, he added.

"And of course the people would sure hate to see you be mistaken about all of this."

It was a tacit threat, but Alec kept his cool.

"Oh well," he broke out with a broad smile as he began walking the sheriff to his car, "don't worry none about that, Bass. I ain't fixin' to run for any public office anyway."

Sheriff Fisher got in his car and left.

⚜

There was an unusually frigid cold snap in the second week of December.

One-armed jailer Orville Bush kept noisily busy, stoking the two Warm Morning stoves which sat on both sides of the courtroom and keeping the coal scuttles replenished.

They were picking the jury for the Inky White murder trial. The two-story brick courthouse, which hung onto the side of Penitentiary Hill on Main Street, was abuzz with people and anticipation.

Circuit Judge Aaron Cates—old, bald, and grouchy—gavelled the proceedings to order and quieted the crowd. It was a cavernous old courtroom, bleak and run down. The windows in the front, opposite from the bench, looked out over the diminutive skyline of downtown Currentville and the gray Cumberland River which slid silently by.

At the counsel table to the left of the bench sat the Commonwealth attorney John Paul Adams, in his late sixties, tall and broad shouldered with a thick shock of gray hair. He looked like the oracle of Greek justice. At his side were Sheriff Fisher and the county attorney.

Across the heavily worn and buckled wooden floor sat the defendant with his court-appointed lawyer, Jefferson Fitzgerald "Droopy" Sanders.

This old lawyer in the baggy suit had long been labeled

such both because of his oversized apparel, which always seemed to swallow him, and his striking resemblance to the Snow White's dwarf.

Droopy, in his seventies, was an ancient drunk whose practice was in shambles. Sometimes weeks would go by when he never turned the key to his little dusty law office next to the courthouse.

During bouts of sobriety he would show up in court, defending other drunks. Sometimes he could be found searching titles in the clerk's office.

What few people outside legal circles knew was that this little alcoholic with mustard stain on his lapels had finished second in his class at the University of Virginia Law School.

In his promising early years he had served one term as county attorney and written a book on the history of the county, which could still be found on the shelves of the school library.

He came from one of the old, affluent families in town. Having survived three stormy and disastrous marriages, he now lived alone in a huge, ancient Victorian house on Franklin Street.

There, hidden by the huge magnolias and oaks, he ruminated and drank.

On sultry summer nights, the scratchy recording of Italian opera great Enrico Caruso floated through the open windows and down the street.

Droopy himself was no slouch at the piano, and was known to serenade the tolerant neighborhood with late-night rhapsodies.

Some neighbors claimed that on occasion he would climb upon a huge tree stump beside his front porch, and while in a drunken stupor recite the speeches of Mark Antony, Lincoln, and William Pitt.

No one doubted any of the most bizarre reports about the eccentric and mysterious Droopy Sanders.

Luke Cameron had one of his own.

One summer afternoon, Donkey, Bennie Marshall and he were walking past Droopy's house on tree-lined Franklin Street. All at once a loud voice came booming out from behind the hedge row.

"Hey boys! Hey boys! What day is it?"

The three stopped on the sidewalk in front of the old iron gate hanging half off its hinges. Peering down the narrow brick walkway which led through the shaded lawn to his front porch, they saw Jefferson Fitzgerald Sanders.

He was standing at the top of the wooden steps, dressed in a dirty old pair of seersucker pants and a wrinkled white shirt rolled up past the elbow. His thin crop of white hair was sticking straight up, and he swayed gently back and forth with a full glass of bourbon in his right hand.

"What day is it, boys?" he repeated.

The trio knew it was Saturday. And they knew it was July. But that was about it.

"It's Saturday," Bennie chimed in.

"No. No. Hell no! Not what day of the week it is. I'm no damn fool." His words poured out thick and slurred.

Luke wanted to take leave. But his raising held him to the spot, never to depart from the presence of an elder unless dismissed.

Besides, there was something benevolent, even lovable, about the old drunk, trying unsuccessfully to be belligerent.

Droopy's head bobbed, as though it were on a string, as he squinted and brought the boys into focus. Then looking about his ancient and darkened yard, cluttered with weeds, ivy, bird baths and moss, he seemed to fix his stare upon the narrow beams of brilliant sunlight filtering through.

Slowly his bleary and bloodshot eyes returned to the boys.

"Where you boys are now standing," he spoke in a softer more serious tone, " will some day be ten feet of water. See that old tree?" He spilled whiskey pointing his glass at the huge magnolia crowding the house. "It will be reduced to a giant stump and fishermen from Chicago will be catching crappie off of it."

He let the words drift out to the young ears at the gate, and seemed somewhat darkly amused himself by the thought.

"Now back to the question at hand, me lads. What day is it?" The old barrister seemed to pick up steam.

"Well, I'll tell you what day it is. This day is called the feast of Crispian."

Droopy straightened his back, and threw back his shoulders. His words, still heavy with drink, somehow became more pronounced. "He that outlives this day, and comes safe home, will stand a tip-toe when this day is named, and rouse him at the name of Crispian."

The orator, in full bloom, unsteadily descended the porch steps, and began to stagger up the walkway toward Luke and his friends.

"He that shall live this day, and see old age, will yearly on the vigil feast his neighbors, and say 'tomorrow is Saint Crispian.' Then will he strip his sleeve . . . " with his left hand he tugged at his right sleeve, spilling the brown liquid upon the ground. ". . . and show his scars, and say 'these wounds he had on Crispin's day.' Old men forget; yet all shall be forgot, but he'll remember with advantages what feats he did that day. Then shall our names, familiar in his mouth as household words . . . " and then the rambling intoxicant shocked the living daylights out of his captured listeners who had not the slightest inkling that before that moment Droopy Sanders even knew of their existence . . . "Luke Cameron, Bennie Marshall, Donald Hawkins, be in their flowing cups freshly remembered. This story shall the good man teach his son; and Crispin Crispian shall never go by, from this day to the ending of the world, but we in it shall be remembered . . . "

Droopy had moved slowly all the way up to just behind the gate, only arm's length from the young lads looking on. The strong odor of whiskey enveloped them. Reaching out over the wrought iron barrier, the red-nosed lawyer gently rested his left hand upon the shoulder of Luke. His tortured eyes glistened and in a voice barely above a whisper. . . "we few, we happy few, we band of brothers." Their eyes met, the young boy both captivated and embarrassed by the moment. After staring into the faces of the other two, Droopy quickly withdrew his hand, did a staggering about face, and moved back toward the porch flinging his hands here and there. "For he today that sheds his blood with me," he bellowed, "shall be my brother. Be he never so vile but this day will gentle his condition."

The old barrister shakily negotiated the porch steps and returned to his perch. He turned around slowly to look out upon both his domain and his audience from the diadem of his front porch. Then, as loudly as he could speak, he brought his great speech to a thundering crescendo. "And gentlemen in England now abed shall think themselves accursed they were not here, and hold their manhoods cheap while any speaks that fought with us upon Saint Crispian's day!"

The silence following his flourishing finish was deafening. A distant bark of a dog, the buzzing of a bee, and the cawing of a crow applauded the performance. Then the Shakespearean actor gave a slight bow, turned and lunged once, twice, and finally the successful third time, for the handle of the screen door, pulled it opened, and disappeared to the darkness inside.

Luke and his friends looked at each other in amazement, shrugged, and headed on down the street.

When the drunken barrister got the court appointment to represent indigent Inky without pay, most people figured it was lights out for the hapless defendant.

He tried to get the Commonwealth to allow his client to plead guilty to the maximum sentence on the three burglaries in exchange for their dropping the murder charge.

John Paul would have nothing to do with it.

Droopy was able to gain a favorable ruling from Judge Cates, severing the burglary charges from the murder, leaving the latter to be tried by itself.

So there sat Inky White at the counsel table with his blurry-eyed lawyer, ready for the slaughter.

But the Commonwealth had problems of its own.

John Paul was confronted with a tactical quandary.

If he called the witness who discovered the body, he would bring with him more evidence helpful to the defense than the prosecution.

Best he cover that aspect of their case with Harl Black.

Yet, the jury might wonder. Worse yet, Droopy might wonder.

He'd have to take that chance.

Before John Paul Adams announced ready, he stood and called his witness list.

The name of the person who discovered the body—always a critical witness in a murder case—was not called.

Droopy Sanders was a lot of strange things. But one thing he wasn't.

He wasn't dumb.

On the first recess he casually shuffled into the clerk's office and issued a subpoena for Alec Cameron to appear the next day.

By mid morning they had a jury and the prosecution began its case.

The Commonwealth's evidence went on fairly smoothly.

A witness had seen Inky in the area of Aunt Sodie's two or three days before her body was discovered.

Relatives of the victim gave testimony of Aunt Sodie keeping large sums of cash in an old stocking underneath her bed. One even saw her counting "a wad" the last time she was seen alive.

"About five hundred dollars I'd say," the witness said.

The investigators had found the stocking thrown back under the bed with just a few coins left in in.

When they arrested Inky, he had $467.00 in cash on him.

And of course Harl Black testified to the house being a mess, "like there had been a struggle," and most critical, that the smokehouse door had been buttoned shut from the outside.

When Droopy cross-examined Harl, it was not clear as to which one was responsible for the strong odor of booze hovering around the witness stand.

The coroner, Shelby Dodd, stated he did not see any stool in the shed. But Shelby admitted on cross-examination that it was dark, and he could not really attest to anything which might have been lying around the hanging corpse.

Sonny Jim, the deputy, told about his investigation of the scene the next day, including seeing a small three-legged milk stool on the back porch.

A jail-bird came on last and nervously related that Inky had admitted going up to Aunt Sodie's house to get some money. But the defendant had said no more to his fellow inmate. And it was questionable to the jury that he even said that. Droopy pulled out of the ruffian an admission that he had cut a deal with the Commonwealth for his testimony. The witness stopped short of saying anything more.

Almost as an afterthought, a different relative insisted that the alarm clock found in Inky's hideout was "just like" one that Aunt Sodie had owned.

But the big item was the money.

So by the time booming John Paul Adams announced "closed for the Commonwealth," it all stacked up to a pretty good circumstantial case.

The defense began its case the next morning with Inky taking the stand.

He was dressed in blue jeans and a flannel shirt. His long black hair, which was combed straight back, hung down over his collar.

Although he appeared nervous and spoke softly, he slowly found his own rhythm and made a pretty good witness.

His answers were direct and forthright as he responded to Droopy's questions.

Yes, he had been convicted of many felonies.

Yes, he had known Aunt Sodie all of his life, growing up not far from her on Pea Ridge.

And yes, he had been to her house shortly before her body was discovered. He went there to see if she needed any work done. No one was there. In fact it was a little spooky, so he left without ever going in the house.

But no, he had never laid a hand on Aunt Sodie—he did not kill her or know anything about how she died.

"I've known Aunt Sodie all my life. If I had asked her for money she would have given me all I needed. Why would I need to kill her?" Inky concluded.

Droopy left it at that, and the Commonwealth attorney got up to begin his cross examination.

The spectators in the courtroom got ready for the kill.

John Paul circled the witness like a big cat, pulling out bits of information a little at a time, building up to the knockout blow.

"So . . ." the big raw boned prosecutor drawled out in his deep voice, ". . . you got out of prison in the spring I believe. Isn't that right?"

"Yes, sir."

"April . . . is that right?"

"Yes, sir."

"You did not have a regular job."

"No, sir. Just some odd jobs around town."

"Did not have any regular income?"

"Not regular . . . no, sir."

"Did you make any money at all?"

"Well, I made some. I hauled a little hay, set some tobacco, mowed some yards, did some painting . . . "

"What did you do with your money?"

"Gave it to my mother. I was staying with her. I gave the money to her for groceries and things . . . "

"So you didn't keep any . . . didn't put any back for your-self . . . ."

"No, sir."

"Anyone give you any money – friends, family, church, or charity?"

The lawyer was standing with his hands folded behind him, staring out the window, letting the full force of his questions fall upon the jury.

"No, sir," the defendant said, barely audible.

"I'm sorry, I can't hear you," John Paul bellowed.

"No, sir," Inky spoke up.

"So . . . " the Commonwealth attorney turned from the window and strolled toward the jury box, searching the faces of the twelve men sitting there, "...you made no money, had no money given to you . . . isn't that right?"

"Not any that I did not give to my mother."

The prosecutor walked to his table and picked up the wad of money bound by a rubber band which had been introduced as a Commonwealth exhibit.

He charged toward the witness and held it directly in front of Inky's face.

Then the old prosecutor violated the cardinal rule of cross-examination. One does not ever ask an open-ended question to which one does not know the answer.

He exclaimed in a loud booming voice, "Then please tell this jury where you got this money, Inky!"

He paused to allow the question to reverberate throughout the courtroom.

There was a long expectant moment of silence.

Then Inky spoke, calmly and as if the question didn't phase him a bit.

"One hundred and fifty came from Charlie Clark's pool hall. About two hundred from Mr. Ladd's feed store. The rest came from Willis Towns' grocery."

There was some light tittering in the court room.

John Paul took the bait and crashed forward.

"You mean to tell this jury that you got this money by the commission of three burglaries upon business establishments within this community?" he asked in mock surprise.

"Yes, sir. And I tried to plead guilty to them and you wouldn't let me. Because I am guilty of those things. But I ain't guilty of killing Aunt Sodie."

There was a deafening silence.

The experienced prosecutor tried to recover. But before he could, Inky went on.

"Look through those papers you got on your desk over there Mr. Adams. I'm a thief. I've always been a thief. But old Inky has never hurt anyone in his life. Go look in your papers and see."

John Paul, trying to compose himself, did exactly what Inky suggested. He strolled over to his counsel table, shuffled his papers, and bent over to confer with the county attorney.

He then asked two or three totally ineffective and wandering questions and sat down.

A big silly smile came across Droopy's face as he scanned the jury box.

It was then Droopy's time to breach the rule of every good trial lawyer.

He put a witness on cold—that is, without ever talking to him.

Alec Cameron was called to the stand.

Droopy slowly led him through the events of that evening, up to the time Alec stood in front of the smokehouse door.

The defense lawyer paused for a few seconds.

"So . . ." Droopy continued in his slow drawl, ". . . let me see if I have this right. You're the one Harl Black came and got to go with him?"

"Yes, sir," Alec answered.

"You the one who thought of going by the locks to pick up grappling hooks?"

"Yes, sir."

"You the one who led the way through the house looking for Miss Sodie?"

Alec gave a slight shrug, not knowing the significance of it all.

"Yes, sir."

"And you the one who directed Harl to look in the cistern while you looked in the smokehouse?"

"Yes, sir."

"Looks to me you were pretty much in charge of this search." Droopy concluded his sentence just before the Commonwealth attorney made it to his feet.

"Objection, your honor. He's leading his own witness."

"Sustained." Judge Cates came alive long enough to make his ruling.

Droopy then headed down the stretch through one of the most critical parts of the trial. And he did so blindly, not really knowing into what wilderness he was wandering.

"Now Alec, when you saw the door to the smokehouse—was it latched from the outside or unlatched?"

There was a moment of tomblike silence in the courtroom.

"The button was straight up and down. The door was not latched," Alec testified assuredly.

A slight murmur went through the gathering.

After the witness told about his ghastly discovery, Droopy

asked him to describe the inside of the building. Alec obliged, to include the turned over three-legged milk stool.

Droopy, discovering that his hunch was right about the Commonwealth's omitted witness, pressed on with renewed confidence.

"Now Alec, you're under oath. Are you sure where you saw the stool?"

"I'm positive," was the firm reply.

The witness was then taken back into the house and asked to describe what he saw.

"Did you notice anything unusual about the inside of Aunt Sodie's house, Alec?"

A rather inept and dangerous question by the former UVA honor student.

For the first time a look of uncertainty came over Alec's face.

The question stumped him.

Of course the house was a mess, and to that extent unusual. At the same time Harl told him in passing that it was typical of the old woman's housekeeping.

"Well . . ." Alec struggled to answer, ". . . it was pretty messy inside the house. But. . . . ."

"But what?" Droopy pushed, with a slight irritation in his voice.

" . . .but Harl said that wasn't unusual."

"Objection, your honor! I object to the hearsay!" John Paul bounded to this feet.

The objection was sustained, the jury was admonished not to consider the last answer.

But the damage had been done.

Like a blind hog that roots long enough, Droopy had found an acorn.

After conferring with his co-counsel, the prosecutor opted not to ask Alec any questions.

The judge excused the witness and he stepped down off the stand.

"Oh! I do have one last question, your Honor." Droopy

jumped up feigning an afterthought.

"Go ahead," Judge Cates said gruffly.

"Alec, did you receive a subpoena from the Commonwealth to come and testify in this trial?"

"No, sir," Alec replied, standing awkwardly between the witness chair and the jury box.

"Hmmm. . . ."Droopy walked around the counsel table with his chin resting on his chest, and pulling on his big nose.

"I wonder why the Commonwealth of Kentucky didn't want the main witness in this case to testify...."

"Objection! Objection!" John Paul yelled.

Not only did Judge Cates sustain the objection, but gave Droopy a good tongue lashing in the process.

The old defense lawyer took the blows humbly and respectfully. But he could not hide a silly grin as he took his seat.

The case finally went to the jury at 5:20 p.m.

By 6:30p.m., Inky White was at home eating supper with his old mother.

Chapter Eight

Richard

The golden promise trips not from the lips,
but is borne on the wings of the heart.

Freewill, the black section of Currentville, was only a long fly ball from Luke Cameron's front porch. Across the street, through the row of houses, backyards, and gardens, and you were there.

But it was a world away in this segregated town.

This separate community—which got its name from former slaves living there after the War Between the States of their own "free will"—was a small settlement of shabby unpainted houses, a one-room school, and a church. It was nestled in the valley between Penitentiary Hill and the wooded high ground just north of the city limits.

As close as he was to where they lived, Luke only knew the Negro people of Currentville from a distance.

They would come out of Freewill in small groups, heading for town, laughing and talking loudly and happily as they passed Luke's house.

Often at night they would go to the picture show, where they were required to buy their tickets at a separate window at a lower price, use their own entrance, and sit in the balcony.

Separate. Always separate.

Two water fountains existed at the courthouse. One, the tall electric cooler, which produced an ice cold stream, was marked "Whites Only." Next to it, attached to the wall closer to the floor, was the dingy porcelain bowl with a spout. A sign hung above it: "Colored."

The restrooms were marked "Whites Only" and "Colored."

Luke knew some colored people, but only by first name.

Old man Ison, with the crippled right hand, came around daily and collected the slop for his hogs from the bucket nailed to the tree out back.

He knew the names of several maids that worked in the more affluent homes in town. Sudie, Mary Belle, Lottie May, Betsy Jean—all passed by his door, immaculately clean and starched, on their way to or from work. Some took in washing for white families. Hefty black women, dressed in long flowered dresses, marched regally down the street, a large basket of freshly turned laundry perched magnificently on their heads.

Of course he was well acquainted with Ola, the warm, friendly and matronly housekeeper who cleaned house for Birdseed's family.

He knew this race of people. But he didn't know them.

They were there amongst them. But still separate, always separate.

The black children went to their school in Freewill. When they reached the high school level, the county board of education paid their tuition and board and bused them to Lincoln Ridge Boarding School for Colored two hundred miles away in Louisville.

A bus would take them up in September. Go get them for Christmas. Take them back in January. And bring them home in May.

That is for the ones who chose to go to high school. Few of them did.

Their little church overflowed on Sundays, and the wonderful singing and shouting could be heard easily at Luke's house.

And Luke knew several of them by first name from their passing down the river road by his house to fish.

Occasionally he would sell them catalpa worms off the two trees in his front yard.

And of course there was Papa Joe.

He was an old black man, tall and erect, with a long white beard which came down to his waist.

Papa Joe was always neatly dressed in overalls and blue work shirt, and wore an old railroad engineer's cap.

His bearing and demeanor were dignified, almost regal, enhanced by the corn cob pipe always lit and clenched between his teeth.

Loaded down with fishing gear, he would pass down the river road almost every day.

Besides selling him worms from time to time, Luke would go down to the river and visit with Papa Joe while he fished.

On summer evenings, several blacks from Freewill would line the bank below the lock and dam and fish way into the night.

It was a nice time to be on the river. By midnight the oppressive heat of the day had given way to a soft river breeze. A row of lanterns painted circles of light in the darkness. The low roar of the dam and the soft murmur of conversation created an air of enchantment—a haven from the bright and searing summer heat.

One night, while engaged in a rather serious conversation with Papa Joe, Luke asked him a question he had wondered about all his life.

"Papa Joe, why do colored people eat carp?"

The old man remained silent for a long, awkward moment.

Then he asked in return, "Why do white people not eat carp?"

Good question, Luke thought.

So he asked his father.

"Because carp are scavengers. They feed off the bottom of the river."

Seemed like a good reason to Luke. Until years later when

he came to realize that catfish—a regular staple of their kitchen table and one of his Dad's favorite—was just as much a scavenger.

Luke's Dad talked of "good niggers" and "bad niggers."

"Knowing their place" and "uppity."

"Large black buck" and "high yeller."

They were terms casually thrown around in his household. Luke attached no particular significance to them.

One Sunday summer afternoon a Negro couple pulled into the river road beside their house. The woman proceeded to ask Luke for directions.

They had a brief conversation.

After the visitors had left, Luke's Dad, who had been sitting in the swing observing, sternly rebuked him.

"The next time I hear you say 'ma'am' to a colored woman I'll wear you out!"

The fierceness and venom in Alec's voice sent chills down Luke's spine. The experience indelibly marked him.

So in this small burg, two groups of people lived together without really knowing each other.

Their only communications were commands and responses. No dialogue. Even with master and servant—the conversations were perfunctory, directive, submissive and steeped in the ages.

No one, literally no one, ever gave a single thought to its changing.

⚜

Graham's old wooden grocery store sat next to the school.

During the winter it was a hangout for the kids, especially the older ones, who gathered there before school and on dinner break to smoke.

In the summertime, business nose-dived and was limited pretty much to the two and three item neighborhood grocery trade.

And to the baseball boys of summer.

Luke and his friends would often spend an entire summer

day playing baseball on the ball field across from the school.

They would retreat from the heat to the shady front porch of the store and cold drinks. Dinner consisted of baloney and crackers, with bottled Pepsi from the water-cooled drink box. They'd wash it down with water from the hydrant in Mr. Graham's front yard.

On this day, eight to ten of them—stripped to the waist—were sitting around on the white wooden benches with the Bunny Bread signs on the back. They had polished off the crackers and baloney, and for some, a moon pie.

With baseball bats, gloves, and a ball piled on the long wooden steps, they were down to their last swigs of soda. The conversation had tapered off to nothing.

Jack got up, killed his drink, and set the empty bottle on the wooden porch rail.

He stood for a moment looking down the street.

"Who's that little colored boy mowing Miss Aggie's yard?"

All eyes followed Jack's two houses down to the clacking of a manual reel mower.

"His name is Richard," Luke answered, and leaned back on the bench.

"You know him?" Jack continued to study the boy mowing the yard.

"Yeah, I know him." Luke shrugged. "I mean, I know who he is. He comes by the house fishing."

There was a pause, and then everyone turned back to the business at hand, that being finishing up the dinner break and getting back to the ball field.

Everyone, that is, except Jack, who kept staring out across the lawns toward the black boy.

"I wonder if he plays baseball," he mused.

"Baseball?" Luke inquired curiously, wondering along with the rest, why Jack had all of a sudden found Richard so interesting.

"Yeah. Baseball. Baseball. You know, pitch—hit—throw....what we been doing all day." Jack exclaimed.

"Yeah. His real name is Jackie Robinson," Donkey chimed in to a smattering of laughter.

"Hey! I'm serious. Colored people are great baseball players. Look at the ones in the major leagues. Willie Mays, Hank Aaron . . . Jackie Robinson. Even the Cardinals have some colored players now. All of them can play. They have . . . they are natural at it. . . . " Jack had the floor, and the rest were enjoying the speech.

He stopped and once again looked down the street.

"Luke......go see if he will play baseball with us." Jack turned and looked directly at his friend.

The porch went dead silent.

All eyes turned to Luke. He felt very uncomfortable.

"Ask a colored boy to play baseball with us? Come on Jack. You're crazy." Luke finally managed to say.

"We're not asking him to marry your sister, for crying out loud," Jack scoffed, "just to see if he wants to play some baseball."

"Go ask him Luke. What can it hurt?" Perky Perkins jumped in with what was clearly the sentiment of the whole group.

"Okay. Okay. Okay!" Luke finally gave in, swept up his baseball glove, and stomped down the wooden steps.

He headed for Miss Aggie's yard.

"Hey Richard, how ya doing?" Luke caught him by surprise.

He stopped his mowing and turned around.

"Hi Luke."

Richard was stripped to the waist, and his upper body was glistening with perspiration. His lean ebony form was just beginning to take on the muscular lines of adolescence.

His black face, now sweating profusely, was marked by a square jaw, high forehead, and perfect teeth.

If Luke could have looked past the color, he would have seen a strikingly handsome young man.

"Looks like you're about finished with the yard..." Luke noted as he nervously glanced at the store.

A pack of young eyes was watching.

"Uh . . . we . . . were wondering if you'd like to play some baseball?" He spat out nervously.

It was Richard's time to look toward the white boys on the

front porch of the store, baseball gloves and bats in hand.

"Baseball? I ain't played much baseball," he responded.

"That's alright . . . " Luke reassured him, ". . . you want to play?"

It was clear that Richard was not sure. No one knows what thoughts went through his head. But he was thinking.

Finally, "Alright . . . I have to finish here first."

It only took him a couple of more runs with the mower.

He then wheeled it to a shed behind the house and placed it inside. After a couple of knocks at the back door, Miss Aggie appeared and put some silver coins in his hands.

Then he and Luke were off to the ball field.

There were no introductions. In fact, Luke felt like his friends had somewhat betrayed him. They didn't even say hello to his black companion.

"Grab that glove, Richard, we'll go out in the field." Luke instructed.

Richard stuck it on his right hand.

A lefty.

Lefties were few and far between.

Maybe this wasn't such a bad idea after all, Luke was thinking.

Almost immediately a ground ball was hit right to the newly recruited left hander, bounced over his glove and into left field. Richard chased it down and threw it to Luke.

He threw like a girl.

There were looks among the regulars.

Another error soon followed.

Maybe he can hit, they were all hoping.

He couldn't hit either. In fact, he swung like a girl.

In short, he was awful. Worse even than Birdseed.

It didn't take long for interest in Richard to wane.

But he battled on gallantly, until after the four o'clock whistle sounded and the boys began to head for home.

No one spoke to him as he walked off the field. He began to make his lonely way up the street.

Luke gathered his glove and bat and joined the rest of the

pack for the walk back toward town and home.

But the sight of Richard, walking off alone pained him.

He had been against bringing him into the group. It was a stupid idea.

And he had been treated shabbily.

Luke's group moved toward town, keeping a constant distance behind the black pedestrian.

Boys began to drop off to their houses. By the time Luke reached Charlie's Pool Hall, he was alone.

Richard was in front of the post office just beginning his ascent of Penitentiary Hill.

Free of peers, Luke ran after him.

"Richard! Wait up!" he yelled.

"Thanks for playing ball with us," he gasped, out of breath.

Richard remained silent.

Luke tried desperately to make conversation, but it was difficult.

Finally he hit on a common chord.

"How many yards do you mow?" he inquired.

"Three whites. Three colored."

"Who are the whites?"

Richard told him.

"You have a mower?" Luke was curious.

"Naw. I use theirs."

Luke explained his and Jack's lawn-mowing arrangement and the yards they had.

They moved past the front of the prison where Pikeen was closing down the leather stand to go back inside for the night.

Luke had a brainstorm.

"Hey Richard. How would you like to mow a few yards together? Jack's going to have his tonsils taken out next week. He'll be out of action for a couple of weeks. You could help me with mine, I could help you with yours. We'll split the money. I got a power mower."

Richard didn't answer.

Luke had to press him.

"Well . . . you want to?"

After a long pause, Richard answered.

"Naw. I don't want to."

That was that. No explanation.

His answer kinda killed the conversation. Soon they reached Luke's house.

"Well, see ya, Richard."

"Yeah, see ya."

Richard headed for Freewill and Luke went inside the house, smelling okra frying on the stove. He was glad his Dad was not sitting on the front porch.

❧❦❧

It was early one morning about a week later when Luke's mother came into his room to wake him.

"Pumpkin, there's a little colored boy out back. He wants to see you."

Luke had all but forgotten about Richard. He drowsily got out of bed and slipped on some trousers.

He found Richard sitting on the long flight of steps which led up to the back porch.

The morning sun was just beginning to hit the side of the house.

"Well . . . " a big broad grin broke across his black friend's face, ".....you gonna sleep all day? Or are we gonna mow some yards?"

After splashing some water on his face, pulling on his worn tennis shoes, and grabbing two cold biscuits off the stove, he headed out to join his partner.

For the next two weeks, Richard and Luke mowed yards together.

At first Richard used the old reel type manual cutter which Luke had used before his Dad had purchased the gasoline power mower the summer before. But it was much slower, and the yards they cut were uneven.

So Luke managed to borrow Birdseed's power mower, and

he and Richard motored along nicely together.

Jack's tonsillectomy was complicated by an infection, and he was laid up longer than expected.

"I hope that boy mows better than he plays baseball," he said grumpily from his couch when Luke paid him a visit.

There had been a lot of rain, and the grass business was good.

Sometimes they would mow five yards in a day.

And they spent a lot of time together in between.

Hot and tired, Richard and Luke would head to Wrinklemeat's store at their end of town for cold drinks and shade.

One day as he swigged on his Pepsi, Richard commented that he had to go home and chop wood.

"Chop wood?" Luke exclaimed in surprise. "Why are you chopping wood in the middle of the summer?"

"For cooking," was Richard's simple reply.

So Luke volunteered to help him with the chore and made his first trip to Richard's home.

It was a typical house in Freewill—unpainted and with a rusty tin roof. The yard was full of weeds, with chickens picking out a living.

Richard's mother, Selina, sat on the front steps stringing beans, barefoot and clad only in a soiled calico dress. Her three little girls, dressed only in diapers and panties, crawled and tottered over the rotting boards of the front porch.

There was no sign of a father.

Richard and Luke chopped and hauled wood from the back yard to the kitchen, sweating mightily in the burning sun. Before they were finished, Richard's mother began to stir up the fire in the four-eyed cook stove for dinner.

When they sat down to eat, Luke was famished from the labor and the wonderful smell of green beans cooked with a large clump of hog fat. There was also fried bacon and cornbread. He ate feverishly, washing it down with a large glass of buttermilk.

A bent and withered old woman came out of the back room to eat with them. Her wrinkled skin looked like worn dark leather.

She spoke not a word, and was not introduced. Luke assumed it was Selina's mother.

After dinner they shot Richard's slingshot—made of a forked stick, a leather pocket, and narrow rubber strips from an old inner tube.

There were mongrel dogs everywhere, most of them snoozing in the shade. Their ribs stuck out from their hides—each of them a walking, living allegory of want.

Some neighbors came by to visit Selina and the girls. All of them sat on the front porch—literally on the porch, because there were no chairs—and visited. They laughed and talked in loud voices, waving at others who drove by, a genuine and joyful fellowship of kindred spirits.

Luke and Richard sat in the shade, leaning against the base of the cistern, drinking tepid water from fruit jars.

Although Luke could sense it, he would not be able to explain. There was a certain flow to the life in Freewill that was easy and pleasant. Yet at the same time, poignant.

He suddenly realized he didn't even know his friend's full name.

"What's your last name, Richard?" he asked, somewhat embarrassed he had not asked days before.

There was a pause.

"Well..." Richard began haltingly, "....Watson. E'cept when I'm visiting in Louisville with my uncle. Then it's Mayberry."

Luke was totally confounded by the answer. He opened his mouth to inquire. Then, for some reason, he simply let it drop.

The sun was angling to the west and the afternoon was far spent when Luke began to make his way home.

His father was home from work, and in his familiar summer evening pose—reading the paper in the swing on the front porch.

"Hey, Pumpkin," he cheerily greeted his son.

Sensing his good mood, Luke decided to sit for a visit, and flung himself down on the glider.

"Whatcha been doing today?" Alec inquired without looking up from his paper.

"Oh, mowed a couple of yards and messed around with Richard."

Luke felt an inner urge to get the whole Richard matter out before his Dad, for better or for worse.

"Richard who?" Alec asked matter-of-factly, still not taking his eyes off the print.

"Oh, Richard's a little colored boy who's helping me mow yards, now that . . . uh . . . Jack is not able."

"Uh huh. How is Jack?" Alec raised his head and looked squarely at his son.

"Had some infection. Gonna be laid up a while longer. May not be able to play any more ball this summer, or mow yards," Luke explained.

Whatever his Dad might think of Richard, he now knew about it. And didn't seem to mind. Other days, in other moods, it might well be different. But on those days, Luke would manage, and those topics pregnant with controversy would never be broached.

He had told him. That was his only duty.

Alec shuffled and folded the paper.

"Saw some bugs on the potatoes while ago. Better go over them tomorrow. Use a can of coal oil to put the bugs in."

"Yes sir," Luke obliged, and bounded off of the glider and into the house.

They had finished off old Miss Grayson's huge, rambling yard full of bushes, hollyhocks, and sporadic and precious asparagus stalks. Luke and his black friend were sitting next to her hydrant after drinking their fill.

"Whew . . . " Luke exhaled, "this yard is a bear!"

Richard did not reply.

Luke thought for a moment.

"Well Richard, I don't know about you, but I'm ready for a swim."

Luke jumped to his feet.

"Want to?"

Richard finally replied, "I can't swim."

"You can't swim!" Luke was astonished.

His friend nodded, as the town's best swimmer continued to stare in disbelief.

After a long pause Luke announced, "Okay, Sir Richard, let's get these mowers home, and you are going to be taught how to swim."

It took some real coaxing and cajoling for Luke to get Richard down to the river.

But down to the river they went.

They found some shallow slackwater, between two sandbars. After stripping nude, the lessons began.

It would prove to be a slow, grinding process, stretching out for days and days.

Richard was terrified of the water. It took the entire first lesson just to get him to wade waist deep into the stream and splash water onto his face.

Luke was uncertain whether he could ever teach him to even get his head wet, let alone swim.

He was sure that the first day would do him in, and he was not going to push. But to his surprise, Richard showed up at Wrinklemeat's the next day at the designated time for his second lesson.

It was painful for Luke—who couldn't even remember learning to swim—to see someone struggle and strangle so gallantly.

A duck was teaching a chicken how to swim.

But this chicken had heart. Richard would go under, fight the water frantically, come swinging to the surface, gasping—his face in painful contortions, blowing mucus from his nose, and coughing violently.

And, like Tennyson's six hundred, on and on he came.

After the first two or three excruciating days, Luke gave him a way out.

"Richard," he kindly spoke on the way home, ". . . if you

don't want to go on with this . . . I mean . . . I won't mention a thing if you want to quit . . . it will be between you and me."

His friend did not reply. He just continued to show up on time.

Contending with it daily, Luke did not recognize that after a week Richard had made amazing progress.

Luke now had him holding on to a small log, kicking across the slackwater, breathing in and blowing out under water.

From there it was only a short but dramatic step to dog paddling.

When he made that leap, Luke's frustrations subsided and he began to feel the quiet satisfaction of a teacher who has taught a student who has learned.

And they talked about swimming while they were mowing yards, while lying in the shade on breaks, and at Wrinklemeat's.

"The water wants to help you. It wants to hold you up . . . but it can't hold you when you fight it." Luke would instruct in a professorial tone. "Fear, Richard. That's the thing you must overcome. 'The only thing you have to fear is fear itself.'"

He glanced at his student with a grin, but there was no sign of recognition of the quote.

But his black friend listened intently, and continued to learn.

"Richard," Luke said with an air of solemnity as they finished up a rigorous work out, "tomorrow, you are going to swim all the way across the slackwater."

He let the pronouncement settle in.

"And you will do it, too. Swim, dog paddle . . . underwater, on top of water . . . any old way you can . . . you're gonna make it across."

Richard was obviously nervous the next day as they prepared for the final exam.

"Okay, Richard, you get three chances to make it across. Don't panic. Don't get scared. Just remember. It's no big deal. The water's only chest high. And you got three chances. If you make it . . . you pass the test, and the classes are over. You've learned how to swim. If not . . ." Luke let his voice drop, ". . .

then it's back to the old classroom."

The distance was about one hundred feet of stagnant, muddy water from one sandbar to another.

It had been their classroom for almost two weeks.

Richard stood erect on the opposite side, waiting for Luke to give the signal.

"Remember Richard, just keep your head about you. Paddle and breathe and try to relax. Okay. Hit it!"

Richard jumped forward and began to churn the water. He held his head high with his eyes wide open. All the rest of his body was in frenzied motion.

Periodically his puffed cheeks would blow out, and he quickly gulped enough air for a few more moments of life.

Somehow, he managed on the first try to make his way across the lagoon.

Luke motioned and cheered him on.

At times Richard would sink down in the water, almost to his ears, and it appeared that he was going under.

But with a surge of new energy and flailing arms, he would rebound and come charging on.

Closer and closer he came. Over half-way now.

Sinking and rising, sinking and rising. Eyes agape, cheeks sucking and puffing.

"You're gonna make it on the first try, Richard!" Luke yelled. "Keep on comin'!"

If he got close and failed, Luke knew, he would be physically spent and his confidence squandered. The subsequent bouts would be futile.

Closer and closer he got.

Ten feet away.

Five feet.

His drenched sable face carried the look of a horrible death.

But Luke's was pure joy.

Richard's muscular arms reached out, and his hands dug into the sand and rock.

Luke screamed and yelled and pulled Richard up by his arms.

The two of them hugged, laughed and danced around on the riverbank like two drunken prospectors who had just struck it rich.

For the first time in Luke's presence, Richard was totally uninhibited.

He sang. He danced a jig. His face was aglow with his magnificent smile. There was something mystic in his countenance.

Richard and Luke carried on for a long while, falling all over themselves and finally onto the sandy bank. There they came to rest, lying on their backs, exhausted, smiling, and staring at the beautiful sky.

"Well, Sir Richard . . . " Luke finally spoke, "you're not going to be swimming in the Olympics. But you can sure save yourself now." He let out a satisfied sigh of an accomplished teacher. "I could use something to drink. I'm thirsty as a gourd," he concluded.

A long silence followed.

Then Richard sat up and looked out upon the placid stream slipping by. His face was aglow with pride.

His eyes narrowed and he spoke slow and profoundly, "You know what I'd like to do now?"

Luke shuddered. It had been quite a struggle teaching Richard to swim. But to teach him to play baseball would be an impossibility.

"What's that?" Luke asked hesitatingly.

Still staring straight ahead with his eyes ablaze, Richard reported, "I'd like to drink out of that water cooler at the courthouse."

It took a moment for the message to sink in.

Luke sat up. "What are you talking about?"

"That water cooler. The one for whites. You know the one that hums like a refrigerator. Old Jigger Cates use to clean up at the courthouse. He say it has a great big stream of ice cold water . . . ice cold water with no ice . . ."

Luke looked in Richard's face to make sure he was on the level.

He looked as serious as a heart attack.

Both of them pondered the thought.

"Well, Richard," Luke got up to gather up his clothes. "You'd better forget about that. You'll get yourself in trouble."

With that the conversation ended. The two friends dressed and headed for home.

For some reason Richard's comments about the water cooler kept coming into Luke's head that evening.

He was lying on his bed while Bobby Joe was getting dressed for his date.

"Bubba, you ever wonder why they have two water fountains at the courthouse, one for colored and one for whites?"

Bobby Joe turned from the closet and slipped the shirt over his smooth and muscular upper body.

"Nope. Never thought about it in my life," he responded curtly and continued to dress.

He tucked the shirt into his jeans and moved over to make one last check in the bureau mirror.

He glanced at the alarm clock on the bedside table and turned to leave.

"I'm late. Sarah Jean's gonna throw a bitch."

He opened the door.

"The Cardinals are on in five minutes," Bobby Joe reported as he left the room. "Vinegar Bend's pitching. Be sure you turn the station back to Trenton when you're through listening."

It was big brother's way of saying, "You can use my radio, kid, to listen to the game." Even though Luke always used it anyway, with or without permission.

But he was always careful to put it back on Trenton. Big Bubba wanted his music and his station when he sleepily turned on the knob first thing in the mornings. And Luke knew better than to get on the bad side of his big brother.

※※◎※※

The summer became dry. Most of the yards began to burn

up.

Jack recovered from his tonsillectomy and was back on the job.

Luke saw Richard less and less.

Late one afternoon he was making his way home from town. Walking up Penitentiary Hill in front of the courthouse, he spotted jailer Orville Bush. The amputee was sitting alone on one of the wooden benches under the large maples on the courthouse lawn.

Spontaneously and without reflection Luke suddenly turned and headed up the steps to the sidewalk which led to the front door of the courthouse.

Orville sat on the edge of the bench with his legs crossed and a broom leaning against his thigh.

He was taking a break from his courthouse cleaning and enjoying a hand-rolled cigarette which hung soggy and smoldering in his right hand.

Orville had lost his left arm in World War I, and had returned home to become permanently entrenched as jailer. From time to time he would have opposition. He campaigned with only one old worn and tattered candidate card, which he would show to a prospective voter, then retrieve for continuous use.

His "one card" campaigning was such a novelty that the *Nashville Banner* and *Louisville Courier Journal* had once done stories on it.

The old jailer's one-armed dexterity was legendary too. It included many tales of his besting rough and tough jailbirds with just one arm.

To Luke it was no small feat as how he was able to roll his own cigarettes—curling thin sheets of paper, spreading the tobacco from a drawstring cloth bag, and sealing it with a lick—all with just one hand and his teeth.

"Hi, Orville," Luke said as he approached the benches.

"Hello Luke," the gravel voice replied.

Before he turned to sit down on the bench with the jailer, Luke glanced through the open doorway, down the darkened hallway, to the water fountain.

He sat down and leaned back.

"Been a hot one, hasn't it Orville?" he said casually.

"Yep."

An awkward moment passed.

"Orville, you do an awful good job keeping this old courthouse clean," Luke commended, having no idea how good a job he did.

". . . and I bet it takes a lot of time."

"Quite a bit," Orville replied stoically.

Once again Luke glanced furtively through the open doorway.

"What time do you lock up this place, Orville?"

"Usually I lock the doors around five. The offices close at four and they are usually gone right after that. In fact, if you're standing around the hallways at four o'clock there's a good chance you'll get run over."

A sardonic smile creased his gray stubbled face.

"I clean up for about a hour. Except when circuit court's in session. Then I may be here longer."

"When's that?" Luke inquired.

"May, September, and December," was the reply.

It was all Greek to Luke—the courts, the courthouse, the different offices. He passed through the building only now and then—to get a drink of water, or use the stinking and filthy downstairs bathroom by climbing through the open window. The rest of it was a maze of stale-smelling offices, which smacked of grownups and boredom.

Luke got up and went into the courthouse.

There it was, a brown colored, electric water fountain. And yes, it was humming—louder now in the eerie silence of the empty building. The basin was clean and ceramic white, the spout and attached handle silvery bright. In front of the fountain was a small wooden box, about a foot tall, on which short-legged youngsters could stand to get a drink.

Above it on the dirty wall was the sign: WHITES ONLY.

Luke leaned over and turned on the stream. It sprung into a thick translucent arch. His lips surrounded the surge and he easily gulped mouthfuls of the frigid and refreshing drink.

"Ice water without ice," Luke thought as he drank.

He finished, and wiped his mouth with the back of his hand.

His eyes fell downward to the porcelain bowl attached to the wall beside the water fountain.

It was much closer to the floor, where the tall, not the short would have problems.

Pipes led up the wall to the fixture. The lever was underneath, the COLORED banner above.

Luke stepped toward it, cautiously casting a glance out front to where Orville still sat, peering down over the town.

Slowly Luke reached for the crank and turned it.

A narrow flow—smaller than the size of his little finger—trickled out.

Luke placed his hand under the tepid stream. It was tap water.

He quickly moved back out front.

"Well, Orville, see ya later."

"Yeah. See ya later, Luke," Jailer Bush rasped, as Luke moved down the steps and back onto the sidewalk.

⚜

Late one afternoon about a week later, Luke ran into Richard at Wrinklemeat's grocery.

They sat on the wooden decking of the front porch with their legs dangling off the front and talked.

The yard mowing had about played out. Richard had been cutting wood and tending to some hogs for a neighbor. He was going to visit his uncle in Louisville soon.

Luke tore open a brand new packet of baseball cards. He offered the thin pink slice of gum to Richard. He declined, and Luke pitched it in the weeds.

He despised bubble gum, and hated to be around people when they were chewing it.

The slick picture cards were colorfully adorned with face shots of major league baseball players—some well known, most not so well known.

Luke felt a sense of excitement each time he eagerly searched out a new crisp pack. A slight scent of bubble gum hung onto the cards.

He shuffled through the deck of white faces . . . Gus Zernial, Elmer Valo, Andy Pafko.

Unexpectedly the deep black face of Sandy Amoros leaped from the stack.

"Hey," Luke exclaimed excitedly, "that's the guy who made that great catch in the World Series last year."

He shoved the card into Richard's face.

Richard glanced at it and nonchalantly took a swig from his pop.

He might as well have shown Richard his fingernail. Luke shrugged and continued to study the cards.

Finally he leaned to one side, and stuck them neatly into his back pocket.

The wailing sound of the four o'clock whistle began to rise and fill the air.

As the mournful sound subsided, Luke leaped from the porch, "Hey Richard, what are you doing right now?"

"I'm drinking a Pepsi." Richard responded, the charming crooked grin breaking across his coffee-colored face.

"Naw, I mean . . . have you got a few minutes? There's something I want . . . something I want you to see." Luke implored.

"What is it?" his friend inquired curiously.

"Come on. It's . . . well it's over in town." Luke moved out.

Richard drained his drink, and fell in beside him.

They moved quickly up the sidewalk, past the lane to Freewill, past Luke's house. On up the steep hill in front of the warden's house they climbed with little conversation. Walking rapidly, Luke and his dutiful friend moved past the brooding and overpowering form of the penitentiary.

Past the Catlett house, and at the corner of Oak Hill, they began their descent down Penitentiary Hill into the main part of town.

But they did not make it to the bottom of the hill.

At the courthouse, Luke turned sharply to the left, and bounded two at a time up the long flight of concrete steps.

Richard was on his heels.

Beside the benches on the front sidewalk they stopped.

"Okay Richard . . . " Luke turned and spoke, slightly out of breath. ". . . wait here just a minute."

He moved through the open doors and a short way down the corridor of the empty courthouse.

Where the hallway turned to the right toward the courtroom steps, he stopped and listened.

He heard noises from upstairs. Orville was sweeping the courtroom and moving furniture around.

The rest of the building was still and deserted.

Quickly he retraced his steps to out front where Richard was waiting with a puzzled look on his face.

"Okay Richard . . . this is your chance . . ." Luke spoke softly, but could not suppress the proud grin on his face.

He pointed inside the courthouse to the waiting water fountain.

Richard's eyes leveled on the target, and then glanced back into Luke's face.

Their eyes locked for one long and knowing moment.

Slowly his black friend—the inept baseball player, fledgling swimmer, mower of yards—walked inside the courthouse.

Luke followed him to the door and waited. He watched Richard climb the three steps into the main hallway, move to the water fountain, and stop. He looked, for what to Luke seemed like an eternity, at the bold proclamation on the wall above it.

Then he put one foot on the wooden box, placed his right hand on the silver coated lever, and turned it. He stood and watched the watery arch cascading before his eyes. Finally, he leaned over and took a long and powerful drink.

It seemed to Luke like time stood still. Finally Richard was back beside him and they turned to head back down the steps.

"Wait a minute," Richard mumbled and abruptly went back into the courthouse, and to Luke's amazement took another drink from the fountain.

This time he hurriedly exited the building, and he and his white confederate scampered down the steps and up the hill toward home.

They said nothing until their pace slowed to a normal walk in front of the prison.

"Well Richard," Luke broke the silence, "what do you think?"

It was a rather lame question, Luke thought. But it was the best he could do.

Richard looked straight ahead, his eyes dancing. There was that same glow in his face as when he swam the slackwater.

"Okay....Okay...." was all he could manage.

They walked on together in silence, both enjoying the unspeakable quest which they had shared.

Near the warden's house Luke turned and asked, "Richard . . . why . . . what made you go back . . . for another drink?"

There was a long, thoughtful pause.

"My grandma . . . " Richard began, ". . . she died last week. She told me one time . . . she told me someday I would drive a car. Someday . . . someday I would have a television."

Luke turned to look into his face, moved by his tone of voice. Richard was talking differently than he had ever heard him. There was eloquence, there was tremendous feeling in his words.

". . . someday, she say, I would live in a house with . . . water . . . a bathtub. Maybe even a real stove . . . a 'lectric stove. Someday . . . she said . . . someday . . . " his voice tailed off, and his eyes looked out over the wide sunlit river bottom.

". . . someday, she say, I would have lots of things. So . . . so I went back in and took a drink for grandma."

Luke felt a tingle up his back. "That's nice, Richard. That was really nice."

School started and Luke hardly saw Richard at all. They moved back into their totally separate worlds.

One day when he came home his mother handed him a brown paper bag.

"I found this lying inside the front door this afternoon," she explained. "I think it's for you."

Luke opened the sack and pulled out the present. It was a homemade slingshot made of a forked stick, leather pocket, and narrow rubber stips of an old inner tube.

He smiled and tucked it safely away in his drawer, along with the wallet made of cigarette packages given to him by an inmate.

Summer turned to autumn, and autumn to winter.

Luke was busy with school, basketball, and working at the paper office on Thursday afternoons folding papers.

He and Jack went from mowing yards to hauling in coal for the many old widows in town, nickel a bucket.

Birdseed and Luke built forts on the riverbank, searched for arrowheads, played Monopoly, and occasionally did their homework together.

Luke squirrel hunted alone, with the long 32 inch single barrel shotgun handed down to him from his grandfather.

Time passed quickly.

Thanksgiving came and went. And then Christmas.

It was a cold and gray afternoon between Christmas and New Year's. A dismal light drizzle was falling.

Luke was at home rummaging through his drawer when he ran across the slingshot.

His thoughts turned to Richard.

He bundled up and headed down the street toward

Freewill.

By the time he reached the narrow lane, the light rain was mixing with sleet.

Mac's taxi came driving by him, artfully dodging the giant potholes filled with water.

Luke watched the car go the completed length of Freewill and turn into the driveway of a bootlegger's shabby hovel. Mr. Atkins, an elderly and reputable citizen of town, got out of the back seat and went into the house. Mac remained in the vehicle with the motor running. In about three minutes, Mr. Atkins came out the door with a small brown bag in his hand. He got in the taxi and they returned down the lane.

Both Mac and Mr. Atkins gave Luke a sheepish wave as they passed.

He reached Richard's house and walked up on the porch. A baby was crying inside, and through the grimy window he could see a fire in the grate.

Selina opened the door on the first knock.

"Hello Luke," she greeted him warmly.

"Hello Selina, is Richard here?"

"No. Richard's gone to live with his uncle in Louisville."

They both stood staring at each other for an awkward time, neither knowing what else to say.

"Okay. Uh . . . well . . . tell him I said hello," Luke finally managed.

"I shore will," she replied as a little black face appeared at her side, big round eyes peering up at the boy on the porch.

Luke moved off the porch and across the ragged yard to the street.

He felt deeply disappointed, and depressed.

At the edge of the lane, Luke stopped and looked around.

Stripped of the camouflage of summer foliage, Freewill did not bear up well in its winter dress.

On both sides of the lane were leaning and unpainted huts, black smoke streaming out of chimneys. Some had no chimneys at all, but only the stove pipes extending through the tar-paper roof.

The yards were enmeshed in brown winter weeds, cluttered with old tires and dismembered cars. Outdoor privies waited at the end of narrowly worn paths.

Some yards were slick with mud, polished to a shine by the constant bombardment of dishwater.

Chickens pecked around for a living underneath the floors, which were supported only by corners of stone or concrete block.

In one yard, hogs rooted all the way out to the road.

At the end of the draw were the one-room school and the church—both the color of dirty water and badly in need of paint.

The air carried the odor of wood fires, mingled slightly with a tinge of raw sewage. Up on the hillside Luke saw billowing white smoke from an open fire. Straddling the flames was a large black kettle. A crooked old black woman hovered over the fire, stirring lye into the hog fat for soap.

Finally he turned and started down the dreary lane in the falling darkness.

Somehow he now felt better. Like losing a friend to heaven after a long and painful death. Luke felt comforted, knowing that Richard had gone to a better place.

Chapter Nine

Bailey Martin

The most important promise is the one you make to yourself.

It was January, 1953. Chickasaw County High School had not won a basketball game in two years.

The drought had passed the embarrassment stage and graduated into community humor. In the barber shops, restaurants, and gas stations of the county the jokes finally got around to the ball team.

A winter snowstorm caused a game to be canceled, and many called for a victory celebration. The flu bug hit the school one week and it was reported that most of the ball team had been stricken. "How can they tell?" was the chuckling retort.

Only a handful of faithful fans—mostly families of the players and cheerleaders—attended the games in the little cracker-box gym in Catawba.

Most of the people had become accustomed to laughing instead of winning.

All except the new school superintendent Les Hall, that is. He found it humiliating. At the meetings of school administrators of the region, the conversation would always get around to basketball. He would cringe and fend off the good natured but grating barbs about the Chickasaw County Indians.

Les had played on the great teams of the mid forties, one of which won the state championship in the school's only trip to the big show. He was a winner, and the lackluster program he had inherited was totally unacceptable.

Charlie Russell, a misplaced biology teacher, was the coach. He approached the job as if he would rather be cutting up frogs. Mild mannered, soft spoken, and well liked, Charlie possessed the intensity of a snail. He knew just enough basketball to be dangerous.

After much thought and reflection, Les Hall knew exactly who he needed to turn the basketball program around.

Bailey Martin had once been a household word in Chickasaw County. As a wiry, sharpshooting guard, Martin had led the Indians to the state championship. He was an incredible ball handler, and won all state honors as well as a full scholarship to Memphis State. Bailey starred in college ball, and afterward even hung on in the pros for a couple of years.

But booze and women got the best of him. Soon he was back in Memphis coaching high school basketball. Les had kept up with his old teammate from time to time. As a coach, Bailey had done well. But his personal life continued to be a mess. At last report the old Chickasaw star was still fighting the bottle and watching his third marriage go down the drain.

The old timers of the community remembered Bailey Martin's great skills. But Les Hall remembered him for something else—his tremendous will to win and his fierce pride, which always simmered just below the surface.

One particular incident was burned indelibly into Hall's memory.

They were playing a road game at Sparta. Bailey beat the living hell out of a teammate who had yelled a taunt out the bus window to a crippled man walking down the street.

With his terrified and vanquished victim's face pressed against the floor of the bus, Bailey Martin lashed out with rage, "What in the hell do you think that man saw when he heard that?

Your stupid face and silly grin? Hell no! He saw Chickasaw County written all over the side of this bus!"

The old alma mater was in bad need of a good dose of Bailey Martin.

It did not take much coaxing for Les Hall to persuade his old friend to come for a visit. Bailey had always liked Les. Even though they had drifted apart over the years, they would occasionally talk over the phone. Bailey Martin's father had died, and his mother had gone to live with his older brother in Texas. He had no other people there and it had been years since he had paid a visit. It would be a good chance to get away from Memphis and kick back a little.

So they agreed on a Saturday when the Indians would be playing at home and Bailey's own team would be idle. He would drive up in the afternoon, go to the game, spend the night and return to Memphis the next morning.

After much thought and reflection, Les began his mind game upon the former all-stater. He assured Martin he would really be impressed with the old school, and especially the exciting basketball program.   His charade continued after Bailey arrived, attempting to whet his expectation.

Then Les, his wife Margaret, and Bailey attended the game. The gym was cold and dreary, with so few people in attendance that one could hear the players talking to each other. No pep band, lethargic cheerleaders—even some of the lights were out on the battered old scoreboard. The locals were smeared. It was so bad that even the opposing coach was embarrassed and wished he could have substituted with a third team, or a fourth team, or a fifth team . .

Back at the Hall home after the game, Les and Bailey plopped down in the living room while Margaret rustled up some coffee.

"Well, what did you think, big Bay?" Les inquired innocently, using his friend's old nickname.

A knowing grin broke out on Bailey's face. "Nice team," he replied. "I especially like Charlie's game plan—try to keep their team on their end of the floor shooting at their basket. And it worked. They didn't score a basket at our end all night."

They both laughed.

Then Les began the sales talk of his life.

"Well," he grew serious. "It's awful, Bay. I couldn't believe how bad it was. It's a disgrace. For a school with such a rich heritage, it's shameful. I'm going to turn it around...... and you are just the man who can do it."

Les paused to let the words sink in and try to read the expression on Bailey's face. He could detect nothing, so he continued.

"We couldn't pay you what you're getting now. It's not the big school with all that exposure. But.. . ." he paused as Bailey's eyes turned to meet his. "....it might just be the thing you're looking for at this stage of your career. A challenge. A chance to get away from the the big city and enjoy the small town a little. I know you love to hunt and fish. With Kentucky Lake nearby and the land between the rivers.....Well it all might be just what you need right now."

Les wasn't sure just how far to venture into Bailey's ruptured personal life. He only wanted to throw a little bread upon the water. Margaret brought the coffee, and sat down on the couch next to her husband.

Bailey leaned forward, picked up the steaming cup, and cradled it in his big hands. He sat there quietly for a few moments, staring into his coffee.

Finally he spoke softly. "I can tell by the way you're talking that you know that my personal life is pretty much a mess."

He took a deep sigh and continued. "I have a good team. We're winning—had three straight real good seasons. But my old lady and I have split, and she teaches at the same school. It's not a good situation. To tell you the truth, I'm sick and tired of Memphis."

Bailey took a long sip of coffee, put his cup down in the saucer, and stood up. Les and Margaret studied his face anxiously, sensing that he was wrestling with his own thoughts.

He stuck his hands in his pockets and moved over to the window. There Bailey Martin stood for a long moment staring out into the dark night.

Finally he took a deep breath and exhaled, "But God, this place is dead!"

≈≈◎≈≈

They had a nice visit. But Les and Margaret Hall were left with the distinct impression that Bailey Martin was more likely to go to Russia and coach than he was to return to Chickasaw County. There did seem to be one flashing moment when he may have considered it as an interesting idea. But it appeared to have passed as just an intriguing and curious notion.

Weeks turned to months and Les began to look elsewhere for a savior of the basketball wreckage.

Then one night in late March the superintendent received a call at his home from Bailey Martin. The caller got directly to the point.

"I've been doing a lot of thinking, Les, and if your offer is still open, I'm willing to come."

Les was ecstatic. "That's great Bailey!" he exclaimed.

"There's just a couple of things . . . conditions, I guess, Les, that I have to have met before I come," Bailey interjected.

"Okay. Shoot."

Les Hall waited.

"Well, the money's okay and all. But I need two assurances to make it worth my while. First, I need five years, Les, guaranteed. It will take five years to turn the program around, or at least take it to where I want it to go....where you want it to go. Second, and this is probably the most important, I must have complete, unrestricted authority and control over all basketball in Chickasaw County."

Les Hall had won pretty much a blank check from his board of education.

He quickly responded. "No problem, Bay. We accept your two conditions."

Then the superintendent of schools took a deep breath.

"Bay, we have one condition of our own."

He waited for what seemed like a long time.

"What's that?" Bailey asked with just a bit of edge in his tone.

"No booze, Bailey."

"What?" Bailey yelled out in mock surprise. "You mean no iced-down beer in the locker room? No big cocktail parties before the big games? No Saturday night bashes with the wild women of Chickasaw County? That's what's wrong with your program, Les, the kids need to lighten up a little!"

A broad smile broke across Les Hall's face. After a moment or two of silence, Bailey Martin spoke in a serious manner.

"Les, I've been sober eight months, twenty-two days . . . " there was a pause as he counted, " . . six hours and . . . thirty-six minutes. I can stay sober for five years. No, I will stay sober for five years. "

"Then it's a deal, big Bay." Les could hardly contain himself. "Let me know when you want it released and we'll send you a contract."

꙳

Coach Bailey Martin arrived in Currentville alone in late June. He rented a room at Miss Sadie's boardinghouse on tree-lined Franklin Street. Immediately he plunged into his job like a man obsessed.

First, with the full support of his friend, Superintendent Lester Hall and the Board of Education, he supervised a major refurbishing of the high school gym in Catawba. Bailey even labored alongside the workers repainting the walls and bleachers, sanding and revarnishing the floors, and overhauling the moldy old locker room underneath the stage. A new scoreboard was installed, additional lights hung, and glass backboards replaced the old wooden standards. "Hell, Les," Bailey laughed, "y'all ever heard of the twentieth century?"

Late one hot afternoon the two old teammates stood in the gym admiring the gleaming new floor, and especially the handsome Indian head painted in maroon at mid-court. After a moment of reflection, Bailey casually remarked, "I once played with a full blooded Indian at Cincinnati. He was one heck of a guy."

"How did you like playing with the colored?" the school superintendent inquired.

There was a long pause as Bailey pondered the question.

"Never really gave it much thought," he finally answered. "We were all too busy trying to hang on to worry about that stuff." He glanced around the empty gym. Then with a grin and nod of his head, "We could use a few of 'em here."

Coach Martin spent a great deal of time digging through old photographs in the school principal's office. From the the dusty old boxes he recovered team pictures of the past, as well as individual shots of stars from the golden years of Chickasaw County basketball. He took them to the newspaper office in Currentville and had enlargements made. They were framed and strung up along the old hallways of the school, all the way out to the gym which was attached to the main building. Old championship banners were discovered and hung from the rafters. He replaced ones that had been lost. The trophy case was refinished and moved into the entranceway of the gym.

His mission was clear: bring back the glory.

Charlie Russell was not sent out to pasture. "I need him, Les," Bailey implored. "The boys like him. He's a good soldier. I'm gonna need some bodies to help me with the program." So the former coach picked up another biology class and agreed to coach the junior high over at Currentville.

With the facilities upgraded, new equipment ordered, and August almost gone, the new coach turned his attention to his team.

He took the score books from the past two years and camped out in the *Signal* office poring over the old papers. Bailey studied the tally sheets, the accounts of the games, and the box scores, looking for clues as to what he had inherited. Bailey noticed an interesting trend. In a large number of games, especially against similar-size schools, the Indians hung tough for almost three quarters. Then they would get whopped. Fouls accumulated late in the games. Sitting in the corner of the noisy and dirty press room, Bailey sipped on bottled cokes and munched Payday candy bars. Patiently and laboriously the perceptive coach waded through the large bound volumes and made his deductions. The team was either out of shape or playing against teams much bigger and simply being worn down—or both. His grueling and intensive conditioning program would take care of one problem. To combat being outsized, he would have to develop depth, be able to go nine or ten deep into his bench. It was a notion ahead of its time, but he had employed it well in Memphis.

Coach Martin was ready to get the show on the road.

School started, and Bailey comfortably swung into the routine. The kids didn't know what to make of the new coach at first. He kept a proper distance—friendly enough, but not chummy. They were a bit intimidated by his legendary past. But slowly, his worldly ways and subtle sense of humor won them over.

The first basketball meeting was in late September, with tryouts beginning the following week. Bailey had learned from Les Hall and others that they did not have much coming back. So he started out tough and mean, trying to run off those who had been infested with the losing habits of the past—especially the juniors and seniors. Those who survived would have the mental toughness to lend something to the cause.

Defense. That would be the road to recovery.

He expounded to Les and Margaret over supper one night: "Strangling defense can bring good teams to their knees. And you don't have to be loaded with talent to play good defense. It takes guts, grit, and determination. And a lot of pride in the gutter work. But it does wonderful things for you. You can't hustle on defense without hustling on offense. So it flows over into every aspect of your game. Most teams play just enough defense to get by. That's because it's the most grueling facet of the game and requires the greatest self-discipline. Hell, kids love to shoot. They go out in the barn lot and shoot all day. But give me the kids who will take pride in stopping another team cold, of taking a few charges and cutting off the baseline, and I'll win you some games. Most important, good defense builds cohesion. You can't play good defense without talking to your teammates, helping each other out. You're constantly looking out for your teammate, how to help him with his man . . . " Bailey's voice would grow soft, his face beaming with a passion for the game, ". . . helping him out, pulling him out of tight spots, looking out for each other."

So after the cuts, the practices got even tougher. Conditioning, conditioning, conditioning. Wind sprints, side shuffles, full court, "one on one" defensive drills, and run, run, run.

Talking. Talking, Bailey preached, was the key to good defense. "When you're on defense, you ought to be chattering like a baseball infield," Bailey exhorted. After a while their practices were alive with chatter. The gym sounded like an auction barn.

"Pick right. Pick right. Switch. Switch. Check him! Check him! I'm through! I'm through! I've got him, take mine!"

Men at work.

The baseline was sacred territory. Any defensive player giving up the baseline ran ten laps. "Overplay just a step. Push 'em toward the middle. Push 'em toward the middle. They get past you on the baseline, they're through the back door. Force 'em to the middle and your teammates can help you," Coach Martin yelled. There were some mean hits, and some players were knocked into the stage. But fewer and fewer drove the baseline.

Almost immediately there was a new mood both in the school and on the practice floor regarding the basketball program. No one expected to go to the state tournament, but there was a sense of excitement, of expectation. Things were going to get interesting.

The Chickasaw County Indians were four games into the schedule when the long, winless drought finally ended. They beat a fairly decent Trigg County team in a thriller. The fans went bananas, mobbing the floor and celebrating as if the school had just won the state championship.

Coach Bailey Martin sequestered his team in the locker room, and with stomping and hollering still going on outside, quickly wiped the broad smiles off the faces of his happy players.

"What in the hell are you celebrating for? Because we win our first game in two and a half years?" he was yelling. "There was a day in this grimy little old dressing room when winning was routine. And that's the way it is going to be again. That's why we suit up in these things," he reached down and pulled a fistful of sopping wet jersey away from the bony back of Roy Staples. He let the words sink in, and paced back and forth in the steamy little locker room. The outside noise filtered into the tomblike locker room, mingling with the solitary sound of a dripping shower. Finally, he lowered his voice. "Okay. Get showered. Home and bed in thirty minutes. Morning practice at seven." He then walked briskly out of the room, and up the old rickety steps.

Only after he was alone in his car driving back to Currentville did Bailey let a broad smile break out across his face. It had been a long, long time since he had felt that good.

As his initial season rolled along, the excitement continued to build. The Indians were still losing most of their games. But the little gym was filling up, and even in losing, there was an excitement in the air. Their tenacious defense kept them in striking distance in most games, and the intensity and drive of the players were contagious.

One day in a school pep rally Coach Martin casually told the gathering of students, "We are the best defensive team in the region."

One could almost see the shoulders lift on his players. Seemingly, they realized for the first time there was something in which they could be first. Maybe they were, maybe there weren't. But this was something in which they could take pride, a realistic goal for which to strive.

Bailey Martin built on it. Before each game he would recite the number of points the opposing team had scored in its last outing. "We will hold them to ten points less. Fifteen less and no practice tomorrow."

On tough defensive assignments, Bailey offered rewards. "You hold this kid to less than twenty, Tommy, and you've got a steak dinner at Moore's."

Another time he promised that if the team held their mighty opponent to less than 60 points he would shave his head. The enemy scored sixty on the nose. So Bailey showed up at practice with a burr haircut but not shaved," You got close. I got close."

The kids loved it.

One Friday night the very powerful Barlow High came to town. On the previous Tuesday night they had scored 92 points in rolling to victory. The Chickasaw Indians flat got after them. Barlow scored only 51 points, beating the home team by only 4. If not for three straight turnovers made in the last minute, the Indians might have pulled off a tremendous upset.

The next day at practice Bailey conducted them through a light workout, and then set them down for some lavish praise. "Sometimes success and winning do not go hand in hand," he told them. "Last night we did not win. But we were very successful." He then took them to the drugstore for milkshakes.

But even with the progress being made at the high school level, for Bailey it was only the tip of the iceberg. The program— next year's team, and then the next year's team—depended upon basketball being taught and played well in the lower grades.

The junior high school in Currentville consisted of the seventh through ninth grades. Any semblance of basketball there had pretty much vanished. The freshmen were thrown together in a loosely fitted team which played a ragtag schedule of only five or six games, and dressed out for the junior varsity at the high school. The seventh and eighth grades had nothing.

Bailey Martin changed all this. Knowing that this was his farm system—the feeding tube of his program—he spent a great deal of time restructuring and revitalizing youth basketball in Chickasaw County. The freshman team tripled their number of games played, and a junior high team of seventh and eighth graders was re-established and slated for twenty encounters. At the seventh grade level, Bailey borrowed a technique learned from some of the larger schools in Memphis. He divided it into four separate intramural teams, with ten kids to a team—forty seventh graders in all playing basketball. They played their games each day at noon during the lunch break. This Seventh Grade Conference was evenly balanced and stirred up a lot of excitement in the little gym, which had been the Currentville high school home before consolidation. Kids on their lunch break packed the crackerbox with yelling and whooping, giving the players extra incentive and some valuable experience of playing before crowds.

Each day at lunch, Bailey, munching on a baloney sandwich, would drive the two miles to Currentville and supervise the seventh-grade games. Then, he would use his free period to stay and assist Charley with the freshmen and junior high practice.

The place was humming with activity. One could almost hear the hammers and saws busily constructing a new basketball program for Chickasaw County.

In the eighth-grade class Bailey Martin found his vein of gold. There were half-a-dozen boys in that group blessed with extraordinary basketball skills.

And the gleaming nugget was a lean and lanky thirteen-year-old by the name of Bobby Joe Cameron—Luke's older brother.

It took Bailey less than thirty seconds to know that this kid would be the rope by which the Chickasaw County Indians would be pulled back to the top.

He was ambidextrous, able to handle and shoot the ball with either hand. His passes would thread a needle, and the youngster possessed what coaches call "floor sense"—the uncanny ability to be at the right place at the right time all the time. His smooth, easy style camouflaged a catlike quickness. This unselfish leaper would clear the boards, dribble past various defenders the length of the floor and dish off to an open teammate for a basket. His long, soft jumpers arched high into the air, almost skimming the ceiling of the little gym, before nestling gracefully into the white netting. Bailey had seen his kind before. People would pay to watch him play.

Where he gained such skills was anyone's guess. Genetics

and a love for the game combined to create one promising young ball player. And he was not alone. Bobby Joe was accompanied by several teammates who were well above average.

So while things were looking up at the high school, where the seats were filling up once again, the tiny little gym at Currentville packed in just as many.

The eighth-grade team of Bobby Joe Cameron and company went through the season undefeated.

By the end of Bailey Martin's first season at Chickasaw County, the Indians had won eight games and lost fifteen. The talk at the barber shops, restaurants, and Charlie's pool hall was once again mostly basketball. But the jokes were gone. Now it was about the scrappy varsity, that super junior high team, and Bailey Martin. "That guy's one helluva coach," was the consensus.

The crowning touch of the season came late in March, some two weeks after their season was over. Bailey sleepily glanced over the sports page of the daily *Paducah Sun-Democrat* one Saturday morning. A sip of hot coffee hung on his lips as his eyes caught an article at the bottom of the page. The Chickasaw County Indians had led the region in defense, holding their opponents to an average of 51.6 points per game.

The following year, the program continued to climb. The varsity broke even, and the ninth graders packed people in early for the JV contests.

In Bobby Joe's sophomore year, he led the team in scoring, and a squad laden with tenth graders soared to a record of 22-9 and went to the regional tournament.

Bailey was satisfied with the progress, but somewhat mystified by the accolades showered upon him. There really wasn't that much to it, he thought. The problems were obvious, and the answers all lying right out there before him. It was, in his own mind, just the fundamental task of dedication and preparation. Or, as the sign he had posted over the locker room door proclaimed, "THE DIFFERENCE BETWEEN CHAMP AND CHUMP IS 'U.'"

Bailey Martin's personal life during all this time was somewhat of an enigma and shrouded in mystery. He kept mostly to himself, but little of his time was spent in the drab little boarding-house where he lived. An avid hunter and fisherman, he would often disappear for days into the woods and rivers of West Kentucky. A lot of trips were made back to Memphis to visit his little girl and to Texas to be with his mother. Very seldom was he seen around town or mixing socially. Les and Margaret Hall were about the only friends he visited. Still, he was friendly enough to the locals, many of whom had known him all his life. Not aloof or distant—just out of sight mostly.

He was known as a strict coach. But it wasn't really by design. Bailey discussed his coaching style one gray winter morning with Les Hall in a duck blind on Kentucky Lake.

"I don't try to be a hard ass, or a nice guy," he explained. "I'm just myself. To be successful, a coach must simply bring his own personality to the job. Otherwise, if you try to be something you're not, kids will see through it and lose respect for you."

But Bailey's own personality, the white-hot intensity and desire to excel, radiated a certain aura which intimidated others, without even trying. His players respected him to the point of doing him reverence. Yet at the same time, they felt comfortable around him. They came to learn it was not their mistakes which set him off, but their lack of will, the slipshod effort. So his practices were grueling and intense, but not overly long. "Get in and do the work, and go home," he explained to Les.

Not often, but occasionally, he would erupt in a fit of rage, kicking the basketball up into the stage curtains and spewing a stream of invective that would peel the paint off the wall. His ass-chewings were dreadful.

He especially loathed players feeling sorry for themselves, lying on the floor in disgust or hanging their heads.

"Damn! Damn! Damn!" his face would turn crimson, "Get that head up! Get that head up! The other team is looking at your face for the score!"

But he never left a kid down. Somewhere and sometime before the practice was over he would lift him back up. "That was a great defensive move there, Bobby," and all would be right with the world for the young hoopster. Or if he had been especially hard on somebody during the day's workout, he would casually make his way through the steamy locker room. There as he passed the row of lockers he would playfully and quickly scuff the head of his tormented player. "You'll make somebody pay tomorrow," he would offer under his breath. The young athlete's shoulders would lift. He mattered. A little praise from Coach Bailey Martin went a long way. As Bailey liked to say, "You can't lift the shoulders of a kid without lifting his heart." As explosive as he was, as animated his outbreaks, he never laid a hand on a ballplayer. "You can buy into a lot of trouble touching a kid," he wisely confided to his boss Les Hall. "Although I've had a few I'd like to murder."

Sometimes his tactics were amusing. In one particular practice the Indians were simply performing horrendously. Without saying a word, Bailey went to the back of the stage, came out with a ladder, and went up into the large steel beams support-ing the roof. There he climbed up as high as he could go and calm-ly sat upon his perch and looked down on his team. Finally he explained to his totally bewildered team, "Just keep on playing, guys. I just want to get as far away from you this afternoon as I can get."

His authority went unquestioned. His directions were quickly obeyed. Once Bobby Joe turned his ankle in a weekend pickup game. On Monday morning during study hall he paid a visit to the gym, where he soaked his foot and had his swollen ankle taped. "Go light on this in practice today," coach Martin instruct-ed, " and no wind sprints." At the end of practice that day, while the rest of the team was gasping and groaning through the floor length running drills, Bobby Joe utilized the time by shooting free throws.

"Why isn't Bobby Joe running wind sprints?" one of his teammates asked another, not knowing that coach Martin was standing directly behind them.

"Because," the booming voice responded, "I like him. And I don't like the rest of you guys. Any other questions?"

The message was clear: you do the playing, I'll do the coaching.

But as devoted as Coach Martin was to winning, he never

let his players forget it was only a part of life. His own personal setbacks in life had made him a better teacher as well as coach. "This is Life 101," he would often say when a player would have an off night.

"Seize this moment!" he exhorted in one of his skull sessions. "This time next year some of you guys are going to be pumping gas and digging holes in the ground. And you're going to need more than money to get you by. A few good memories won't hurt."

Communication. To Bailey Martin the most important thing in coaching was being able to reach through to his players. "If you can't communicate with a kid," he would say "you can't motivate him and you can't teach him." He spent a lot of time one on one. Many times, as the squad tromped off the floor at the end of practice, he would beckon, "Jimmy Don, stay up here a minute." After the others had showered, dressed and were heading out of the gym, he and his selected player would be casually sitting in the bleachers talking.

It was important to Coach Martin that each player knew where he stood. "Your time is coming," he would reassure one of his scrubs, "until that time you're not going to play much except when we're routing or being routed."

On the other hand, he would often substitute off the end of the bench when most of his starters were still in. "That gives the kid quality playing time—playing with the regulars, time that really helps him. That comical stuff you see when it's their scrubs against our scrubs is good for morale, but not much good for anything else."

He had a way of making every player feel important—even down to the last guy on the totem pole. "Watch that cough, Billy," he would say to a lowly sub in passing. "It could turn into a cold and knock you out of a game or two."

He emphasized the importance of role playing and being ready when your time came. "Failing to prepare is preparing to fail," he preached over and over. To his bench jockeys who were getting limited playing time, "Some night we will pile up the fouls early, we will stink to high heaven. I'll look down to the end of the bench and see your eager little face and think, 'God, anything will beat what I'm seeing.' And then you'll get your big chance—be ready!"

As much as basketball meant to him, he knew that it should never dominate the life of a growing boy—the storytelling should not be bigger than the story. At the end of Bobby Joe's sophomore year, a team meeting was held just before school was let out for the summer. Coach went over some of the things they could expect when they came back in the fall and basically told them he expected the next season to bring them a trip to the state tournament. They had just come off of a tremendous campaign and were still charged with excitement. One of the players asked if they could get a key to the gym so they could continue to play during the summer.

"I don't want you touching a basketball between now and September," he lectured sternly to the startled gathering. "Go out and chase girls, fish and hunt, work, help your Mom and Dad, play baseball . . . " and then, glancing over at Bobby Joe, he dead-panned, ". . . Bobby Joe, I wouldn't fool with the baseball. I hear you're not worth a damn at that either."

It brought down the house, as Bobby Joe tried to keep from blushing and smiling at the same time.

Bailey thought too much of a good thing was not good. "A sixteen or seventeen-year-old boy can physically play basketball twelve months out of the year. But mentally, he can't maintain the type of intensity I want unless he has a healthy break. They're trying that summer crap in Memphis now, and by January the kids can't wait till the season is over," he explained to some interested parents.

So, Chickasaw County basketball and their highly touted coach Bailey Martin headed into the 1955-56 school year with hopes flying high.

The Indians did not disappoint.

Bailey had spent a great deal of time lining up a tough schedule so that the team would be well tested by tournament time. Even so, Bobby Joe Cameron and company rolled.

By Christmastime his team had rolled up ten wins to one

loss. That loss came in double overtime in the finals of the prestigious Paducah Christmas Tournament.

There was standing room only at their games in the little crackerbox gym in Catawba . The pending talk of a dam and relocation of the county's two villages got lost in all of the excitement of the high school basketball team. Defense was still a strong suit of the resurrected program. But now it was a well-balanced scoring machine which was making it a team to be reckoned with. The muscular six-foot-two-inch leaper, Luke's older brother—was the tallest player on the team. He swang between forward and center. Only because the Indians were blessed with ample and outstanding guards were his great skills in the front court not utilized. In short, he could do it all.

When pressed to talk about his star, Coach Martin demurred, insisting instead that every individual on the team had an equally important role to play. In private he expressed his tremendous admiration for his star athlete to Les Hall.

By the first week in February, the Chickasaw Indians were 18-4.

It was then that the bottom fell out of Chickasaw County High School.

One cold Monday morning as the students began to arrive at school, they sensed a dark and foreboding mood hanging over the halls and classrooms of the old two-story wooden building. There were low whispering conversations throughout the nooks and crannies of the old firetrap, each of them repeating in their own rendition rumors and counter-rumors which had floated in over the weekend.

The essence of this gossip was focused on their basketball coach.

Bailey Martin was in trouble.

It had something to do with Memphis—serious allegations arising out of his former job, some four years before. He was under investigation for sexually assaulting a student, who was now in her early twenties and bringing charges.

The student body somberly and quietly moved through the early morning motions of first period, wondering if and when some verification or explanation would be forthcoming. Not until the hour before lunch was there some break in the tension. The announcement from the principal's office crackled over the public address system directing all varsity basketball players to report immediately to the gym for a team meeting.

Nervously, eleven of them assembled—one was home with the flu—on the cold wooden bleachers next to the steps which led down into the home team locker room. The two managers were also present.

No one spoke. Quietly they waited for what seemed like an hour, but was only two or three minutes.

Finally Bailey Martin emerged from his office to the left of the stage and moved slowly down the steps and across the floor. His step lacked the usual spring, and his face was drawn. It was apparent right away to these young men who had grown up with him that something was terribly wrong.

Plunging his hands into the front pockets of his pants, he came to a stop in front of the squad. He ducked his head and began to pace. His steps echoed throughout the quiet, cavernous hall. Faint sounds from the schoolyard of the lower grades at recess mingled with the heater, which kicked on above their heads. The savory scent of rolls cooking in the school cafeteria mingled with a slight odor of tape and adhesive balm emanating from the locker room.

"I've got something important to tell you," coach began at last. "It's not the most important thing I've ever told you . . ." he was struggling for the words. Not a player moved, their eyes burning into his face. "The most important thing I ever told you . . . that would have been three or four years ago . . . over at Currentville. That first day when I gathered a bunch of scraggly looking eighth graders together in the old gym." He stopped and looked up, honing in on one of his pupils. "Joe Dan Logan... you didn't even have tennis shoes. You were playing in those old brown canvas shoes with the crepe soles." A faint smile of recognition floated across the sea of faces.

Bailey continued, " What I told you then was not to look at what you were . . . but what you could become. Through dedication and hard work you have become what you are today . . . winners. It's the same way with life. Dedication and hard work, pride in winning, striving to be the very best you can be will make you a winner. Oh, it's not going to guarantee you will be state champions, or that you are going to make a living playing for the Boston Celtics, or later on become president of the United States. You can't put in what God left out. But you can go places people never thought you could go, see things you never thought you would see . . . become something only God thought you could be . . . "

It was a religious moment for a man they never thought of as being very religious.

"......those were the most important things I ever told you. But what I'm about to tell you now is important, probably more important to me than to you. "

He paused, looked down at the floor, and took a deep breath.

". . . I've got a problem in Memphis that I've got to go take care of. I wish I could tell you more, but . . ." he hung his head shamefully, "my lawyer told me not to say anymore."

Then, looking down at his watch, he went on.

"Effective at noon today, I will no longer be your basketball coach."

If anyone else had been there, they would not have noticed. But for those few who were, they would forever swear thenceforth that all sound, noise, and life was frozen in place for a long numbing moment.

Coach Bailey Martin continued on with his remarks for a short time, thanking them for their effort, their loyalty, and their devotion. But thereafter no one would be able to recall exactly what was said, as their senses were blurred and anesthetized by the ponderous announcement.

Bailey quickly wrapped it up, turned, and walked briskly back to his office. No handshakes. No embraces. Just like that, their common quest was over.

One by one the bewildered young men arose and made their way back to the classroom.

Only the sound of rubber basketballs against hardwood could be heard in practice that afternoon. Charlie Russell sat quietly in his folding metal chair on the stage and looked out over the young athletes going through the motions, wondering how he was going to possibly pick up the pieces. He spoke softly and incoherently to them for just a few minutes at the end of the short workout. But no one really listened—each of the players was absorbed in his own thoughts.

The mighty Chickasaw Indians lost two of their next three games, and played listlessly and miserably in all of them. The entire community was stunned and dejected. This bright and promising star of a basketball team was falling before it had reached its zenith. Throughout the small county there was an oppressive downpour of gloom. It was the time of the year when teams were gearing up for the stretch run, and tournament time. But now, people were trying desperately to think of other things.

But while they did, surveying stakes with red flags began to appear here and there and government men dressed in suits began to call upon landowners to discuss the value of their land. It was not the best of times for Chickasaw County.

The reports drifting back into the county on Bailey Martin were a mixed bag of half-truths and rumors. He was being charged with the rape of a high school student. No, it wasn't a student, but a teacher. And it wasn't rape, but some lesser kind of sexual assault. Then, yes, it was a student, but she was of age. No, she wasn't of age, at least for some of the misdeeds. If Les Hall knew, he wasn't saying.

After their third miserable outing, poor old Charlie Russell—heir apparent to the great Bailey Martin—pulled up his courage once again by conducting another team meeting before practice. In his own low-keyed and mumbling way, he made a gallant effort to remind them of their mission, of what Bailey Martin would want them to do.

Then, in the middle of his talk, as the gathering twilight pushed against the windows of the little gym, a sound interrupted him in mid-sentence. It was a sobbing sound, low and rhythmic at first, and then louder like a rising storm. All eyes moved up the bleachers to the top row where senior Billy Hill sat, his head buried in his arms folded across his bare knees. He was heaving and crying, trying desperately to stifle his own pain.

A long awkward pause ensued, as the gathering stared on in empathy without knowing what to do.

Finally Bobby Joe Cameron stood and spoke, " Uh, Coach . . . if you don't mind . . . uh . . . could you give us a few minutes by ourselves?"

The decent Charlie Russell made the coaching decision of his career. He nodded, and walked out of the gym.

No one else ever knew for sure what went on in that closed meeting on that winter evening of February 20, 1956, in the old rickety Chickasaw County High School gym.

A few things did become known, however.

It lasted almost two hours. And each player there not only spoke, but also swore never to discuss what was said.

And the basketball team which Bailey Martin built was revived and transformed. That was known almost instantly.

For this band of friends went on a tear, winning the remaining four games of the schedule and and ripping through the district tournament, winning the championship game by thirty points.

It was a miraculous resurrection, and even ole Charlie Russell—in spite of his modest and shy denials—got some of the credit. Smiles and laughter returned to the barbershops and restaurants, and the talk at Charlie's Pool Hall was once again of basketball.

Only Coach Russell noticed when his happy troops disrobed in the victorious locker room the small inscription inked into the shirt tail of each sweat-soaked jersey, "The difference between Champ and Chump is U."

It was a secret fraternity of boys coming of age. And Charlie Russell, for all his lack of charisma, was smart enough to just let it happen.

March Madness. It was on to the Regional Tournament in Madison, a town of about 25,000, five times the size of Chickasaw County. The cathedral of basketball was enormous, holding more than 5,000 screaming and delirious roundball junkies.

It was not a seeded tournament. So there was consternation and disappointment when the pairings were announced. Chickasaw County and Madison, the two powers of West Kentucky, were in the same bracket, and would clash before the championship if each got by their first-round opponents.

The Indians cruised by comfortably in the first game of the tournament. But the Madison Bobcats had to sweat it out in overtime before advancing to the big matchup.

And what a matchup it was. The two teams had split their regular season encounters, both nailbiters. Now, most sports pundits and media hounds predicted this contest would decide who would represent the second region in the state tournament. Too bad it was not the championship game—a strong argument for seeding.

And so the throngs arrived for the appointed evening. The showdown was the second game on the card, and the first went into thrilling overtime—setting the stage for the big bout.

Standing room only, the place permeated with the mixed smell of stale perspiration, human beings, popcorn, and an occasional wisp of whiskey. Bands played, gorgeous cheerleaders prissed and twirled. Fans of all ages and sizes adorned with colorful streamers and placards, from tough farmers and hyperactive kids to bankers and rogues. It was basketball—Kentucky—Americana.

Starting lineups were announced and the lights were doused, except for those directly over the hardwood. The stage was set, the hour struck, and both teams—Indians in road maroon and the homestanding Bobcats in white—moved to center circle. Bobby Joe Cameron manfully shook hands with his taller counterpart at center and then proceeded to out jump him by a good four inches to control the tip. The Indians—to a tumultuous roar of the evenly divided crowd—scored on the first trip down.

The battle had begun.

And what a battle it was.

Back and forth, back and forth—trading baskets, trading fouls. Seasoned sports writers would later report it as the most magnificently played, hotly contested high school game they had ever witnessed. But it was also punishing for the teams, with Bobby Joe taking a beating underneath against the much larger Bobcat front line, and the Indian guards piling up the fouls. By midway through the last quarter and with the game tied, the starting guards for Chickasaw County were gone. But because of their depth—"a touch of Bailey" it was later called—their replacements played superbly.

With less than a minute to go in the game, Bobby Joe tipped in an errant shot to put the Indians up by one. Thirty seconds later a Madison guard turned the ball over.

The Indians had the ball and the one-point edge with twenty seconds to go in the game. They went into a weave to freeze the ball, or as Bailey Martin often called it, "letting the air out of the ball." To their good fortune, the Bobcats were out of timeouts, so their coach had to wave and holler frantically from the bench for them to foul. Amidst the ear-splitting noise and bedlam of the frantic crowd, the Madison players seemed to be mesmerized by the splendid ball handling of the Indians.

Finally, with five seconds to go, the ball was knocked loose from a Chickasaw County forward. A mad and desperate chase ensued, with players diving and scrambling after a basketball which seemed to be electrically repelled by human hands and knees. As the big scoreboard moved from 01 to 00 seconds, a referee's whistle stopped the clock. The huge crowd, uncontrollably wild seconds before, grew stone silent so that even those in the far reaches of the cavern could hear the official's call.

A foul was called on the same Chickasaw Indian forward who had let the ball slip away. It was on Roger Catlett, a solid performer who had been like a rock the whole season. Now he had pulled the boner of a lifetime.

With no seconds left on the clock, a Bobcat player would have one and the bonus.

With thousands on their feet—men hollering hoarsely, boys shaking cow bells and girls screaming with tears in their eyes—the din reached a deafening pitch. Then, as casual as if he had been kicking tin cans from the road, the incredibly cool and gutsy little Bobcat guard sank them both. Madison by one, 67-66.

The Madison fans, about half of the gathering, swarmed the floor in wild celebration.

Immediately the two referees were in front of the scorer's table. Then with the help of several state policemen they began the ponderous task of clearing the floor.

The horn had not sounded, and the Indians would have the ball until it did.

Confident that their celebration was only momentarily postponed, the happy crowd moved back into the seats. The stunned Chickasaw County fans stood in their place, hardly believing their cruel fate and not at all consoled that they were being given less than a second to live.

The Indians called time out to decide what to do. How much time was left? No one knew. Presumably only the split second which would be left after the clock was turned on and the horn would blow.

Charlie Russell drew out the only plan in his head. He X'ed Bobby Joe in directly under the basket. Billy Hill, the team's strongest arm, would take the ball out and throw the ball, football style, the length of the floor. The team's star would have to leap into the air, grab the ball, and get off a shot. It was a Herculean, downright superhuman feat being requested of the sixteen-year-old junior.

The horn blew the teams back out onto the floor and the roar of the crowd began to rise toward the climatic end.

Of course the Madison coach had anticipated exactly what the Indians would do. So as Bobby Joe moved toward his spot on the floor he was boxed in by a tight little two-two zone drawn in around the lane. The extra defender was sent to detract and harass the passer preparing to launch the floor-length prayer.

Billy stepped up next to the referee holding the ball just outside the end line ninety-four feet away from the Chickasaw Indian goal. The man in stripes blew the whistle—though Billy could hardly hear it for the noise—and handed him the ball.

Peering down the bright and shiny oaken hardwood, Billy could see nothing but a sea of white. His heart sank, as he drew the ball back in his right hand to hurl his missile. Bobby Joe was completely hidden by a forest of tall timber.

Then, out of the corner of his eye, he spotted a little substitute Indian guard standing on the extreme left at mid-court. It was a maroon uniform standing on what looked like an acre of open ground.

Billy Hill's basketball instinct took over and he heaved the ball to the open man who was at least fifty-five feet away from the basket.

Little Stumpy Duncan had never done anything important in his life. But what he would do in the next split second would make him immortal in Chickasaw County.

He caught the ball just behind the midstripe, and all in the same motion pivoted, crouched, and then let fly a two handed shot exploding from his chest.

The orange sphere headed up into the dark stratosphere of the smoke-filled arena. As it finally started its downward trek, the air went out of 5,206 people.

It was going to be long, Bobby Joe Cameron would later remember thinking. Too long.

It was long. But not too long.

The ball came crashing down upon the glass within the square above the rim, and banked back through the basket.

Only the two alert officials had heard the sound of the horn as the ball had begun its downward trajectory. Looking at each other in total astonishment, they simultaneously extended their left arms and made a sweeping downward motion with their right hands.

It counted.

Pandemonium broke out. The Chickasaw County fans stampeded the floor, while the Madison fans—so exuberant only minutes before—now stood numb in disbelief.

The bedlam went on for a good fifteen minutes. Before the players could make their way to the locker room, they were bruised and scratched. Bobby Joe lost a shoe. Stumpy Duncan had his jersey torn off of him.

Silently the Madison crowd started shuffling toward the

exits, with the sad but resigned acceptance that God had intervened.

Back in Currentville, which was thought to have been drained of its population by the big game, porch lights began to flick on. Those people, mostly the elderly, who been listening to the game on the radio began to move out of their homes and onto the sidewalks. Dressed in pajamas, bathrobes and gowns, they gathered on street corners talking and laughing excitedly. Out of nowhere cars appeared on the streets, horns blaring and people yelling.

At Charlie's Pool Hall, where a small group of old men had hovered next to the Philco, a loud whoop erupted and a round of cold drinks was ordered by all. The phlegmatic old Charlie Clark, never one to show emotion, could not, as hard as he tried, wipe the wide grin off his face.

By midnight, when the yellow team bus crawled up the long hill in front of the school in Cawtaba, over one thousand people had gathered, screaming and shouting.

"Stum-pee! Stum-pee!" came the chant.

Bobby Joe Cameron, whose brilliant evening of 27 points and 15 rebounds had seemingly been forgotten, was happy to shove the little hero out of the bus first and onto center stage.

Lester Hall was there. Speeches were given, all to the continuous roar of the jubilant gathering. Only Bobby Joe Cameron soberly reminded everyone that the job was not finished. The championship game was still to be played.

At close to one in the morning, the mass rally finally came to an end.

Those who had feared a letdown by the Indians had wasted their worry. The next night in the championship game, they could not have been beaten by the Boston Celtics. It was like Stumpy Duncan's miracle had spread into the life and limbs of the rest of the players. By halftime, the Indians had built up a thirty point lead. The final margin was whittled down somewhat, only because the scrubs played the entire fourth quarter.

For only the second time in history, and just four years after a winless season, the Chickasaw Indians were going to the state—"The Sweet Sixteen."

There were parades and pep rallies, and all kinds of hoopla surrounding the trip to Louisville, to include the county schools being recessed for the duration of the tournament.

Two games into the state tournament, the Chickasaw Indians were simply outmatched by a large Louisville school, and their dream season came to an end.

"We weren't beaten by a better high school team," Charlie Russell bitterly announced. "We were beaten by a junior college."

As spring came knocking, things returned to normal at Chickasaw County High School. Well, not really back to normal. The little school still basked in the warmth of all those memories of a momentous basketball season. That glow hovered over the dilapidated old wooden structure and adjoining little brick gym, until one cold winter night some five years later the whole thing went up in flames. All the trophies, plaques, and pictures melted and disappeared in the ashes. Bulldozers buried the debris and the Army Corps of Engineers bought the land.

Solid information finally arrived about the plight of Bailey Martin. He had been charged with statutory rape of a student. But then it was discovered that the willing victim was not under-age. After some tortuous legal encounters, the indictment was finally dropped. At last report, the former Chickasaw County star and coach was teaching and coaching out West.

Bailey Martin had been a broad beam of sunlight which had shone down upon Chickasaw County for a while and then disappeared behind a cloud.

There was no darkened sky for Stumpy Duncan. That one dramatic and miraculous basket would make him a ton of money selling insurance in Chickasaw County.

Many years later at a class reunion, the old ballplayers gathered around and got into their drinks. "You know what," the balding and plump Stumpy Duncan reflected, misty eyed, "I've relived that moment thousands of times. And you know who the real hero in that game was? It was Billy Hill. He could have played it safe and followed the script and thrown the ball into nowhere. That's what the play called for, right? Think about it . . . if I had air-balled that sucker, they would have skewed ole Billy alive.   But I remember that look on his face when he saw me standing out there at mid-court, wide open.   He had that excited look, just like . . . well, just like I was standing right underneath the basket wide open. I mean, he looked so . . . so . . . elated," and here Stumpy stopped and swallowed, "I mean, that look on his face . . . like . . . he knew it was just a matter of me putting it up. Like I said... I've relived that shot a thousand times, and you'll think I'm crazy . . . but I knew I was going to hit it. Billy Hill . . ." he nodded and stared reverently into his drink, ". . . he's my hero."

Chapter Ten

Revive Us Again

Standing on the promises that cannot fail,
by the living word of God I shall prevail.

It was revival time. And Luke dreaded it as much as the devil dreads holy water.

Church.

That one word summed up a great portion of Luke's life. Not religion necessarily, or even doctrine. But simply church.

Church, and all the trappings of religion which attended it, was the one area of Luke's family life where his mother Esther reigned supreme. Alec, who was raised in a family where Sunday morning might mean church or it might mean craps, went along with her without a whimper, glad to be rid of this one responsibility of raising children.

Esther, on the other hand, came from a rigidly devout clan of Southern Baptists, her father following a mule all week and leading singing on Sunday.

So Esther Cameron's family attended the First Baptist Church of Currentville. That's what it was called formally, with the designation apparently being used to distinguish it from the Negro Baptist Church in Freewill.

And Luke and his family were in the little brick church every time the doors were opened.

On Sunday mornings for Sunday School and Church.

On Sunday nights for Baptist Training Union, better known as BTU, and preaching.

On Wednesday nights for prayer meetings.

Royal Ambassadors for the boys.

Girls' Auxiliary for the girls.

Also throw in Bible School in the summer, periodic study courses on books of the Bible, and church socials.

And, of course, every single night of a revival.

Baptist preachers became like members of their family.

There was a common thread which ran through them all.

Baggy suits, stiffly starched white shirts and faded ties, scented down with cheap after shave. Whether from the larger towns or the country churches, they were similar in dress and mannerisms.

Most were limited in education—being certified to preach normally required only to have heard "the call." A few were sophisticated enough to have attended the Southern Baptist Seminary in Louisville.

Their pulpit technique included a raging and literal interpretation of the Bible, and fundamentalist adherence to the rules and regulations of God's word. Hellfire and brimstone, mingled in with gripping deathbed stories, laced their sermons.

Generally, they were good and well meaning men. Quick to love and forgive, and at the same time to brazenly give the head deacon a tongue lashing for mowing his yard shirtless.

Most of them possessed a certain amount of charisma, rough-hewn as it sometimes was. This was begot by the dynamic, eloquent, and highly inspired passion of their sermons.

Bigoted and narrow as a rule, there was still something learned and scholarly about them. They were accommodating with the men, charming and slightly flirtatious with the women.

And there was a little mystery there. A stumbling, ignorant plow boy would seemingly be transformed into a learned and articulate evangelist immediately after receiving "the call to preach."

"The call" could come at any time or almost any place.

At a young age, it would normally come during a heated summer revival, at which time he would be jerked from the complacency of the back seat all the way up to the altar during the soul-wrenching invitation.

Or "the call" might come after the service, out under the old apple tree when the young man hears the voice of God beckoning him to become a fisher of men.

But the time and place were unpredictable.

Middle-aged men might get "the call" while putting up hay or suckering tobacco, and spend the rest of their lives splitting time between growing corn and "bringing in the sheaves."

Regardless of the forum, God would always have his way, sometimes after months or years of torment. Then a man would become more than a man. He became an ambassador for his King, filled with such spiritual exuberance that he literally became a different human being.

Luke and his family encountered one preacher, however, who did not fit this common mold.

He was called by the congregation to be the pastor of the Currentville First Baptist Church.

From the minute Brother Josh Boyd came to town from Arkansas with his wife and two young daughters, everybody loved him.

He was young, with a hefty mop of curly black hair and boyish good looks. His crooked smile, Ozark drawl, and L'il Abner ways charmed the entire congregation.

In the pulpit, he was a disappointment. An uninspired speaker, he simply stumbled through his sermons with little enthusiasm, and would quit just before his listeners fell asleep.

But no one is perfect, the membership rationalized, and it was more than willing to tolerate the poor preaching in exchange for his winning ways.

And Brother Josh's habits were a little unorthodox for a Baptist preacher. Not only did he not condemn smoking, he even chewed tobacco himself and puffed on a pipe occasionally. In fact, he was rarely seen outside of church without a big wad of sin bulging out his cheek.

The keen observer could discern that this maverick went though the motions with the doctrine and the form, but really didn't take it as seriously as even his deacons did.

Amazingly, his occasional irreverence did not seem to offend the staunch and rigid born-again Christians of his church.

He got away with it like a favorite son.

Once when the backwater was up, threatening to run everyone from their homes, he met Brother Ollie Ladt, the Methodist minister, at the post office.

The old Methodist graybeard was lamenting to Brother Josh that he could not get the Red Cross to come and move him out of his parsonage.

"Cuss 'em, Brother Ladt! Cuss 'em!" he implored, trying to keep a straight face. "Naw, on second thought, you let me cuss 'em. You can fall from grace, but I can't."

The people loved him.

All the people.

And that included the town drunks.

Actually they were not drunk all the time. Only about half the time. The rest of the time they spent sitting around town, with puffy eyes and sour breath, on benches or on the stoop in front of the pool hall.

Shabbily dressed, usually in faded overalls with dirty old caps pulled down on their heads, they would watch their dreary world go by.

The sidewalk combo consisted primarily of three lost souls.

Stonewall Jackson was by far the youngest of the group, about the same age as Brother Josh. He had been on booze since a kid, and could be a mean drunk. Stonewall oftentimes became belligerent when intoxicated. He was meek as a lamb when sober.

Uncle Harry and Ben Knight were of the same ilk. Both were decorated World War II veterans who could never manage to get their lives back on track after D-Day. They lived on handouts, charity, and small government pensions. At one time they were able to handle part-time jobs—mowing grass, cutting tobacco, sweeping out stores. Now they did nothing but lord over the amber-stained sidewalk by day, and drink Four Roses whiskey at night.

Brother Josh befriended them from the very first.

On muggy summer nights, and early on Sunday mornings, Brother Josh would saunter down town and sit on the stoop, chew, and talk with the drunks.

At first the old sinners were rigid and tense, not really knowing what to make of a preacher who came and visited them without mentioning church. After a short while, however, they were put at ease by his charm, and he became a welcome partner to their gab if not their booze.

Brother Josh would tell yarns about Arkansas, jokes about preachers, fishing stories, and the virtue of planting by the moon. When he wasn't sharing a twist of his favorite chew, he would stoke up his old pipe. The preacher of the Ozarks would pull on its stem while his eyes danced in merriment as he listened to Ben and Uncle Harry kid each other about German women.

Not one time in all those conversations did Brother Josh invite them to church. Not one time did he talk to them about the Good Book or their need to be born again.

At first they awkwardly waited for him to bring it up, to slip in a plug for his business.

But it never came. And finally they relaxed, accepting him as a man rather than a preacher. And he accepted them for what they were.

Brother Josh had been in Currentville for over two years as the little Baptist Church prepared once again for its annual revival.

A large banner was hung high over the pulpit announcing the campaign slogan for the revival:

TWENTY-FIVE FOR CHRIST

It was a heady goal to win that many people to Christ during the week-long meeting.

But when the revival began on Sunday night with a packed house, anything seemed possible.

There was excitement in the air and the lights were beam-

ing through the opening windows in the gathering dusk. The heat
was stifling as the ceiling fans moved at rapid speed in a futile
attempt to cool the sultry air. Cardboard fans, with a picture of the
Last Supper and compliments of Sanders Funeral Home, were
whipping back and forth in front of almost every face.

The choir loft, which was just to the left to the elevated
stage and pulpit, was full of eagerly awaiting singers.

It was 7:30 p.m., time for the opening pitch. Folding
wooden chairs were being brought in as latecomers still poured in.
The rest of the congregation waited for the procession to come
forth from the door behind the pulpit. There were coughs, shuffling feet, the whimper of infants, and the steady hum of the overhead fans.

The air was alive with anticipation.

Then the back door swung open and out came the starting
lineup.

Brother Josh, in his baggy suit, led the way, with an elfish
grin on his face. He was followed by the revival preacher from
Dyersburg, Tennesseee, Brother Leonard Hackworth Barnes, a tall
gray-headed reverend in black, his small Bible tucked up under his
left arm. A far away, mystic look was in his eyes, as he peered majes-
tically out over the congregation.

Leonard Hackworth. L. H., for "Living Hell," was the
label for this charismatic evangelist around the circuit.

Last out of the chute was a young guy with a blond flat top.
It was Tom Jackson, the church choir leader. He was a music major
at Murray State University forty miles away who drove over and
serviced the church on Sundays and at revivals.

Tom went to the pulpit.

"Let's begin this great crusade for Christ," he bellowed in
his deep baritone voice, "this wonderful week for the Lord by raising our voices in song, sing it like you mean it, number 155,
'Revive Us Again'!"

Brother Tom raised his arms, palms up, and the sweating
crowd rose to their feet.

Miss Lillian pounded the first chords on the piano, and the
earth began to shake.

We praise Thee, O God! for the Son of Thy love,
For Jesus who died, and is now gone above,
Hallelujah! Thine the glory, Hallelujah! amen;
Hallelujah! Thine the glory, revive us again.

The little church vibrated with the sound. It was magnificent.

All the voices of heaven could not have entered this small brick church and given it more spirit. The fervor was warmer than the summer night. The music and the emotion were electrifying.

Brother Josh welcomed everyone.

More songs. Long prayers.

Prayers. These works of oratory were a big part of all church services of the Southern Baptist faith.

Deacons in the church, called upon in the order of their age and service were asked to rise from the congregation and lead the gathering in prayer.

Ancient and withered Mr. Hale, close to ninety and chairman of the deacons, always got the honors to open up the revivals. Old and slightly bent, the beloved old gray beard would rise, and to a full house of expectant ears, give a ten minute petition to the Almighty.

On this evening, old Mr. Hale actually prayed twice. First when he was called upon by Brother Josh. At another time when he wasn't called on by Brother Josh.

The immaculately dressed old man was hard of hearing and sometimes drifted off from what was going on. When Brother Josh was making the announcements in between prayers and songs, he proclaimed, "A deacons' meeting has been called for tomorrow evening at 5 o'clock by Mr. Hale."

At the sound of his name, Mr. Hale arose once again and began to pray. The kids snickered, the grown ups bowed their head reverently, and Mr. Hale was no doubt honored by the double dip.

In the very back of the church against the wall and underneath the cathedral windows was a long pew. It was where the ushers sat.

Every Sunday night (and opening night for revivals were no exceptions), the young boys of the church served as ushers and took up the offering.

Usually there were two.

On this night, with the big revival crowd, there were four.

Luke, Donkey, Bennie Marshall, and Marvin Lee Foote had the honors on this simmering August evening.

Marvin Lee was a farm boy from Pea Ridge, with a large shock of blond hair and ruddy complexion. He was as bright as a tree full of owls, and as shy as a mail-order bride. On this night he was scrubbed and combed clean, his red cheeks aglow.

Taking up offering was old hat to the other three. But it was Marvin Lee's first time. Luke had assured him it was a piece of cake and all he had to do was follow their lead.

He forgot to tell Marvin Lee about the offertory prayer.

Tom Jackson announced that the offering would follow the next hymn, a cue to the youngsters in the back.

They grabbed the hymnal and followed the song. On the chorus of the last stanza, they began their march—tramp, tramp, tramp—two abreast, down the middle aisle.

> *At the cross, at the cross where I first saw the light,*
> *And the burden of my heart rolled away,*
> *It was there by faith I received my sight,*
> *And now I am happy all the day!*

The four handsome lads moved through the standing crowd and arrived at the front just as Miss Lillian pounded the song to an end.

Luke and Marvin Lee in front.

Donkey and Bennie behind them.

Brother Josh took the two big wooden plates from the altar table and held them in his hands.

"Now we'll ask Brother Marvin Lee to lead us in our offertory prayer."

Poor Marvin Lee jumped like he had been shot with a bolt of electricity.

He looked around in panic, searching for help. But Brother Josh had already bowed his head and closed his eyes.

No help there.

Reverend Barnes had bowed down on one knee beside the pulpit on the platform, just an arm's reach from Marvin Lee. His head, too, was buried in his chest, his eyes tightly shut.

Luke, empathizing painfully, cut his eyes over at his hapless and terrified partner.

There was a long, awkward silence. A nervous cough from the sweating mass hovering behind them. The humming fans overhead seemed to grow louder.

At last, a sound came from Luke's right.

"Dear God. . . ."

It was Marvin Lee. He had managed to begin.

" . . . we uh, thank you for this money . . . I mean . . . we thank you for this revival . . . uh, bless brother Barnes and uh, this meeting. . . ."

Brother Barnes let out a low "Amen!"

Marvin Lee stopped dead in his tracks and looked into the pious preacher's face.

"What?" he whispered.

Luke cut his eyes over and saw Marvin Lee looking at Brother Barnes, waiting for a reply.

Finally, after what seemed like a long time but was actually only a second or two, Marvin Lee looked back at the floor and continued.

. . . we know that there are people here tonight Lord who are not saved . . . uh, we need to . . . we pray that you will . . . uh, save them here tonight. . . ."

Again Brother Barnes chimed in, just above a whisper, "Yes, yes Lord . . . we pray to God. . . ."

Again Marvin Lee stopped.

"What?" he implored, looking straight at the preacher from Tennessee, and almost in a normal tone of voice. "What do you want? What do you want me to say?"

Marvin Lee was now not only nervous, but growing highly agitated, thinking that the evangelist was trying to tell him what to pray.

Brother Barnes, hearing Marvin Lee's plea and sensing something was going amiss, opened his eyes just enough to look into Marvin's sweating face. Then, apparently aghast at what he saw, shut them again.

Marvin Lee was in agony, close to a stroke. Kids were beginning to snicker and the grown-ups to wonder.

Tension was at the kindling point.

Time hung suspended.

"Amen!" Luke blurted out loud and clear.

He grabbed the wooden plate from Brother Josh. Marvin Lee—as if reprieved from a death sentence—did the same. Miss Lillian began to play. The people took their seats as the young ushers began to pass the plates.

The crisis was mercifully over.

Marvin Lee Foote's shirt was wringing wet.

As the preaching began, Brother Leonard Hackworth Barnes really turned on for opening night.

He began in a low voice, like a distant rumble giving hint of a gathering storm.

His Biblical text, which he read slowly and distinctly was from the book of Luke. It was the story of the rich man and Lazarus.

"There was a certain rich man, who was clothed in purple. . . "

Luke shivered, knowing what was coming.

". . .And in hell he lifted up his eyes, being in torment..."

When he was through reading, he then retold the harrowing account in his own words.

Like most Baptist evangelists, Brother Barnes was a great storyteller.

Amens were raining down from throughout the congregation.

Poor Lazarus, starving and diseased, the dogs licking his sores. He begged merely for the crumbs from the rich man's table.

Then the rich man died and went to hell. Lazarus died and went to heaven.

With his voice slowly rising, Brother Barnes began to paint a graphic picture with words and phrases, of the horrors and agony of hell.

Luke and his fellow ushers could feel the flames, see the grotesque faces, and longed for a drop of water.

The preacher then very skillfully transferred the spellbinding scene to Currentville, to that evening, to that very place. He spoke of the people with sin, in that very congregation, who were as guilty as the rich man, and who were destined to the same horrible fate.

Even those without sins of great consequence faced fire and brimstone unless they were born again—even if their new birth was not substantially better than their first. All people everywhere, unless washed in the blood of the Lamb, were in the same class with the rich man.

With graphic description he then related one story after another of terrible scenes he had witnessed.

The cursing and drunken lumberjack on his deathbed, who screamed out in excruciating pain when he felt the fires of hell already engulfing his feet before he had even drawn his last breath.

Of the lost soul in a past revival who turned down a last chance to accept Christ and was mashed to smithereens by a train that very evening on the way home—cast away into eternity, lost and condemned.

On and on it went. The perspiring preacher removed his coat, rolled up his sleeves, mingled admonitions with memorized verses from the Bible he held high in one hand.

There were amens from throughout the mesmerized gathering. Everyone was either enraptured, scared to death, or both. Even the babies didn't dare to whimper.

Finally, after a good hour, he began to build to the crescendo—like a great classical conductor. The waves of oratory ebbed and flowed, his voice reaching such levels it could be heard through the open windows for a half-block away.

Tears flowed down his cheeks, mixing with the dripping sweat. A small white handkerchief, neatly folded, was pulled from his back pocket and mopped across his brow.

Then, he humbly bent his head, and lowered his voice.

"There are people here tonight who need to come. There are people here tonight who are bearing the weight of sin. There are people here tonight under conviction."

Luke knew—thank God—that the end was drawing nigh.

"Brother Tom will come and lead us in our invitation hymn. Brother Josh will be standing here in front. I beg you not to let this chance go by. It may be your last chance. Eternity may be only fifteen minutes away. You may meet your maker on the way home from church tonight . . . or in those wee dreadful hours of the morning . . ."

Tom Jackson announced the number. The congregation rose and Miss Lillian began to play.

> *Just as I am without one plea,*
> *But that Thy blood was shed for me . . .*

Brother Barnes continued to plead, his strong, compelling voice overlaying the music with masterful effect.

People began to go down front. Youngsters, old people, all kinds.

Brother Barnes kept calling for one more stanza. Through all five of "Just As I Am," and then to another song.

> *O why not tonight? O why not tonight?*
> *Wilt thou be saved? Then why not tonight?*

The spent and exhausted minister raised his hand.

"One more verse and we will close. This is the last chance some of you may ever have to save your soul from hell. Just one more verse, Brother Tom . . . "

Finally it was over.

Eight people had come down front.

Five for profession of faith—to be saved.

One for a change of church membership—to request a letter from another church.

Two for the purpose of rededicating their lives.

The invitation had lasted thirty-five minutes.

Everyone sat back down.

Brother Josh introduced the penitent souls.

Then he did something that Luke's father liked. Unlike all other pastors before and contrary to church doctrine, Brother Josh did not ask for a vote of the congregation whether to accept the new converts. He simply asked that "all who would welcome these fine people into our membership, please stand."

Of course everyone stood.

It was a nice little touch.

The long first night was closed with a long prayer, and hand shaking with the folks down front.

Luke and his friends burst through the back door and out into the wonderfully fresh air of the hot summer night.

On the way home, Luke related to his parents the incident with Marvin Lee at the altar.

"That will teach the preacher to keep his mouth shut when someone else is talking to God," Alec chuckled.

⚜

Revival time was an all-out frontal assault upon sin.

It was war.

And as in war, there were strategies, objectives.

The pastor, revival preacher, deacons, and different organizations of the church all helped to put together an outreach program where the maximum number of people were notified and asked to come to the revival meetings.

It was called "witnessing," and few people in town escaped the dragnet.

Of course evangelism was a year-round, day-to-day practice for the priesthood of believers. The Sunday night BTU weekly attendance card, filled out by all in attendance, had a category labeled "contacts" to encourage everyone to seek out new members, if not converts.

But the annual church revival was the gigantic pep rally for evangelism.

The generals of this brigade of Christian soldiers, the clergy, targeted key sinners of Currentville to pursue. They didn't even have to be sinners, just notable people who were not Christians, or who had never joined a church. Either way, in the eyes of the crusaders, they were lost.

One such object of attention was Sedmon Peck.

Sed was a local entrepreneur who dabbled in varying kinds of investments, but mostly in run-down rental property on Oak Hill. He was also known to bootleg, shack up with an assortment of ladies with soiled reputations, and generally live the life of a reckless libertine.

And he was pretty well off, scoring big from time to time up at the horse races at Henderson. He always dressed in fancy clothes with dazzling jewelry and drove the latest cars.

Sedmon Peck was in his early sixties and dyed his hair jet black. He smelled of cheap cologne and wore dark shirts with light-colored ties.

But for all of his debauchery and sin, Sedmon was a charming piece of work. He was always smiling and glad-handing people, like a politician running for office. And in spite of how much people might disapprove of his way of life, it was hard not to like ole Sed.

For all these reasons, he always became a target of revival preachers, who tried to bring the town's chief sinner into the fold. It would be a bright feather in some pulpiteer's hat.

And it was an odd thing. Sed never darkened the door of a church except at revival time. Then, it made no difference whether it was the Baptist or the Methodist, or even the tiny little Church of Christ, he would make it for the first night and then no more.

But Brother Josh and the Reverend Hackworth Barnes had really worked on him this time.

On the second night, he was back, moving up a couple of rows from the back seat.

He was obviously impressed with the fervent and passionate preaching of Brother Barnes.

If the people were astonished and excited about his return on the second night, they were downright electrified by his appearance on the third night, sitting only about three rows from the front on the right side.

All the congregation was abuzz with the prospects of exceeding their goal for converts—-they now already had close to twenty—and landing the biggest fish of all in Sedmon Peck.

Songs were sung and prayers were given.

Once again both the overhead fans and the cardboard ones worked overtime in the stifling heat. The outside air clung against the screens in the open windows. Moths circled the lights.

Finally, with bated anticipation, Brother Barnes arose and began his sermon.

He moved through the scripture and into his oration.

His humble eyes moistened with tears, and his face glowed. Sweat dripped from the tip of his noise as his booming voice grew louder.

It was plain to all that on this night, the Tennessee evangelist was truly possessed of the spirit. Raging and crying, he moved back and forth on the platform. He had the look and power of an Old Testament prophet.

Off came the coat, and he slung it across the choir railing.

Then he was down off the platform pacing in front of the crowd, and even up and down the aisle.

His shirt was darkening under his arms from the perspiration.

Later, no one could remember exactly what he said.

But he had just reached the crescendo of one of his rolling alliterations where there was a split second of deafening silence.

Sedmon Peck suddenly leaped to his feet and yelled, "Hell! Let me out of here!"

Then, in a panic, he stomped across the feet of the people sitting on his row, hit the aisle, and almost in a trot headed out the back of the church.

The effect was overwhelming.

There was chilling silence as the retreating man's exclamation was still echoing off the walls.

But Brother Barnes, a man possessed with the Holy Ghost, was totally at ease with the situation, almost like it had happened to him many times before.

With the sweetest, kindest look on his face, he raised his hand and spoke softly.

"Brothers and sisters," he began in a hushed tone, contrasting dramatically from his loud and powerful voice of just a few moments before, "we have just witnessed the terrifying movement of the Almighty's hand. Brother Peck is under conviction. He has come face-to-face with his own mortality and his own sins.

"Let us bow our heads . . . all of us now . . . right there where you are . . . and let us pray for this poor wretched soul. Let us pray with a fervent voice for this tormented brother, that he may find peace . . . that he may find Christ this very night. . . ."

With all heads bowed, Brother Barnes prayed what Luke Cameron thought was the most beautiful prayer he had ever heard.

Tears came to Luke's eyes. For one of the few times of his life, and certainly during this revival meeting, he felt the loving and forgiving side of his faith.

At the conclusion of his prayer, Brother Barnes asked the congregation to keep their heads bowed.

"As Brother Jackson leads us in the invitation number, I want you to keep your heads bowed and pray not only for Brother Peck, but for all of the others here tonight who are in need of the saving grace of God."

The choir, led by Brother Jackson, began to sing.

> *Softly and tenderly Jesus is calling,*
> *Calling for you and for me.*
> *See on the portals he's waiting and watching,*
> *Watching for you and for me.*

They came up that night in droves.

> *Come home, come home, ye who are weary, come*
home.

Some came on a profession of faith. Others, including

Luke, who had been baptized when he was nine, simply went up to rededicate their lives.

It was one kinda night.

Luke never saw Sedmon Peck in church again. Not even on the first night of revivals.

※⊚※

There was talk of extending the meeting for another week.

But the church budget and Brother Barnes' prior commitments scotched the idea.

After the climatic Sedmon Peck night the fervor ebbed and the number of converts slackened.

So "Living Hell" Barnes wrapped up the week-long revival on Friday night with a stirring curtain call from the Book of Revelation.

Exhausted and spent, the perspiring servant of the Lord humbly took a seat in one of the large chairs on the platform after the final invitation. He mopped his brow with his handkerchief and peered out over the flock with that look of eternity in his eyes. Brother Josh extended to him the heartfelt thanks of the Currentville First Baptist Church in a moving farewell.

On Saturday morning sad news came that Brother Josh's father had passed away in Arkansas.

He and his family had to leave town, and the scheduled baptismal service set for Sunday night was up in the air.

Because of the large number of converts—mostly children ranging in age from nine to fifteen—they were going to be baptized in batches, on three consecutive Sunday nights.

But now the death in Brother Josh's family had placed the first round of submersions in jeopardy.

As a courtesy, and because one of the candidates for baptism was his young granddaughter, Brother Josh had invited the Reverend Albert Boone, an elderly minister from one of the country churches to assist him on that first Sunday night.

In a hastily called meeting before he left town, Brother Josh and the deacons decided to go on with the rites as planned, with Brother Boone doing the honors by himself.

So on Sunday evening the baptistry was ready.

The pulpit, and the chairs on the platform were moved aside, and the floor was literally picked up and moved. Underneath was the concrete basin which was filled with water.

Bobby Joe and a couple of his friends had once gotten into big trouble by slipping into the church one Sunday afternoon after Mr. Holland, the custodian, had filled the pool with water. They dumped several boxes of red dye into the waiting waters. The coloring had settled to the bottom until the baptismal services stirred the waters. Then everyone began to turn red—preacher, candidates, all—washed in the blood of the lamb.

That was the last time Luke remembered Bobby Joe being skinned alive by his father.

On this night the baptistry was filled with clear and placid waters and surrounded with potted ferns.

Baptismal services were a lark for Luke and his friends. There was no preaching. And all the young lads of the church crowded up on the front row to watch the dunking.

There they would snicker and point at those poor subjects who choked or sputtered during the submersion. And it was always a treat to see how the preacher would maneuver some obese convert. The most giggling and gaping came after the girls were soaked and exiting the pool with their revealing dresses clinging to their breasts and backsides.

It was this bit of lewd gawking which caused a curtain to be hung from the ceiling in front of the baptistry that was pulled as the baptized made their way out of the pool.

It was time to start, and the curtain was closed. A packed house waited in the sultry heat as crickets chirped through the open windows.

Miss Lillian began to play. Luke heard the door behind the baptistry, which led to a Sunday School room open.

Then he heard Brother Boone moving down the steps and into the water.

The musical prelude did not drown out the sound of

swirling water as the minister moved into position.

It was a quiet and soothing scene.

Brother Boone moved over to the front of the basin where his Bible was lying open on the floor at about chest level. Lying next to the open Bible was the reading lamp, which had been detached from the pulpit.

The large, raw-boned old preacher reached for the lamp to pull it closer to the Holy Word. Then, piercing the hush, came the sound of splashing water and the loud voice of Macon Carr from behind the curtain.

"Turn the current off! Turn the current off!"

Macon threw back the curtain, his face ashen and distorted.

"Turn the current off!"

Pandemonium broke loose as the congregation surged forward to see what was going on.

There floundering in the water was poor Brother Boone, kicking and shaking, his eyes bulging out of his head, and the lamp stuck in his right hand.

Alec Cameron had been sitting on the aisle next to Esther about halfway down toward the front.

While others swarmed and screamed around him, rushing to assist, he walked briskly to the electric outlet in front of the platform and pulled the lamp plug.

Spitting and choking, Brother Boone bobbled to the surface and regained his footing.

He was visibly shaken and upset, as some of the men led him out of the water and into the back room.

The crowd, now buzzing with excited relief, returned to their seats. In a few minutes the song leader, Tom Jackson, walked out to the edge of the baptistry and announced in very solemn tones that Brother Albert was apparently alright. But out of an abundance of caution, it had been decided to postpone the baptismal services.

So, with a hymn and a long prayer of thanksgiving by Mr. Hale for the deliverance of dear Brother Boone, church was dismissed.

While driving home that night, Alec suddenly began to laugh.

"What's so funny?" Ester inquired.

Alec explained, "I was just thinking . . . I wonder what those poor candidates for baptism standing back there were thinking, seeing poor old Brother Boone about to be electrocuted right before their eyes . . . I mean that would have been a shock to your newborn faith. . . ."

Luke's mother failed to see the humor.

≈✿❀✿≈

A steady and bone-chilling drizzle fell upon the town of Currentville. It was a gray, late September morning.

The large yellow moving van was backed across the sidewalk, and up to the front porch of the Baptist parsonage.

Brother Josh and his family were moving back to Arkansas. He had been "called" to pastor at a Baptist church not too far from his home town.

Of course, as Brother Josh had told Luke's dad with a grin and a wink, "I never knew any preacher to ever be called to a church which paid less."

His leaving saddened the community, but the people understood how he wanted to get back to his widowed mother.

Mrs. Boyd and the girls had already departed in the family car. Brother Josh was finishing up with the movers and would soon be leaving with them in the truck.

Three men, shabbily dressed and stooped, made their way down the tree-lined avenue to the house beside the church.

Soaked from the steady rain, they moved in under the large sugar maple at the corner of the yard.

There the three old drunks removed their caps and waited.

In a few minutes Brother Josh spotted them there and came bouncing off the porch to greet them. Smiling broadly, he cheerfully pumped each of their hands and invited them inside.

They meekly declined.

Out of his trousers he pulled his pocket knife and a plug. He carved the pieces and passed them out.

Under the shelter of the dripping limbs they chewed and talked.

He told one last joke.

"A guy was on his first parachute jump. He jumped out of the plane and started looking for his rip cord. Couldn't find it. He was tugging and pulling frantically. Got about five hundred feet above the ground and he met a man on the way up.

"'Hey,' he hollered at the man on the way up, 'you know anything about a parachute?'"

"'No,' the man answered. 'You know anything about lighting a gas stove?'"

They grinned and chuckled, tobacco amber trickling out of their toothless mouths.

After some more conversation they put their caps back on their matted heads, shook hands with Brother Josh one last time, and shuffled back down the street.

He stood and watched them until they reached the corner. They turned toward town, and disappeared out of sight.

Chapter 11

The Big Fight

Fear gives way to a promise well made.

At the beginning of Luke Cameron's seventh grade year in school, he and his classmates were having a ball.

They had moved from grade school into junior high at the old two story brick building in Currentville. Graduated grade schoolers from all over the county came together for the first time. That meant his class—along with the eighth and ninth graders—changed rooms on the hour, had home room where they assembled briefly in the mornings, and hadfour different teachers and study halls. The top three grades were over at the high school at Catawba. Even the studies seemed more interesting. And the girls, for some reason or another, definitely seemed more interesting. It was all new, different, and exciting.

Adding to the magic was the employment of a new principal.

Mr. Blake—"Blistering Blake" as he was known by the fearful students—had moved over to the high school.

His replacement was Mr. Stevens, a steely eyed little man

with curly hair, much younger than his predecessor. And while he maintained the dreaded wooden paddle, in the top drawer of his desk, he used it more infrequently than had "Blistering Blake."

As soon as school had started, misbehaving students began their doleful trips to the principal's office—sent there with notes from fed up teachers. In the past it had meant an automatic paddling by the schoolmaster—the number of blows and severity of which depended on the seriousness of the offense.

But Mr. Stevens employed a brand new means of discipline. He saved the beatings for only the worst of crimes. For the misdemeanors—excessive talking, throwing paper wads, tardiness, and the like—he imposed the punishment of doing "thousands." It was based on the penal premise that "an idle brain is the devil's workshop." The purpose was to give errant students something to occupy their time—since they were obviously not spending it on lessons.

If a student was given "five thousand" for his punishment, he would have to figure on paper from the top number down to zero, by subtracting three and adding two. It was a grueling, mind numbing and time consuming exercise which cut deeply into after school and nightly leisure time. "Two thousand" due by the close of business the next day could put a real hurt on a guy. The initial and joyful acceptance of this alternative punishment soon gave way to somber disappointment as reality settled in. They should have known, each agreed, that it wouldn't be easy. Some even preferred the paddling. At least it was over with in a matter of minutes—after the sting worked its way out of the breeches. But "thousands" put a crimp on the most precious thing for a 13 year old boy—free time.

It wasn't long into the school year when Luke got hit with his first fine. He blew milk out of his straw into Tommy Grogan's green beans in the lunch room. Everybody thought it was a hoot except Tommy—and of course Mr. Stevens, who just happened to be standing, arms crossed, right behind the table of roustabouts.

"That will be two thousand, Luke, by Friday noon," came the stern sentence from the principal.

Luke dutifully worked on the math during his classes, care-

ful to hide the work under his book.   Birdseed looked on curiously, unable to keep the amused smirk off his face.   That night he
came down to Luke's house to see how he was doing.

"About finished up," the tired youngster sighed at the
kitchen table. "Mom and Dad think I've really turned over a new
leaf and doing a lot of studying."

Birdseed poured himself a glass of water from the sink and
plopped down at the table. He silently studied Luke's figuring.

"Why don't you try something Luke?" he finally said with
just a tinge of interest in his voice.

He continued, "You're down to three hundred almost.
Why don't you do the last three hundred in hundreds?"

Luke thought about it for a minute.

"I mean....think about it." Birdseed's brilliant little head
was turning. "He assigns a thousand, say. Well, that's ten hundreds, right? Doing it by hundreds would be easier, less figures you
have to put down."

"Yeah, I guess," Luke was skeptical, "but what if he doesn't
want us to do it that way?"

"You actually think he studies these things?" Birdseed
exclaimed incredulously.

"He probably glances at the first page—maybe the last, to
see that you worked it down. He may look to make sure there's
enough paper work of figuring. Anyway, try it. It's worth a try.
We could see. It's not much of a risk. All you have to say is you
didn't know. He probably won't even do anything but tell you not
to do it again."

"Okay," Luke acquiesced, "What the heck."

As Luke wound down his work, Birdseed continued to
think. Suddenly he became excited.

"Luke! I just came up with a great idea!" he proclaimed,
his face beaming.

"What?" Luke was taken back by the sudden shift in his
friend's mood.

Birdseed was leaning back in his chair, tilting it away from
the table. He was staring straight ahead with a smile on his face.

"Yeah, it just might work," he mumbled halfway to himself.

"Okay Luke, I can't tell you now. But let me know how this goes. I mean if we get by with hundreds and all........" his words trailed off. "Let me do some more work on this. I may have a great idea but I want to hold off on telling you until I clear some more details."

"Okay," Luke shrugged and went back to work. He was used to these great ideas that would suddenly pop into Birdseed's head—these thunderbolts of inspiration. Most times they came to nothing.

To his great relief, Luke's work passed muster. Mr. Stevens glanced at the folded stack of papers and cast them aside.

The "Birdseed method" caught on immediately. The author of the procedure advised the convicted students. Being the smartest kid in his class, he never got in trouble. A close shave every now and then, but generally speaking, "such a darling little boy" as far as the teachers were concerned. Little did they know.

To camouflage the new technique, he suggested that the first page be done in the conventional way, converting to groups of hundreds afterwards.

Teachers now had began to adopt the "alternative punishment" to a large degree on their own and without the necessity of a trip to the principal's office. The punishment was at an epidemic stage. The teachers even turned their heads when the figuring was done in class, relieved that trouble makers were at least subdued during their hour of guard duty. Consequently, not a day went by that several students in the three junior high grades were not saddled with numbers to do for punishment.

Then, only a few days after turning in his punishment for the lunch room offense, Luke got tagged again. This time by the science teacher, Miss McDermott. He took an eraser from the board and powdered Norma June Jackson's desk seat with a good layer of chalk dust just before she sat down. Prissy Miss Norma June was not amused when her dark blue skirt became both blue and white. Neither was Miss McDermott. Luke got "the big grand."

"Stupid! Stupid!" Luke lamented to Birdseed on their walk

home that afternoon. "I've already got into more trouble this year than I did all last year. I don't know...Norma June always prissing around putting on airs. I just.........I don't know..."

"Hey Luke," his friend offered, "We all thought it was great. She had it coming......always smirking over her good grades, looking down her nose at everybody and constantly putting on that stupid lipstick....."

"Yeah," Luke retorted uncomforted, "but y'all don't have to do the thousand."

There was a moment of silence as they began their climb up Penitentiary Hill.

"Luke, you remember the other night when I said I had an idea about.....well, about doing thousands?" Birdseed spoke in a low tone, like the whole town might want to eavesdrop.

"Well," he continued, "now is the time for it. I'll come down after supper and......well, just let me say this. Your troubles are over. And we may very well have us a money making business."

Luke listened but he didn't understand, and he didn't feel any better about the situation.

Birdseed showed up that night as promised. Luke's mother was cleaning up the kitchen and his dad had gone to Masons.

"Where's Bobby Joe?", Birdseed inquired as he stormed into Luke's room, closing the door behind him.

"I don't know. Sara Jean's I guess." Luke looked up from his paper work spread out across the bed.

Birdseed was carrying a small flat box in his hand.

"Okay Luke, feast your eyes on this." Birdseed laid the container down on the bed and gently removed the top.

It contained a neat stack of black, shiny paper.

Carbon paper.

He had seen it before, was intrigued by it. Luke had picked it out of the waste can at the lock house where it had been discarded by the lock master after making his typewritten report to Nashville. It seemed almost magical the way you could put it between paper and duplicate things. He had even used it one time when he had to write sentences in the sixth grade.

But what Birdseed had was obviously a brand new box of

it, glossy and unused.

"Where did you get that?" an astonished Luke inquired.

"From my Dad's office. He's got a lot of it. Won't even notice that it's gone," his friend answered.

Luke thought for a minute.

"Well, we can't use that stuff........I mean....the numbers......it won't work...," he injected.

"Of course we can," Birdseed spoke excitedly. "That was the whole point of breaking down the numbers into hundreds. Now it will work with carbon. We can duplicate the hundreds. One page of one hundred will become two hundred!"

Luke pondered the idea. It was too good to be true. The teachers could tell the carbon numbers. And Lord help them if Mr. Stevens noticed.

"I don't know, Birdseed...," he expressed his doubts, "I mean....they will be able to tell the carbon......"

"No they won't. This is real good carbon paper. I'll show you."

He pulled out a slick piece, took some of Luke's notebook paper and with a pencil and the aid of the flat surface of a geography book demonstrated the quality of the paper.

Luke looked and let out a low whistle.

"Boy! That is really good," he exclaimed, unable to hide his glee.

"Here. This piece is your's. You can knock out your thousand in no time. Turn it in to Miss McDermott. If it flies, we're on our way."

Birdseed then laid out his scheme. They would bring in a couple of more—Jimmy Don Baker and Norris Trapp maybe. Real good, solid kind. Donkey and Jack wouldn't work because they were both in the eighth grade and more interested in impressing the ninth graders than anything else. Besides, it would be hard to co-ordinate things with them.

Anyway, it would be a partnership. With the use of the carbon paper, they would all four work at doing thousands by the hundreds, stockpiling them and selling them. They could work on them during school, especially in study hall.

"I've even found a place where we can stash them away," Birdseed summed up feverishly. "You know the old, closed-in wooden steps leading out of the basement to the window? It's a fire escape, never used, right? Well there's a crawl space underneath. Has a door on it. I believe they used to keep supplies under there. Anyway, there's a hasp on the door. I'll get us a combination lock for it. Only you and me will know the combination. I'll take the one off my locker."

Luke was trying to take it all in. Birdseed was beside himself and talking so fast that it was difficult to follow him.

"We'll set a price—50 cents a thousand. It will be a gold mine."

Birdseed could see that his friend was skeptical.

"Okay, okay," he reassured Luke. "Just leave it up to me. I'll handle the business part of it. You and Jimmy Don and Norris just do as I tell you. Primarily, just turn out the numbers. I'll take care of the rest."

A sly grin broke across his face and his eyes sparkled through the large lens of his glasses. "Just try to stay out of trouble will you? You'll eat up all our profits."

If the teachers were suspicious, they did not show it. But almost immediately there were four boys in the eighth grade who became unusually quiet in class. The foursome—Birdseed, Luke, Jimmy Don, and Norris penciled busily during most of their classes and study hall. Hiding the carbon paper and figuring under the cover of their notebook, they furtively piled up the numbers. As they did, Birdseed began to deposit them in a shoe box underneath the steps—behind the combination lock. He then went to work quietly, working with those who fell victim to student discipline.

The word went out throughout the three grades. Birdseed could get you numbers—in a hurry. Within a week he was meeting two to three people each morning in the basement next to the fire escape. Contraband math exchanged hands for gold in these brief, clandestine encounters. The firm cranked out the numbers, as Birdseed kept the boys supplied with crisp, new carbon paper and handled the finances.

Business hummed along well for the first week, and on

payday the crew divided up the profits. They made a dollar and a half apiece.

Toward the end of the second week they ran into their first wrinkle.

The chairman of the board passed around a note in last period study hall. They needed to meet after school.

The four of them congregated at the corner of the school yard and began their trek up Main Street to town.

"We got a problem," Birdseed somberly got straight to the point. "Corky Smith owes us money and won't pay."

Corky Smith was a ninth grader, a rough neck from the bad part of Catawba who was old enough to be over at the high school. He was short—stunted by cigarette smoking no doubt—but as stout as a bull. Corky had a nasty reputation as both a trouble-maker and ferocious fighter. In spite of his stature, most everyone was afraid of him. His surliness and blackened teeth only added to the menacing persona.

"I made a big mistake," Birdseed went on to his muted partners. "I gave him three thousand on credit. Said he'd pay later. Now he says he ain't paying nothing."

They walked on in silence, all of them letting the full weight of Corky Smith press down upon their shoulders.

"I'd say forget it," Luke finally spoke. Jimmy Don and Norris nodded in agreement.

"I mean, you made a mistake. Why in the world would you ever trust Corky Smith? It was a terrible risk.....like a....well, like a bad loan I guess that banks make some times. Besides, the guy's into so much trouble, he'll need us again. We can sock him then."

"Well," Birdseed responded, "it's not quite that simple. I mean...." he hesitated for a moment. "We have some other people who owe us......."

All of them looked at Birdseed in astonishment.

"I mean not many...just a couple. But we can't let Corky get away with it. Listen, a lot of the guys can't come up with that money when they need the goods. I mean—Turtle Adams got five thousand the other day, plus five licks with the paddle—for throwing a rock at the school bus and chipping a window. I mean, how is he going to come up with two dollars and a half before he needs the numbers? If we are going to do business, stay in business, we're gonna have to do some credit."

The others listened intently.

"Okay," Norris finally chimed in. "I got an idea. Birdseed, you go up to Corky and say, 'Corky, you big piece of crap...either pay up or I'll stomp your ass.' "

They all laughed.

"Here's my idea," Birdseed returned to business. "I say we hire someone to collect the debt. Someone who can handle Corky—I mean really handle him. We give them half to collect it."

"Who in the world could we get to take on Corky Smith?" Jimmy Don inquired.

"Maybe Jack," injected Norris.

"Jack and Corky are big buddies. I see them at the store together at dinner. Besides, Jack would think it was crazy. Kinda like I do," Luke explained.

Birdseed heard them out, and then spoke, "I got the man. Randall Harper."

Randall Harper was a big, raw boned, red headed farm boy from out in the county. He was muscular and strong, and had already whipped a couple of ninth graders.

"He's poor. You can look at his clothes and tell he needs the money. We all know he can do it." Birdseed argued.

There was a long silence as the boys neared downtown and Charlie's Pool Hall. A fleet of yellow school buses blew past them. A couple of them were headed for Catawba. On one was Corky Smith.

"I don't know guys," Luke was skeptical. "I mean, I think we're going overboard with this thing. We're making a mountain out of a mole hill. So Corky Smith owes us money. He probably owes half the school money. Who's gonna bug Corky Smith? I mean......" his doubts trailed off.

What he didn't say, but what he was thinking was that Birdseed had been reading too many gangster stories. He was surprised he wasn't munching on a cigar and talking like James

Cagney.

"Fine. Fine. Just forget it. If we don't collect this debt we might as well fold up the operation. Either we follow through on this, or.........." Birdseed was almost yelling, his face contorted with rage..... "or I quit."

The proclamation fell hard upon them. A few moments passed.

"Okay Birdseed...." Norris spoke up, "you take care of it, and we'll go along with it. Right Jimmy Don......Luke?" They both nodded reluctantly.

"I'll take care of it," Birdseed ended the conversation with a firm assurance.

The very next afternoon Luke ran into Corky Smith after school. Their nemesis was waiting to board the school bus to Catawba. Corky stood under a mulberry tree taking a last few drags off of a cigarette while the other kids loaded onto the golden carriage. Luke was heading across the corner of the school yard toward town. Standing there all alone, Corky looked approachable. Luke decided to give it a try.

Nervously he walked over and tried to strike up some conversation with the strong man. Luke barely knew Corky except by reputation. Good enough to speak—if Corky ever spoke. But basically they were strangers. It was an awkward situation for him. Luke would not be able to even remember later how he struck up the conversation, nor how he broached the subject of the debt. His heart was pounding, his mouth dry, and his mind was a jumble of disconnected thoughts. His words were incoherent and it seemed like his voice was coming from somewhere else. He knew Corky was listening because his eyes burned into Luke with a fierceness that reflected unknown demons from within. But there was no response. After a very short while, Corky flipped the butt of his cigarette to the ground disdainfully, and crushed it with his foot. Without a word, he turned and got on the bus. He had hardly acknowledged Luke's existence.

Shaken and relieved, Luke turned and headed down the wide gravel driveway toward the street. At least he had given it a try. While he now had second thoughts about the effort, at the time it had seemed like the thing to do. Try to talk it out. Now all he could remember about the conversation was that Corky Smith was already shaving.

On the following Monday there was one helluva fight at the store during dinner.

Luke had been playing basketball on the outdoor goals up behind the school. He saw the debris of the encounter, however, in the middle of fourth period class when Randall Harper returned to class from the principal's office.

Randall was a mess. His shirt was torn in half—even the white undershirt was soiled. His lip was busted and swollen, and his left eye was frozen shut and blown up the size of an egg. Blood was still caked under his bloated nose.

Luke had already received the other bad news. Corky Smith received not a scratch.

It was a day which would live in infamy for Luke. From that time forth, and for several weeks, his life would become one of torment and agony.

For some reason—perhaps because he had approached Corky himself about the business debt—the school yard terror was convinced that it had been Luke and Luke alone who had hired Randall Harper to do his dirty work. Consequently, Corky Smith placed Luke Cameron on his most wanted list.

Corky first sent word that he wanted to see him. Thinking it might be about the money, Luke met him at the store before school. Corky proceeded to challenge Luke to a fight. Petrified with fright, Luke backed down under Corky's taunts and the snickering of the gathering. Humiliated, Luke retreated to the safety of the school. Corky smelled the fear of his prey and proceeded to terrorize him at every turn.

In the hallways between classes, the bully went out of his way to either bump him with a shoulder or utter some obscenity at Luke under his breath. The store was now off limits to Luke, unless he wanted to be smeared by Corky Smith. He lingered in the school in the afternoons until he knew that his nemesis was on the school bus for Catawba and safely on his way out of town.

Luke was a coward, and he knew it. Worst of all, his

friends knew it. Worse than even that, the entire student body—including the budding young girls—knew it.

Fortunately for Luke, he and Corky were not in the same class. Also, Corky lived in Catawba so Luke's weekends were free of the menace—except for the dread of Monday mornings. Then, high school basketball games began at Catawba. He and his parents would go to watch Bobby Joe play. Luke stayed close to his mom and dad, cowering under the glare of Corky Smith from across the gym.

With each passing day, it became an increasingly miserable life.

Luke had been afraid before, but he had never lived in constant fear. It was his first encounter with the paralyzing and inescapable shadow of dread.

He made a gallant effort to be brave, to be the strong silent type and not even talk about it with Birdseed. But soon he had to have some relief for his pent-up anxiety. So the two friends began to talk about the problem—periodically at first. But then it became almost the full measure of their conversations. Luke did most of the talking, bemoaning his plight. Birdseed listened sympathetically.

On one occasion, Birdseed screwed his courage to the sticking place and offered to throw himself into the fire for his friend.

"Maybe I should tell Corky," he spoke timidly "......I mean, we know it was me who put Randall Harper up to it. It really wasn't you. It really isn't fair....I'll just tell him the truth......and....." his voice trailed off into fearful silence.

Luke's first reaction was to jump at the offer, his agony was so intense. It was only fair. It was all Birdseed's fault. Luke had been against the crazy scheme from the start. Let Birdseed reap the harvest of his own machination.

But he looked at his wimpy little friend and knew it would not do.

First of all, Corky Smith might beat the hell out of Luke Cameron. But he would *kill* Richard "Birdseed" Barrett. The thought of it made Luke cringe. Also, Luke had this gut feeling that Corky would not believe it. He was too set on his target, enjoying the stalking and torturing of his subject too much. Corky Smith would not even consider the diminutive little bookworm with the glasses worth a second thought. Worse yet, he might just brutalize them both at the same time.

"That's a nice gesture, Birdseed," Luke replied, "but I really don't think that would do any good. Might only make it worse."

Birdseed did not argue, and Luke detected a huge sigh of relief from his friend.

One afternoon, Birdseed, Jack, Donkey and he were trudging home down Main Street, just a short distance from the school. The yellow school buses rolled past. There in the back of the Catawba bus, staring out the window, was the infamous visage. A sinister smile crossed the face of Corky Smith as he raised his middle right finger and flipped an obscene gesture, directed at the group, but, without doubt, intended only for Luke Cameron. All of them saw it, but no one spoke a word.

Jack and Donkey split off to their homes.

"Birdseed," Luke calmly spoke, "I can't go on like this. I've been thinking about this a lot.......and....well, I'm gonna have to face the music."

Birdseed knew what he meant and turned to study Luke's face. There was both a look of resignation and relief. A sense of purpose was in his voice, even a hint of bravery. Birdseed was a bit mesmerized by the look in Luke's eye. He continued to examine his friend.

Funny thing, Birdseed thought to himself. You grow up with a guy, see him every day, practically live with him. But you hardly ever look at him. Really look at him.

An uplifting realization came over Birdseed.

Luke Cameron was no slouch of a boy. He was an outstanding athlete, strong swimmer, and as hard as a rock. Luke was getting tall, actually taller than Corky Smith. Even though he would be considered skinny, Luke was broad at the shoulders now thickening from hours behind a push mower, garden plow, and stemming the surging currents of the Cumberland River sand bars. His arms were long, if spindly, and his hands huge for his age.

While he might not be a match for the Catawba pugilist, Luke Cameron was capable of causing a lot of hurt.

"You're right, Luke," Birdseed said, "You're gonna have to fight him once and for all. And the only way you can be rid of him once and for all is that you give him enough of a good fight so that he won't want to make you a regular meal."

Luke began to feel the spirit in him rise. He was tired of being a coward. It was unbecoming of a Cameron. His dad would have been enraged. For the first time the oppressive weight of fear began to lift, challenged now by an embryonic anger.

"I may not be able to whip Corky Smith, Birdseed, but I can make him wish he had never picked on me." There was a cold, steely hardness in Luke's voice. "You wait and see."

The worm had turned.

Luke's problem with Corky Smith was far from over. But he could now see an end to his nightmare—however painful that end might be. A sense of commitment and determination replaced his consternation. He would be ready.

Suddenly Luke and Birdseed flew into a frenzy of words and ideas.

A mission was forged. Luke would go into training.

The back room of Luke's basement turned into the gym. It was pretty grim—concrete floor, musty smell, and a single light bulb hanging down from a cord. But soon it hummed with activity.

They recovered Bobby Joe's old home-made weights—a pipe anchored on both ends by discarded paint cans filled with concrete. Birdseed moved his punching bag over to the basement from his house, and they mounted it on a wooden frame. Norris donated a set of tension springs with handles for chest exercises. A jump rope, rubber ball for squeezing, and a feed sack filled with sawdust hanging from a wooden beam made up the rest of the equipment. Birdseed brought in a large ginger ale bottle, bound to the neck with surgical tape for their water jug. Just like the real boxers.

On the wall they placed a small blackboard on which they listed the daily regimen and kept tabs with the workouts.

Each night after supper, Luke and Birdseed would meet in the gym—the latter coming in through the window.   With his neighbor's encouragement, Luke began to pump the iron—or concrete as it was—and jump rope. After some effort, he learned to punch the bag with the rhythm of a pro.   Each night he increased his repetition and kept up with his progress on the blackboard. An old alarm clock measured each segment of the workout. Although it was now winter weather and the basement dank and cold, Luke always worked up a heavy sweat.

The strenuous activity was doing wonders for Luke's morale. He suffered the daily humiliations and degradation with aplomb now, knowing that he was preparing to put an end to it all.

He got caught up in the drama of it. Even at church, he hooked in emotionally for the first time to some of the Biblical accounts of personal courage and heroism, such as David and Goliath. The stirring anthems seemed to be written just for him.

Luke began to think deeply about the quest upon which he was afloat. He became curious about the emotional pull and take of fear, challenge, and courage.

A couple of years back Bobby Joe had heroically bested a detested and overbearing bully in his class. One night Luke gingerly maneuvered the conversation with his older brother around to that grand encounter.

"Tell me about the time you whipped Oran Moxford," he inquired.

"What about it?" Bobby Joe casually responded.

"Well....what happened?" Luke persisted.

"Not much to it. He called me a bad name.....actually called your mother a bad name, and I beat the hell out of him."

Pretty simple.

"Were you scared?" Luke pushed on.

"Scared of what?" big bubba asked quizzically.

Bobby Joe was no help.

In preparing himself mentally for the big event, Luke spent hours alone hiking along the river bank. He did a lot of praying, mostly for courage.

On a Friday night in early December, he had been in training religiously for several weeks. It was raining and the weather unusually warm. Luke and Birdseed sat on a wooden bench in the gym just after a rigorous work out. Luke was mopping the sweat from his face. The moist night air seeping in from the open window was refreshing. Their conversation was easy and relaxed, caressed by the gentle cadence of the winter shower.

Luke knew he was much stronger from the training. The number of curls and lifts of the weights had tripled since he started. Same with the jumping rope. The spring, taut and difficult at first, was now easy work. All in all, he felt good about himself.

After a lull in the conversation, Luke made the announcement.

"One more week Birdseed, and I'll be ready. I want to get this over with before Christmas."

"Yeah, you're right, Luke," Birdseed agreed, " I think you're in great shape. And you don't want this hanging over you over the Christmas vacation."

They were both quiet for a moment. The silence of the big old house hanging over them seemed to envelop the young warrior and his trainer. Only the steady fall of the rain could be heard.

"How are you going to do it?" Birdseed inquired.

Luke knew what he meant and gave it some deep thought.

"I don't know. Guess I could just go over to the store at dinner. I'm sure he'd take care of the rest. Maybe send a message and have him meet me after school."

Birdseed pondered it.

"I say after school. That way, no matter how it comes out Corky will at least miss his bus home." Birdseed spoke airily with just a trace of a grin.

Luke smiled. They sat there for a long while in silence, lost in their own thoughts, pondering the epochal struggle in which they were engaged.

Finally, Birdseed bid good-night, climbed through the open window and headed home.

Luke pulled the chain on the light and sat in the darkness for a long time.

The next day was a Saturday. In the afternoon, Donkey,

and Perky Perkins and Luke shot pool until the 3 o'clock drawing. There they ran into Birdseed, returned to the pool room and sat on the stoop and talked. After a while Birdseed and Luke decided to go home and shoot some basketball.

The matinee crowd was just getting out of the picture show as they headed up the steep slope of Penitentiary Hill. Near the top of the hill, while Birdseed was babbling on about something, Luke saw him.

Corky Smith.

He was standing with two of his friends thumbing a ride to Catawba.

Luke's heart leaped against his chest, and his arms and legs went limp. About that time Birdseed saw Corky and stopped talking in mid-sentence.

"Well, Birdseed," Luke was resigned to his fate, "we won't have to wait another week."

The two moved on up the sidewalk toward "hitch hike" corner in front of the Catlett house—straight into the eye of the storm.

Luke and Birdseed were almost upon the three hitch hikers when Corky spotted them. A nasty look of delightful recognition swept across his face. Good fortune had brought his spineless and skulking adversary right into his path.

"Well, look who's here, boys," he intoned to his smirking friends. "If it ain't old pantywaist and his weirdo friend."

You could almost hear Birdseed's frightful moan.

Luke kept walking up the sidewalk to where the three were standing. Corky stepped in his path.

"You'll have to pay a fee to use this sidewalk, little boy," Corky boldly declared. His friends were grinning, enjoying the fun.

Luke stopped just over an arm's length away.

"Okay, Corky," his voice was quivering but strong, "You want to fight? Then we'll fight."

Luke immediately took a fighting position, boxer-style. His left fist was raised in front of his face, with his right fist raised to the side. It was somewhat of a comical pose, like that one would see on old boxing posters—more for show than for effect.

But to Luke, he was bracing for the real thing.

With a sneer pasted on his face, Corky moved in closer and began to circle his prey. His hands were still down to his side, as if to mock Luke's readiness.

Birdseed looked on in sheer terror. Corky's friends watched in amusement, waiting for the kill.

And then, Corky Smith did something which was totally incredible. Something which his foes and friends alike would wonder about forever—something unbelievably stupid.

Apparently to further mock and humiliate what he considered to be an unworthy foe, he raised his right leg, wind-up style, high into the air and brought it down upon Luke's raised right fist. One must only assume—for Corky would never explain the purpose—that he was so disdainful of Luke's exaggerrated fighting stance that he would simply use it for a bit of showing off. For whatever reason, it was a bizarre and shocking maneuver which even startled his friends.

Corky Smith was no rocket scientist. But Luke Cameron was. And therein was the difference in the encounter.

As soon as Corky's leg came down upon Luke's fist, he instinctively grabbed it behind the knee with his right hand. The image of that moment would be forever frozen in the minds of the three spectators to this dramatic event. Corky Smith, proud victor of numberless fights, somehow now standing on only one leg, the other hiked high into the air, and held firmly by his combatant.

For one flashing moment, the eyes of the two fighters met. Corky's had the surprised look of a wild animal knowing that it had ventured one foolish step too far. Luke's had the exalted look of knowing, that regardless of the final outcome of this fight, one thing was certain. Corky Smith was going down.

And down he went. Hard.

But not before he joined Sputnik in outer space.

All of the frustrations and pent up tension Luke had experienced during Corky's reign of terror burst forth with a mighty surge. He stepped forward and thrust his loaded arm upward with a violent push. His victim's body was projected high into the air, the feet kicking at the heavens before the human missile started back to earth, head first.

Corky finally landed on his back with a crunching thud.

Life was undoubtedly going on around them—cars passing, birds singing, the water surging over the dam below. But for the four young onlookers at "hitch hike corner," time was frozen in place.

At first Corky did not move. Luke's first impulse was to plunge upon the heap at his feet and pulverize it into a bloody mess. Then the prostrate form began to slowly roll back and forth upon the ground as Luke stared straight down into the face.

Where Corky's eyes had just seconds before revealed surprise, they now were open wide in sheer terror. He could not breathe. Only a low guttural moan escaped the gaping and breathless mouth.

The urge to pounce upon his enemy was now displaced with a strangely incongruous feeling of compassion. Luke recognized the damage he had caused. The breath had been knocked out of Corky Smith—an experience most every growing boy endures at some time or another. At any time the ordeal is painful and frightening, but the first time is undescribably frightful. You know that one needs air to live. You know that you are not able to get air. Therefore, you know that you are going to die.

It was obviously Corky Smith's first encounter with the monster. He thought he was dying.

Luke knew also that it would pass. That almost as quickly as it went, breath would return to the rigid, desperate torso. There would be no lasting injury or impairment—a minor and temporary discomfort. Momentarily, the fallen adversary would be fully recovered.

If damage was to be done, it had better be done quickly. But Luke remained standing, hovering over the body. Staying him now was another feeling which came crashing in on top of his pity. If he had come this far, waded through the agonizing weeks of fear and trepidation, he would not give in to a cheap victory. The opponent lay paralyzed and helpless—easy picking. A sense of chivalry constrained him. It was undoubtedly misplaced upon this uncaring soul who had unmercifully tormented him. But it persisted nevertheless. It was a matter of sportsmanship. With the adrenalin coursing through his body, Luke was now ready to suffer the worst, toe-to-toe, hand-to-hand. But by all means—after enslavement to cowardice—absolute release, full liberation.

All of these thoughts, emotions—fragments of the soul—passed through the young lad's head in a flash, as he stood on the verge of victory, staring down into the loathsome, gasping face of Corky Smith.

Finally the victim's diaphragm collapsed into rhythmic breathing, as air—wonderful, life-giving air—began to course through Corky's frame. The horror in his eyes was transformed to a blank stare.

"Are you all right?" the words came from Luke Cameron, instinctively, without thought.

"Yeah, I'm all right," was the equally spasmodic reply.

But one could tell that Corky was not all right. Something undefinable was different. One demon had been replaced by another. He rolled over and slowly returned to his feet.

Luke stepped back, resuming his exaggerated fighting stance.

Corky faced his opponent again, not disdainfully now but with an almost puzzled look upon his face. A look of uncertainty. Luke sensed it. The fear which had been encased in his body had somehow been transplanted to Corky's. Not a trepidation easily defined nor appearing to arise from a newly acquired respect for his opponent. It was a subtle yet clearly discernible metamorphosis of the spirit. Like one coming to terms for the very first time with his vulnerability, maybe even his mortality. And that had been the only difference between the two all along-a varying perception of the same situation.

Corky looked at Luke through different eyes—not friendly, but no longer with contempt.

Then with a wave of his hand and with a false bravado in his voice he announced, "We'll call it a draw."

No one at the time recognized the humor of it.

With that startling announcement, he turned to his

stunned confederates and they began to move away.

Luke remained anchored to the spot, unwilling to leave the field of battle first. He didn't have to wait long. The Catawba trio caught a ride with the very next car, climbed inside and were off. Luke and Birdseed stood and watched the vehicle move past the penitentiary and disappear on the other side of the hill.

"Whew!" Birdseed was finally able to breathe.

"Whew! Why didn't you plaster him when he was down Luke? Why didn't you smash him to pieces?" he talked excitedly as he and Luke began to walk toward home.

Birdseed rattled on so ecstatically that he could hardly contain himself. He recounted every single word, every move, the looks on the faces of Corky's friends.

Luke hardly heard anything he said. With the momentous weight off of his shoulders, he floated home on clouds.

The victory over Corky Smith was countered by the sudden and disastrous collapse of the numbers business at school.

Terry Rogers was a struggling ninth grade student biding his time until he could reach the drop out age. He got into trouble and needed two thousand numbers. Terry approached Birdseed who cut the deal. In last period that day Birdseed passed Luke a note.

"Can you meet Terry Rogers after school and give him two thousand and take the money? I've got to get to band."

So Luke, who usually never got involved in that end of the business, met Terry at the basement steps, unlocked the door and completed the transaction. Little did he know it would be the last hurrah for the thriving business.

Everyone knew Terry Rogers was not long on gray matter. But Luke never dreamed that he would turn in his numbers the very next morning. They weren't due for a week.

Logically, Mr. Stevens was suspicious. He checked the work closely and discovered the counterfeit carbon. Terry was called into the office.

If Terry was short on brains, he was even shorter on backbone. He was quick to give up his dealer.

Luke Cameron took his place sitting nervously in the wooden chair in front of Mr. Steven's desk.

At first the principal was going to inflict three licks with the paddle. Then he thought a more poetic punishment would be three thousand numbers. And he would personally check them for foul play.

Dejectedly, he carried the bad news back to Birdseed and the board of directors. Without as much as a voice vote, they immediately dissolved the business, destroyed the evidence, and left Luke hanging with his three thousand to do.

That night Birdseed came down to check on his friend who was bleeding from every pore as the sacrificial lamb. Birdseed found him at the kitchen table, doing numbers under the dim light of the hanging bulb. Books were stacked up around him to camouflage his clandestine figuring. Bobby Joe was onto the "strange math" as he called it. But he maintained a brotherly silence.

Birdseed sat down sheepishly at the table. Luke glanced up from his work. If looks could kill, Birdseed would have been one cold cadaver.

Finally, "I'm sorry Luke."

Silence.

Birdseed fidgeted. Then, "Uh......I'll help you with them if you want me to."

Luke looked up in astonishment .

"Are you kidding?" he exclaimed. He shook his head in disbelief. Then he began to vent.

"Look, Birdseed. I'm going to do every single one of these numbers myself. Not by the tens, not by the hundreds, but by the three thousand. See!" He held his work up and stuck it into his friends face.

"Then......" He glanced at the door. Realizing that his raised voice might carry to his parents in the living room, he lowered the octave.

".......Then, I may even do an extra five hundred just for

good measure. When I finish, I'm going to take them to Mr. Steven's office. I'm not even going to fold them. I'm going to bow and crawl along the floor.......I'm going to grovel, and beg that he give me ten thousand more and ten licks with the paddle for my sins....."

His venom spent, he then turned away from his friend and returned to his "funny math."

Almost under his breath but loud enough for Birdseed to hear, he concluded "........and then......I'm going to join a monastery."

Chapter Twelve

The Raft Trip

A dead promise will come ghosting.

They were in the dog days of summer. Mid-August, with school still nearly three weeks away.

The weather was hot and dry. The parched grass and drooping trees seemed to simmer under the hazy, cloudless sky.

The river was low and tepid. Swimming in it was like taking a warm bath.

Fishing was awful. Baseball season was all but over. The lawn-mowing business had literally dried up. Gardens had either played out or burned up. The Bisbees had come and gone. The circus had come and gone.

Screen doors seemed to slam, and dogs seemed to bark in slow motion.

The only thing that thrived were flies, and they were everywhere in large numbers.

Luke, Donkey, and Jack were walking up the road from the ferry toward town. They were identically clad in blue jeans and black canvas tennis shoes—Jet high tops. They wore no shirts. Their backs were August brown.

It was mid-afternoon and they had been across the river and up to Penitentiary Springs to look for a good camping spot.

An occasional car moving down the gravel road toward the ferry would choke them with dust.

There was very little talk, and each of them was looking forward to the cool darkness of the pool hall and a cold Pepsi.

They were in behind the DX station and just a short distance from Main Street and their destination.

"See those oil barrels over there?" Luke pointed casually. "If they still have the ends in them they make a good raft. I saw a boat dock made with them one time down in Tennessee."

"Let's go see," Jack calmly responded, somewhat to Luke's surprise.

They moved through knee-high weeds to the back of the service station. Old tires, used oil filters, and a rusted tire rim littered the roasted ground.

Three empty oil barrels stood against the concrete wall which was the back of the service bay.

"Hey, all three still have the ends, and the plugs are still in them too," Luke exclaimed with some excitement. "You don't see that very often. Most ones I see have the whole end cut out."

Jack kicked one to make sure it was empty.

"Let's take 'em," he said.

Luke and Donkey looked at him quizically.

"We can take 'em. Keep 'em. Who knows, maybe we'll make a raft," he insisted.

"I think these things are expensive," Luke interjected, "I mean, I think they have to pay the oil company for these things, or . . . like deposits on drink bottles . . . or something . . ."

Jack surveyed the premises. Luke could tell his mind was turning.

Then in a lowered voice, "We could come back here at night and steal them."

All three were silent, thinking.

"But we need about three more for a raft," Luke said, as much to himself as to the other two. "Let's go ask Fish about it. Maybe he can give us a good deal on them, and get us three more."

They hurried around to the front of the building.

Fish was sitting in a cane-bottom chair leaned against a shaded front wall of the station, between the two open service bays.

He was close to thirty-five years of age, and his long brown hair was slicked straight back. He was cramming a Payday candy bar into his mouth with one hand while holding a half-filled Pepsi bottle in the other. His teeth were black with decay.

An old Philco radio with the cover missing and parts exposed was blaring out Pat Boone's "Love Letters in the Sand" from the workbench in the back.

Fish was a friendly guy, well liked by all the boys.

Luke was right. Fish told them the oil company credited him two dollars for each barrel he turned back in. It would cost them two dollars apiece.

He'd have a couple more ready on Monday.

Now energized by the prospects of a new and exciting project, they headed for the pool hall, where they bought their cold drinks. They sat down on the stoop out front, where they swigged and talked.

"How much money can y'all come up with?" Luke inquired.

"Right now? Maybe two bucks," Jack responded.

Donkey concurred.

"Me too. But that leaves us three barrels short," Luke observed.

They thought and discussed. Times were hard. No lawns to mow. No coal to take in. No catalpa worms to sell. Nothing.

"I say we go back tonight and heist 'em," Jack proclaimed.

"Are you crazy?" Luke argued, "Ole Fish may not be no Einstein but I think he could figure that one out. Then we'd be cooked for good."

There was silence. Then they talked some more.

Finally the conversation dried up like the grass, and they went home.

The next day, which was a Saturday, manna fell from heaven.

First of all, Birdseed won the drawing—first place.

Five bucks was the prize. It was the first time any of Luke's friends had won first prize. Luke himself had won two dollars once—the third place prize.

The three didn't even have to discuss the matter among themselves. Immediately after the drawing, when the crowd was heading back to town from the riverbank, they instinctively converged on Birdseed.

Quickly they told him of their plans to build a raft.

They talked about material. They talked about the barrels. Then they talked about costs.

Birdseed got the picture. He liked the idea. He was in.

Most important, his newly acquired wealth was in.

"But where are we going on a raft? New Orleans?" he asked sarcastically as an afterthought.

"Who knows? Let's get it built first. Then we can worry about that," Donkey explained to everyone's satisfaction.

Manna continued to fall.

Later on that day, on their way home, Donkey and Jack saw another barrel with the top still in behind the Standard Station. They checked it out, and to their amazement and joy, the owner said they could have it for free.

"He must have a different deal going," Jack quipped to Donkey as they quickly grabbed it and rolled it out the street to Donkey's house.

On Monday the new barrels came in. The day was filled with frenzied activity. After the money was paid, they began collecting their wares and grouping them down on the riverbank.

After some reflection and discussion, it was decided that the raft needed to be constructed downriver, below the lock and dam.

"I thought your old man told you that they had to lock anything that wanted to go through even if they were riding on a log," Jack teased Luke.

"That's right," he retorted, "but why take a chance? Besides, it could get complicated. I mean, it might come apart in the locks."

So with great effort they rolled the metal cylinders downriver—across the lock wall, up the high embankment, along the edge of the cornfield, and finally into the heavy thicket of weeds which hovered over the river's edge. There at last they proudly hid them in a small clearing.

Sweating from the work, they threw themselves upon the ground and rested.

The first stage was completed. Now the fun began.

Planning and building the raft.

They talked about how they would proceed. The plan was simple. A wooden frame with a lip which would collar the barrels and then the wooden decking.

The rest of the day was spent requisitioning the needed lumber—old two by fours, and planks. They broke up into two teams and scoured the town. Most of the needed material was found under Luke's back porch where his father had stacked used but useful old lumber.

The next morning they arrived at the site early with tools from home—hammers, saws, and nails.

For hours the sounds of hammering and sawing echoed up and down the riverbank. The boys ignored the dripping humidity and worked feverishly. Their dogs laid stretched out in the shade of the willows and horseweeds, ignoring the gnats and flies encircling them.

By mid-afternoon the framing and rim part of the decking was finished. It was big, about ten feet square.

On a rest break they proudly surveyed their work.

"Grab the end there, Donkey," Jack said, jumping to his feet.

Donkey and Jack each grabbed an opposite side and lifted. It was heavy.

"Oh boy!" Jack exclaimed as they raised it a couple of feet and dropped it back to the ground. "We'd better get this thing on the barrels in the water. If we finish the decking up here we'll have a helluva time moving it."

They all agreed.

The next step was a lot harder than any of them had imagined.

They rolled the huge barrels down the steep bank, along a narrow sandbar which jutted out into the river a ways. The stream was low and barely moving. Protected by the sandbar was a small embayment which fingered in toward the steep bank—"slackwater" was the river term. There they floated the barrels in waist-deep water.

With great effort they then wrestled the large wooden frame down the bank along the same path to the water's edge. Grunting and swearing, all four waded out into the water with the unfinished raft on their shoulders. The soft, muddy bottom made the job even more cumbersome.

While Jack and Donkey held the frame aloft, Luke and Birdseed tried to group the barrels into place—two rows, three abreast. Finally, after much effort, the frame came down on the buoyant floats and collared them under its weight.

"Looking good!" Birdseed cheered as the crude-looking craft floated on the water.

They pulled it to the bank and fetched their tools and planking.

The four o'clock whistle at the prison groaned out its familiar message. Still the four boys worked on. Finally, with the decking almost finished, they ran out of wood.

After grounding the raft onto the sandy bank, they stripped and went swimming. Frolicking and splashing in the water, they relaxed from their hard day of work. Gradually they begin to wind down, and finally lay down in the sun along the sandy edge.

They grew quiet and closed their eyes.

"Four o'clock whistle blown yet?" Birdseed broke the silence.

"Yep," answered Luke. "About an hour ago."

"No way!" Birdseed leaped to his feet and grabbed his clothes and put on his glasses. "Time to go home."

The others didn't move. Soon Birdseed was dressed.

"My hair look dry?" he asked anxiously. It was a standard check Birdseed made after swimming in the river. Wet hair was a dead giveaway to his parents.

"Yeah," Jack opened his eyes. "But you got mud all over

the top of your head."

As he said it he leapt to his feet and brought a fistful of Cumberland River mush down on top of Birdseed's head.

It was a bad scene. Mud on Birdseed's head and face, and all over his glasses.

Luke and Donkey rolled with laughter.

Birdseed cursed and cried, "You son of a bitch!" Then he ran down the bank with his head bent to the ground trying desperately to keep his T-shirt and pants from being soiled. He made it to the water's edge and cleansed himself of the foul act.

Still fuming and swearing, he finally headed for home.

They were still laughing and putting on their clothes when a boat sounded its horn. It was *The Virginia* coming around the bend and heading up the straight stretch of river to the lock. It was pushing twelve empty grain barges.

The boys sat on the bank and watched her pass. Its big white tow rumbled by, churning the placid river into a white boil. A cook, wearing a large blue apron came out of the door at the back of the boat and threw a bucket of potato peelings into the river. He turned to head back into the galley when he caught sight of the boys. He waved and they waved back.

Three sun-worn boys on a riverbank in late summer, captured for a few fleeting moments by a passing ship.

As the boat moved on up the river, the sound of its mighty movement began to subside. Slowly this common event with uncommon effect began to loosen its spell and they began to stir.

The raft was secured, and they picked up their tools and headed for home.

"See you here in the morning with some more wood," Luke said as he parted company with the other two and turned up the river road toward his house.

"OK," was all the tired couple could muster as they moved up the river toward town.

It didn't take them long the next morning to finish the decking. Birdseed was back without the slightest hint of any resentment for the previous day's dirty deal.

A rope was hooked to the front of the raft and tied off to a leaning willow. They made two heavy oars from two-by-fours and squares of plywood sawed to a rough point. They were long and unwieldy, but with much a do, would turn the raft.

Finished with their work, the boys jumped up and down on the vessel with glee. Its deck sat high and dry about two feet above the water line. It was definitely a fine piece of work, and they could not hide their pride and excitement.

"Hey, you guys," Birdseed exclaimed, as if just remembering something important. He got their attention and thought for just a moment. "You guys wait right here. I'll be right back." With that command, he bounced off the raft and scampered hurriedly up the bank.

"Where you going, Birdseed?" Donkey yelled after him.

"Just hold everything. I'll be right back," was his only reply as he disappeared into the horseweeds.

They looked at each other and shrugged, and then turned their attention to other things.

"Well it's time to start making our plans for the trip, boys," Luke remarked as he lay down on the pontoon and swept his hand over the side and dashed his face with water.

He turned over on his back and closed his eyes. It was so hot and humid that the river seemed to simmer. Donkey and Jack lay down beside him.

There was silence as all three contemplated the possibilities. Several minutes passed without anyone speaking.

Finally Donkey broke the long silence, "How many nights will our folks let us go out on this thing? How far can we go in three days.....two days, or whatever?"

"Paducah. That's a good destination," Jack interjected.

"I don't know. That means we'd be on the Ohio for a while. Smithland . . . that's forty-three miles by water. Maybe three days. Not much current," Luke said.

They all turned at the same time and looked out at the river. It looked like glass.

"I say we just tell our folks, a couple of nights. See how far we get. We could always call 'em and go farther." Luke spoke thoughtfully.

Suddenly Birdseed popped out of the river weeds and bounded down the bank.

In his right hand, he carried an unopened bottle of 7-Up. The three bewildered sunbathers stared at their friend who was winded and panting.

"All right . . . " Birdseed commenced between gasps for air, ". . . it's time to christen this mama . . . "

"What're you talkin' about, Birdseed . . . and where you been?" Jack responded.

"Wrinklemeat's," he answered, still catching his breath. We're gonna do this up right. We're really supposed to use champagne . . . but, well, Wrinklemeat's was a little low on champagne this afternoon," he grinned.

Birdseed was really into it, and his enthusiasm was somewhat contagious. He began to give directions to everyone.

"Pull the raft in here a bit . . . everyone gather around . . . and . . . "

Birdseed flipped the bottle in his hand and held it by its neck.

"It may take a little force to break this thing over the raft, so maybe you ought to do it, Jack. You do the honors."

Birdseed handed the fizzing 7-Up to Jack.

He tentatively reached out and took the bottle by the neck, not really sure as to what it was all about nor what he was supposed to do.

"Wait a minute! Wait a minute!" Birdseed exclaimed like he had forgotten some detail of momentous importance. "We gotta have a name. We can't christen it without a name."

"A name?" They all spoke in unison, with identical quizzical looks.

"Yeah . . . " Birdseed was undaunted. "We have to name it. Think. What would be a good name?"

It was easier to just go along, so they all began to think.

They threw out some possibilities, but all were discarded.

Finally Birdseed exclaimed, "I got it! You know the *Delta Queen* . . . the big paddle wheeler . . . "

They nodded.

"We'll name this . . . the *Delta Dream!*"

Birdseed beamed with pride.

"Sounds good to me," Donkey quickly answered, more to end the matter than enamored with the name.

"Okay, Jack. Raise the bottle . . . " Birdseed seized the moment. "You gotta break it across the bow."

Everyone watched attentively as Jack. raised the bottle high over his head.

"I christen thee—the *Delta Dream!*" he announced and signaled Jack with a downward motion of his hand.

Down came the 7-Up bottle, striking the wooden decking with a heavy thud.

It didn't break.

Without hesitation Jack raised it again. This time he brought it down with greater force.

The bottle broke. 7-Up, glass and blood flew everywhere. Jack yelled and quickly discarded the jagged neck of the bottle.

Jack's wound was gushing crimson, dripping onto the deck of the raft in mighty drops and even into the water.

"Good grief!" exclaimed Luke for all of them. They stared at the gory scene.

But Jack was the least affected. He peered at the bloody index finger, and then sunk it into the water beside the raft.

After a quick rinsing, he lifted his hand toward his face and surveyed the damage. Donkey, Birdseed, and Luke all crowded around with concern.

There were anxious moments as they all stared.

Jack pulled apart the deep gash which half encircled the finger at the middle joint.

"Looks pretty bad . . . " Luke finally spoke. "May need some stitches."

"Naw . . . " Jack spoke matter-of-factly, "a little coal oil will do the trick." He moved to his clothes on the bank and jerked a handkerchief from the back pocket of his jeans. He carefully wrapped it around the finger and tied it. The blood at first found its way through the bandage, but then ebbed to a stop.

"It's okay," Jack insisted and the swimmers began to put on

their clothes.

"I say we leave on Monday and tell our folks that we will be gone for two nights," said Jack, getting back to business.

They all nodded in agreement, tied their shoes, and began to move up the bank. A quietness settled over the group as they realized the moment of truth had come. It was time to get clearance at home for the maiden voyage of the *Delta Dream*.

❧

Luke studied his father closely at supper that night.

Bobby Joe, as usual, had wolfed down his meal, excused himself, and headed for his girlfriend's house.

That left Luke and his Mom and Dad finishing up the evening meal.

He listened to the casual conversation of his parents, pacing himself as he nervously waited for his father to finish.

A slight breeze came off the river and through the open windows, offering some respite from the heated kitchen. The late evening sun filtered through the tall sycamore hovering over the back porch and covering the open doorway. An eager chorus of katydids were getting a head start on their nightly requiem.

Finally Alec took a last sip of his coffee, pushed his chair back from the table, crossed his legs and lit up a cigarette.

Luke's Mom rose from her chair and began to collect the dirty dishes.

"What are you gonna do after supper, Dad?" Luke asked as nonchalantly as he could.

"Don't know," Alec took a drag off his Camel, exhaled, leaned forward with his elbows on the table, and with just a hint of a smile looked into Luke's eyes. "What do you want me to do, Pumpkin?"

Luke was right about his Dad's mood. Anytime Alec called him Pumpkin, he was in a good humor.

Feeling more confident, Luke pushed on. "Well, I'd like to show you something."

"Okay. Bring it in," Alec said good naturedly.

"Well . . . it's not . . . it's not in the house. It's . . . down at the river."

"Hmm. Don't tell me you have another possum caged down there . . . or a litter of pups," His Dad smiled.

"Naw, nothing like that . . . just something I'd like for you to see. Something I'd just like to show you."

Puzzled, Alec reached over and killed his cigarette in a saucer.

"Well, let's go take a look."

Father and son headed down the river road now shaded by the mingled growth of full-grown corn and weeds on each side.

They reached the river, and turned off on the dirt path leading downstream. Shortly, both were in the world of horse-weeds and Johnson grass, until they reached the top of the river-bank.

There, a few feet below and secured to the sandbar, was the raft.

Luke pointed, "What do you think of that?"

Alec peered down only for a moment, and then with the agility of a teenager, he bounded down the bank, across the sand-bar and onto the vessel.

He surveyed every corner, obviously amused. Like some kind of ship inspector, he bounced up and down in the middle and stepped on the corners. The raft hardly broke the water.

Luke beamed.

After a few more moments of inspection, Alec inquired, "Where'd you get the barrels?"

Luke explained.

He could tell that his father was impressed. Alec kept walking around the raft with a discernible twinkle in his eye and a slightly turned up corner of the mouth.

"What're you gonna do with it?" he asked, genuinely inter-ested.

It was the critical question. Crunch time. Luke proceed-ed cautiously, with his heart in his throat.

"We . . . uh, we would like to take it downriver for one or

two nights . . . " He had gotten it out.

"Who's 'we'?" came the response.

Luke told him.

Alec then silently began the universal agony of father-hood—the timeworn process of parental decision making. His forehead furrowed as he considered the petition with its risks, dangers, hazards, and awful possibilities. Weighing all within the space of a few moments, an ordinary decision with potentially extraordinary consequences. On the rational side of the scale is the heavy weight of concern—the prospects of bad things, nightmarish possibilities, doubts, and the needlessness of it all.

On the other side of the scale is nothing. Nothing, that is, except that part of a father which is still a boy, and thinks like a boy.

It is a mighty weight.

Luke was waiting breathlessly, for what seemed like an eternity.

Alec lit up a cigarette, took a long drag, and exhaled. Finally he spoke. "Well . . . whatever you do, don't take this thing out on the river after dark. You understand?"

He peered sternly at Luke, who could hardly conceal his joy.

"Yes, sir," was the quick reply.

The day broke clear, and the pale blue sky gave promise of another day of searing heat.

Four creatures moved along the riverbank in single file, the morning dew soaking their pant legs up to the knees.

Three of them were laden with camping gear, making them look like ants, with loads disproportionate to their size.

To no one's surprise, Birdseed's parents would not let him go.

But he was coming along cheerfully to bid his friends adieu.

Donkey had resorted to deceit in the oldest con game

known to childhood.

He had told his folks he was going fishing and spending the night with Jack. They were advised that he and Jack were camping out the second night up by the cemetery.

Only Luke and Jack were carrying legitimate passports.

Excited, they dumped their gear on the *Delta Dream*, spreading out their sleeping bags and blankets. Their duffel bags and packs containing food and other provisions were stacked in the middle. This protected their wares from falling overboard and also provided backrests on which to lounge.

Birdseed was a pitiful sight, although he valiantly attempted to keep up a good front.

His friends were kind.

"Don't worry about it Birdseed. We'll probably all drown and you can tell everyone how you tried to keep us from taking such a foolhardy trip," stated Luke.

"That's right," chimed in Donkey, "it's going to be hotter 'n hell out there anyway."

At a little after seven, they picked up the large oars and shoved off. With some effort the bulky vessel moved out of the slackwater and toward the thread of the river.

"Send me a postcard," shouted Birdseed good naturedly from the bank, "and watch out for the naked women."

"There you go, Birdseed," answered Jack as he wrestled with an oar, "always thinking about sex."

There was hardly any current as the vessel sluggishly moved along at the low summer pool. The high banks and trees blocked the early morning sun and shaded the stream. A slight mist was rising to be inhaled by the eager sun.

The raft drifted slowly to the point where Birdseed appeared dwarflike. Still he remained on the bank, his eyes fixed on his departing friends.

Fully under way, the deckhands of the *Delta Dream* laid their heavy oars aside, and fell jubilantly back on their blankets and sleeping bags. They propped themselves against their makeshift back supports.

It was a wonderful and exhilarating feeling—on the river,

liberated from parental control, and off to unknown sights and adventure—youthful Caesars lounging on their summer couches, watching the river scene pass by.

They jabbered excitedly and incessantly about the trip, gazing out at the banks which went ever so slowly by.

The first bend in the river took its toll as Birdseed began to slip behind the willows and out of sight. Silence fell upon the crew as they peered back for a final look at their less fortunate friend.

Finally, Luke broke the spell. "You think Birdseed knew all along he wouldn't be able to go?"

"Yeah, he knew," Jack stated flatly.

"But . . . he showed such enthusiasm, such . . . I don't know . . . it was like he knew he was going. He was so excited," Luke continued on.

"It was all a show . . . " Donkey interjected, "....or maybe he was just excited for us. Birdseed . . . with his parents . . . he had to know he would never make this trip."

Once again they fell silent. Birdseed, the lock and dam, the penitentiary, and Currentville all vanished from view as the curtain closed.

Now they felt a keen sense of release.

Around the bend, on their first stretch of river never seen before.

The *Delta Dream* rode high above the water. All three could walk around at the same time, and it would hardly give.

Apples were pulled from the bag, and they chomped away as their eyes soaked in the passing vista.

This river, in the early morning, while still shaded by the convoluted banks, had a certain aura—a combination of scents and smells. It was a mingled odor of mud, fish, plant life, and water.

A long legged crane pulled out of its muddy mooring and flapped across the river in front of them. A few crickets were still refusing to give way to the rising light.

The sun began to cover the western bank and within minutes it enveloped the entire stream. Soon the raft and its passengers and cargo were basking in the hot morning sun.

Trot lines—marked with dark brown Purex bottles—slid

past.

Weather-beaten old wooden skiffs and john boats were occasionally spotted, tied off to the bank under overhanging willows. Slick and narrow paths snaked through the weeds away from the vessels toward a distant house where dogs barked and roosters crowed.

Jack pulled his .22 rifle from under his pack and they took turns shooting at targets on the bank. The head of a menacing cottonmouth was seen moving along the top of the water. It disappeared under a hail of bullets.

A grisly old fisherman, clad in soiled overalls and a baseball cap, made his way upriver holding onto the throttle of a small outboard motor with one hand. A homemade cigarette hung from his mouth. He gave the lads a slight nod as he sputtered by. It was like he passed three boys on a raft every morning.

The shooting stopped and the sun began to heat up the river. They stripped to their swimming trunks and settled into easy conversation.

They wondered what their friends were doing.

What about the Cardinals? How long would Musial last? Who would be his replacement?

Charlie James? No way.

Their thoughts turned to girls and sex. The ones who were developing big boobs. Which ones they were looking forward to seeing when school started. Fantasizing over the high school cheerleaders.

They even talked about politics.

"What's the name of the guy running for sheriff against Bass Fisher who was a Japanese prisoner of war?" asked Donkey.

"Sandy Hooks?" responded Luke.

"Yeah. They said he ate grasshoppers to stay alive."

They fell silent and contemplated the horror of it.

"Speaking of Bass Fisher," Donkey broke the spell, "Is 'Bass' his nickname or real name?"

No one responded, so he went on. "I mean, what mother in her right mind would name him Bass? Bass. Fish. Fisher. Bass Fisher?"

After thinking on it a moment Luke responded, "Probably his real name. You know there's Bass Logan at school."

With that, they left politics behind.

"Okay, Luke—time for the question game," Jack chirped during a lull in the conversation.

The "question game" was a conversational lark of impossible questions and silly answers. It was played in times of long talks and little action.

Luke was a master of the game.

He plopped back on his pack, looked up at the sky and pondered.

Jack and Donkey continued to chat.

In a few minutes Luke bolted up.

"Okay, here's the question . . . what date did people write on their checks before Christ?"

"On their checks . . . I don't get it," Donkey said quizzically. "I mean . . . they didn't have checks before Christ . . . "

"Yeah they did . . . assume they did . . ." Luke implored.

Both Donkey and Jack wore blank faces.

"Okay," Luke explained, "if you write a check now you put 1958, right? Because it's one thousand, nine hundred and fifty-eight years after Christ. Well, what did they put on their checks before Christ was born. I mean, like 300 B.C.?"

"Well, they put 300 B.C." Donkey took the bait.

Luke and Jack looked at each other and then burst out laughing.

Donkey blushed and then countered, "Well, what did they put?"

"They didn't put nothing . . . and all the checks bounced. And that's why they had to run around living in caves and wearing bearskins," Luke answered emphatically.

Jack jumped to his feet, "That's bad Luke. Real bad."
And he dove off the raft into the tepid water. Donkey and Luke followed suit.

By late morning they drifted by the neighboring town of Catawba. There was no love lost between the boys of Currentville and their counterparts two miles downriver.

Some young Catawba roughs were swimming in the river, diving off Silver Cliffs.

The *Delta Dream*, slipping by on the opposite bank, received derisive taunts from the boys of Catawba. Luke and his friends returned the insults with some pretty mean stuff of their own, the ribbon of water between them bolstering their courage.

And then, slowly, Catwaba and the rowdy swimmers faded out of sight.

For the noon meal they downed sardines, crackers, and Kool-Aid.

Throughout the afternoon, the merciless sun and heat drove them periodically onto the bank, where they tied up under the canopy of a huge cottonwood or elm. There they swam, drank iced tea from a a large thermos, and reclined in the refreshing shade.

They would then push on until the flaming orb and smothering humidity would drive them to land again.

A cloud about the size of a bushel basket made a cameo appearance.

They began to look forward to night when they could escape the intense heat. Sometimes they would nap, only to wake in a pool of sweat, bleary-eyed and feeling miserable.

The river took on a dull, simmering sameness to it. Each bend was answered the same as the last.

Still they moved on sluggishly, but surely, throughout the long summer afternoon.

Only two tugs with tows, one going upstream, the other downstream, interrupted the tedium. The raft was safely out of the main channel both times and easily rode out the waves generated by their large propellers.

Finally shadows began to form along the west bank as the sun began to head for home.

They moved the craft into the corridor of shade along the edge of the stream. Refreshed and encouraged by the respite from the sun, the drifters began looking for a place to camp.

It was a rugged stretch of river, and the banks were steep and covered with undergrowth and trees. It was like a jungle.

The crickets had already begun their evening chant when they spotted a grass clearing sloping gently to the water.

It looked perfect, nestled beneath large trees and next to what appeared to be either a creek or a slough which emptied into the river.

Slowly and with great relief, they pulled their bulky craft into the bank.

Excitedly they leapt off and secured the vessel. Then they bounded off to reconnoiter the area. They shouted and bounced about gleefully, proud to be released from the ship and able to stretch their muscles in the cool forest.

After the brief interlude of frolicking, they returned to unload the provisions from the raft.

But not before they stopped to survey the creek which edged past the grassy knoll where they had landed. With the river at its lowest summer pool, this tributary was now just a stagnant pool of water with green algae floating on its surface.

It was getting dark as they prepared their campsite, laying out their bedding and building a fire.

A few fireflies appeared.

And then, just as the first flames of their fire began to take hold, the onslaught began.

Mosquitoes.

Just a few scouts at first, giving the boys nothing to be overly concerned about. Mosquitoes—especially at this time of year—were a part of camping. Unconcerned, Jack reached for the can of insect repellent and laid down a heavy fog of spray.

Still they came, heavier than before.

Their numbers were increasing, and their bites painful. The famished voyagers hurriedly prepared their food, smacking and yelping as they ate.

Luke attempted to build up the fire in an attempt to run them off.

The flames seemed to attract them.

It was now totally dark and turning more miserable by the moment.

The spray can was emptied.

"They're coming from the slough," Luke painfully intoned. "The place is a breeding hole for them."

"Look at these sons of a bitches," Jack slapped three at one time on his forearm, "they're as big as horseflies."

"We gotta get out of here," yelled Donkey as he grabbed his blanket and, in spite of the hot night, tried to cover up completely under it.

"We can get back on the river. That's the only way we can get away from them," suggested Jack.

"Can't get on the river at night," Luke admonished, remembering the stern warning from his Dad. "We'll have to tough it out. Maybe they'll let up as the night wears on."

But they didn't.

It was unbearable. The fire, raised to a conflagration, was making them sweat which in turn seemed to draw more of the vicious insects.

The campers were unable to keep still, having to move about, swatting and waving their hands, fending them off—or trying to fend them off.

Finally, Jack could take no more.

"We're leaving! I can't take this anymore."

Luke opened his mouth to protest, but his heart wasn't in it. They were right. It was a choice of evils.

"We can get on the raft, get out to midstream. It will be cooler on the water and we'll be rid of these bastards." Jack was already packing his gear.

"I'm all for it. Let's do it," Donkey threw in with Jack and began to gather his belongings.

"Okay," Luke gave in. "I will agree to do it if we do two things. First, we have to take turns keeping a watch all night for barges. And second, we have to keep the lantern going."

"That's fine. Let's get out of here...son of a bitch!" Jack swore as he slapped the back of his neck.

Hurriedly, they threw their things on the raft and put out the fire.

Luke lit the lantern and they pushed off.

Relief came almost immediately. Once they cleared the

bank and moved away from the creek, the attackers vanished.

Still, they moved out to midstream just to be sure. They had escaped. Wonderfully relieved, they collapsed on the deck.

There was even a slight breeze stirring on the water.

Sprawled on their bedrolls like spent fighters, they stared up at the wide sky, studded with diamonds.

"What were those things?" Donkey broke the silence.

"I have never seen such creatures in my life. I lost a quart of blood," Luke replied.

They all laughed. The delirious laugh of relief.

"See Luke," Jack chided, "this wasn't such a bad idea, was it?"

They sat up and looked out on the river. In spite of the clear sky full of stars, the night was pitch black. The dark rim of the banks could barely be discerned.

The lantern cast a cozy ring of pale light across the raft.

They were afloat on a sea of darkness, with the sounds of night beyond their vision, and a canopy of summer night's sky overhead.

It was delightfully peaceful and beautiful, made even more so by the misery they had left behind.

The river at night takes on a personality of its own.

Far down the river, Luke spotted a small white light blinking in the inky darkness.

"One . . . two . . . three . . . one . . . two . . . three." He counted off the seconds.

"What is it?" Donkey inquired, peering downstream.

"Navigation light marking the right bank," Luke responded.

"Right bank? Looks like it's in the middle of the river," Jack interjected.

"River turns to the left. It's the right bank. It blinks once every three seconds. Count it. One . . . two . . . three. If you see a light on the left bank it blinks twice . . . one, two . . . and then three seconds."

Jack and Donkey listened intently as they watched the light. It had a certain tranquilizing effect.

Because of his Dad, Luke knew more about the river than any other kid in Currentville.

Luke grew up with river talk every night in his kitchen. River friends of his Dad often stopped to visit. Topper Adams, a pilot for one of the larger boat lines was one of Luke's favorites.

He was an old man with a large shock of white hair and still piloting the crooked Cumberland, as well as other rivers in the Southeast. Many times, while his boat was tied up waiting for a locking, Topper would climb ashore and come up to Luke's house and eat supper. Alec loved the old man, and they talked endlessly about navigation, common friends, and river gossip.

One thing always struck Luke as odd about Top. Every time the old man came to their house, he would walk into the kitchen pantry when he left—thinking it was the outside door.

They would suppress their laughter until he left and then wonder how ole Top could navigate the tricky currents and sandbars of the rivers of the Southeast, but had trouble negotiating his way out of their house.

Luke had spent a great deal of his boyhood loitering around the lock house listening to the lockmen and observing river trade. It was a warm and cozy place to be on winter nights, with the two-way radio crackling with boat traffic and the smell of freshly brewed coffee permeating the place.

On summer nights they would sit out under the stars on the grassy lawn. From that lofty plateau, they could look down on the river from bend to bend, serenaded by the the low roar of the water cascading over the dam.

Luke wanted to be a riverboat pilot when he grew up. And he absorbed everything he heard or read about the river.

There on the raft, in his element, he conducted class for his interested friends.

"Of course in the daytime you've got the buoys. The can buoys, the black and white ones, mark the right bank as you look downriver. The nun buoys, the red and white ones, mark the left bank."

He explained to them about the navigation signs, mile markers, dredging of the channel, shifting sandbars, fords, and such.

"Big Horse Ford is not too far from here. It got its name long time ago when in late summer you could ford the stream there if you were riding a 'big horse'. That's all changed now with all the dams on the rivers which keep what they call a nine-foot pool. Even so, Dad tells me that every now and then when the water really gets low—like right now—a big tow will get caught up on Big Horse Ford. The pilot will radio the lock and they will have to drop some wickets in the dam which will release more water down below and lift the boat off the bottom."

Luke was a good storyteller, embellishing his accounts a bit to make sure they were interesting.

So he continued on into the warm summer night, as his two friends listened intently, interrupting only to ask questions.

He related tales he had heard from lockmen and pilots—close scrapes with death, shanty people, haunted parts of the river. Of particular interest were the stories he had been told by Jess Langston, the Corps of Engineer diver who would come down from Nashville from time to time. His job was to go down to the bottom of the river and repair malfunctions in the lock. His staging area would be from an Army "Duck," and he would descend into the gray, murky waters encased in his diving helmet and a bulky canvas suit.

Needless to say, Jess had some hair-raising experiences to tell.

And they talked about floods, dwelling upon the accounts they had heard about the granddaddy of them all—the deluge of 1937.

"Hey, Jack," Donkey interjected with a big smile, "have you ever heard the story of Hack McGregor falling in the backwater?"

Jack shook his head negatively in the pale lamp light.

"Tell him, Luke."

Luke chuckled, stretched his legs and then brought his knees up against his chest, settling in for the story.

"Well, it was a couple of winters ago and the backwater was way up, almost in the main floor of our house. And it was cold. I mean real cold.

"Dad decided it would be a good time for us to cut a few limbs off the big old mulberry tree down behind the garden. It was beginning to spread a little too much shade in the summer on our garden. And the water was way up in the tree. I mean it was probably ten feet deep in there. We could just cut the limbs, and let 'em float off.

"So Daddy took Bobby Joe and me and we all got in a skiff and rowed out to the tree. Daddy and Bobby Joe had hand saws and I was just sitting in the boat watching. My job was to hold the boat into the tree while they did the cutting.

"I mean it was bitter cold. Cloudy and cold, maybe even spitting a little snow.

"About the time Daddy and Bobby Joe started to saw on some of the limbs we heard old Hack yelling out from the bank.

"'Hey Alec! Come and get me and I'll give you a hand.'

"Well, Daddy....now he thinks the world of old Hack, loves him like a brother and he's lived just a couple of houses down as long as I remember. But Daddy's really not too crazy about having Hack out there in the way....you know how fidgety and nervous Hack is, always rattling on about something.

"So I hear Daddy say something under his breath . . . you know . . . swear a little bit. But old Hack standing there on the bank so anxious to help and looking so pitiful . . . well, anyway, we go back in and get him.

"As soon as we get back out to the tree, Hack takes Bobby Joe's saw away from him and starts in cutting limbs like crazy. I mean he did just like he does everything . . . just full speed ahead. That cigarette's hanging out of his mouth like it always is and he's working like crazy. He gets up on the side of the boat with one foot in the boat and another on a limb . . . I mean he's in a heck of shape. Bobby Joe and I look at each other and Dad tells him to be careful.

"But he starts sawing away.

"Well, what old Hack was doing, and no one realized it 'till it was too late, he was cutting a limb with the saw, but the tip of the saw was dipping down at the same time and cutting the limb he was standing on."

Luke laughed and shook his head.

"Well . . . just about the time he was almost through the limb, we heard this loud crack and off into the water Hack went.

"I mean he cleared the boat, tree, everything, and went in head first. He went completely out of sight. Then up he came grabbing for the side of the boat.

"I will never forget the shocked look on his face, and his eyes wide open, scared to death. And there lying flat on his chin, was the soaked and limp cigarette still hanging out of his mouth."

Jack and Donkey rolled with laughter.

"Well, we got him back in the boat. Of course his teeth were chattering and he was freezing to death. I mean I don't know how cold that water was . . . near freezing . . . and we started rowing him into the bank.

"Polly must have seen it all happen from her back window, because by the time we got to the bank, she was waiting there with a blanket which she wrapped around him and led him back to the house.

"I tell you this much . . . that boat ride in from the tree was the only time in my life that I have ever seen Hack McGregor not talking."

They laughed, regaled by the story, and then grew quiet.

Luke turned the conversation to more serious matters. They touched upon a little religion and philosophy.

"I got a question. Something I don't understand," Luke stated. "There was a poem we read in school—I forgot the name of it or who wrote it—but there's a line—'two roads diverged in a wood' . . ."

"Robert Frost," Donkey interrupted.

"Yeah, Robert Frost," Luke continued. "Well, anyway, 'two roads diverged in a wood and I took the one less traveled and that has made all the difference.' Well, what does that mean? Made what difference?"

They gave it some silent thought, and then Luke continued, "I mean if he had taken the road most traveled it would have made the same difference."

The subject was too heavy for them.

It was late, and now, in the gentle drift, they were growing sleepy, exhausted from their long first day on the river.

"Time to hit the sack," Jack announced, and began to spread out his bedding.

"Okay. We gotta set up our shifts to stand watch," Luke admonished.

"I'll take the last shift . . . the one from six to seven in the morning," Jack joked.

They discussed the routine, and decided it would be best to work on hour shifts. Two hours sleep, one hour watch. Jack pulled his watch from the pack and held it near the lantern.

"Almost the bewitching hour of midnight," he proclaimed. "I'm bushed. Call me for the third watch."

Without debate, he slid into his sleeping bag.

"I'm bushed," Donkey mimicked, "Call me for the second watch." He stretched out on his air mattress and threw his blanket down around his feet.

"Okay . . . give me your watch, Jack."

Luke took the timepiece, laid it by the lantern, pulled his pack up behind him, and leaned back to begin his watch.

"Hey, by the way," he mentioned as an afterthought, "green lights. We're looking for green lights. A green light means barges. If you see a green light we have to row like hell."

"Row like hell to where?" a muffled and tired inquiry came from a sleeping bag.

"To the bank. As fast as we can get there," Luke answered.

The raft fell silent.

Luke felt around in the dark till he found the thick handle of each of the large oars. He checked the lantern. Reassured, he settled back, peering downriver into the darkness.

The cacophony of a summer night surrounded him— crickets faintly chanting on the distant shore, an owl hooting, and a bull frog occasionally bellowing.

And from the darkened waterway came reminders to Luke that he did not have the river to himself. Periodic splashes and flutterings gave evidence of aquatic life which was not sleeping.

Floating in the pale circle of light, time and place became suspended. It was surreal.

Then a huge, dark form came out of the water toward the raft.

Luke jumped, frightened out of his wits.

It reached the light of the lantern and became clearly visible. And then slowly the huge black and white cylinder passed by so close to the vessel that Luke could have reached out and touched it.

It was a can buoy. Strewn along the river in the daytime, they appear small, almost toylike. Up close, however, especially unexpected in the dark of night, they loom big and even menacing.

Luke's only companion on this lonely vigil were his thoughts. And they cast about in every direction.

The summer, which was now drawing down to a close, baseball, the Cardinals, Bobby Joe's amazing athletic ability, Savannah Johnson—all were images floating along with the raft through his mind.

He kept returning to Savannah Johnson, like a warm and sunny haven to his lonely reverie.

A flush of excitement, and then the calming beauty of her face, the fragrance, the smile.

But Luke's attention was also given to the deeper things of life, to which the inky midnight scene lent itself.

Daylight, darkness. Good, evil. The staggering change in the river from daytime to night.

God. Preachers. Deathbed stories. The terror of the unknown. Doubts about the known.

Friends. Luke thought about his friends, especially those sleeping beside him. Jack. Donkey. A warm sensation, not as intense or sensual as with Savannah Johnson, but something similar. A sharing, teammates. Maybe he loved them, Luke thought.

Weird.

It had cooled down considerably, to the point where it was comfortable. As the night wore on, well past the midnight hour, the dampness on the river seemed to increase. Small patches of fog would pass through the raft and its crew, like some wandering spirit hastening upstream.

Donkey was restless, constantly moving about.

Finally, with about ten minutes to go on Luke's watch, his relief sat straight up and looked around.

"What time is it?" Donkey asked.

Luke held the watch near the flame.

"Almost one."

Donkey sat up straight and pulled his legs in toward him and crossed them. He reached into his pack, pulled out the water jug, and took a long quaff.

He looked like he had been dragged through a forest.

"My eyes feel like two burnt holes in an Army blanket," he lamented and looked out over the river like he was seeing it for the first time all night. The light from the lamp reflected off his face, leaving his eyes in shadows and giving him a spooky look.

"Did you sleep?" Luke wondered out loud.

"I guess. But not very well," Donkey replied.

They heard a fish jump in the water.

"I wonder if you could catch any fish out here?" Donkey inquired.

"Probably. If you had a line and a hook."

Luke leaned back on his pack.

"I have a line. I have a hook. And I have baloney," Donkey suddenly remembered and began rummaging through his pack.

He held the canvas pouch down close to the lantern to shed some light on his search.

"There's the line . . ."

He pulled out some fishing line, wrapped snugly around a used Popsicle stick.

". . . and here's the hook."

"Good grief, Donkey, what'd ya bring such a large hook for? You could catch a whale on that thing," Luke exclaimed as the hardware appeared.

"Damn," Donkey swore under his breath, "the eye is broken off of this thing."

Their heads came together and they peered intently at the hook which Donkey was holding close to the light.

"So much for that," Luke sighed. "You ready to take your watch?"

"Yeah. I'll take it from here. Go ahead and go to sleep. I'm gonna get this hook fixed and a line out yet. We'll have fish for breakfast. You just wait and see."

Donkey pulled a pocket knife out of his jeans and moved the lantern to the upstream side of the raft. There, with his back downstream, he hunkered over the light and began working on the fishhook. His form practically blocked all the light from the front of the raft and cast it into darkness.

Luke laid down and closed his eyes.

He had trouble going to sleep. Each time he opened his eyes and changed positions, he saw Donkey working intently with the hook, hovering over the lantern like some mad scientist.

Finally Luke began to drift off to sleep, moving ever so slowly down that long slope of mingled and fragmented thoughts which lead to unconsciousness.

Deeper and deeper he went, fading away from the sights and sounds of the summer night. He was falling softly down a vast shaft of darkness without sound.

Without sound, except for a low purring which was gently lulling him on toward slumber.

His drift downward slowed, however, when the tranquilizing sound began to hum.

Still he lay suspended, not in this world, but still not yet out of it.

Almost imperceptibly, the hum became louder.

"Bum, bum, bum, bum, bum . . ."

Now, instead of falling softly on his brain, the rumbling became irritating.

"Bum, bum, bum, bum, bum . . ."

Then a lone embattled neuron armed with a conscious thought banged loudly on the door.

"A barge!"

In one motion, Luke leaped to his feet and stared downstream.

What he saw sickened him.

There, no more than a hundred yards away, bearing down on them was the dreaded green light mounted on the right side of a barge. Directly across from it, about seventy feet, was a red light. The span was the width of two barges. The lights were sitting high. Empties.

"A barge! A barge!" he screamed with all the sound he could muster.

Donkey was still sitting exactly where Luke had left him. Hunkered over the lantern, blocking all meaningful light from the beacon, he had become mesmerized by his project of preparing a fishing line. In his endeavor he had become less conscious of what was going on around him than Luke.

Jack shot up and onto his feet. Amazingly he grasped the severity of the situation immediately.

"Get to rowing! Get to rowing!" Luke yelled as he reached for an oar.

Jack grabbed the other one.

"Donkey . . . get that lantern up and wave it as high as you can!"

Luke was taking charge, his heart racing and his mind afire.

"Bum, bum, bum, bum, bum . . ."

The barges moved closer.

Slowly the clumsy raft began to move as Luke and Jack dug the heavy cumbersome oars into the water.

But the vessel was moving around and around in a circle.

Jack was rowing one way, trying to take the raft toward the right bank. Luke, perhaps instinctively, was rowing toward the middle of the river and the left bank.

Once again he quickly eyed the oncoming barge, seeing for the first time, the lights of the tow downriver behind the massive flotilla.

"You're rowing us into the channel!" Luke screamed, "Right into where the barge is going. Row this way . . . out of the channel!"

Jack was unconvinced. It was easy to be enticed by the

nearest bank.

But Luke was right. The channel up which the tow was churning was near the right bank at that spot in the river.

The escape route was to the middle of the river.

Jack went his way, pulling with all his might. Luke pulled the other way, yelling for Jack to follow suit.

The *Delta Dream*, now a nightmare, continued to slowly spin, like a huge top.

They were losing critical time.

Desperately, Luke glanced again at the oncoming barge, the monster with the green and red eyes.

Then he felt an indescribable sinking sensation in the pit of his stomach.

He realized that he was going to die.

There were no flashbacks, no spiritual revelations or poignant regrets. Just the cold, lonely reality that this was it.

The lights were now so close that Luke could even see the edges of the barge reflected by their glow.

Donkey, apparently frozen with fear, was standing like a statue on the front of the raft, holding—not waving—the lantern high up in the air toward the oncoming vessel.

They had only one chance to survive.

"We gotta swim for it!" Luke yelled at his two desperate friends.

With that command, and knowing that time was of the essence, Luke immediately dropped the oar and dove into the water.

Just before he cleared the raft, however, he managed one last bit of instruction.

"This way!"

He didn't know if they had heard over the rumbling of the tow. Or, if they heard, whether they would follow.

Luke knew that if they went the other way, they were doomed.

The muscular youth had never swum as he swam that night.

With his head down, he simply knew he had no time to

even breathe. He had to move.

Panic driven, Luke cut though the water, his arms pulling in an almost circular motion, his legs and feet kicking for life.

He heard the loud pounding of the tow coming closer and closer. His whole body was in a frenzy, every muscle burning and straining. Only when his lungs pained for breath, did he gulp for air.

His mind was exploding with terrible fear, expecting any moment that mountains of steel would drive him down into the watery deep, where the slashing propellers would grind him into sausage.

The terrifying noise grew louder and louder, and then held constant against his ears.

In a daze he continued to do all that he could do.

Swim like hell.

Swim for his life.

The noise began to lessen.

Then, like a fever breaking, Luke felt danger passing.

He continued to pull through the water, slower and slower as he tired and the adrenalin left him.

Finally he stopped, filled his lungs with air, and turned in the water to look back.

To his great relief, he saw the boat safely passed and churning its way upriver. The stern and the water being plowed white by the propellers were alit by the rear running lights. "Port of Cincinnati" was proclaimed on the rear, just above the water line.

Slowly the sound faded as the monstrous ship began to move around a bend.

The big waves from the boat arrived, lifted him, and then washed around him. Still recovering, Luke began to look around the dark waters. He could see nothing but blackness.

"Jack! Donkey!" he yelled, when the pounding diesels of the tow quieted to a murmur.

"Jack! Donkey!"

"Luke!" came Jack's reply, so close that it startled him. "Over here."

He breast-stroked upstream toward the sound, trying to

keep both ears above the water.

"Where are you?" he yelled as the natural sounds of the night returned to the river.

"Right here," Jack responded in a normal tone as they met.

"Where's Donkey?" Luke inquired.

"I don't know. The last time I saw him he was still on the raft, holding up that damn lantern. He looked like the Statute of Liberty, not moving at all, but just standing up straight holding up that lamp. I think he was in a daze."

"Donkey!" Luke's call echoed off the opposite bank. An eerie silence fell upon the water.

Jack tried. "Donkey! Where are you?"

Still nothing but the crickets and the movement of the water.

Although they were much closer to the left bank, they began moving toward the other side of the river, back toward the channel and the waters from which they had just moments before desperately fled. Back toward the home side of the stream.

"When did you leave the raft?" Luke asked after a while.

"Right after you. And in the same direction," Jack said, and Luke resisted the urge to reply.

"Maybe Donkey's on the other side, and just can't hear us." Luke tried to sound optimistic.

But he was scared. They were both scared.

Doggedly they plodded on toward the other side.

At about mid-stream Luke's right hand hit something solid and metallic and he flinched in terror. Then it struck his face and he flung out his hands and grabbed it.

It was a barrel from the raft.

Their spirits sunk.

They had hoped that some way the raft escaped the barge, that Donkey had ridden it out and was safe.

Now they knew one thing. The raft was gone.

And probably Donkey.

After a laborious and dreary time, the dark mass began to grow closer.

Finally, the totally exhausted and spent swimmers reached

a sandbar jutting out from the bank, and pulled themselves out of the water.

After he had rested a few moments Luke got to his feet and tried to make something out of the surrounding darkness.

"Donkey!"

This time his voice echoed off the other shore.

"Donkey!"

He sat back down on the bank.

The terrible and somber significance of the tragic event began to overwhelm them.

Neither said a word as they pondered the enormity of it all.

Luke put his head in his hands, wondering what he would say to Donkey's family. He sunk even deeper when he thought about what he would tell his Dad.

Long heavy minutes went by in silence.

Suddenly, a loud voice from behind shook them to their toes.

"You'll wonder where the yellow went, when you brush your teeth with Pepsodent . . . Pepsodent . . . Pepsodent!"

It was Donkey! Jack and Luke sprang to their feet like they had been shot with a charge of high voltage.

"Where you been?" Jack gushed with both excitement and tremendous relief, "We thought you were a goner . . . didn't you hear us yelling?"

"Yeah I heard ya," Donkey replied airily.

"What ya mean you heard us?" Jack asked with some agitation.

"Yeah," Luke jumped in, "you mean you heard us hollering for ya and you just . . . you just . . . we thought you were drowned!"

Donkey nonchalantly plopped down on the bank to rest.

"Well, I thought I'd sneak up on you and scare ya. Then when I heard you come ashore, I thought I'd listen to what you had to say. I mean, you remember the part in Tom Sawyer where they thought him and Huck were dead, and they slipped back in and listened to their own funeral? Well, kinda like that. But you didn't talk much about me. Just set here saying nothing like a couple of dopes."

Luke and Jack could not believe the levity which Donkey was bringing to the whole harrowing situation. And this was the guy who had totally freaked out on the raft.

"What happened to you anyway? How did you make it?" Luke inquired, as he and Jack both took seats along with their resurrected friend.

"Well," Donkey began his story, "after you two so rudely left me, the barge hit the raft. I was waiting to see where the barge was going to hit so that I could swim the opposite way. Well it didn't hit it square. I mean there were two barges, right? I mean there were a lot more barges but they were two barges across. Anyway they almost missed the raft completely. The left side of the left barge just barely nipped the raft.

"The barges were empties and sat way up out of the water. So just a little part of the raft went in under the front overhang of the barge When the bottom part of the barge hit the raft, the raft just bobbled around to the side.

"Well, that old raft just banged and slid down the side of the barges as the boat kept steaming by. If they hadn't been empties and setting so high up in the water I could have just jumped right over on them. So, the old *Delta Dream* got hit by the barge and survived!"

Donkey stopped to let it all sink in. He was obviously enjoying this telling of his hair-raising escape.

Luke interrupted, "Well, what happened to the raft? I mean we ran across one of the barrels."

Donkey continued.

"Well, all was going well for a while . . . except of course I was scared out of my wits while all this was going on. But it really looked like I was going to ride the whole thing out until we got down to the towboat. You know the tow sat in some from the barges. The raft kinda rolled into the tow off the side of the barge and . . . well, I mean it crashed into the tow.

"When it did, two of the barrels just popped out from under the raft and the whole thing tilted down to one side so everything started rolling off and the low end was in the water. I grabbed hold of the upper edge of the raft and hung on. It bounced a couple of times more off the side of the tow and then.....I got down to the end of the tow and the raft went right in behind it. And here was the scariest part of all.

"The churning and boiling water from the propellers just tore the raft completely apart. The next thing I knew I was in the water swimming.

"And . . . dun de dun . . . here I am!"

The account left Jack and Luke breathless.

"Wheeewww . . . Donkey," Luke marveled, "you're lucky! I mean really lucky!"

They continued to talk about the experience, deliriously happy to be reunited. After a while they even began to laugh about some of it, especially about Donkey and his fishhook and his turning to stone while he was holding the lantern.

They were so relieved to all have survived, that no one even chided Donkey for "going to sleep at the hook."

Luke grew quiet as Jack and Donkey continued to banter.

After a while Luke interrupted.

"Donkey, did anyone see you on the raft?"

"See me? You mean on the boat?"

"Yeah," Luke spoke in thoughtful, serious tones.

Donkey thought for a moment. "Huh, I don't know. I never paid any attention. All I could see were the sides of those barges, the tow, and the .....the white, churning water.....I wasn't exactly checking the boat out for girls, you know . . ."

"Why?" Jack questioned Luke, "What difference does it make?"

"It makes a lot of difference," Luke declared with a disturbing inflection in his voice.

"That boat will be at the Currentville lock in two or three hours, maybe even before daylight. If they saw us, and they know they hit us . . . "

Luke didn't even have to finish the sentence. A stonelike silence fell upon the trio.

"Aw shit," Jack whispered, "they'll report it. And they'll be out searching for us."

Luke was thinking hard. Trying to remember all he could

about the boat.

"He was running on radar," he recalled, almost to himself, having remember seeing the fanlike antenna revolving on top of the pilot house, "and I never saw his spotlight."

"I did," Jack countered. "As soon as I stopped swimming I looked back. He turned on that big spotlight. He swept it from side to side out in front of the barges like he was looking for something. In fact, I thought for a minute he was going to shine it on me. It went around in a . . . well . . . a . . . half-circle, you might say. After a couple of times back and forth, he just shut it off."

Luke pondered, "He knew he had hit something. He felt the vibration, sensed it, or something . . . maybe even saw something. But he never cut his speed . . . just kept on trucking."

"Ah he never knew," Donkey chimed in. "That thing was so big it could have hit five *Delta Dreams* and never known it."

But Luke wasn't sure. He had been in the pilot house of large tows many times, even at night. It's true that he would have been watching the radar screen. But the raft should have shown up on the screen. Large logs, even ducks, showed up on the radar. How could Donkey slide down the barges on the raft, ram into the tow, and not be seen from the pilot house?

But again, why did it not cut its engines and look for survivors?

It was a puzzle. A bothersome puzzle.

"We gotta get home. We gotta get moving." Luke sprang to his feet.

A serious discussion as to their location followed.

They deferred to Luke. "I figure we're a mile or two above Dycusburg. That means the highway is about two or three miles thata way." He pointed with his hand, and even though it was too dark for them to see, they got the picture.

Luke gave the command to move out.

He was barefooted, having pulled off his shoes when he laid down for his ill-fated repose. The other two were shod in tennis shoes, a condition which had seriously impaired their swimming but would now aid their traveling.

They clawed up the steep bank in the pitch blackness.

Once on top, they found themselves in the middle of a cornfield.

Luke led the way as they plunged into the August crop. The dense growth of stalks towered above them and were laden with roast'n ears. Their blades lashed out and sliced their arms and faces, now wet with sweat from their suffocating journey.

It was hard going, and the darkness made it even more miserable. They were able to stay together only by the sounds of their movement and continuous talking.

On and on they trudged, trying their best to keep on a straight line from the river, hopefully toward the highway. But they were full of doubts.

"If we end up back at that damn river, I'm gonna die," Donkey lamented.

It was the largest cornfield in the history of the world.

After what seemed like hours, they stumbled out of the last row and into a clearing.

Then into a fence row, marked with trees.

They felt their way over the fence, piercing their hands with barbs, and then fell down a steep embankment. They lay there on their backs staring up at the stars, and wondering where they were.

Exhaustion and fatigue fell upon them like a mace.

After a few short moments and some mumbling, they were all asleep—the deep sleep of the weary.

Luke was having a nightmare. He was back on the raft, and he was again hearing the rumbling of the oncoming tow. Except this time it was much louder, it was much nearer, and a metal clanking had been added to the sound. It jarred him loose and up on his feet he came.

All three of them stood terrified, looking up to the top of the grade where a train was roaring by at fierce and noisy speed, only about twenty feet from where they had been lying.

Quickly it passed, the well-lit caboose moving out of sight down the track.

"Damn! Damn! Damn! Damn! Damn! Damn! Damn!" Jack started screaming uncontrollably, "Damn! Damn! Damn! You son of a bitch!"

He bent over and grabbed up handfuls of grass and weeds and was throwing it at the train which by now was safely out of sight and sound.

"We get hit by a barge! We almost get hit by a train! I guess when we get to the highway we'll all get squashed like a possum!"

He was letting it all out, jumping up and down and shaking his fist.

A long silent moment passed, and then Donkey and Luke began to laugh.

Jack saw them fall back down on the grass and begin to roll around holding their sides.

". . . squashed like a possum . . ." Luke managed to get out between gales of laughter.

Then Jack began to laugh. All three allowed the tensions of a long fearful night to erupt into a boisterous outpouring of mirth.

After the euphoric interlude of several minutes, they grew quiet. Then they realized they could see each other. A few birds were chirping. The gray dawn, long sought for by these three young soldiers of fortune, had finally arrived.

From the railroad track on top of the slope, they could see lights from cars on the highway about two miles away. The cornfields in between they would skirt this time, even if it made for longer distance.

Their spirits lifted, and off they went.

The sun was up, and the morning was already beginning to warm up when the reached the road. Under the familiar pale blue sky, they caught a ride with a young carpenter on his way to work. He took them as far as Catawba, where they walked through town to the intersection of the Currentville road.

There a farmer Jack knew and who was driving a truck picked them up. They rode in the back the last two miles of their return trip home.

As they crossed the Depot Bridge and started around the long curve leading into Currentville, the tension began to rise.

Luke silently prayed that things would be normal, and that

the town, and more especially their families, would not be wringing their hands in grief and desperation over the news of their mishap.

He had the driver let him out at Wrinklemeat's grocery, at the edge of town.

After a thanks to the farmer and a wave to his confederates, he went behind the store and slipped through the backyards and gardens of the houses leading up to his home.

There in the garden next door he bent down in the tomatoes and surveyed the scene.

His mother was out in the yard hanging up clothes on the line. The radio was blaring out a popular tune through the open windows, ". . . cause you got, personality, smile, personality, walk, personality, talk, personality . . ." He heard Bobby Joe yelling out to his mom about some missing jeans.

He heaved a great big sigh of relief. All was right and normal with the world.

Luke bounded into his yard, slipped up and grabbed Esther from behind. He planted a big kiss on his mom's cheek. She turned around in amazement.

"What on earth are you doing here?" she asked as Luke headed for the house, trying to get away before she started asking questions, especially about his shoeless condition.

"I thought y'all were going to stay a couple of nights. What are you doing home so soon?" she called after him as he headed up the back porch steps.

"The mosquitoes drove us crazy!" he explained as he disappeared into the house.

Chapter Thirteen

Grave Robbers

A broken promise is a lie dressed up for church.

Luke looked out the study hall window, day dreaming, when he should have been studying for his science test coming up the next period. It was late February of his eighth-grade year. Dark clouds were forming, and the wind was kicking up dead leaves in the schoolyard.

Suddenly a paper airplane crashed into his chest. He looked around and spotted Birdseed seated at a table on the far side of the large room. His friend was pointing toward the library, a sign for a meeting.

A small room off the larger study hall area housed the library books under the domain of Miss Fletcher, the school librarian. Students in study hall were allowed to enter the library two or three at a time with the permission of the teacher supervising the study period.

Luke raised his hand, pointing to the alcove, until stern-faced Mrs. Gray gave him the permissive nod. He jumped to his feet and headed for the reading room. There were two or three students already there browsing around, so he nonchalantly grabbed a book off a shelf and sat down at the table, acting like he was reading and waiting for Birdseed to come aboard.   Old Miss Fletcher sat behind her desk, gravely peering through her bifocals at a stack of paperwork in front of her. If a person laid low, and kept down the noise, he could hide out in the library for the entire hour, flirting with one of the female student librarians who ostensibly helped Miss Fletcher but in reality just tried to look important and flirt back.

In a short time, after a couple of the kids cleared out, Birdseed arrived on the scene and slid into the seat beside Luke. He brought his large loose-leaf notebook with him.

"Luke," he whispered excitedly, "I want to show you something."

He pulled an old battered book out of his notebook.

"You know who Matthew Lyon is?" he inquired of his listener.

Luke thought. "Yeah, that guy Miss Virginia's always talking about in history class. A friend of Thomas Jefferson who helped settle Currentville. Buried up on Pea Ridge."

"That's right. Now lookie here." Birdseed turned to a well-marked page in the book. He pointed to a paragraph and began to read.

"'As a token of his friendship, Jefferson gave Lyon a Masonic ring which had been converted from a gold band presented to him by Ben Franklin. Franklin had brought back the original piece from France. Lyon wore the ring until his death.'"

Birdseed looked up at Luke with a euphoric glow, his eyes dancing through his horn rimmed glasses.

"Okay. Got that? Gold ring from France. Belonged to Ben Franklin and Thomas Jefferson."

Luke nodded, wondering what riddle Birdseed was cooking up.

His friend shoved the book aside, and quickly pulled out several sheets of notebook paper from his folder.

"This is a copy of the will of Matthew Lyon. I went to the courthouse and copied it word for word."

Unlike Luke's terrible scratching, Birdseed's hand writing was impeccable.

"Now look here," he smoothed the folded papers out in front of Luke. "Here is a listing of all his property. It goes into great detail. That's the way they did their wills back then. Here is all his land, house—Matthew Lyon was a wealthy man . . . then he starts listing each of his belongings, one by one. See here . . . " Birdseed was pointing down the page. ". . . here's a list of everything. He even has his slaves listed by name and who he wants to have them. Look . . . riding crop, saddle bags, old army sword used at the Battle of Fort Ticonderoga. Look here . . . a silver mug 'given to me by General . . . ' I can't make out the name. But it goes on and on." Birdseed shuffled the papers.

"Now Luke, do you see anything missing?"

Luke scanned the writing, looking and thinking.

Finally, "The ring."

"Exactly," Birdseed pronounced with a big smile.

"So, maybe he gave it away before he died," Luke shrugged.

"Not so," Birdseed countered. "Remember . . . " he opened the book again and read, "'Lyon wore the ring until his death.'"

Luke was growing impatient. Besides, Miss Fletcher was giving them a hard stare.

"Okay Birdseed," Luke leaned back in his seat, "what's the point?"

"Luke! A gold band, worth thousands of dollars! It belonged to Ben Franklin. It belonged to Thomas Jefferson. And it's buried right here in Currentville! It had to be buried with Matthew Lyon."

Slowly the picture came into focus.

"You mean go and rob the grave?" Luke queried incredulously.

"It's not robbery, Luke. There's nobody there to rob—after all this time it's just dust. The ring is just lying there in a pile of dust. It's abandoned. Like buried treasure. Like treasure on a sunken ship. They go down and get that stuff all the time. Nobody thinks anything about it." Birdseed's high whisper was rising even higher with excitement.

Luke pondered the incredible idea.

"I don't know, Birdseed. It's like stealing. I mean if they buried the ring with him . . . it's meant to stay with him. There's something not right about it." Luke was shaking his head.

"Listen Luke," Birdseed lowered his voice, taking a quick glance at Miss Fletcher, "the ring is valuable. It's lying up there not doing anybody any good. We could take it, sell it to the Smithsonian, use the money for something good. People would be able to see it . . . and it would make Currentville famous. They might even put it in *Life* magazine."

"What's the Smithsonian?" Luke asked, having heard the name but not quite sure.

"It's a big museum in Washington. They keep all kinds of things there....like George Washington's wooden false teeth, Charles Lindbergh's plane. They'd die to have this ring there. A ring that Benjamin Franklin brought back from France and gave to Thomas Jefferson!"

And then as a second thought, "Or we might be able to sell it for more to some other place."

About this time Miss Fletcher moved into the picture. Luke and Birdseed were booted from the library.

Birdseed would not give up on the idea. He was like a man obsessed. That night he called Luke on the telephone.

"Luke, I've been reading up on some of this stuff. Old Matthew was buried in a wooden coffin, right? Water builds up under them at times and pushes them up. After all these years, the coffin may only be three or four feet below the ground. Of course it's crumpled to nothing. It would be easy pickings."

Luke could only conjure up images from the horror comic books he had read—grave-robbing ghouls wallowing around in slimy burial places, feeding off horribly grotesque and putrefying corpses. Although he didn't want to admit it to Birdseed, the idea scared him.

"What do you think is left of old Matthew, Birdseed?" he asked airily.

"Probably nothing," his caller responded. "Like I said, it's probably just a pile of dust."

"But what about those skeletons down at Wickliffe?" countered Luke. Down there at the Ancient Buried City. Those are Indians who have been dead hundreds of years. And what about that place in Rome—the picture in our literature book—what's it called?"

"The catacombs." the human encyclopedia spit out.

"......yeah, the catacombs. Those skeletons are in pretty good shape."

"So what?" Birdseed intoned impatiently. "So if there is still a skeleton in there. You're being silly . . . you're not scared, are you, Luke?"

There was just a bit of mocking in the question.

"Naw, I'm not scared. Just curious. I've never dug into a grave before. I suppose you do it every day," Luke remarked sarcastically.

Luke would try to change the subject, but Birdseed would continually return to the grave of Matthew Lyon.

This went on for days. Luke was captivated by the idea. But at the same time it didn't feel right. There was something wrong about it. And even though he would not admit it to Birdseed, going into a graveyard and digging up someone's grave was also more than a little bit spooky. Finally, in a saner moment, he made up his mind not to do it. He told Birdseed while they were shooting basketball in his backyard.

"Okay," his friend quipped nonchalantly, as if it were no big deal. "I'll just have to get someone else. Maybe Jack. Or Donkey."

They fell silent. Finally Luke inquired, "Have you told either one of them about this . . . thing?"

"Nope." Birdseed answered sharply, flinging the ball up toward the goal.

"I did tell one other person though . . . " He let the revelation hang in the air.

"Who?" Luke inquired with obvious interest in his voice.

"Savannah Johnson."

"What?" Luke yelled, hardly able to believe his ears. "What in the world made you tell Savannah Johnson?"

"Oh, I don't know," Birdseed was playing it cool, "we were

just talking. I told her it was your idea."

"My idea! Why did you tell her that? Now she's going to think I'm some kind of . . . some kind of . . . ghoul."

Luke had stopped playing around with the basketball. When Savannah Johnson's name came into the conversation, he lost all interest in anything else.

"Not really. In fact she was kinda impressed. You know what she said? She kinda smiled that shy little smile of hers and said, 'Luke is the only boy I know who is smart enough and brave enough to do something like that.'"

The words carried a tremendous wallop, and Luke stood there turning them over and over in his head.

Birdseed Barrett had set the hook.

It was a long quiet minute before Luke finally began to come out of the haze. He grabbed the ball and took a couple of shots.

"Okay," he said at last, breaking the silence. "I'll do it."

✳❋✳

That night after supper they met at the cherry tree midway between their houses.

"It will take most of the night to pull this off," Birdseed noted, "so we'll have to do it on a Friday night."

"This Friday night," Luke chimed in. Now that he had made the commitment, he was anxious to get on with it.

He continued, "We'll need a shovel, a pick, and a lantern. I can get all three from the basement."

The more they discussed the project, the more excited they became. Not only was Luke now fully in the hunt, he was taking command. "We'll have to slip out as soon as we can after our folks go to bed," he instructed, "because we've got to be sure and be back before they get up in the morning."

They covered every angle, every possibility, every wrinkle which could develop. It was, they decided, a very simple task.

"What's the closest house to the cemetery?" Birdseed asked.

They both went into deep thought.

"It would have to be Ollie Bennett's house," Luke surmised. "It's a good piece down the road, toward town. I don't know. If we stay low, at that time of night, they shouldn't be able to see us."

"Luke," Birdseed said in a serious tone as the meeting was about to wrap up, "if we pull this off, we will be famous. I mean, at least famous for this place."

They talked about the venture periodically throughout the week. At school on Friday morning, Luke reported the first wrinkle.

"Bobby Joe's coming in from college this weekend," he told Birdseed. His older brother was in his first year of a combination basketball and baseball scholarship at Ole Miss. He had unexpectedly gotten a weekend off at the end of basketball season before he joined the baseball team.

"It will complicate me slipping out," Luke explained, "but I'll think of something. I'll meet you at the cherry tree between eleven and twelve with the tools."

On Friday evening the weather was mild and cloudy, with a soft breeze. Bobby Joe hit town and was showered with love and affection by his Mom and Dad. He had only been home for three days at Christmas.

Luke's big brother had changed since he had gone away to college. Now on his trips home he seemed to enjoy the company of the family. He lingered for a long time over supper talking to Alec and Esther about a wide range of topics. Bobby Joe was even friendly to Luke, and seemed genuinely interested in what he had been doing. Luke began to understand what his father had said after an older sister had left the nest. "You began to lose them when they turn thirteen, and get 'em back when they leave home."

That night after catching up with the family, Bobby Joe prepared to go out and visit with some of his old friends. Luke was sprawled across the bed with Cocoa, talking easily with his brother, who was sprucing up in front of the mirror.

"Well Bubba, tonight you will probably get in before me," Luke interjected casually.

"Why's that?" Bobby Joe inquired as he tucked in his shirt.

"Jack's Dad is taking us coon hunting. We will be out real late."

"That's good. Taking Cocoa with you? He could introduce you to some of his friends," Bobby Joe joked with a grin. And then, "Never been coon hunting this time of year." Luke picked up just a slight tinge of suspicion in his brother's voice. But the star athlete let it pass, said good-bye, and left.

Before his parents went to bed, Luke went down into the basement and slipped the shovel, pick and lantern outside and placed them underneath the cherry tree. He didn't want to be stumbling around in the dark down there later on. He then made sure to stick some matches in his coat pocket.

By ten-thirty the house was dark. He lay in bed waiting for the old clock in the living room to strike eleven. There was no danger of him falling asleep. The adrenaline was pumping overtime.

When he arrived at the cherry tree, Birdseed was nowhere to be seen. So he waited.

Finally, after almost an hour, his partner in crime arrived.

"Sorry I'm late. I didn't think they would ever go to bed. And it takes my Dad a long time to go to sleep. I wanted to bring his army flashlight, but I couldn't find it."

As planned, and to avoid being seen on the streets of town, they took the long way around to Pea Ridge and the cemetery. Through Freewill, up through the woods, past the prison dump, and in behind the penitentiary they hiked. Only because they had walked this route so many times before were they able to make their way in the darkness. The lantern remained unlit. No need to take a chance on being seen. Luke carried the shovel and the lantern. Birdseed packed the pick.

Finally, after about thirty minutes of challenging terrain, the pair started up the last wooded hill before coming to the graveyard. The sleeping village of Currentville lay down in the valley behind them. Soon they reached their destination.

The ancient burial ground was marked by towering cedar trees and magnolias, some of which had been there for two hundred years. Wrought-iron fences marked off various family plots.

The venerable tombstones were of all shapes and sizes, the oldest being thin slabs with curved tops. Some were leaning grotesquely from age, while a few were broken or lying on the ground. The cemetery began a short distance down the hill, and then climbed up to and over the crest. Luke and Birdseed were working their way to the plateau where the community stalwarts were buried under the moss-covered ground. They moved slowly, feeling their way around the markers.

Just as they arrived at the top of the slope where the ground began to level off, they encountered wrinkle number two.

A car was parked in the middle of the cemetery.

Both of them dropped to the ground and out of site.

"Who in the world is that?" Birdseed whispered.

"I don't know. Too dark to tell. People come up here and park all the time," Luke answered in the pitch blackness.

They both lay on the ground and thought.

"What are we going to do?" Birdseed implored anxiously.

" There's nothing we can do but just wait till they leave." Luke sighed, raised up on one elbow to take another look, and then dropped back onto the grass.

"We could run them off . . . scare them . . . or something," Birdseed was thinking out loud.

"Birdseed," Luke was lying on his back staring up into the blackened sky, "to be so smart, sometimes you're not so smart."

"You're right," Birdseed exhaled in resignation and stretched out on his back. "Wonder what time it is?"

"Around midnight, I'd say. I hope it's some high school kids who have to be home at a certain time." Luke's mind was turning. "Oh well, there's nothing we can do but relax. If they stay too long we might have to put it off to another night."

"What do you think they're doing in there?" Birdseed inquired lasciviously.

"I don't know," Luke was not in the mood to speculate. "I hope they're thinking about going home."

Silence fell upon them. Luke, lying on his back with his legs stretched out straight, crossed his hands on his chest in peaceful repose.

He began to think about all the other people lying around him. Just a few feet away, inches actually, lying there just like him, probably in the same position, looking skyward. But they were cold, lifeless, rotten, dust . . . and he was warm, breathing, alive. There were old ones, and young ones . . . mothers and fathers . . . long, muscular farmers, short and plump housewives. His mind was searching for something from school, some poem in English class . . . about a country churchyard. He couldn't remember the name of the poem, or the poet, but a certain phrase had stuck in his head—

> *For them no more the blazing hearth shall burn,*
> *or busy housewife ply her evening care.*
> *No children run to lisp their sire's return,*
> *or climb his knees the envied kiss to share.*

After a while they began to drift off.

The roar of an engine brought them to life. Bright beams from the headlights struck the trees above them, receded, and then disappeared.

Luke and Birdseed jumped to their feet just in time to see the taillights heading down the hill, past Ollie Bennett's house.

"Okay Birdseed, light the lantern. Let's go," Luke commanded enthusiastically.

A pale circle of light emerged as the wick took hold, and the globe was lowered. The two boys moved up the hill into the main part of the cemetery. Spooky shadows from the markers and trees danced and weaved around them.

Then came the third wrinkle.

They could not find the grave of Matthew Lyon. All of the old tombstones, with their sloping tops and faint etchings looked alike. Lichen and moss, blackened by age, covered the faces of the ancient markers.

"I've seen that grave a thousand times!" Luke complained.

"I thought there was a special marker of some kind," lamented Birdseed.

"There's one out on the road—-one of those special, what

do you call them . . ." Luke explained.

"Historical markers."

"That's right."

Time and time again they would hold the lantern close to one of the silent tombstones, kneel down, and rub away the veneer of time.

Luke glanced anxiously down toward the Bennett house a quarter mile away. Still dark.

Finally they found it:

Matthew Lyon
July 14, 1749 – August 1, 1822

It had taken only ten minutes of wandering among the dead, but it had seemed like hours.

"All right, let's get to work," Luke was speaking barely above a whisper as if they might wake their sleeping companions.

He grabbed the pick, as Birdseed set down the lantern and grabbed the shovel. Straddling what he guessed to be the eternal resting place of Matthew Lyon, Luke raised the mattock and brought it plunging into the sod. It dug deep into the soft earth, scattering fragments of moss which formed a crust over the grave. Again and again, he brought down the iron until the ground began to bleed dirt.

Birdseed stepped in and loaded his shovel.

"Put that dirt in one place Birdseed. We'll need it to fill it back up."

Luke had just given this directive when they both froze. A car was coming up the road.

Instinctively, and as if they had both been shot squarely in the head, they dropped to the ground.

"Put out that lantern!" This time Luke did not bother to whisper.

Birdseed raised the globe and blew out the flame. Darkness once again fell over them. But the lights of the car could be seen bouncing off the trees. Breathless, they hugged the ground as the car came closer.

And then their hearts sank. The vehicle was stopping. Seconds later the engine died. A spotlight came on and began to sweep the cemetery.

"Okay, we know you're in there. Come on out!" It was the voice of Sheriff Bass Fisher.

Without even thinking, Luke suddenly rolled down the slope, jumped to his feet, and took off running. Birdseed followed suit. The spot light raked their backs as they disappeared into the undergrowth.

Into the black forest they charged like wild animals. Down the hill they raced, crashing into limbs, briars, bushes, even small saplings. Never had Luke Cameron moved as he moved that night. He tumbled time and time again, taking falls which would have killed an ordinary mortal. But these were not ordinary times. Onward he kept thrashing his way down the slope toward what he knew was Currentville. His body was flailed and beaten by the dense wilderness whacking away at his face, arms, and legs.

Finally and mercifully the ground leveled out and was clear. But he only ran faster. He knew—only by radar, for the night still blinded him—that he was now in the backyards and gardens of houses on Franklin Street. Soon their forms took shape. He tripped over flower beds and hydrants—once knocking a bird bath off its pedestal. Then he was clothes-lined along the chest, flipping him into the air and onto his back. He could not breathe. Luke knew that he was dying there in the darkness, a convicted grave robber. Moaning and groaning, he rolled from one side to the other. Birdseed eventually arrived on the scene, somehow able to sense him writhing in the darkness. Finally, air returned to his lungs. Luke bounded to his feet and continued the mad dash, Birdseed at his heels.

At Franklin Street, the dim glow of a street light gave them sight. Glancing both ways, Luke sprinted up the sidewalk, down the alleyway behind the Methodist church. He was still running as fast as he could run. Birdseed could not keep up. The streets were deserted of all forms of life, the houses dark. At Main Street, the stoplight switched colors indifferently. Compared to where they had been, the empty downtown area glowed like Times Square.

Craning his neck for witnesses, Luke darted across the street and down the dark alleyway beside the *Signal* office.

At last he was behind the buildings of town and on the riverbank, near the lock and dam reservation. Hidden again by the dark but familiar territory, he threw himself down on the grass.

Luke lay there exhausted, his chest burning, gasping desperately for air. He wondered about Birdseed, trying to remember where he had last seen him. He worried about Sheriff Fisher. It wasn't long, however, before he was joined by another gasping, spent runner. He was too tired to express his relief. Both of them remained speechless as they slowly recovered their wind.

"Did you see anyone?" Luke was finally able to speak, as his breathing leveled off.

"A car coming down off Penitentiary Hill. But they didn't see me," was the reply in the dark.

"Didn't see anything of the sheriff?"

"No."

More silence as each tried to assess their situation.

"I don't think he could have recognized us," Birdseed said, trying to sound confident.

Luke did not answer.

After a few moments Luke sat up. In a slow and somber voice he warned, "We've got real problems."

"Not if he didn't see us. Not if he didn't recognize us," Birdseed argued.

"You don't understand, Birdseed. Our tools—my Dad's tools, the pick, the shovel, even the lantern—are still up there."

For a second Luke contemplated going back to get them. But it was too risky.

"We can go back up there and get them tomorrow," Birdseed assured.

"If they are still there. If Sheriff Fisher didn't pick them up." It was not a promising prospect to Luke.

"Besides," continued Birdseed, "he won't know whose they are. There's no way he can link them to us. When do you think your Dad will miss them? He may not miss them until the summer. Then we can have some kind of story cooked up. He won't even know that you took them."

"He'll ask me," Luke declared. Then with an air of resignation, Then he'll know."

They carefully negotiated the rest of the way home. Bobby Joe was already home and sound asleep when Luke quietly slipped into his bed. He lay in the dark, his mind racing madly. Then he prayed.

Early the next morning, the two desperadoes made their eager way back up to the cemetery. It was raining, a slow drizzle. This time they traveled the conventional way—up Franklin Street to where a path led to the base of the hill. There the old stone steps led their winding and convoluted way up through the woods to the summit.

To their dreadful disappointment, neither the tools nor the lantern was at the gravesite. With forlorn, even pitiful faces, they stood and looked down upon their night's work. In the full light of day their digging looked like little more than a muddy incision in the ground. The dripping trees, melancholy stones, and soggy ground were appropriate props for their blackened mood.

Without saying a word, they turned and headed back down the hill. At the bottom, under the protection of a vine-colored arch, Luke sat down on a step.

"We need to think and talk this out, Birdseed."

Birdseed eased down beside him.

If Luke felt any resentment toward his cajoling friend, he did not show it. Neither recrimination nor blame raised their venomous heads. Here were simply two friends—sitting in the rain on a dreary winter morning—in one helluva fix.

"I don't think we are going to beat this thing, Birdseed," Luke reflected glumly. "It's just a matter of time."

"But time is on our side," Birdseed offered hopefully. "We need to cool it. Act normal. Deal with the tool problem when it comes up. Who knows, your Dad may not ever mention it."

Luke did not think that such wishful thinking merited a reply.

"Listen, Birdseed. Think about this. Sheriff Fisher has my Dad's shovel, pick, and lantern."

Birdseed interrupted, "Maybe. Maybe not. Somebody might have gone by there this morning before us and picked them up."

"Sure, Birdseed. Loads of people were strolling through that old cemetery between midnight and now," Luke chided. "Why, they might have even had a couple of burials already."

Birdseed nodded in recognition.

"No, Bass has the tools. 'There was an attempted grave robbery at the Currentville Cemetery on Friday night. The culprits were caught in the act and ran off. Sheriff Bass Fisher, our brave and heroic sheriff, not only stopped this terrible deed but has the tools of the crime in his possession—a shovel, a pick, and a lantern.' Those words will be in the *Signal* next week. My Daddy will read it."

They both gave thought to the consequences.

Weary of the futility of it all, Birdseed shifted gears.

"Wonder how Sheriff Fisher knew to come up there? I mean, you don't think he just happened to be driving by, do you?"

Luke pondered.

"It must have been when we were waltzing around with our lantern blazing looking for Matthew's grave," Luke speculated. "Mr. Bennett must have seen us and called the sheriff. It's the only thing I can figure."

They thought about that for a while.

"Well," Luke let out a big heavy sigh and picked himself up off the stone step. "Let's go home. I guess we'll just have to play it by ear."

≈✨≈

Bobby Joe Cameron got up early on Sunday morning to go back to Ole Miss. Luke lay in bed and chatted with him as he dressed and packed. For the first time, he noticed how much his brother looked like their mother. This cause an unexplainable stirring within him. This was not just the All-State baseball player. This was not just the All-State basketball player. It was not the local legend, the unbelievably gifted icon, or the Chickasaw Clipper, as the West Kentucky media liked to call him.

This was his brother. Born of the same parents. Raised in the same home. Sharing the same sisters, fearing the same father, loving the same tender Mom. All his life Luke had walked in the shadow of this larger-than-life athlete, finding himself looking on in awe along with others. But he also loved him deeply, and was indescribably proud of him. It pained him now, as he watched his idol preparing to leave home again, that he had never once told him of either.

"Bubba," he sat up in bed. "I have this problem . . . I'd like to talk to you about. If you have a few minutes before you leave."

"Sure thing, Pumpkin. We'll walk down to the river after breakfast." It was a conversation that would never have happened one year before.

The two brothers walked down the lane. It was the first of March and the morning was gray and cool, with a chilly breeze sweeping up the river bottom. The broad sweep of cornfields and tree lines were stark, barren of life. Winter winds and swirling floodwaters had drained the vast valley of life. Broken and withered cornstalks stood like surviving skeletons of a catastrophic battle with nature. The river was swollen from the early spring rains, running its course just below the rim, the lock and dam under water. Deep, surging currents and large chunks of entangled driftwood raced by. High on the hill, lording over this colorless valley, was the gray brooding presence of the penitentiary.

It was a bleak landscape desperately crying for spring.

Luke envied his older brother, who would in just minutes be leaving this grayness, this shabby, dying town, and heading into the life of a much brighter world. By noon, about the time of the fourth stanza of the invitation song at church, Bobby Joe would be passing through Memphis. Before dark he would be in the land of ivy-covered buildings, green lawns, bright and noisy dorms, pretty girls, and athletes.

"Y'all play Kentucky this spring in baseball?" Luke asked as they neared the river.

"Yeah, they come to Oxford at the end of the month. They

don't have much. We should win the conference," his brother declared matter-of-factly.

They climbed up on the trunk of a huge sycamore lying on its side. It had been uprooted and washed downstream and deposited on the bank by the receding water. Luke joined his brother with a greater effort. There they sat, perched among the limbs, looking out over the stream.

"I know you are in a hurry," Luke started nervously, "so I will try to make this quick."

He then proceeded to lay out the whole unseemly story.

Bobby Joe listened patiently. From time to time Luke searched his brother's face to see if he was frowning, scowling, amused, or asleep. But he was encouraged to find that he was listening intently, though without expression.

Luke concluded the tale and waited.

"What in the world made you do such a harebrained thing anyway, Luke McCuiston Cameron?" Bobby Joe finally asked in a stern voice.

It was a family habit. Anytime someone in the family used a person's full name, it meant that person was in trouble. Like they were getting ready to formally read their death sentence off a verdict sheet. Put in the full birth certificate name to make it legal.

"How come you gave in to Birdseed?"

Luke decided to bare all, to throw himself upon the sword. So he told Bobby Joe about Savannah Johnson.

Surprisingly, it seemed to soften him. His brother said nothing for a long time, his eyes fixed on the horizon. Then he began climbing down out of the tree.

"Well, there is only one thing left for you to do now, Pumpkin," he declared. "You've got to tell Daddy the whole thing. And you'd better tell him as quickly as possible. You'd better tell him before he finds out."

Then, giving it further thought, "He may already know."

Bobby Joe read the startled look on his little brother's face.

"He has a way of finding out things. Don't ask me how he does it. It's weird. Another thing. Always tell him the truth. You know that terrible whipping I got over putting the dye in the baptistery? The reason it was so bad is because I lied to him. I've never known him to whip any of us kids when we told the truth. He's got this hang up on truth."

Bobby Joe stopped and looked his little brother over until their eyes met. It was like he was taking only the second really good look at him. The first was when the older kids were brought home from the neighbors to see a wrinkled and squalling little piece of human being cradled in his mother's arms.

Suddenly a half-grin broke across Bobby Joe's face. He shook his head, wondering to himself, "What would this family do for excitement without this kid?"

They headed back up the road from the river. Near the house Bobby Joe chuckled under his breath, "All I got to say is Savannah Johnson must be one helluva woman."

Luke knew his big brother was right. He had to tell his Daddy. But when? And how? It was a time of agony and dread. During this period of torment, Luke avoided Birdseed. He really didn't want to be bothered with all of his blustery blabber about "riding it out." Birdseed didn't have to live with the missing tools.

He thought about going up front at church on Sunday morning, making a full confession in front of the church. That way there would be witnesses. His father surely wouldn't kill him if there were witnesses. Or maybe surrendering to the ministry. He could explain that all of it had been part of God's plan to drive him into preaching—kinda like Jonah having to be swallowed by the whale before he surrendered.

But those ideas passed, as he continued to live in the shadow of death. Luke gave a lot of serious thought to how he got into this cauldron in the first place. He pondered the influence, the sway of Savannah Johnson. He did not understand why this girl, this gorgeous and delectable human being, caused his knees to weaken, his heart to quicken, and his stomach to feel queasy with anticipation at the mention of her name. But now he had learned of the danger lurking in the excitement of this great mystery. It would bode watching.

On Monday night after supper Alec was working in his wood shop in the basement. He was sanding down a small bookcase he was refinishing for Esther.

Luke decided this was the time.

He descended the rickety wooden steps, passed the coal room, and walked into the combination washroom and workshop. His father was working under the pale glow of the hanging light bulb. At supper Alec had been quiet. Not a good sign. But Luke was determined not to put it off any longer.

"Hey, Daddy . . . I need to talk to you about something," he began, his heart pounding and his throat dry.

"Okay. Let's hear it," his father replied sharply as he scrubbed one of the shelves with sandpaper. Definitely not a good sign.

". . . well, Birdseed and I did something kinda stupid." Luke dropped his head, ". . . actually it was real stupid."

Alec kept right on working, making it really tough on Luke.

"On Friday night we took your pick, shovel, and lantern and went up to the cemetery."

The words caught in his throat. He stood in quaking silence. In the history of the world, had any thirteen-year-old boy ever stood in front of his father and confessed to grave robbing? The magnitude of such a historical happening overwhelmed him.

". . . anyway, we had heard that there might be a valuable ring in the grave of Matthew Lyon and we decided to dig down in it to see."

Here he almost lied. He was tempted to tell how they were going to sell the ring and donate the money to hungry children. But he forged on down the rocky road of truth.

"So we went up there. Slipped out of the house after you and Mom had gone to bed. We got up there and started digging. About that time Bass Fisher came up there and started shining his spotlight. So we ran off."

Alec had not changed his work pace, nor his expression, the whole time. It was terribly unnerving to Luke. He was struggling desperately to unload this terrible burden, and his father gave no indication whatsoever of what dire consequences were in store. Alec just kept sanding and listening.

"We left your tools up there," Luke plowed on. "On Saturday morning we went back up there, but they were gone."

There. For better or for worse, it was out. He had thrown himself upon the rack. Now the prisoner waited in terror for the verdict.

It was a cruel and excruciating wait.

His father continued to sand the wood, saying nothing, giving no indication whatsoever that he had even heard his young son painfully bear his soul.

Luke stood there, twisting and turning in the wind. Waiting. Waiting.

After Luke had seen his entire life pass before him—after the long punishing pause, his father finally dropped his hands and stood up straight. He placed the sandpaper on the shelf and inspected his work. Then, with his eyes finally leaving the bookcase, he walked slowly to the wall.

He reached up and pulled down the shovel from two nails.

Expressionless, and without a word, he examined the end of it and returned it to its place. Then he took down the pick, walked to the work bench, picked up a rag, and calmly cleaned the point. Then he slowly and deliberately placed it back on the wall.

Luke stood speechless. Dumbfounded.

At long last, Alec Cameron turned and looked into the eyes of his young son.

"Bass called me on Saturday morning. He recognized you both. I went down to the courthouse and picked up the tools. I was waiting to see if you would come clean."

Luke dropped his head and stared at the floor. His father turned and went back to his sandpapering.

"Be in Sheriff Fisher's office as soon as you get out of school tomorrow," Alec sternly concluded the conversation.

The next day, Luke and Birdseed got their first big break with Sheriff Fisher. Just as they nervously settled into their chairs and Bass reached down and spit amber into an old coffee can, a deputy came running in. There was a shooting between-the-rivers. "Y'all don't do a crazy thing like that again, y'all hear!" he bellowed gruffly as he headed out the door.

Birdseed was confined to his room for a thousand years and required to copy pages and pages from his history book.

As for Luke, something incredible happened.

Neither his father nor his mother ever mentioned the grave-robbing incident again.

It was not until summer that Birdseed and Luke came to talk about it again. They were lying under the cherry tree one hot night staring up at the stars and talking about everything. They got around to the grave robbing. This time they were able to laugh about the whole ordeal. "We must have really been dumb, Birdseed," Luke bellowed. "I mean, even if we had been successful and got the ring out of Matthew Lyon's grave, people would have had to find out we were guilty of grave robbing." They laughed some more.

"Luke, I got a confession to make," Birdseed said in a serious tone. "I lied to you. I never told Savannah Johnson about the grave robbery plan. She never said those things about you."

Luke lay on the grass and stared into the sparkling galaxies with mixed emotions. He was disappointed that she had not said those things about him. But he was relieved that his chances with Savannah Johnson did not depend on his success as a grave robber.

It was many years later when the topic once again raised its ugly head. In the midst of the pounding confirmation inquisition of the U.S. Senate, the future Supreme Court Justice received a note of encouragement from Bobby Joe. In the postscript, big brother couldn't resist getting in his dig. "Do they know about the grave robbery conviction? I can be bought!"

Chapter Fourteen

Buildings

A house without people is like a promise without hope.

It was a long haul from Luke's house to school. From one end of Currentville to the other.

He would leave his front porch and head up Penitentiary Hill, walk in front of the prison, and steeply down the other side into the business district. Leaving the stores and Charlie's Pool Hall behind, he would continued to trudge out tree-lined Main Street, passing old houses along the way. Finally, just a short distance from where the town ran out, he would arrive at the large two-story brick school on the left. The baseball field was across the road on the right.

Most of this trek he would make alone. Before he graduated, Bobby Joe had caught the school bus in front of the house going the other way to the high school, two miles away, in Catawba.

Birdseed, ever the overprotected child, was dropped off by his father at his grandmother's house next door to the school early each morning.

So Luke made the mile-long trip alone, sometimes with

Soldier at his heels. For the most part he enjoyed the hike, even when loaded with schoolbooks and gym gear. The rare exceptions were those coldest days of winter when the frigid wind off the river would blast him as he reached the summit of Penitentiary Hill. There were days when he would suffer terribly. He came to know that there were 1,264 steps from his front porch to Willis Town's grocery in the middle of town. On those single-digit mornings his only goal in life was to make it there before he died.

First there was tingling in his hands, feet, and face. Then the arrival of pain—pounding, aching pain. It cut so sharp into his frame that every step was like a crank upon the tortuous rack. That's why he knew the number of strides to his rescue station— he counted each one in order to divert his tormented thoughts from the stabbing cold. School buses laden with country kids would pass, the snug, happy faces of the passengers peering out at his suffering. Their toasty comfort pained Luke even more. There was a grave injustice here somewhere, Luke pondered resentfully during these frigid moments. Most of these country kids would leave their cozy kitchens when they saw the bus coming down the road, walk thirty yards to the mailbox, and then board the yellow cocoon which transported them comfortably to school. But the town kids had to battle the cold, sleet and rain—even backwater at times—on foot, slogging the long and bitter way to school—a place where he would just as soon not be in the first place.

Finally, and mercifully—when he could no longer feel anything but the frosty air cutting into his nostrils—he would make it to the store. There he would stagger through the door and to the glowing coal-burning stove in the rear. While some of the local men loafed and gossiped, Luke stood near the fire and let the blissful heat seep into the frozen tundra of his small frame, slowly bringing it back to life. Rescued and rejuvenated, he soon took heart again, and lit out on the last leg of his embittered journey.

The return trip in the afternoon was quite different.

When the bewitching hour of 3 p.m. hit the drowsy hamlet, it came alive with the sounds of children, disgorged in packs from the big brick building at the edge of town. A fleet of golden angels dispersed from the school, motoring their precious wares to all parts of the county.

Luke and his small knot of friends ambled back toward town, jousting, wrestling, and joking as they moved in the general direction of home. By the time they reached Charlie's Pool Hall, some had fallen off to dwellings perched on the ridge or nestled in the back streets.

Weather and the time of the year guided Luke's daily homeward journey. On most days, from Charlie's Pool Hall on in, it was a solitary way. When cold weather set in, he took in coal for some elderly widows, as well as the *Chickasaw Signal* newspaper office. He got a nickel a bucket, and during spells of low temperatures—brief and unpredictable as they were—it would keep him busy till dark. At times the duty was critical. Confined to their large drafty houses heated only by open grates, these old women would—on bitterly cold days—depend upon Luke literally for their lives. And he never failed them.

There, in the gathering gloom of a winter afternoon, he would find these shabby and wrinkled old ladies entombed near their glowing fires. With his arrival they would quicken momentarily in dim delight, encouraged in the assurance that their coal buckets would be full for the long dark night ahead, buoyed briefly by the wonderful sound of a human voice in their lonely world.

"I'm afraid one day I'm gonna find one of them sitting in there dead," Luke confided to Bobby Joe one night.

"How would you be able to tell?" his older brother dourly replied.

He and Jack had separate clients. When times demanded, they would cover for each other. Sometimes, when spending the night with each other—or on ballgame nights—they would work them together.

On Thursday afternoons, Luke also worked at the *Signal* office folding newspapers. All this combined with chores at home kept him busy after school.

But the days of autumn—late September and October— allowed him some respite. He enjoyed his walk home from town, through a world dressed in colors of gold, scarlet, and bronze. He peered at this world through an amber screen, inhaling the smoke of burning leaves. On top of Penitentiary Hill was a huge walnut tree which dropped its beautifully rounded fruit. Luke would scrape the green shell along the low wall in front of the prison. Placing the bruised pellet to his nose he ingested the rich, earthy scent of fall. He also discovered that walnut stain was good for warts.

Many times during this season of splendor Luke would take the river route home, tasting ripe persimmons, searching for the fork and spoon in the seed.

There was a painful melancholy about fall, however, which Luke could not fathom. Such awesome beauty, a magnificent kaleidoscope of color framed against an azure sky; a bright warm sun which did not burn but seemed to be constantly waning. Browning fields, orange pumpkins, turnips, and early nights with harvest moons—all of it glorious and splendid, while at the same time whispering-ever so softly and subtly—an unsettling message of death. It would be a long time before the young boy would fully understand his grandfather's perceptive quip, "Peering at the splendor of fall is like looking into the face of a beautiful woman. You know she will break your heart."

It was early on one of these golden and frosty mornings when Luke first noticed that something was wrong at Dr. Carey's house.

The large two-story antebellum home sat back off Main Street behind a rolling lawn of sugar maples and magnolias. It was sandwiched incongruously between the feed store and Jennie's Resturant. Out of this brick structure with the white columns, the tottering old physician practiced medicine on the first floor and lived on the second. Out back, across the alleyway which meandered from Main Street across backyards and behind old houses, was the old slave quarters. Dr. Carey used the outbuilding to store his ample supply of assorted junk and keepsakes.

On his way to school this morning, Luke casually glanced through the yellow and green foilage up to the stately mansion. There was something amiss, a peculiar look to the place which his mind, still a bit groggy from sleep, failed to fully comprehend. The impression simply raced through his head, into his consciousness, and back onto the street, as he hurriedly turned toward school.

That same afternoon on his return trip from school, he took a much more measured look up the winding driveway toward the ancient landmark. Suddenly it dawned upon him. The big old house was empty. This historical centerpiece of town, the bustling Bethesda of Currentville, was now vacant, cold, and lonely.

Mesmerized by the startling revelation, Luke stood for a long moment and stared. Slowly he began to walk up the driveway to get a better look at the abandoned home. There was a strangeness to the stillness, and an unwelcome feeling as he approached the spacious portico. Marring the elegance of the slender columns was a cardboard sign nailed to one of its number. "CONDEMNED BY THE U.S. ARMY CORPS OF ENGINEERS" was embossed in large black lettering, followed just below by smaller print, "No Trespassing." The familiar red castle, which Luke recognized from the caps of the lockmen, adorned the top of the proclamation.

Wind whipped up some leaves at Luke's feet as the embattled old monument stared down upon him in silence, a muted hostage to change. After a few moments of heavy reflection, the young schoolboy moved away from the ghost and stole away home.

Luke learned that Dr. Carey had moved his practice and home—lock, stock, and barrel—to a rambling old house up on the ridge. In that dwelling he continued to peer into opened mouths, punch around the glands, scribble out prescriptions, and hit the bottle as soon as the last patient departed. He was incredibly endowed mentally, compassionate, and made regular house calls. But he was old, widowed, and saw little use in doing anything else but getting out of the floodplain to hang on a day at a time.

Each day as Luke would pass the old home, he would look upon it in wonder, not only about its long and celebrated past, but its murky and uncertain future. In reality, its future was neither murky nor uncertain. The historic landmark was soon going to be history.

One day around Thanksgiving Luke noticed activity at the

place. A navy-gray Corps of Engineer truck was parked in the driveway near the house. Two men dressed in khaki were walking around in the yard, staring up at the roof and eaves of the house. The tall one scribbled notes on a clipboard he was carrying. They conversed with each other, pointing here and there, and after a while got in the truck and rode off.

The Carey place was no ordinary antique homestead. Anchored in the middle of town, it connected the community to its cultural, historic, and social past.

A portion of the structure had been built in 1809 as a river tavern and hotel. The bricks had been made by slaves in a kiln located just behind the house, where what was now just a low spot on the ground covered in weeds. It even served for a while as the county's first courthouse. Over a period of time it was enlarged as additions were made, until it was slowly transformed into a stately mansion.

During the War Between the States it was owned by a wealthy landowner named Augustus Yates who sent six sons to fight for the Confederacy. These included the youngest—a lad of only fourteen years of age—who took off with an older brother and served as a drummer boy in the closing days of the war.

Luke, though quite small at the time, could remember when this last of the surviving Rebs—who was Dr. Carey's uncle—celebrated his one-hundredth birthday. It was a festive occasion at the mansion, as the whole town turned out. The high school band came to play on the shady lawn, speeches were made by leading citizens, and the frail and withered old drummer boy was rolled out onto the front porch in a wheelchair to receive a giant birthday cake decorated as a Confederate flag.

During the war, while his sons were away fighting for the gray, Mr. Yates and his proud home suffered two indignities which left permanent scars upon the family residence. One of the Union gunboats moving up the Cumberland River toward Fort Donelson and eventually Shiloh, spotted the flag of the insurrectionists flying proudly from the roof of the Yates home. Without slowing down, the war vessel lobbed a shell through the front wall of the house and right into the finely furnished dining room. Undaunted, the owners repaired the damage. But the new brick used to patch the hole never quite matched the old, and evidence of the wound remained as long as the house stood.

The unkindest cut of all, however, was inflicted upon the soul of both the house and its master.

When the Union troops moved in and occupied the strategic little river town of Currentville, they commandeered the largest building in town, the Yates mansion, for their headquarters. Troops pitched their tents and bivouacked in the yard. The commanding officer—a cocky little captain—slept in the master bedroom located on a corner of the ground floor. Not only was the family relegated to limited parts of the house, but they and their property were treated with disdain for their contribution to the Southern cause. For several weeks Augustus Yates simmered in silence, both humiliated and incensed. Finally, after doing substantial damage to the premises by insolent and willful neglect, the troops moved out and headed south toward Dover.

The day that the Yanks departed, Mr. Yates closed the shutters of the Captain's vacated bedroom and nailed them shut. "Never again," he proclaimed solemnly, as he watched the windows being sealed by his house slaves, "will the sunlight shine into that room."

And so it was to be. The Russians had launched a sputnik into space. But the shutters on that room remained as defiantly shut as the day the Union soldiers rode off.

Only now, the Feds were back in force.

After the November winds had stripped the trees of most of their leaves, the lonesome old house seemed to have taken a couple of steps up closer to the street. One day at school in Mrs. Wilson's class they studied Joyce Kilmer's poem, "The House With Nobody In It."

> *I suppose I've passed it a hundred times,*
> *but I always stop for a minute*
> *And look at the house, the tragic house, the*
> *house with nobody in it.*

Of course all the kids could relate to the words of the poet. There were a growing number of empty houses in Currentville.

One sunny afternoon on his way home from school, Luke decided to explore.

He went up the driveway and climbed the steps of the portico. The large oaken door stared at him. Looking closely, he was surprised to see that it was slightly ajar. Pulling back the screen, he reached in and grabbed the bronze knob. With a slight nudge, the door opened easily.

Glancing around, and suppressing second thoughts, he quickly moved through the doorway. It was cold inside, shivering cold. Although the outside temperature was mild, the cavernous shell had encased the chill from colder days.

The aging hardwood floor, which had borne the muddy heels of the Union troops, sagged under the load of time. Luke was in the large waiting room, now empty and bare, but once full of fidgety and fearful tots clinging to their mothers who stared dully into space, or thumbed mechanically through old magazines. A faint scent of formaldehyde and ether still lingered.

Slowly he began to edge toward the next room to the right, the floor, squeaking and popping with each of his steps. The tomblike silence permeated the giant edifice. The walls of the structure must have been three feet thick, blocking out all sounds from the outside. It was spooky.

Luke now stood in what might have passed as a kitchen. Ivory colored tile climbed up the wall from the linoleum floor halfway up to the ceiling. Beams of afternoon sunlight streamed through the pane windows above the sink. A constant dripping of a faucet had etched a brownish-orange stain into the milk-colored basin. Empty wall cabinets flanked the window and the sink, their doors flung open. In this room the smell of medicine still carried a mighty whiff. Luke remembered this place—the examining table, eye chart, a Norman Rockwell painting, scales—now all gone. He almost winced, thinking of sharp needles and the pain of inoculations.

With his mind always possessed with dread as to what instruments of torture might be forthcoming, he had never noticed the narrow doorway and steps to the left which led upstairs. He moved to the opening and stared up the shaft. These steps, steep and cramped, had provided back access to the second floor from the kitchen which had once been located in a separate building out back. The house slaves used them as the avenue to service the upper parts of the mansion. Seldom did the cooks and the house-boys use the grander and sweeping stairway leading up from the huge front living room.

Here, at the bottom of the steps, Luke hesitated.

The long almost ladderlike ascent was enticing—a passage-way to the unknown mysteries of the upstairs. Yet at the same time he felt like an intruder, a trespasser, and was somewhat fearful. The deeper into the bowels of the rambling abode he went, the more difficult and ensnaring the retreat. He looked around, heard noth-ing of course—for there was nothing to be heard—and then start-ed up the steps. There was no trouble seeing his way as the bare and towering windows of the house poured in plenty of the day's bright light.

At the top of the steps he found himself in what had been a large bedroom. Through the rectangular windows he could see the giant elms and oaks, now mostly naked, in the side yard. Old newspapers and some coat hangers were strewn along the floor of the empty room.

Luke turned to look through the open door to his right.

Suddenly he froze and his hair stood on end.

There in the other room was a human being. The man, shabbily dressed, was seated on the floor with his back to the wall, his knees pulled up to his chest. His head was buried in his arms folded across the knees. A shaggy mop of graying hair gave him away.

It was Stonewall Jackson.

Within a split second, Luke's options tumbled through his racing mind.

He could beat a quiet and hasty retreat, backing down the steps and out of the house. Or he could continue on with his quest, searching out the rest of the house, ignoring—if he could—Stonewall's presence.

But fear paralyzed him. He had always been a little bit afraid of drunks—even the seemingly innocuous and sometimes comical town sots. There was something of the unknown, the unpredictable, about those not totally in control of their faculties which made them monstrous. One never knew what they would do.

Luke had friends whose fathers were given to the strong powers of drink. He had been at their homes when they staggered in, out of control, raging, and sometimes abusive. It was frightening for him, but he had the opportunity to escape, to steal away home. His friends did not. Luke's father was not an unabashed enemy to drink, even though his mother looked upon whiskey as man's chief enemy. From time to time, Alec would slip around behind Esther's back and imbibe a little. Maybe a couple of beers at the ballpark in Nashville, or a pint of bourbon hidden away in the basement at Christmas time. But, for marital harmony if nothing else, he was delicately discreet and temperate. So Luke was not accustomed to drunks up close.

Nevertheless, for some reason, he took the road less traveled and stepped into the room with Stonewall.

It occurred to Luke that Stonewall could be sick. He might need help. A boldness, closely akin to courage, arose from within the young lad. The vagrant ceased to be an object of contempt or fear, and became a victim who needed help. A victim of what, Luke was not sure. Only that he was aware of a strange and peculiar sense of togetherness. Though his boyish mind could not have fashioned the thought, it was as if he were somehow guided by an unseen hand, and, for some inexplicable reason, these two lives had come together on this winter afternoon in this vast and lonely house doomed for destruction.

Moving in closer to the object on the floor, Luke soon stood directly in front of him. He noticed a slight scent of fresh booze, layered over a stale and sour smell of liquor breath and soiled clothing. On the floor to the left was a dead bottle of Four Roses whiskey.

"Stonewall!" Luke spoke, in a tone not unlike that of a schoolteacher waking up a sleeping student.

For a long moment there was no response. Then slowly, without any apparent question or surprise at being found here in this hidden corner of earth, Stonewall raised his head. His bleary and tortured eyes focused on the diminutive inquisitor until his muddled and mealy mind could process the information.

"Hello Luke," he finally said as matter-of-factly as if they had just met in front of the post office. The voice had the drag and distortion of a phonograph spun to the slower speed.

"I'm just resting," he added as a groggy afterthought, and his heavy head went back down upon his knees.

Convinced the patient was okay, Luke turned to leave. The conversation had kinda dried up. As he reached the door, Stonewall raised his head once again.

"Hey Luke," the bloodshot eyes searched the room until they rested upon the boy. "I'm waiting for Dr. Carey. Tell him I'm here, will ya?"

"I'll tell him, Stonewall," Luke promised.

Having lost his adventuresome spirit, Luke hurried back down the steps, through the house to the front door. There at the doorway he stopped. For some unexplainable reason he turned and looked back into the giant maze and listened to the stillness. Then he bellowed at the top of his voice, "Dr. Carey! Stonewall Jackson is here!"

The proclamation thundered through the corners and crevices of the empty chambers, even falling, no doubt, upon the pair of ears in the faraway corner of the house.

With a slight grin on his face, Luke turned and left.

Those were the last words ever spoken in the Carey mansion. Two nights later it burned to the ground. Arson was suspected, but then forgotten.

After all, how could one murder a corpse?

***

The DX station at the main corner of town was a sorry piece of work.

Perhaps at one time, long before Luke was born, it had been bright, clean, modern, and attractive. The concrete block building certainly claimed a prime location. It sat on the river side of Main Street at the town's only stoplight. Beautiful, tree-lined Franklin Street intersected with downtown at this junction. But on the other side of Main Street, where it passed the DX station, the road quickly turned to gravel. This was the ferry road, placing the filling station not only in a prime location for the town's drive through trade, but for the between-the-rivers traffic as well.

But whatever glory years of commerce it may have experienced were now long gone.

The building itself was a two-tone color, with the dull brownish outer coating almost completely chipped off, revealing its earlier dirty white. From atop a tall metal pole on the corner, the familiar diamond-shaped sign, faded and rusty, dangled at an angle. There was only one service island with two pumps, one for gas and the other for kerosene. On the left side of the building were two service bays, almost always empty. Their outer doors, which pulled closed from overhead, were each adorned with a row of windows coated with dirt, grease, and grime.

To the right of the service bays was the dingy little customer service area. A large plate-glass window, also layered with dirt, looked in on the money end of the business. The glass counter contained a few candy bars, Moon Pies, chewing gum, and cigarettes—Camels and Lucky Strikes only—with a huge, cast iron cash register on top. There were a few new tires stacked near the door, and a few other items for sale pitched here and there—sunglasses, motor oil, window scrapers, tiny tins of aspirin, and various other things with a long, long shelf life. Over to the left of the counter, underneath the window, was the battered old drink box. Under the sliding lid, standing up to their necks in refrigerated water, were bottles of Pepsi, Coca-Cola, and RC.

But the hub—the soul—of this establishment was the area behind the counter against the back wall. At the center was a pot-bellied stove. Its black stem reached upward, and then crooked into the brick flue. On one side, close enough for warming purposes, sat a tattered old back seat out of a car. To the right were a couple of cane-bottom chairs, the seats unraveling from wear. Several wooden drink boxes stood on end in a semicircle to provide additional seating. To the back of the stove, against the wall, was a huge open box partially filled with lumps of coal the size of grapefruit. From time to time, the wooden holding bin was replenished with scuttles of fuel from the pile out back.

The floor around this heater was most times dirty and unswept, coated with a ghastly mix of spilled ashes and tobacco amber.

But it was an enticing place to loiter, especially in winter, for the more forlorn and hopeless street people of the town. It was here where the marginal figures of the small community congregated to while away their idle time, nurse themselves through head-pounding hangovers, burn up lost dreams and ambitions within the winter fire. Town drunks, the destitute, the jobless, and some other old men who felt more comfortable with the rabble and the rude, made this their downtown office.

There was an unannounced and unwritten caste system in the town's loafing spots. Men of means, jobs, positions, statute, respectability, warmed their hands and backs at the stove in the rear of Willis Town's grocery. And the soldiers of drink did not feel welcome at Charlie's Pool Hall. Sometimes there was a thin line between being sober and being under the influence, and Charlie was not one to give the edge to the consumer. So that left the DX station, where the very environs seem to attract decadence and demise.

Yet the place did some business. Nothing like the cleaner, brighter Standard station catty-cornered across the street. But cars came and went, and there were the occasional sounds of banging and clanging from the service bays, where vehicles hung suspended on the lifts.

Luke watched all this from a distance, passing by on the way to school each day on the other side of the street. He could see through the sooty windows, the convention of wayward souls hovering near the stove, the thick black smoke billowing out from the roof. It was there where he next saw Stonewall Jackson after the Carey house encounter. He was shuffling through the front door, around the counter, and finally—after some effort—settling unsteadily upon the end of a wooden drink case. There his shoulders dropped as he leaned forward toward the warming grate. Others already there greeted him with the customary grunts and glances.

It was Bennie Marshall who first noticed it. Luke had met up with him and Jack one morning on the way to school.

"The DX is closed," he stated nonchalantly, and pointed across the street.

Sure enough, the seedy gas station was locked up tighter than a drum. It was empty, and no smoke came from the chimney.

"Yeah, I saw them moving stuff out over the weekend," Jack added.

That was all that was said, but each of them knew the consequences. "Closed" no longer carried the conventional meaning in Currentville. It did not mean to be reopened under new management, or a different business. It did not even mean that it would cease to exist, and the land would be sold to a new owner with perhaps different purposes. It did not even make it unique—shutting down, failing, going under, while others survived and flourished. It simply meant that this business, this home, this building, was "the next to go." The cardboard sign attached to the front door with the ever-familiar Corps of Engineers castle boldly proclaimed that this was the newest victim of the systematic execution of a town. This block building with an inglorious past, a haven for vagrants, would fare no worse than the regal and romantic Carey house a block away.

It was just a couple of days after the Christmas vacation when Luke noticed something strange about the dead DX station. By coincidence, he was once again with Jack and Bennie Marshall walking to school. At first they thought the building was on fire. But then they realized that it was just smoke pouring out of the old chimney.

"What's going on over there?" Luke asked, pointing above the roofline.

They all stared in wonderment.

"I don't know. Let's go take a look," Jack urged, and headed across the street. Luke and Bennie followed.

The old building still appeared vacant and deserted. A filthy old "Closed" sign was still hanging from the door and the Corps condemnation notice had been torn slightly by the wind.

Each of the three schoolboys moved cautiously up to the large, filmy window and cupped his hands to peer inside. After their eyes adjusted to the darker inside, they saw life forms within the cemetery.

The potbellied stove was ablaze and three manly figures were seated around it, their shoulders hunched and drawn.

One of them was Stonewall Jackson.

The entire room was empty and bare with the exception of the stove, and the familiar seating around it. At the back was an old wooden door, slightly ajar, through which the trespassers had made their entry.

After only a few moments the boys resumed their trek to school.

"Those old coots," Bennie commented as they headed back across the street, "they'll be sitting there with the water lapping up around their feet."

Luke and Jack somberly nodded in agreement.

⁂

There was nothing more peculiar about this shabby, run-down little river town than Charlie's Pool Hall.

It was located halfway between the elegant Carey mansion and the battered old DX on Main Street. The concrete block building was clean and well kept, with a green metal awning hanging out over the sidewalk from above the doorway. Large plate-glass windows with neatly painted frames flanked the door. It was so that mothers and wives could easily peer through the glass in search of their men. Three tables sat end to end, cue racks on the wall to the left. Toward the rear was the counter, with assorted candies and snacks displayed for sale. The well-stocked, ever-popular drink box was to the right.

Running down the right side of the wall, after the pinball machine and jukebox, were wooden benches elevated upon a narrow platform. They provided excellent viewing for the continuous games of rotation, eight ball, bank, and sixty-one. During peak times, the smacking of ivory clashed with the bells and bumping of the pinball machine.

It was pool, and it was in Currentville.

But it was not "trouble in river city."

And for that reason it was peculiar.

While it carried some of the looks and smells of most all small town pool halls, it was not a place for swearing, gambling, and hidden bottles of cheap bootleg whiskey.

The proprietor of this unusual establishment was an odd little man himself: Charlie Clark.

Mystery surrounded Charlie, at least as far as the town boys were concerned. He spoke with a Northern clip in his speech, and lived alone on one of the hidden back streets of town. Short and stocky, in his mid-sixties, he was always impeccably dressed in expensive slacks, neatly pressed shirt, and well shined shoes. Never did he remove—even inside of his shop, summer or winter—the narrow-brimmed straw hat fixed squarely on his head. He wore thick, tinted glasses, adding to his enigmatic ways. But he was friendly and talkative, even as he protected his own privacy. Charlie had someone to open up the pool hall in the morning. He would arrive on the job at high noon, whistling softly, his brown-bagged supper and thermos under his arm. There he would remain until closing time—eleven on week nights, midnight on weekends. Closed on Sundays.

No one knew anything about Charlie Clark's personal life. He belonged to no clubs, had no close friends, was never seen anywhere in town outside his own business, and never darkened the doors of a church. It was like he vanished at midnight, and on Sundays, off the face of the earth, reappearing at high noon each day—fresh, cool, and unchanging.

Of course rumors surfaced periodically. He had a wife in Princeton. He was wanted by the FBI for a crime he committed in his youth up in Michigan. He had a demented and deformed old mother whom he kept tied in the back room of his house. All false. But one thing was true. He had run the pool hall in Currentville for so many years that anyone under forty could not remember when he wasn't there. Another thing was undisputed. Little Louis Dawson was only twelve years old when his abusive and alcoholic father pulled a knife on the jailor one night and was shot dead. Charlie took Lou under his wing, putting him to work opening up the pool hall each day when he wasn't in school. This was many years before Luke was even born. Lou Dawson grew up to become a prominent businessman and one of the most respected citizens of the town. The older people of the community gave Charlie Clark a lot of credit for that.

There were two things which remained ever constant about Charlie Clark. No one really knew him. And everyone liked him.

And his pool hall was a shining anachronism—a strangely wholesome and virtuous entertainment center, in the middle of a rough and decaying old river town.

Children under twelve were not allowed to play. Once a young boy reached that magic age, his father could make the ritual visit and sign the permit for him to play pool. It was a rite of passage.

No gambling allowed. No profanity allowed. No drunks allowed. No one even with the smell of drink was allowed. No horseplay or wrestling allowed. If anyone got out of hand, Charlie—armed only with his change apron and wooden rack around his arm—would step over and softly whisper something in the delinquent's ears. Each time the offender, sometimes as big and rough-looking as a lumberjack, would quietly rack his cue and leave. It was a place to which any man's wife, mother or sister could go looking for their man, and not have to worry about what they might see or hear.

"There's more religion in Charlie Clark's pool hall," Luke once overheard his Dad tell his preacher, "than there is in all the churches in Currentville."

It was hard to argue the point.

Charlie also kept his domain spotless. In down times he was constantly sweeping, dusting, and otherwise policing the area.

The long room buzzed with activity. There was a spirit to the place—lively, noisy, smoke filled, frequented by all ranks and types and yet, in a peculiar way, clean and wholesome. Blaring music from the juke box, ringing bells of the pinball machine and the cracking of ivory mingled with laughter and lively conversations. Here within a most unlikely place there was vibrancy, life, bedlam, energy. It was—in this moribund village—like the strong heart of a comatose animal, pumping life throughout the trunk and limbs of a body already dead or dying.

The pool hall awakened at seven in the morning, and within an hour it was already filling up with high school kids congregating at the downtown bus stop. Some of the callow youth played pool, while others looked on sleepily, munching their breakfast of Lance crackers washed down by Yoo-hoo chocolate drink. Others stood around with hands in back pockets staring out the front windows onto Main Street. Always a cluster hovered over the pinball machine, concentrating on the small silver sphere rolling and ringing down the colorful display. The player looked down intently, flipping and gently shaking the machine.

Then in a flash the place would be empty as the last school bus for Cawtaba pulled up outside.

Schoolboys were quickly replaced by the army of local merchants, clerks, and mechanics, ducking into Charlie's for a lighthearted game of billiards before moving on to the drudgery of work.

Business would drag—especially in winter—through the balance of the morning. At noon, with Charlie's arrival, came the courthouse crowd. County Judge John Ryan Cartwright, Sheriff Bass Fisher, and others would noisily make their entrance, laughing and joking, grabbing cues from the wall and crashing the ivory. After a boisterous hour of spirited play and jousting, the county leaders paid up, slapped Charlie on the back, and made their exit.

Then, in the afternoon—even in the summer—the cavern of fun would drowse with inactivity. Only sobered drunks, old men in retirement, and Cowboy Curtis, the town imbecile, hung tough.

No one knew for sure how old Cowboy really was. That

part of him was almost as much of a mystery as Charlie. It seemed that he had been in the same grade at school with everyone at one time or another. He would slip back, while others moved on. The old yearbook showed him in the grade school pictures for a decade. Finally, at some age, he disappeared from school and hit the local haunts as the full time sentinel of the streets. He wore a spot on the bench in Charlie's Pool Hall to a shiny sheen.

Plump and toothless, Cowboy was plagued by a severe speech impediment. He talked incessantly in a high pitch and grating tone. Only those who had known him all their lives could understand a word he said. That included almost everyone. What he would say was not exactly idiotic, but just childish chatter, which constituted nothing more than noise.

"Two buses stopped here this morning. Herky Rose first one on bus. Tommy Barker was last one on bus. He rode on back seat yesterday. That bus number 18 . . . " And on and on. His was the mind of a five-year-old.

For hours Cowboy would stand around in the pool hall talking to Charlie, rattling on and on, spewing out a steady stream of nonsensical verbiage. Little Charlie would stand patiently watching a game of pool, nodding his head kindly to the clatter, even occasionally offering a polite response.

"Cowboy must have pictures on Charlie," growled Sheriff Fisher. "Nobody could be that damn patient!"

At night, the pool hall lit up with activity, especially on weekends. On Saturday nights the downtown stores remained open until 10 o'clock. Charlie's Pool Hall would jive with a packed house of country men and boys, mixed with the regular locals. Songs blaring loudly from the jukebox mingled with the roar of the crowd and the cracking sounds of pool.

Summer Saturday nights were especially festive, as hardworking men enjoyed the rare respite from the punishing sun. Charlie's large floor fan at the back of the hall stirred up the humid air and rushed it toward the front, under the slowly revolving ceiling blades, and through the open doors.

Charlie was an inveterate St. Louis Cardinals baseball fan. His loyalty was unfailing. Regardless of the score or their place in the standings, he listened to every single inning on the little Philco radio sitting atop an old refrigerator at the back of the pool hall. It was reported—rumored if you will—that Charlie played ball in the Cardinals' organization and was a friend of one of the old Gashouse Gang, Pepper Martin. No one knew for sure, and inexplicably, no one ever asked.

Charlie would stand with his left arm draped up over the corner of the icebox. Peering out over the commotion of the crowded room, he would listen intently to the rich and exciting voice of Cardinal announcer Harry Caray. To this place, in the sleepy shantytown nestled in the steamy Cumberland River Valley, came the sounds of major league baseball. In the hot, muggy air of a summer Saturday night at Charlie's Pool Hall, one could almost smell the hotdogs and cigar smoke of old Sportmen's Park many miles away.

At 9:40 p.m., Charlie's business was bustling. The Cardinals were batting.

"It's a 2-2 tie in the bottom of the ninth," intoned Harry with his familiar flair for the dramatic.

Charlie, with his ear only inches away from the battered old receiver, intently watched the game of eight ball drawing to a close on the back table. A deeply absorbed look covered his face.

"Musial opened with a double, and went to third on the ground out by Boyer. He's there now with two outs."

With "Stan the Man's" ringing double, the players at the table had been drawn to Charlie's side. There they stood, in between shots, ears bent to the radio. Their attention to the game upon the felt slowly giving way to the game upon the grass.

"Wally Moon, facing Ed Roebuck . . . the Dodger relief hurler . . . Moon has worked the count to two and one." Harry's voice, like the rising crescendo from a great pianist, was adeptly staircasing the event with magnetic excitement.

Harry Caray, the entertainer, performed as if he knew that drab little places, sleepy little towns, country stores, pool halls, and lonely homes depended upon him to bring a surge of excitement into the grayness.

Just as the eight ball banked into the corner pocket to conclude one game, Harry reported the end of another.

"... the pitch to Moon ... There's a shot to right center, it may drop! Snider on the run ... on the run ... Base hit! Cardinals win! Cardinals win! Wally Moon comes through!"

Even though he was yelling at the top of his voice, Harry's bell-tone inflections flowed smoothly and distinctly over the entire pool hall.

Varying yelps and exclamations of approval erupted from the Currentville gathering. The players on the back table moved jubilantly across the room to rack their cues on the wall. Silver passed into Charlie's hand, which he deposited in his apron. He moved in to pick the pockets and rack the balls.

His face beamed with the Cardinals' victory.

"Thank you very much, gentlemen. Come again, gentlemen," he buoyantly exuded to his departing customers.

All is right with the world. All is right in Charlie's Pool Hall, in Currentville, on this Saturday night in July.

But now it was a dreary winter morning in late February. After a week of unseasonably warm weather, it had turned damp and bone chillingly cold.

Luke made his mindless march to school. He sleepily weaved his way through the large congregation of high school kids standing in front of Charlie's Pool Hall, his mind sluggishly commingling thoughts of basketball, and the English paper due.

After he had cleared the group of silent students and was moving on down the street, he heard his name being called.

"Hey Luke, wait a minute."

He turned and saw Jimmy Cummings, a high school sophomore, coming toward him in a half trot.

"Will you see Wally before dinner?" he asked, half out of breath. Wally was Jimmy's younger brother.

"Yeah, I'll see him," Luke replied.

"Here, give him this. It's his lunch money. Mama gave it

to me to give him. I forgot it and walked out of the house with it."

Jimmy pulled a quarter from his pocket and handed it to Luke.

Luke took the coin, stuffed it in his pocket, and started to turn away.

"Thanks Luke," Jimmy quipped, and then, "did you hear about Charlie?"

"What about Charlie?" Luke turned back in an instant.

"He died this morning. Heart attack."

Jimmy hurriedly rejoined his friends as the large yellow school bus appeared upon the scene.

Luke stood riveted to the spot.

He had not noticed the locked doors and the darkened pool hall as he came threading through the high school kids under the green awning. Like that morning when he first passed the empty Carey house, he sensed something amiss with the large number of boys on the sidewalk standing mute and strangely still. But still, his mind had remained focused on the trail ahead.

Neither had he noticed the large spot of fresh flattened dirt where the Carey house had once stood. Just the day before, the remaining walls from the burned-out hull had been brought down by bulldozers, pushed into a pile and hauled away. The large trees had been cut, sawed into large chunks and burned upon a heap. If he had paid attention, he would have noticed the wide open space, a gaping hole, through which the innards of town—alley-ways, unpainted coal bins, and out houses—were exposed to view. With one fell swoop a historic old landmark, and any remnants of it, had been swept from the face of the earth.

So neither did he notice, as he turned from the staggering news of Charlie's death to continue on his way to school, the pathetic scene across the street. There in the rubble of the destroyed DX station, the old stove remained in place. The stove pipe had been reattached to the rear, and pointed upward, propped in place by a crude tripod of two-by-fours. Out of it rolled heavy black smoke, up, up, up into the drab gray sky. Seated around the stove amidst the debris, finding comfort in it's warm glow, sat three gray forms. They leaned forward, their heads pulled down into their coats, relentlessly trying to survive.

Luke saw none of this, even though it was just a turn of his head from view. His eyes were downward, focused on the sidewalk, pondering the heavy message he had just received.

He could not imagine Currentville without Charlie Clark.

The dark irony escaped him.

There would be no Currentville without Charlie Clark.

Chapter Fifteen

Farewell

A promise to remember has a life of its own.

It was the most beautiful day in Luke Cameron's young life. The first Sunday morning in June.

A thunderstorm a couple of days before had cleared the air of humidity and the sky was a deep cerulean blanket cast over the lush greenery of summer.

The friendly sun smiled brightly upon the town of Currentville, casting sharp crisp shadows on the ground. It would still be a few weeks before its rays would began to scald. On this morning one had to move about a bit to sweat.

It was picture perfect, a day that made even the most apathetic stop for a moment and stare at the sky, or take a deep breath.

Luke was hurriedly making his way down Franklin Street beneath the canopy of full maples and elms which lined the avenue.

He was a little late for church, as he had come by the river to see if anyone was catching fish on such a gorgeous day.

His steps hastened when he saw the familiar family car parked at the curb near the church. He was not much late, but a little too late for his own good. Luke's mom had this sixth sense of always knowing exactly where her kids were on Sunday morning. Like radar, Luke often thought.

Luke was fourteen and had just finished his freshman year.

He was growing tall and thrashing about in the midst of puberty. His face was sharing its space with a few pimples and some fuzz struggling to become whiskers.

He would have been going to school at Catawba that fall where the top three grades were enrolled in high school.

But his parents planned to move to Trenton before the end of the summer.

The government had bought their house. Barkley Dam, eight miles downstream, was well under construction. His father was being transferred to another lock. The town was crumbling around them.

It was time for them to move.

Luke turned right at the church and started down the narrow sidewalk which led to the back of the church and the entrance to the Sunday School classes.

It was then he saw her. She was moving out of the alley along the same direction he was now hastening.

It was Savannah Johnson.

Luke's heart turned over, and his mouth became dry.

She was dressed in a white cotton dress, her dark complexion made richer still by her early summer tan.

Her coal-black hair was pulled back and tied behind her neck—a few strands of the resplendent covering swept down across her face.

She walked—floated, it seemed to Luke— with her head down, like an Indian maiden, clutching her small Bible to her breast with crossed hands.

Every curve of her splendid figure was draped tightly by the clinging dress.

She was stunning.

"Hey!" Luke managed to speak over his pounding heart.

Her soft green eyes lifted and met his. Then they dropped with a bashful smile.

"Hi," came the soft reply.

They came together on the narrow sidewalk and walked side by side toward the door.

Luke stumbled through some small talk, trying to maintain his cool.

But it was nearly impossible, as his head spun to the subtle but intoxicating trace of her perfume.

Their bodies touched ever so slightly as they strolled arm to arm, her warm softness electrifying him. As he talked, Luke kept glancing at the dazzling face. His eyes could not keep from dropping to the plunging neckline of the dress and to the ample cleavage hidden just below its white border.

His heart ached with desire.

He held the door open as they entered the first floor of the Sunday School annex.

There was the paper and woodlike smell of church which sobered him to some extent.

Luke and Savannah moved up the steps and down the hall to the assembly room for their class.

The gathering of teenagers was already singing the first hymn.

> *This is my Father's world, and to my listening ears,*
> *all nature sings, and round me rings, the music of the*
> *spheres . . .*

Mr. Barney Kilson, head of the Intermediate Department, was leading the singing, throwing his hands up and down and wagging his head.

Savannah moved in and stood with her friends up front. Luke headed for the back of the large room where the boys congregated in front of the open windows.

The song ended and the group sat down in the wooden folding chairs.

Luke looked out the windows into Miss Jessie's vegetable garden, teeming with birds and insects. Bees buzzed in and out of the stately hollyhocks which bordered the patch of neatly lined rows of beans and corn.

He longed to be outside with nature in the bright sunshine, under the vaulted blue sky.

He glanced toward the front where Savannah Johnson sat gracefully, with her head bowed.

Luke's soul quickened with excitement, fed by the dazzling sunlight on his shoulder and the beautiful girl in white.

After some scripture reading and announcements, the group broke up into their respective Sunday School rooms.

Luke's class of thirteen- and fourteen-year-old boys was pure chaos.

Meek and mild Mr. Lester Timmons, a spectacled little man who sold insurance, was no match for the boundless mischief and energy of these eight roughneck youngsters.

The teacher spent the first ten minutes of the class trying to coax Bennie Marshall and Tommy Joe Barnett off the roof and back through the window.

Finally the class took on some slight semblance of order as Mr. Timmons began reading from his Sunday School book. Still the members fidgeted, popped their knuckles, took turns punching each other on the shoulders, and made obscene sounds by cupping their hands inside their shirts against the armpit and pumping wildly. For any teacher, getting through this Sunday School class was like getting through a sunrise with Dracula.

Luke, who was normally not above adding to the bedlam, was quiet and subdued. He sat in reverie, his mind a couple of rooms away. The scent of her perfume, her movement, the white clinging dress, lingered in his head.

Finally and mercifully, the bell rang and Sunday School came to an end.

It was a dead heat as to who was the most relieved, the boys or Mr. Timmons.

A stampede ensued.

Yelping and giggling, boys and girls exited the Sunday School rooms into the hallway and—tumbling over each other—down the stairs and out into the glorious outdoors.

The younger kids swirled around the churchyard playing

various games of chase and tag. Most of the teenagers scattered, and those staying for the main church service knotted in small groups and talked.

Out front the grown men stood and smoked waiting for the preaching to begin.

Luke hurried down the sidewalk away from the Sunday School rooms to the corner of the main building. Glancing toward the street, he saw Savannah walking down the sidewalk away from the church.

His spirits plummeted.

"Hey!" he yelled instinctively, and moved toward her.

She turned to wait.

"You not staying for church?" he inquired.

"No," she purred simply and softly.

Luke was perplexed, momentarily at a loss.

Finally, "Can I walk you home?"

He had said it without even thinking. Of course he couldn't walk her home. He had to stay for church.

"Don't you have to stay for church?" she asked with a look of slight surprise on her face.

No grown man, let alone a fourteen-year-old boy in the midst of puberty, should have to make the choice between church and a beautiful woman on a stunningly bright summer morning.

He took a furtive glance at the men standing out front.

His Dad had gone in.

"Oh, well . . ." he soft-soaped it, "it won't hurt to miss one Sunday."

Luke was not convincing.

"You sure?" Savannah asked, coquettishly.

"No, not really."

Luke's smile plainly said he would bravely accept the consequences.

So with the fateful decision made, they turned and began walking down the street.

They made small talk as they passed large old homes on both sides of the thoroughfare.

"Old money," Luke's Dad called the owners, mostly elderly widows, who would dress in their Sunday best each afternoon and hold forth from the large rambling front porches.

"Let's walk down by the river and see if they are catching any fish," Luke suggested enthusiastically as they reached the first intersection.

Savannah acquiesced and they went straight toward Main Street and the river.

In the second block from church, things began to change. Empty houses with overgrown yards began to appear. Small signs nailed to the front proclaimed them condemned by the Corps of Engineers. Weeds sprouted up ankle high from cracks in the street where rocks the size of a fist were scattered upon the pavement.

On the right the jail had been reduced to rubble. Prisoners were now being housed in an adjoining county.

It had been a long time since Birdseed and Luke had forged an all-out attack on the surveying stakes around town. In spite of their uprooted and hefty collection, the government had charged relentlessly on.

Their efforts now seemed rather juvenile to Luke.

Across from the courthouse, the blackened ashes and burnt remains of the picture show remained undisturbed from the winter's fire which had destroyed it.

At the post office, Savannah and Luke turned left onto Main Street and began walking through the business district.

Most of the buildings still stood, though several were empty, dust layered upon the storefront windows.

One building had been recently razed, the remaining debris piled up in the center of the lot, awaiting the torch. A bull-dozer sat idly by, like a large tortoise snoozing in the summer sun.

In front of the pool hall, Stonewall Jackson sat on the stoop in the soothing sun, watching Sunday morning coming down. At his side were Uncle Harry and Ben Knight.

Shabbily dressed, they smelled of soured whiskey and mildewed clothes. Bleary-eyed and forlorn, they looked up at the young, sun-kissed couple as they passed.

Luke spoke, calling them by name, and they greeted him in return.

Citizens of a common ruin moving in opposite directions on a brilliant Sunday morning.

Across the street stood the seedy Currentville Hotel. The two-story concrete block building was badly in need of paint. From an open second floor window came the voice of Buddy Holly, flooding the downtown area.

> *The sun is out . . . the sky is blue,*
> *There's not a cloud to spoil the view . . .*
> *But it's raining . . . raining in my heart.*

At the stoplight, they turned right onto the ferry road, which they would follow the short distance to the river.

On the corner to the left as they turned was a pile of rubble which had once been the DX station—the same gas station which had spawned the raft trip.

On this June morning, the stove still sat there, cold and lifeless, without friends.

> *Oh misery, misery . . .*
> *What's gonna become of me . . . ee?*

The dusty lane ran parallel with the stream for a short distance. Off to the right was the grassy bank, punctuated with fishermen.

Hesitantly and with some anxiety, Luke reached for Savannah's hand to guide her off the road and across the uneven terrain.

To his relief and delight, she locked her hand in his.

There was Papa Joe, standing erect and serene, staring out at the line which stretched from the rod and reel he held in his hand. Around his feet were two or three cane poles angled at the ready, their strings taut to the water.

Brightly colored dough balls lay in an open bucket. Next to them was an old coffee can full of black dirt and earthworms.

"Hey Papa Joe," Luke greeted him as the two moved in beside him. "Catchin' anything?"

"A few." Papa Joe answered without moving his eyes off the water. A thin wisp of smoke from his corncob pipe curved around his head.

Luke glanced down at the stringer staked out at the water's edge. Just below the surface he could see a good morning's work.

Some carp. Some catfish.

They were standing above the lock and dam. In the early summer the pool was high, and the fishing good. Later, as the water level dropped with dry weather, the regulars would move back below the lock and dam where the whitewater made for better chances.

Luke and Savannah stood and stared out at the beautiful scenery.

The placid river, now a gray-green, moved slowly by. Across the way on the opposite bank were acres and acres of rich farmland, its earth newly turned and basking in the sun.

A large John Deere tractor clattered along the river's edge pulling a plow through the ankle-high corn. Black puffs of smoke belched from the green machine.

Way down the river on the opposite bank against the far horizon was the stately, miniature outline of the old Lafayette house.

Upstream a bit, the ferry groaned its away across the channel.

The bucolic vista of blue sky, miles of freshly plowed river bottom falling off to the green banks, and the graceful stream, all bathed in sunlight, was mesmerizing.

After a few more exchanges with Papa Joe, the teenage couple moved off and began to stroll along the bank, downstream.

The grassy knoll would soon give way to river weeds and trees.

Before they reached the rougher terrain, they stopped once again to survey the panorama.

Not far from where they stood, the river widened slightly and pooled behind the lock and dam.

Most of the wickets were up, narrowing the spillway in the middle to only a few feet. The concrete lock on the right bank flared a bit, as its outside wall extended at an angle upriver.

Just above the lock, hanging onto the right bank and still on the government reservation, was another wall by which the boats would ease toward the lock chamber.

It had been a false start for the original construction. When bedrock could not be found for the outer walls of the lock, the site was moved a short distance downstream, leaving the inside wall behind as a navigational aid.

"See the upper lock wall?" Luke pointed it out to Savannah.

She nodded.

"That's where ole Gordon Gray pulled his caper. We swim there a lot. We used to swim in the nude until Miss Annie, who could see us from her window on the hill, complained to the lock crew."

Savanah blushed a bit.

"So we had to start wearing bathing suits down there. We leave them up there at the edge of the horseweeds when we are through. You can imagine what kind of shape they are in by the end of the summer.

"Anyway, the current can get pretty swift there this time of the year. And there are only two ladders. By the time you dive off and come up, you're already past the first ladder. So, you'd better catch that last ladder. If you don't you can get carried into the lock chamber....or maybe even over the dam."

He made it sound pretty dramatic.

"'The Last Ladder' . . ." Savannah pronounced, "sounds like a good name for a short story. Why don't you write it, Luke?"

"I hate writing," Luke protested.

"Why Luke Cameron . . . you're a terrific writer."

"I know. But I don't like to."

The matter was dropped on that serious note.

They strolled on, hand in hand.

Suddenly Luke chuckled.

"Artie Ledford bet Bobby Joe ten dollars that he couldn't hit a baseball halfway across the river off that upper wall.

"So one Saturday morning a couple of years ago we all

gathered down there for the big show.

"Jimmy Don Moore swam out to where both Artie and Bobby Joe agreed was about halfway across. They gave Bobby Joe three baseballs—he got three shots at it."

Luke stopped talking to leave his rapt listener in suspense.

"Well?" she beckoned "Did he do it?"

"Well . . ." Luke drawled, with obvious pride in his voice, ". . . let's put it this way. They didn't have to waste two of the balls."

Savannah laughed with delight.

Luke was surprised with how little the black-haired beauty knew about the river.

He explained how the locks worked. The wickets which made up the dam were a little more complicated.

"See, the dam is in sections. Big cast iron sections. They're like . . ." he struggled to think of a comparison.

". . . like . . . staples for a stapler. Think of each section being shaped like a staple. But tops are about three feet wide with hooks or handles on the top, and they spread out as they go down and are anchored and hinged on the bottom of the river.

"So when they want to widen the dam, they hook onto the wickets and pull them up out of the water to fasten to another section which is already up. When they want to lower the wickets . . . meaning when they want to widen the spillway, let more water go through, they drop or release the wicket down into the river . . . it's a little complicated."

Savannah was polite. "I understand. You're doing a good job explaining. Since you don't want to be a writer, you can be a teacher."

She smiled, but Luke let the comment drop.

"They get a call from Nashville, 'raise so many wickets' or 'drop so many wickets.' It doesn't make any difference what time of day or night . . . or weather. In the middle of the night in ice and snow . . . they have to go out there and raise or drop wickets."

Luke was awed by the process himself.

"You can walk inside those wickets when they are up . . . walk inside the dam."

A look of amazement came over Savannah's face.

"Walk inside the wickets?" she exclaimed.

"Yeah. You know sometimes in the late summer when we have a water shortage? Dad will take Bobby Joe and me inside the wickets for a shower."

"For a shower?" she asked incredulously, totally engrossed in this young boy and his strange story.

Luke went on, with her flashing green eyes searching out his face.

"You see, you come down the steps by the lock wall, step on a narrow ledge, and then go in this open doorway in the first wicket. You can stand up inside. It's like a long tunnel inside. But the water which is rushing against the dam . . . well, the wickets are not exactly watertight. So water leaks through and comes gushing or spraying through the top. It's like a gigantic shower.

"So we take a nice shower."

Luke grinned and went through the motion of washing under his arm.

She playfully slapped him on the arm.

"It's true. I swear to God."

It was true, but Savannah still wasn't sure as they neared the tall horseweeds.

"Come on. I want to show you something."

With that, Luke pulled Savannah toward a large swath which had been cut in the jungle of weeds.

Immediately they were onto a path about four feet wide. The high horseweeds towered over them, blocking out the sun. A slither of blue sky hovered overhead. The way was cool and still damp from the morning dew.

It was a maze, as the passageway cut a circuitous route to its destination. Secondary trails led off the main route.

"We tried to make this complicated so as to confuse the little kids and people we don't want coming in here," Luke explained.

"Including girls," Savannah opined.

"Ha! I've never seen a girl on the river in my life," Luke proclaimed condescendingly. "What do you girls do in the summertime, anyway?"

"Oh, girl stuff," she replied, now following behind Luke in the narrow aisle, wide-eyed with expectation.

"What do you mean, 'girl stuff'?"

"Oh, cleaning house, talking on the phone . . . fixing our hair . . . watching television when the reception is good."

"Great summer vacation. No wonder you girls love school," Luke deadpanned.

"Sometimes we go downtown to the drugstore . . . spend the night with someone. Lay out to get a tan. Sometimes Mother will take a bunch of us over to Kentucky Lake."

Savannah was trying to fill in the gaps.

Suddenly they came to a large opening, right at the water's edge.

The ground was carpeted with soft grass, shaded by a large cottonwood.

It was cool and inviting, with a large stretch of river opening up in front of them.

"It's our fishing hole," Luke explain proudly as he watched her look around.

"It's wonderful, Luke." Savannah was impressed. "It's so peaceful, so . . . hidden. But you still have such a great view of the river and the other bank. It's just perfect."

She walked around the clearing, inspecting and admiring the hideaway.

Over to one side, at the edge of the horseweeds and partially hidden by weeds, she spotted something.

"What's this?"

She looked down at a pile of wooden stakes, stacked neatly on top of a pile of paper or cardboard. They were weather-beaten, and had obviously been there for a while.

Luke walked over to look.

"Oh," he sighed, "that's Birdseed's stuff. Well, really mine and Birdseed's."

"What is it?" she pressed.

Slightly embarrassed, yet resigned to the fact he would have to explain, Luke bent over and picked up one of the wooden objects.

"These are surveying stakes. You know how the Corps has surveyed and staked out around town? I don't know, I guess to mark where the water is going to come with the dam. Or maybe where they are going to buy. Anyway . . ." He was becoming more than slightly embarrassed.

". . . we pulled these things up whenever we saw them. Some we would drive back down in different places. Others we collected and brought here. I don't know . . . I guess we thought maybe it would delay the coming of the dam . . . kinda silly, really."

He fell quiet, and then dropped the stake.

"These are the signs that the Corps posted on the buildings they had condemned." Luke bent over and picked up a torn cardboard placard. The lettering was barely visible. The ones underneath, protected from the weather, were much more legible.

CONDEMNED BY THE
U.S. ARMY CORPS OF ENGINEERS

There was the bright red castle, the Corps emblem.

Luke dropped the sign and stared down at the debris.

How long ago it now seemed.

The buildings came down almost as soon as the signs came off.

He sighed.

"Oh well," he turned and chirped in a much lighter tone. "We fought the good fight. Let's have a chair and enjoy the view."

They moved back to the bank. Luke sat down on the soft grass and crossed his legs.

Savannah gracefully eased down on her knees and sat back with her feet under her.

She appeared pensive as she ran her hand across the velvety grass.

Luke looked longingly out over his beloved river.

"See the sun shimmering off the surface of the water?"

She nodded.

"My Dad always told us that was the twinkle in God's eye."

Savannah smiled, obviously intrigued by the metaphor.

Luke fell backward on the soft sod and stared up through the leafy branches of the cottonwood and into the deep azure sky.

"This sure beats church," he exhaled softly. "I'll be glad when I don't have to go to church. When I can do what I want to on Sunday morning. Won't you?"

Luke turned to Savannah for a reply.

"I don't have to go to church," she stated calmly.

"What?" Luke was up on one elbow, wide-eyed and unbelieving. "You don't have to go to church? You mean you don't have to go to church . . . and you go anyway!"

He was incredulous.

He didn't give her a chance to answer.

"Why?" he drove on. "Why do you go if you don't have to?"

She thought for a moment.

"Oh, I don't know. I like to go to church most of the time. I like to dress up. See people. Sing, listen to the music."

She grew serious.

"I love to hear God's Word."

Luke was moved by her sincerity.

He laid back down though, still in disbelief.

Why would anyone go to church if they didn't have to?

Luke closed his eyes and let the sounds and smells envelop him.

A slight but exciting scent of Savannah's perfume drifted with the breeze into his senses. He heard the distant clacking of the tractor; the call of a crow; the cacophony of singing birds; the refreshing murmur of the dam.

This, Luke thought, must be what heaven is like. An eternal summer Sunday morning, with your favorite girl—and no church.

The reverie was broken by Savannah's soft voice.

"You'll be moving soon," she said matter-of-factly with just a touch of sadness in her tone.

"Yep. I guess so," Luke responded.

"High school won't be the same next year without you,"

Savannah murmured.

And with those words, a dark cloud of despondency rolled in across Luke's soul. He felt his mood plummeting down into a pit, far away from what had moments before been a euphoric summer day.

It was hard to imagine that all of this would be gone. This place. This town. These friends. This girl.

Even where he now lay his head, the lazy stream beside him, the trees overhead, Papa Joe fishing not far away—all would be gone.

Where he lay would be the bottom of the lake, covered with water. Forever.

He felt himself floating downward. Away from the sunlit morning, down, down, into the mud and the mire. There he lay in the darkness covered by Barkley Lake. It was cold, lonely, airless. He was suffocating.

Suddenly he sat up. Trying to shake off his mood, he chirped thoughtlessly, "Oh, I'll have my license in a couple of years and be able to come back and visit the new town all the time."

"Besides," he went on with forced bravado, "you'll have boys falling all over you, just like you do now. You won't even miss me."

"I'll miss you," Savannah was still moving her hand across the grass, searching.

An awkward silence followed.

"You're different," she said, still not looking up.

"What makes you say that?" Luke inquired.

Savannah thought for a minute.

"Well . . . you know, just like a while ago when you said something about the sun shimmering on the water . . . "

Luke turned and peered out across the river as the green tractor made a turn on the opposite bank.

She went on.

"And last winter, we were playing Trigg County there. It was a very cold night. You got back on the bus after the game and sat next to me. There was heavy frost or ice formed on the outside of the windows. As the bus began to warm up inside the ice began to melt. For some reason it formed some unusual configurations on the glass . . . and silver designs . . . like a . . . like one of those things you look in . . . " She formed a tube with her hands.

"Kaleidoscope," Luke chimed in.

"Yeah, like a kaleidoscope. Anyway, it looked really neat when car lights hit it. You looked at it and pointed and said, 'That's beautiful.'

"I looked into your face, and there you were with a swollen and busted lip, and dried blood still on your chin where someone had elbowed you in the game. And you had hit two free throws at the end to help us win the game. Yet there on that noisy and rowdy bus, you were the only one who noticed the beautiful figures on the windows. My mom calls it 'passion'—she says you have a passion for life . . . Oh, I don't know, I don't know how to explain it . . . "

She raised her head and looked him straight in the eye. "You're just different, Luke Cameron—that's all!" she exclaimed as she threw up her hands in frustration.

There was a look of exasperation on her face, as if she were both put out with not being able to explain, and also put out that Luke was the way he was.

Her green eyes burned with intensity, contrasting beautifully with her darkly tanned face and black hair.

She leaned to one side with her legs underneath her. The hem of her white cotton dress had slipped up above her knee, sensually revealing her beautiful and richly tanned thighs.

She was adorable. So adorable, so utterly exquisite that Luke's heart both jumped with excitement and ached with desire.

His head began to spin and his face felt a flush of heat.

Trembling, he raised his left hand toward her face and gently touched her soft cheek with the back of his fingers. Then he stroked the side of her face ever so softly and brought the back of his hand down under her chin.

He leaned toward her—his heart racing—and they kissed.

After more trembling and awkward groping, they embraced and rolled over onto the grass, their lips wedded and their bodies joined.

"What time is it?" Luke asked as he led Savannah by the hand back through the winding horseweed corridor.

She looked at her watch.

"Twelve thirty," she reported solemnly.

"Well, I'm in big trouble," Luke said, and one could not tell by the tone of his voice if he was glad or sad.

"Church's been over for thirty minutes now."

They cut across the field behind town and moved away from the river to the ferry-landing road. There they turned left and followed it into town where it intersected with Main Street.

Luke turned Savannah's hand loose.

"Well, I'll call you when I get out of prison."

She grinned and lowered her head in her special shy way which drove boys wild.

". . . or the hospital, whichever it is," Luke added.

Their eyes met affectionately, and with a wave Luke turned and headed up the street. Savannah headed the opposite way.

After only a few steps, Luke turned. "Hey!"

Savannah stopped and looked back.

"It was worth it," he said softly, his words barely loud enough for her to hear.

"Thanks," she said in a near-whisper.

Luke didn't look back until he had reached the top of Penitentiary Hill. From there he stopped and peered out over the little broken-down town snoozing in the mid-day sun.

It was a pitiful sight, really, and Luke saw it for the first time as it really was.

A grouping of empty buildings, along with some that were still hanging on to some purpose. Vacant lots, holding the debris of recent razings. A town—yet not a town. Like a shell of a dead tortoise—a turtle, but not a turtle. The streets were deserted, grass growing ankle high in the sidewalk cracks.

Only the trees—the giant sugar maples, oaks, and elms, maintained their stately watch along the avenues.

He looked down old Main Street, past the burned-out theater, into the main business district, and past the drunks still sitting on the stoops in their own spittle. Leaning old structures sat with dark holes—like eye sockets in a skull—-where windows had once been. The stovepipe stood like a lonesome sentinel in the DX ruin.

The ferry puttered its way across the river in the upper-right-hand corner of his picture.

He followed with his eyes the road—Main Street, actually—on out to where it disappeared over a rise.

There in the distance moving along the shaded sidewalk—floating like an apparition—was a girl in white.

He watched her disappear.

An overwhelming sense of loneliness rolled over Luke. A loneliness of such dreadful weight that he could almost feel his shoulders sag, and his knees buckle.

He turned and headed for home.

The punishment which awaited him there for skipping church would be light compared to the gaping hole in his heart.

⚜

It was mid-morning in early July. The sun was already blazing hot in the pale blue sky. A large commercial moving van was backed up to the front porch. The big old house was almost empty, and the front screen door was propped open with a broom.

Alec was assisting two muscular men wrestle a large piece of furniture onto the back of the truck, which was now almost full. Luke was helping his Mom, carrying bedclothes and bath towels to the car. He stopped on the front porch for a moment to gaze out over the neighborhood.

It looked like the wake of a tornado.

A few of the houses, including Birdseed's, were standing with people still living in them. Others stood vacant, weeds waist high in the yard. But most had just recently been demolished, the jagged and dusty debris piled high in the morning sun.

Johnson grass grew high along the side of the road, and the

cracks in the sidewalks had given birth to a virtual botanical walk-way.

As Luke peered across the street through open spaces where houses had once been, he looked right into Freewill, still mostly intact. He was startled by how close the little settlement had been to his own home. So near, yet so far away. He wondered briefly about Richard. Where he was, what he was doing, whether he would ever see him again.

Then his gaze moved up the hill toward the penitentiary. This gray, somber castle stood unchanged. Like a Sphinx on the Nile, it stared unflinchingly over the tremendous upheaval taking place in the valley below.

Luke was searching the summit, squinting into the scorch-ing sun, looking hopefully for any sign of friends coming one last time. He and Birdseed—who had left for the Smoky Mountains with his parents earlier that morning—had said their farewells the night before, after a long and serious conversation under the cher-ry tree.

Seeing nothing at the top of the hill but the monolithic prison, Luke continued on with the job at hand—helping Esther pack the car. Footsteps echoed and reverberated off the floors of the hollow wooden structure. The inside—four rooms, a hall and a bath—where Luke had spent his entire life, all seemed so much bigger now. Bigger and somehow unsettling. Like looking at his grandfather in the coffin. It was his grandfather, but it wasn't his grandfather. It was his house, but it wasn't his house.

Luke's Dad had not quibbled with the price given to him for the house. Unlike many others throughout the town, he did not want the hassle. He managed to buy the house back for only a hundred dollars, and then sell it again to a salvage dealer for a profit. So it was not really Luke's house any longer anyway. But as he moved about inside, memories came tumbling across his mind, unwanted and uninvited. So he chased them off, vaguely afraid of what pain they would bring.

Then on another trip to the car, he glanced again to the top of the hill. This time he saw them, side by side, their white T-shirts reflecting brightly in the morning sun: Donkey and Jack. They moved down the hill and crossed the street in front of Birdseed's.

"I'll be back in a minute, Mom," Luke yelled back into the house. He bounded off the porch, down the steps into the side yard. Jack and Donkey moved through Birdseed's front yard, down the embankment toward the boundary cherry tree. There, the three old friends came together.

"We waited 'till you had all the heavy stuff loaded," Jack joked as they ducked under the limbs and came to a halt.

"Good timing," Luke replied. "We're just about finished."

There was an awkward moment, none of them knowing exactly what to say. They stood there with their hands tucked in the tight front pockets of their jeans.

"Where's Bobby Joe?" Donkey finally broke open the impasse.

"He's working in Oxford this summer," Luke explained, "playing on a local baseball team. The coach wants to move him to third base next year. He wanted him to stay around this summer so he could work with him."

"Well, I guess you told him you were moving, didn't you?" Jack inquired with a smile, and they all laughed.

More awkward silence.

"Well, Luke," Jack strained to make conversation, "I'll have my license next year and we'll come see you."

"Yeah, and I'll be back to visit. Wherever you are," Luke assured them.

Jack's house was up on the ridge, out of the impoundment area. Donkey's family were still dickering with the Corps, not sure where they were going to move—probably to the new town being laid out a few miles inland.

"We might even play you in basketball this year," interjected Donkey. "Trenton has one helluva team."

"Yeah, I know. I hope I can make the varsity," Luke, who would be a sophomore in the fall, spoke wistfully.

"You'll make it, Luke," Jack proclaimed. "You're going to really help their team over there before you're through. Just go easy on us when you play good ole Chickasaw County High."

They thought about it in silence, each finding it all very

strange.

Jack straightened up and looked out over the river bottom, green now with tasseling corn. "Well ole Cocoa won't be going to Trenton with you."

He had spotted the small grave at the back of the garden. The lovable pet had been killed by a car just a few weeks before, sending the entire family into grief.

"Naw. Daddy said ole Cocoa wouldn't have liked the city anyway. It's just as well," Luke spoke with both resignation and sadness in his voice.

"Well, Luke, I guess we'd better be going," Jack said after another lull in the conversation.

He stuck out his hand.

For the first time ever, Jack and Luke shook hands. A surge of melancholy coursed through him. Jack's large, powerful hand and long arm, now marbled with manly muscle, held Luke fast. Their eyes met, the grip tightened, and then the hands dropped. Donkey extended his hand, and the heartfelt ritual was repeated.

"I got something for you guys," Luke said as they dropped their arms.

He reached into his pocket and pulled out two envelopes. Inside of each was an identical note for his friends. The night before he had intended to write them each a letter, in case they did not show up that morning. He would have left it with Birdseed to deliver. But he could not think of anything to say which would not be corny or mushy. One line he had heard from some distant English class had stuck in his mind and found its way onto the paper. Luke was like that. He had a tremendous memory for verse, rhyme, moving phrases. But he could never remember their source. Donkey, on the other hand, had the peculiar trait of not remembering the verse, but once said, could quote the source. An affliction most strange.

Luke handed each of his friends an envelope.

"There's no money in there," he quipped with a grin. "Just a few last words for you to read after I'm gone."

Jack and Donkey looked at their envelopes and stuck them in their jeans.

There were a few mumbled words between them that none of them would remember, and Jack and Donkey turned and were gone.

When Luke returned to the house, he found that the moving van had already departed. He walked through the empty house for the last time. His mother was in the kitchen. Esther was doing something which struck Luke as very peculiar. She was busily sweeping the floor clean, raking the fine dust and small bits of trash out the back door. He thought it was incredible for her to go to the trouble, considering the circumstances. Luke opened his mouth to inquire. Strangely, the question caught in his throat, and was never asked.

Last, they loaded Soldier, two cats, and a caged parakeet into the crowded back seat of the Ford. His Dad made one last check through the dwelling, closed the front door and slid in behind the steering wheel. The three of them, Luke riding shotgun and his Mom in the middle, pulled out onto the street and started out of town.

Past the ruined tenements and weeded yards, slowly at first and then picking up speed. Past Wrinklemeat's store, now closed and partially demolished. Quickly they were out of town, past the Currentville city limit sign with the bullet hole through it. Within seconds they were in the country and gone.

Jack and Donkey reached the top of Penitentiary Hill. In front of the inmate leather shop, and overlooking the lock and dam, they stopped. Simultaneously, and as if on silent signals, they pulled the envelopes from their pockets.

Each tore open his envelope and read the short message from their departed friend.

"If we do meet again, why, we shall smile; if not, why then, this parting was well made."

Jack's arms dropped to his side.

"Where in the world does Luke come up with all this stuff?" he inquired with a chuckle.

His friend was still staring at the paper. Donkey raised his eyes to meet Jack's. "Shakespeare. From *Julius Caesar*, I think," he stated, unsmiling.

"Well la le da," Jack countered with mock admiration. "Aren't you the smart ass!"

They tucked the notes in their jeans, turned, and headed for home.

Chapter Sixteen

Homecoming

God looks for men of promise, not promises.

The young law student drove his red Volkswagen beetle onto the gravel parking lot at the Jumpin' Joe Restaurant.

Luke Cameron was on his way home to Trenton from law school to spend the weekend with his parents. Just a few hours before, he had dropped Carolyn off at the Lexington airport to fly home to North Carolina for a week with her folks.

It was a bright but cold February day.

He had passed by the town of New Currentville several times between Trenton and Lexington, but this was the first time he had stopped. The four-hour drive had made him drowsy, and he needed a cup of coffee.

Plus he was more than a little bit curious.

He cut the engine, surveyed the half-full parking lot of pickup trucks, and moved inside.

He casually looked around the place, not knowing whether he would see familiar faces or a sea of strangers.

It was a sea of strangers, mostly in work clothes and baseball-type hats hovering over cups of coffee and chatting.

He slid onto a stool at the counter and ordered a cup of coffee.

Luke watched the waiter with keen interest, searching the face. He was much older than Luke, maybe forty. He spoke with a Yankee clip. Definitely not a native.

He had just received his steaming cup of Java, and started to raise it to his lips when large hands came down on each of his shoulders, and held him straight.

"We don't let any strangers into this town." The voice, drawling with its West Kentucky twang, was unmistakable.

It was Jack.

Luke wrestled himself loose and turned around.

There he was—his boyhood pal—now a grown man with a big round face, flushed red from both the cold and too much beer on the weekends. His billed cap, advertising DeKalb corn seed, fit snugly around the black hair in need of a trim.

His broad beaming smile and twinkling eyes had not changed.

They embraced, and exchanged greetings.

Luke picked up his coffee and joined Jack in a booth.

It was awkward at first. Feeling each other out—what they were doing, who they had married—a rough but manageable conversation which in its own way brought them up to date on each other.

Jack had dropped out of high school before his senior year. Worked here and there, and was now laboring the second shift driving a truck at a nearby stone quarry. Making good money. Married a girl who Luke could only vaguely remember. Had two kids. His mother had died. His father, elderly, was getting along.

"Last time I heard you were in Vietnam," Jack interjected.

"Yeah, then I did a tour in Germany where I met my wife. Got out last summer, started law school in the fall." Luke tried not to dwell on himself, as he was interested in other things.

Then they started down that memory lane of names.

Billy Mason was up north somewhere, hadn't heard from him in years.

Perky Perkins was teaching at the local high school.

Bennie Marshall had done well in real estate.

Marvin Lee Foote had gone to college and gotten a degree in agriculture and was now in Georgia.

And Donkey. Donkey had gone into the Navy, married a wealthy Texas girl, and had ended up in the Lone Star State. He owned some car dealerships. Made it big, came back in from time to time, driving big long cars and taking everyone out to eat. Donkey was still good old Donkey—good old rich Donkey.

Tommy Grogan? Folks moved away with the dam, never heard from him again.

On and on he went.

Finally, as if both of them had wanted to avoid the topic, and after a brief silence Jack said, "You heard about Birdseed, I guess."

"Yeah," Luke said softly as he looked down into his coffee. "I was also 'in country' when he was killed," he said, barely above a whisper.

"You were?" Jack was surprised.

"Yeah."

Nothing was said for a few moments. In that brief time, the years between them faded away. Once again, they were buddies.

"Funny thing," Luke took a deep breath and continued, "incredible, really . . . I ran into him not long before.

"I was in Can Tho, down in the Delta, and another officer and I had gotten off the compound one night and gone downtown for a beer. I was on a special assignment down there from up north, and this officer pretty much knew where we could go. I mean, there were some places you didn't dare go.

"We walked into this bar and were downing a ba muoi ba—a Vietnamese beer—at the bar.

"Then I heard this loud voice from the back, 'Luke Cameron! Unless I'm dead or crazy drunk, it's my old buddy Luke Cameron!'

"I turned and peered through the dimly lit, smoke-filled bar toward the back. There in the very back, sitting at a table with a bunch of good-looking Vietnamese whores all around him, was none other than Birdseed."

Jack laughed with amusement.

"I couldn't believe it. He was sitting there all by himself with all these girls. The table was full of empty beer bottles and he was having the time of his life.

"My friend and I joined him and we had a merry reunion.

"We sat there drinking beer, talking—mostly about old times—and laughing. The girls, seeing they were pretty much wasting their time, slowly lost interest and slipped away, one by one.

"Finally my friend—the one I had come with—left by himself, leaving Birdseed and me there by ourselves.

"We drank beer, talked, and laughed—even talked about you."

Jack gave a quick chuckle, took a sip of his coffee, and begged with his twinkling eyes for Luke to continue.

Luke paused, reflecting.

"I remember . . . while we were there by ourselves . . . this little Vietnamese boy comes in. You know, a little beggar . . . they were all over the place. They would come into the bars and ask for money.

"Well, this one, I'd say about nine or ten, was a little different. He was selling paintings. Ones he had done himself. A regular little capitalist. Quick way to the GI heart, you know." Luke smiled and so did Jack.

"Anyway, paintings—water buffaloes, a pretty girl in a traditional Aui Dai, things like that—they weren't bad actually. There were five or six.

"Birdseed looked them over. Then he pulled all the money he had . . . I mean all the money he had . . .Vietnamese dong of course . . . out of the wallet and handed it to the youngster.

"'We'll take 'em all me lad,' he said.

"The little boy could hardly contain himself. It was a bonanza for him. He happily took the money, bowed and bowed again, thanking Birdseed, and then ran out of the bar. I bet it was twenty-five dollars there at least.

"Birdseed threw the pictures on the table. 'The kid's sister is probably whoring, his mamasan's cleaning hooches and spying on the compound, and papasan is somewhere out there in the night in black pajamas as we speak . . . But the kid, he's only trying to survive.'

"Then he shoved them toward me. 'You can have 'em, Luke. You'll probably be back in the world before I am anyway.'

"I took 'em. Still have 'em, somewhere tucked away in my trunk at my parents'.

"Anyway, it was close to midnight . . . the place was empty, except for Birdseed and me. The owner . . . or the papasan who ran the place came back to our table. 'Almost curfew, GI. If you go . . . need go now.'

"There was something in his face, the way he said it, that Birdseed and I . . . well it's hard to explain . . . we got the message. So we left, said our farewells. He went back to his unit. I went to mine.

"The next morning I heard that some heavy shit went on down there . . . some people were killed . . ."

Luke stopped. He fell deeply into his own thoughts.

Jack broke the spell. "If you have time, we could go out to Birdseed's grave. He's buried out at Pea Ridge. And I could show you some of the new town."

Luke smiled. "Sure. Let's go."

≈≈✹≈≈

They slipped into Jack's clean and late-model pickup truck and pulled out of the parking lot.

It was a strange-looking town, Luke thought. It didn't even look like a town—scattered and spread out over a slightly rolling, treeless landscape which had not long before been cornfields.

Wide streets, a house here and there, new curbs and drains, fire hydrants half-hidden by weeds. It reminded Luke of a military installation where an MP would not have looked out of place out on the main road, waving people in.

The houses were nice and neat for the most part. There were ranch types, modest but clean and new—almost all adorned with a carport on the side and a small stoop with wrought iron rails, which passed for a front porch.

"Jimmy Don Moore lives there. He's the mayor now."

He pointed out others as they rode slowly down the streets. With some names came faces to Luke's mind. With others, only the names.

Each street looked the same. Even the houses all looked alike.

Then they turned onto a gravel street.

"There's the colored section over here," his driver explained.

Colored. Luke hadn't heard the term in what seemed like eons. College. The army. Vietnam. Germany. Law school.

Assassinations. Race riots. Kent State. Charlie Manson. Moon landing. Nixon.

He thought "colored" had disappeared from the English language. Yet it rolled from Jack's lips easily without degradation or disfavor, the same as if he were describing the "business district" or the "school zone."

"Speaking of colored," Jack suddenly said with a look of excitement, "I just remembered. You remember that colored boy in old Currentville we tried to teach how to play baseball?"

"Richard?" Luke exclaimed, surprised that he remembered.

"Yeah, that's him. Anyway, about a year ago he came by here. Drove right in to Jumpin' Joe's, just the way you did here — they serve colored there now, you know. He was driving a big fancy car, wearing nice clothes, had this good-looking wife and a couple of kids. I mean, he stuck out like a sore thumb around here. I didn't even recognize him 'til Joe, who was working at the counter, sent him over to see me. He was asking about you. Let's see, there was something he told me to tell you if I ever saw you..."

Jack cocked his head to one side, frowned, and tried to think.

Luke waited anxiously as he warmly remembered this lost

friend of a world long gone.

"... oh yeah, now I remember." Jack jolted with the recollection. "It really didn't make much sense to me, but he seemed awful proud of it. He said to tell you that his son was on the school's swim team."

A broad and knowing smile broke out across Luke's happy face.

The vivid image flashed across his mind—the contorted mahogany face, glistening wet in the sun, gasping for life and blowing and puffing his way across the slackwater. Eyes agape, nostrils flared. The look of fear. Fear and determination.

Luke gazed out the window, and more to himself than to Jack he uttered, "That kid had guts."

Jack shook his head unknowingly. "You were a helluva swimmer, Luke. Remember the time you saved old Perky Perkins from drowning off that sandbar when we were camping out near Buzzard Creek?"

Luke had forgotten. Now he recalled, "Really wasn't much to it. His feet were scraping bottom. He was fighting the current, trying desperately to get back to where he was. All he had to do was let go and drift with the current into the bank. He just kinda lost his head and I just helped him out."

"Well, maybe so," Jack argued, "but as far as I'm concerned you saved his life. Yeah, you were one helluva swimmer."

Then they were in the business district—a bank, a drugstore, post office, other businesses. They were all one story with flat roofs. There was considerable distance between most of them. Not a walking town for sure, thought Luke.

"There's Stumpy Duncan's insurance office. He's got a big house on the lake." Jack pointed, and a flash of nostalgia ran through Luke, remembering the dramatic shot.

In the middle of the complex on a grassy knoll sat a square brick building.

"That's the courthouse," Jack pointed. "Godawful, ain't it."

It was awful. It had a flat roof with the heating and air conditioning units perched on top.

"Supposed to be modern......huh, it's modern, alright. So modern it's already out of date," Jack said and shook his head.

"A lot of people made money on this relocation, Luke," he continued. "Big money. Contractors, architects, engineers . . . mostly out-of-town people who sold us a bill of goods."

"There's a standing joke about the courthouse . . . there was a Confederate general from these parts, Hylan B. Lyon. During the War Between the States, he went through this part of the state burning courthouses to keep them out of Union hands. People now say, 'Where is General Lyon when we need him?'"

Jack laughed and Luke smiled.

"How do you like living here, Jack?" Luke turned and searched his old friend's face.

"It's okay. I mean, it's not old Currentville. No place to loaf much. People pretty much stay to themselves. As you can see the town . . . well, it doesn't look . . . it hasn't got . . ." Jack was struggling.

"Character." Luke helped him out.

"Yeah . . . character. The town doesn't have much character. But our kids will never know the difference, and I guess it will be home to them."

Character. Luke thought about it as he looked out the window. What gives a town character? Whatever it was, this town didn't have it. The old town certainly did, Luke mused, not only character, but characters as well.

They turned back onto a residential street.

"Right up here on the right, on the corner, is where Birdseed's mother lives." Jack slowed the truck down and nodded. "His Dad died not long after Birdseed. He was the only child, you know. She lives there by herself. In pretty bad health herself and doesn't get out much."

Luke's heart sank.

It was a simple little house. A red brick ranch. A covered carport with no car. A side door from the carport and the front door stoop which only salesmen and strangers ever used.

The yard was neatly kept. A fat yellow cat dozed in the sun on a front window ledge.

There was no other sign of life around the house. Luke looked at the gray roof and thought of the terrible heartache and loneliness it had covered—the long dark nights, the heart-rending dreams, the empty dawns.

It could have been different. Should have been different. There should have been a daughter-in-law proudly announced on the doorstep. There should have been an anxious grandmother looking out the window for Thanksgiving guests. The meager yard should have borne the small feet of grandchildren playing.

"Wanna stop?" Jack's sudden burst made him flinch.

"No . . ." Luke stuttered, ". . . I'll drop her a note."

He quickly made a mental note of the house number near the front door. "Maple Avenue—right?"

Jack nodded.

To Luke's relief, they turned left, and the house faded from view.

They drove out to the intersection on the main highway and turned left again. They picked up speed and headed out into the country, heading south toward the penitentiary and old Currentville.

"What ever happened to Savannah Johnson?" Luke finally asked the question which had been burning in his mind, and tried to be casual about it.

"She married a guy from Clarksville. They went to Nashville, had a couple of kids and divorced. Last thing I heard she was going back to school—to nursing school, I think."

Luke pondered the information. The erotic image of Savannah in a tightly fitted white nursing outfit leapt into his mind: White. In his mind she was always in white. Dark skin, and in white.

Jack went on.

"Boy she was a knockout, wasn't she! They say the guy she married was a real asshole. That's the way it always seems to go. The losers get the best-looking women. And Savannah . . . she was a nice girl, too." He shook his head.

"Oh I don't know, my ole pal," Luke drawled, gazing out at the passing landscape. "You and I got two good-looking gals, and we're not losers."

Luke said this, not having the slightest remembrance of what his pal's wife looked like.

"Yeah," Jack retorted, "but some people may think we are."

They both chuckled and rode on in silence for a while.

"This is some big lake here, Luke," Jack finally chimed in. "A great big son-of-a bitch. Land developers have made a killing. People coming in from the North buying up lakefront property. Some mighty pretty scenery, I guess. But when I look at it, I just think of what's underneath it. Or what's not underneath it, I guess. It's just a big, old man-made lake. Man-made. That makes a difference Luke, you know what I mean?" He looked to search out his old friend's face.

Not able to get a reading, he continued. "I mean, there's some guy down there at the dam, working for the government, sitting up there in his little glassed-in control room staring at a panel with a lot of lights. So, he pulls a lever or two which controls the level of the water. Summer pool. Winter pool. And all kinds of levels in between. Driftwood piles up on the shoreline with all kinds of trash and plastic bottles and junk which makes the place look like a trash heap at low water. They say this lake has a life span of ninety-six years, and then it will all be silted in. Of course that don't make no difference to me, or even my children. But for some reason just the thought of it gives it . . . makes it seem . . ." Jack struggled for the word.

"Artificial," Luke interjected to Jack's vigorous nod.

"Yeah. Artificial."

They turned right at the water tank and headed back toward the Kentucky State Penitentiary and what was left of old Currentville.

After a couple of miles, they turned off and drove along a ridge until they came to the gate of the cemetery.

It was the same old graveyard Luke had known as a boy. The same one of his hair-raising grave-robbing venture. It sat high on a hill overlooking the lake and the back of the penitentiary.

The oldest part, which had graves marked by thin rectangular gravestones over one hundred fifty years old, was in a grove of trees. The ancient writing was hardly legible on the markers.

Jack drove the truck on up the gravel driveway into the newer part which was out in the open, void of trees and left to face the cold winds of winter and burning sun of summer unprotected. It was a rather desolate, windswept place, even in the brightness of the mid-afternoon sun.

He stopped the truck and they got out. The sharp cold breeze took a swipe at them, and Luke pulled the collar of his old army field jacket up around his face.

Jack led the way as they walked past a wide variety of tombstones—large and small—familiar names passing by on marble markers.

They reached their mark.

Jack walked slowly to the large granite slab and looked down.

Luke went to the foot of the grave, squatted down oriental style, close to the ground with his arms draped over his knees. He peered into the face of the marker.

His eyes were on the same level with the writing.

Douglas Lee Barrett
September 25, 1944 — September 25, 1969
HE DIED FOR HIS COUNTRY

"I'll be damned," Luke muttered mostly to himself, "died on his birthday."

"Yeah," answered Jack, "Isn't that a heller!"

Jack pulled a pack of cigarettes out from inside his down vest, moved over toward Luke, and offered him one.

Luke shook his head, and Jack returned to his place next to the stone. He lit up a cigarette and took a long first draw, the smoke streaming out into the winter air.

Then he rested his left hand on the rough top of the granite marker, his right hand holding the cigarette to the side. Slowly he moved back toward the foot of the grave, just a few feet from Luke.

"Ole Birdseed was real smart, you know. He went away to college and made real good grades at first. Made all kinds of lists and stuff. Then they say he just quit. Started staying up all night reading books . . . not schoolbooks, but deep philosophical crap. Slept all day and skipped his classes. Then he got to boozing and partying all the time on weekends, got into pot. Well, he flunked out. Came home and just farted around town."

Jack took a drag and then peered out over the cemetery toward the horizon.

"Me and Birdseed went and took our physicals together. A whole busload of us went down to Nashville. I've never seen so many naked guys in one place in my life . . . all shapes and sizes. There were fat guys and skinny guys, tall and short . . . all lined up, 'turn your head and cough, turn your head and cough.'"

A faint smile of recognition broke across Luke's face.

"They checked us all over real good. Then they had me wait after the rest had moved on through. They checked my heart again. 'Irregular heartbeat,' they said. They gave me a special slip and told me to report back the next morning. Well, there were some other guys in the same boat——blood pressure, funny results on something—and they put us up in a Nashville hotel.

"The next morning the test was the same. They moved me from one clerk to another, and finally I came to the final place where this cranky old sergeant looked over my papers, stamped a thing or two, signed his name and handed me a slip. 'Go kiss your Mama, candy ass. You're 4-F.'

"I held that piece of paper like it was a million dollars and couldn't wait to get out on the street and let out a big war hoop. I was 4-F and exempt!

"There I was. Big athlete. Muscular and strong, and I was not fit to be in the army. And then they took all the little ole pimply-faced scrawny guys that were as pale as ghosts. They even took Birdseed, weak eyes and all. I couldn't figure it, but I sure wasn't complaining.

"So I came home all happy and beaming. The family was just downright tearful they were so glad. It was like I had received a reprieve from a death sentence. They treated me like a king for a few days until it all wore off.

"Well, after a while I began to worry a little bit. Maybe they would call me to be checked again. I'd never had a thing wrong with me. The heartbeat thing . . . well, I knew, or at least I was pretty sure, it was just a flukey thing. Maybe they'd call me back in a few weeks or a few months. Vietnam was heating up real good and I still worried about it. So my happiness kinda faded for a while and turned to worry.

"I kept that 4-F paper in a real safe place like it was something sacred. Course I had it on my new draft card they gave me. But I also kept that paper safely tucked away in my Mama's big old family Bible.

"Then the months passed by, and the years. As all of the stuff went on . . . all the fighting and dying . . . well, I wasn't happy anymore. I wasn't even worried. Then I became . . . well, I started feeling guilty."

Luke looked up. There was something about the way Jack was talking that made Luke know that he was confronting something, relating something, for the first time.

There was a pause as his friend took a last draw on his cigarette, flipped the butt away, and put both hands in his coat pockets.

"And then they sent Birdseed back in a box. I went up to the funeral home. There were his poor old mother and father, now old and feeble, crying and just . . . well, just destroyed. Of course they didn't open the coffin. I remember his poor old mother just kept caressing the corner of the American flag draped over the casket . . . caressing it . . . like it was Birdseed . . . like she might have his hair if he was lying there with a fever . . ."

Jack's voice broke.

Luke looked up again and saw his friend's wet cheeks glistening in the sunshine.

Tears welled up in Luke's eyes as he looked straight ahead.

The inscription on the stone became blurred.

"Guilty. I felt . . . guilty," Jack said, straining to compose himself.

Luke didn't move. He couldn't move. His leaden heart

pinned him to the ground.

Jack recovered. "I still do, to some extent."

Silence. Only the sound of the cold breeze now moving about the stones and dead grass.

"Of course you do," Luke was finally able to speak. "We all do. It was a war of guilt. Ours is a generation of guilt. Those who didn't go feel guilty. Those who went and came back feel guilty. The only ones who don't feel guilty . . ." Luke nodded to the ground in front of him, ". . . are those like Birdseed here."

Jack stared at the ground, unconvinced.

"You went when you were called," Luke went on as he arose off of his haunches. "They didn't want you, so they sent you home. You waited....you didn't hide. You got a job. Paid taxes. Got married, had kids. Obeyed the law. You did your duty, Jack . . . that's all anyone can do. Birdseed did his. I did mine. I suppose those who went to Canada . . ." Luke swallowed hard, ". . . think they did theirs. You did your duty. That's all anyone can do."

Jack brushed his cheeks with his sleeve, sniffed and pulled out another cigarette. He felt comforted.

"Such a waste," he began again after he had lit his smoke. "For what? Birdseed didn't die for his country. I don't even know if he died for anyone's country. Or at least anyone who gave a shit. Why? That's the question I keep asking myself. I'm here. All in one piece. I got married. Take my kids to Grandma's for Sunday dinner. Watch my favorite television shows. Drink a little beer. Make love with my wife. Have a good time. Will probably live to see my grandkids. Then there's Birdseed's folks. Good decent Christian people. Suffering so. So many others just like them. Why them? Why me? Why does God let all this bad shit go on . . . why?"

Luke, gazing at the tombstone inscription like it was a flickering flame on a cold winter night, was now moving about the attic of his soul. He was picking up things . . . thoughts . . . which had been stored away there over time.

"Because God doesn't always win," Luke blurted out.

He squatted back down and looked into the flickering

flame.

"Don't take away His beauty, His compassion, His love... His justice . . . and not even His strength. Just His omnipotence. He's caught up in a universal struggle . . . good against evil . . . as powerful as He is, He is not all-powerful. He needs us just as we need Him. Even in the Bible, they killed His son, murdered His followers, Hitler slaughtered 6 million of His chosen people."

Luke was talking more to himself now than to Jack.

"It's a struggle . . . the God of Good against the forces of Evil . . . it's simple. We take casualties, not by His design but in the big cosmic and unfathomable firefight. Birdseed, his family... kids starving in Africa . . . all are casualties. Why? Because it's a struggle of good versus evil, that's all. Birdseed died just like some nameless V.C. died . . . because they both were struggling to be, to exist, to find a reason, to obey some distant call . . . to seek their own personal duty . . . to make some sense of it all. Yes, to do good . . . as they—in all their different ways—saw it . . . yet . . . evil overcame them both . . ."

Jack kneaded his brow and peered down at Luke.

Luke paused, deep in thought, and went on.

"That's the only way you can figure it, Jack. You either think of it in those terms, or don't think about it at all. Otherwise . . ." Luke's face darkened and his voice lowered to almost a whisper ". . . you'll go mad."

There was stillness. Both had emptied their souls and were spent. Their eyes shared the cold etching of their buddy's name.

Then out of the winter air came a sound. It began as a slow hiss and quickly grew into a low mournful moan. Louder it came, enveloping the air around them. It stayed with them for less than thirty seconds. Then it began to wane and fade away, finally back to a hiss and gone.

It was the four o'clock whistle at the prison.

"Time to go home," Luke said, smiling.

"Yep," Jack looked toward the sun, "time to go home."

The two old friends took one parting glance at Birdseed's grave and silently walked up the hill and got into the truck. Slowly they motored back down the driveway through the cemetery, the same route they had walked as boys with packs on their backs; past the same old mossy stones through which he and Birdseed had fled from Sheriff Bass Fisher one dark and cloudy night.

Chapter Seventeen

A Promise Fulfilled

*All the elements of nature cannot match
the simple majesty of a promise kept.*

The voice of a child jarred Justice Luke Cameron back to the present.

"Excuse me, mister, are you saving this table?"

Luke, momentarily disoriented and confused, looked quizzically into the little girl's freckled face.

"Uh, what? Uh . . . no, no, I'm just . . ." his response tailed off as he looked back up the hill to a car full of family, anxiously awaiting word.

The Supreme Court Justice slowly pulled himself from the table, muscles halting and strained from his long stay.

"I'm just sitting here . . . you can have the table," Luke finally managed to relate to the little scout.

He moved slowly up the hill toward his car.

The galloping family rushed to fill the void. For the first time in American history, a Supreme Court Justice had been unseated.

As he climbed the slope, he heard the excited play of children to his left.

It was the sound of young boys shouting, yelling, and generally having a good time.

He followed the noise. Across the ridge, through picnickers and the acrid smoke of smoldering charcoal, he moved past the clearing into a small forest. A shaded pathway bent downward toward the lake through a dense jungle of vines and undergrowth.

It meandered along a winding way to an overhanging cliff near the old lock and dam. As he came closer to the center of the clamor, the sound of splashing water rose from the din. There was a draw here, an inexplicable magnet pulling him along the trail. Around the last bend, the vast lake came into view.

In the water, and along the edge, some fifteen feet above the surface, was a healthy bevy of young boys ranging in age from single digits to early teens. Some wore swimsuits, while others frolicked in cutoffs and jeans.

From a large cottonwood leaning over the bluff, the swimmers had tied a long thick rope to a top limb. Some were taking turns swinging out from the hillside and over the old lock site where the water ran plenty deep. There in mid air they dropped, twisting and turning into the waters below. Others simply dove or jumped from the rocky crevice. To the right, the bluff gave out and the bank sloped easily into shallow water. There, near the edge, some of the swimmers retreated to splash about and rest.

They were boys of summer, and even though the season was young, most of them sported brown backs and cheeks of tan. There was gaiety in this place—the spontaneity of unfettered mirth recently set free from school.

But when the form of Justice Cameron appeared upon the scene, a dozen sun kissed boys were frozen in their jubilation. The shouting and the movement ceased, as each and every pair of eyes came to rest upon the stranger in their midst. There was a long, excruciating moment of silence. The distant groan of a motorboat and the chirping of birds punctuated the stillness.

Finally a small freckle-faced boy with the rope in his hand broke the spell.

"You with the government, mister?" he inquired. His endearing little face was cocked to one side, his short hair spiked by his recent plunge into the water.

All the others anxiously awaited the all-important answer to the question.

Taken back somewhat by the inquisition and the searing eyes bearing down upon him, Luke still managed to reply.

"No, I'm not with the government." It was an enormous lie, he thought, and felt a tinge of guilt. "Why do you ask?"

The young spokesman shifted slightly, dropping one hand from the rope and quickly glancing at his companions. In an unintelligible flash that only kindred spirits know, he received the unspoken word to go ahead.

"Well . . " the barefoot sprite looked around, ". . . we're not supposed to swim here. And the ranger, and sometimes other government men, give us a hard time."

Luke took a few more steps down the trail.

"Looks like a good place to swim to me," he assured them, taking in the swimming hole with an approving glance, ". . . and I don't see any signs. Why don't they have it posted?"

Smiles broke out on all the beardless faces, and they waited for their spokesman to answer that one.

"Well . . " their leader searched for words. Finally, he turned to a spindly twelve-year-old standing waist deep in water, "Show him, Spider."

Spider grinned, waded to a certain spot, took a deep breath, and then went under. The rippling currents churned and bubbled, and finally Spider emerged with a metal square, rusted and muddy. He proudly held it over his head for Luke to see. He could only make out the edges of some letters, but nothing readable. Spider gave the trove a pitch, and it crashed back into the depths from which it came. The young diver followed it, once more heading for the bottom of Barkley Lake.

This time the skinny kid stayed down much longer. Only Luke seemed to be concerned when over thirty seconds passed without a body in sight. Then, like a geyser bursting forth from the deep, Spider exploded through the surface, water pouring off of his slight frame. Again, he held a large object, the same size and shape as his first recovery. But this time there was no rust, and very little mud. He turned the gray side around toward him, displaying the shiny white front, so fresh that the water beaded on its surface. The sign proclaimed in bold black letters, "POSITIVELY NO SWIMMING—VIOLATORS WILL BE PROSECUTED." Below the lettering was embossed the familiar red castle of the Army Corps of Engineers.

As Spider stood in the water with the banner above his head, all eyes eagerly turned to catch the reaction of their uninvited guest.

A look of amusement swept across Luke's face. Being a law-and-order justice, he managed to stifle a smile. But the twinkle in his eye clearly signaled a common understanding. A chord had been struck.

The group's bold little leader, warming to the occasion, pressed on.

"You from around here, mister?"

He was an inquisitive little squirt, Luke thought. But oozing with chutzpah and charm.

"Yeah, I'm from around here," came his answer. And then to ward off any further inquiry in that direction, he added, "but I don't live here anymore."

"We're not supposed to swing from the trees either." The boy changed gears once again, pointing up to the top of the trees.

Luke's eyes floated up into the overhanging boughs out of which the rope dangled. Several limbs in the upper reaches had been sawed off even with the trunk of the tree.

"A boy fell up the lake last year, broke his back, and was paralyzed," the boy explained. "He sued the Corps for a million bucks. So what does the Corps do? They go around cutting down all our ropes—even cutting the limbs off the trees."

Another thirteen-year-old had moved in beside the main mouthpiece of the bunch. He chimed in. "But we keep coming back and finding new limbs. They even cut down some of the trees." He pointed to a stump nearby. "But," he drew back boastfully, "they can't cut every tree on the lake."

Luke then let his gaze drop from the tall timber to the wide placid lake which covered his hometown.

"I don't know . . ." he took a deep breath and peered at the horizon, "they can take a pretty good whack at it."

His words hung over the congregation of believers, as they patiently waited for his benediction.

Slowly he looked again upon his people, searching the irrepressible buoyancy in their faces. His eyes locked for a magic moment with those of the engaging little leader.

Then from some forgotten corner of Luke Cameron's soul, came the words unsolicited and spontaneous, "But nature will win in the end."

This pronouncement traveled over the heads of his young listeners, who made a momentary stab at understanding.

Finally, after a long silent moment, came the response, "Yeah . . . well, whatever . . ." The little foreman of the recreating crew turned and fixed his hands tightly around the rope and pushed off into the abyss. Far out into the limits of his swing, a good twenty feet above the surface, he released his grip and did an amazing double flip into the water. It signaled to the rest of the gathering that their parley with the stranger was over. Like the surge of a movie from frozen frame to action, the lively play of the young boys was renewed.

Recognizing his presence was no longer welcome, the ignored Supreme Court Justice turned and began his way back up the path.

Quickly he turned a corner of honeysuckle and foliage and was out of sight of the frolicking swimmers. But he was not out of sound.

"Who was that guy?" he heard one of the revelers yell above the din.

"I don't know," came an anonymous response. "He was a little spooky, if you ask me."

Luke laughed out loud. Throughout all his years as a lawyer in the rough and tumble arena of trial practice, through various bruising political campaigns, and even in the grueling inquisition of the Senate hearings, that was one thing he had never been called.

"A little spooky," Carolyn would love it.

The sun was off to the West as he made his way back to his car. The entire area had come alive with the Memorial Day crowd beginning their weekend in the great outdoors.

Happily, he found his car fully in the shade of several large maples bordering the picnic area. Nevertheless, the inside was still scorching as he slid in behind the wheel. Quickly he turned on the engine, and cranked up the knob for the air conditioner. The cold air blissfully blasted out over him, chilling his sweat-stained shirt.

Dodging new arrivals, Luke slowly turned the car around and headed back down the road away from the lake.

Past the prison, down through the valley, and then he started up the long steep grade around Pea Ridge.

Luke glanced at the digital clock on the dash. It read 4:03 p.m.

Instinctively, he reached and turned on the radio for the news.

". . . and will be points for discussion on the President's upcoming trip to South Africa."

There was an amateurish pause by the young student newscaster, with a low hum begging for words.

"Turning to other news . . . In a decision written by Kentucky's Justice Luke Cameron, the United States Supreme Court ruled today that a group of natives of the Pacific island of Bikini have legal standing to challenge the sale and private development of their home islands from which they were displaced almost fifty years ago. In writing for the 5-4 majority, Justice Cameron stated, 'When a democracy takes the property of people against their will, it holds the land in sacred trust. The democratic sovereign must not become a perverted Robin Hood, robbing from the poor and giving to the rich . . .'"

Luke clicked off the radio as the car picked up speed. He knew every single word, jot, and tittle, of the opinion. Justice Luke Cameron wanted to be lost in his own thoughts.

A flood of mixed images came pouring through his mind. Slowly but perceptibly, like the filling of a large urn with water, he became awash in the calming sea of nostalgia.

Tree limbs cut back to the nub. The smell of burning

leaves, coal smoke, and bruised walnuts. Honeysuckles and freshly cut grass, rusty signs, and a carefree youngster in mid-flight
against a powder blue sky. Lazy summer afternoons, and the sound
of a calliope around the bend. Long lost faces, and broken wood-
en bats. Savannah Johnson.

Nature will win in the end.